# IN VINO VERITAS

## *The new Lambert and Hook mystery*

Martin Beaumont is the uncompromising owner of a successful Gloucestershire vineyard. He has built the company steadily over the years, with a small but dedicated team by his side. However, he sees Abbey Vineyards as his company, to do with as he pleases, much to the chagrin of his senior staff members. So when he is found dead in his car, Chief Superintendent Lambert and DS Hook don't have to look very far to find people with strong motives for the murder...

# IN VINO VERITAS

*A Lambert and Hook Mystery*

## J.M. Gregson

**Severn House Large Print**
London & New York

This first large print edition published 2012
in Great Britain and the USA by
SEVERN HOUSE PUBLISHERS LTD of
9-15 High Street, Sutton, Surrey, SM1 1DF.
First world regular print edition published 2010 by
Severn House Publishers Ltd., London and New York.

British Library Cataloguing in Publication Data

Gregson, J. M.
    In vino veritas. -- (A Lambert and Hook mystery)
    1. Lambert, John (Fictitious character)--Fiction. 2. Hook,
    Bert (Fictitious character)--Fiction. 3. Police--
    England--Gloucestershire--Fiction. 4. Detective and
    mystery stories. 5. Large type books.
    I. Title II. Series
    823.9'14-dc23

    ISBN-13: 978-0-7278-9882-1

Severn House Publishers support The Forest Stewardship Council
[FSC], the leading international forest certification organisation. All
our titles that are printed on Greenpeace-approved FSC-certified paper
carry the FSC logo.

Printed and bound in Great Britain by the
MPG Books Group, Bodmin, Cornwall.

*To John, a son who has been a constant source of inspiration when he least suspected it.*

# ONE

It was at two minutes to midnight on the third of March that Alistair Morton first entertained the idea of murder.

He could be very precise about that, for he looked at the clock on the mantelpiece at exactly the moment when the idea came into his head. His wife had already been in bed for an hour, and Alistair had switched the television off at twenty to twelve. Since then, he had been sitting very still in his chair. Ruminating about where he stood in life and what he could do about it. It was a habit he had acquired over the last year, when his existence had moved from being merely frustrated to being embittered.

He sat in the deep, comfortable chair, which no one else ever used, and wondered whether living had any meaning. His life in particular seemed to be completely without purpose. Murder might be the only thing which could bring some meaning back into his existence.

Alistair was a practical man. He was an accountant for a start, and accountants were taught early in life what was possible and what was not. They also learned that imagination was the most dangerous of human properties. It had to

7

be imprisoned within very strong walls and not allowed to escape. Better still, imagination had better be discarded altogether. Left to poets and other misfits like them. Dumped in some neglected garret until disuse starved it out of existence.

Alistair thought he generally controlled his imagination well, but he was aware that it was an unruly and scarcely tameable beast. Of late, it had tended to come out of the shadows late at night. The dangerous time was when his wife was in bed, the television set was switched off, and he was left alone with his thoughts in the quiet sitting room.

Alistair Morton told himself firmly that the concept of murder should probably be no more than a delightful fantasy, an idea to play with and then discard. But instead of abandoning it as his training told him to do, he now proceeded to give it substance, to put bones and flesh upon the skeleton. It should have given him no more than a minor thrill and then been rejected, like a passing spectre upon a fairground ghost train.

Yet the more he thought about it, the more the idea began to seem feasible. That magic accountants' word! Feasible. Instead of seeming upon examination bizarre and impossible, this particular murder began to seem as practical a proposition as tax avoidance. Just this particular murder, Alistair told himself repeatedly. He wasn't saying that murder in general was feasible, or even desirable. But this particular murder was both of those things.

Desirable because the man concerned would be no loss to society. Indeed, his demise would be a positive benefit to many people, not just to Alistair himself. His removal would be a public-spirited act. An act which would make a wide circle of humanity much happier in the years to come. 'Every man's death diminishes me', some fusty old poet or philosopher had said; that was the kind of irrelevant nonsense they tried to fill your head with at school. Well, sod that for a game of soldiers! Alistair had never subscribed to that idea. Even when the idea was first put to him, he had immediately thought of several masters in the school whose death would have seemed positively desirable, whose passing would have diminished him not in the least.

With the passing years, his sentiments had not changed. Hitler and Stalin, and in his own life-time Chairman Mao in China: here were three for a start whose deaths would have diminished no one at all and benefited thousands. This man wasn't a villain on that scale, Alistair wasn't claiming that. But he couldn't see that anyone would suffer by his elimination, whereas there were a whole range of people who would bene-fit. Once you looked at it in those terms, the case for his removal seemed overwhelming. Alistair wriggled his toes in his slippers and luxuriated for a moment in the thought.

In the next few minutes, he confirmed to himself – and this was the thing which appealed to the accountant in him – that the proposition was feasible. Many murders wouldn't be, but this one was. There was no hurry, for a start. With a little ingenuity and a lot of careful planning, this death might be arranged so that no one was ever charged with it. And planning was his forte, wasn't it? Planning was the whole raison d'être of accountants.

Murder wasn't just a matter for the imagination, after all.

That was probably why it was still such a rare crime, once you discounted the impetuous knife crimes of city youth and the domestic killings which were solved within hours. Those weren't proper murders, not murders in the sense which most people had of the crime, where someone was struck down by person or persons unknown.

There were probably a lot more murders than people realized from the statistics, because the most successful ones were never recognized as such. That was both a satisfying and a thought-provoking notion. It also marked a challenge which even an accountant should be excited to undertake.

And even if the police recognized this death as murder, there would be many suspects, wouldn't there, because the victim was such an unpopular man? Alistair decided that he would be well down that list of suspects; indeed, he might not figure on the list at all, if he planned the crime as carefully as he proposed to do. It was a crime, he supposed. Technically, at any rate. But he'd already proved that some crimes were perfectly justified, hadn't he?

When he looked at the clock, he was surprised

10

to find that it was one a.m. Alistair Morton smiled. He wondered when he had last spent an hour in such fruitful and productive thought.

# TWO

The sun was still quite low, but there was scarcely a cloud in the sky. The long lines of carefully trained grapevines stretched away over the hill, straight and regular as columns of Roman soldiers. Martin Beaumont called out a cheery good morning and waved to the visitors as he passed them in his electric buggy. They wouldn't know who he was, of course, wouldn't know that he owned the land as far as their eyes could see. One of the workers would tell them, if they asked. That didn't really matter, but the thought pleased him.

'As far as the eye could see' might be pushing it a bit. Eighty-five acres, to be precise; his land didn't include the long line of the Malvern Hills to the north, or the more distant Welsh mountains to the west: that would be ridiculous. But the strolling visitors he had passed were in the valley. All they could see from there were the long lines of beautifully trained vines running away to the top of the slopes above and behind them, and every inch of that intensively cultivated land was assuredly his. Well, his company's, if you wanted to be pedantic, but everyone understood that that was just a legal technicality.

Beaumont stopped at the highest point of his land. He loved this spot on a spring day, loved to survey the scale of his achievement on this rolling land which was bounded by the historic rivers Severn and Wye, neither of them visible from here but each of them imbued with the turbulent history of England. That history was an appropriate setting for his revival of wine-making in this western corner of Gloucester-shire. The Romans had made wine in quantity in England, as Martin was fond of reminding any-one who would listen. He was reviving an ancient craft. If global warming was giving him increasing assistance, that was but a happy acci-dent. If your mind favoured the notion of a supreme being, the changing climate might even be seen as a sign of approval from a benevolent Providence.

It was the middle of March and the sun was rising a little higher each day. It had real warmth in it now. The swelling buds on the vines were bursting into fresh green leaves on the more sheltered south-facing slopes, heralding the lush green and black grapes which would follow, as summer warmth and Gloucestershire rain swell-ed them towards maturity. Martin loved this time of the year, when summer and its promise were all before them and the earth smelt of growth, whilst each day stretched a little longer and brighter.

He walked over to where two of his men were

screwing wires on to the stout wooden crosses which were to carry the first crops of the new red-wine grape they had planted. 'Morning, Walter,' he said to the older of the men, glad that he was able to remember the name. The man had been one of his first workers here and was now a veteran of viniculture.

'Mornin', Mr Beaumont,' said Walter in his thick local accent. ''E's comin' on a treat, this new 'un.'

Nothing in the local parlance was inanimate: every plant was he or she, and any failure on their part to cooperate was taken as a personal insult. Martin liked that local trait, which meant that even a golf ball had a personality of its own, exhibiting a malignity when it ran into trouble and a friendliness when it bounced favourably for you.

Walter couldn't have much longer to work now. Though his movements had slowed imperceptibly with the years, he never shirked and he gave full value for his wages. He had touched the canvas cap he always wore in acknowledgement of the boss's status, and Martin was pleased despite himself by the gesture. It wasn't very long since ill-paid rural workers here had touched their forelocks to the lord of the manor who was exploiting them. It was surely harmless for today's much better paid workers to acknowledge their employer with a touch of the cap. The habit would die with Walter and his contemporaries; the younger workers didn't see the need for any such demarcation in their status.

13

Beaumont glanced at his watch. The meeting was in ten minutes: he had better get back to base.

He drove the electric buggy swiftly back to the long, low complex of buildings near the entrance to the vineyards. The bricks stretched out further here each year, but there was ample room for additions where once the old farmhouse buildings had sprawled. The dining room and the shop had been extended again during the winter. The single-storey range of rooms which had been built for holiday lets was a lucrative addition to the complex over the last few years.

His own large office doubled as a room for company meetings. He liked this sort of economy, because it showed his staff where their priorities should lie. He was always reluctant to increase office facilities, which he saw as non-productive. The available funds should go to making the shop, restaurant and residential accommodation more attractive, as these areas were self-evidently the source of the profits on which Abbey Vineyards depended.

This morning's meeting shouldn't occupy them for very long. Martin, as chairman, began by telling them that. It was no more than a necessary evil, his attitude implied. His preference was to act as a benevolent dictator, but a meeting of senior staff was one of those diversions necessitated by their status as a limited company. He looked round affably at the five people who sat around the table which had been brought in for the occasion from the restaurant.

There were nervous half-smiles from two of them, but all of them stared down at their brief agendas for the meeting rather than at him.

Martin reported on a couple of items under the heading of 'Matters Arising', then in more detail on the progress of new planting. 'Abbey Vineyards continues to make excellent progress. I look forward to your reports on your individual sections and to highlighting any problems we may have in particular areas, so that we can give our attention to them.' Whether intentionally or not, he made the words seem like a threat to the people who were about to speak. 'First on the agenda is the restaurant. Report from our head chef.'

Jason Knight coughed nervously and said quickly, 'Things are progressing well, I think.' That didn't sound as definite as he had intended it to when he had rehearsed it the night before. He had been determined that when he came in here he would exude a calm confidence, would emphasize how much he was in control of this vital source of profits. But Jason was a practical man, used to achieving results under pressure and driving himself and his kitchen staff hard. Formal reporting like this, in a quiet room full of attentive and possibly critical listeners, was still alien to him.

But Martin Beaumont wasn't in the mood for criticism. 'That's what we want to hear,' he boomed out into the quiet room. 'The extension to the restaurant has given us room for sixteen more covers each evening: I'm sure that as the summer progresses we shall fill the place on most nights. The challenge will be to do that during the winter, when people are less conscious of us and there is less for them to see here. But I'm sure we're all confident of meeting this new task as efficiently as we have done such challenges in the past!' The chairman jutted his chin aggressively at the room. His attempt to stir the blood might have been more effective with a larger audience than five.

Jason Knight said a little defensively, 'People have to be persuaded to drive out here through the winter darkness. There's a lot of competition from the pubs, which is going to increase during this recession.'

'If other people can pull in the punters, Abbey Vineyards can,' said Beaumont firmly. 'We have a wonderful, spacious set-up here. Plus the individuality offered by our own wines. That is a well-nigh unique selling point.'

Alistair Morton looked up from his notes, sensing that there was no way the chef was going to win an argument with the more fluent owner of the vineyard. 'The fact that there is a vineyard around the restaurant has been fully exploited over the last twenty years, Martin. It probably still has some novelty appeal for visitors to our area, but the locals are well aware of it.'

Beaumont's forehead furrowed for a couple of seconds. Then he resumed his upbeat performance, as new arguments appeared to him. 'It is still a pulling point, Alistair. People are well aware that they don't have to struggle into a cramped car park and file into crowded pub dining rooms when they come here. They appreciate the space around them and the expertise which drives this place. That applies even during the winter, when they cannot see the greenery beyond our windows.' He turned and smiled directly at Jason Knight, as a prelude to his concluding argument. 'But of course the biggest trump in our hand when it comes to the restaurant is Jason's cooking. The quality which he and his staff produce in their beautifully equipped new kitchens is second to none. I'm sure that all of us are aware of that.'

There was a polite, slightly embarrassed mutter of approval from the people round the table, whilst Knight stared at his agenda and reddened. Beaumont, sensing that he had taken this as far as he could, glanced at his agenda and said briskly, 'Residential Accommodation.'

Vanda North, a striking woman with a prominent nose and bright blue eyes, was, at forty-six, ten years younger than Beaumont. She nodded and spoke decisively. 'We shall have to face the fact that the residential accommodation is not going to do as well as hitherto in the next two or three years.'

Beaumont glanced quickly at the other faces round the table before he said, 'It's not like you to be gloomy, Vanda.' But he was cautious. Vanda North had been in the business from the early stages. She was his partner in the limited company, though a very junior one in terms of

17

her financial contribution. She was also responsible for the hitherto highly successful operation of the site's en-suite bedrooms, through her management of the residential section staff.

'I'm being realistic, Martin. We don't operate in a vacuum. If people tighten their belts in the world at large, we must expect this sort of stay to be one of their first economies. Very few of our clients use our breaks as their only holiday of the year; we might be their first economy. We shall need to be ingenious to occupy the rooms as fully as we have done in the past. It probably wasn't the best time to extend our provision to twelve rooms.'

Beaumont frowned. 'That was done on the basis of our previous lettings, which had been almost a hundred per cent during the summer months. It made sound sense to extend our plant when we were making handsome profits.'

Vanda North smiled. She was much more used to sustaining an argument than Jason Knight had been before her. 'The extension may still make sound sense, if we take the long view. I'm merely flagging up that I anticipate problems in the next two years. We have to be flexible. The signs are certainly that we'll need to extend our range of bargain breaks. Once we're outside the peak summer season, we're facing a vast range of competition. We'll almost certainly have to accept lower profit margins, to keep the rooms occupied and hang on to the excellent staff we've recruited over the last few years.'

'Well, I'm sure you understand the problems

of this area better than anyone else in the room, Vanda,' said Beaumont shamelessly. This sort of meeting wasn't the place to make policy decisions. Some time in the next few days, he would have a detailed discussion with Vanda North about strategy and how they were going to fill the new accommodation suites. He was better at enforcing his formidable will in a one-to-one situation than in this sort of formal meeting. 'You are right to emphasize that we can't ignore what is going on in the world around us, of course. The worst possible thing any of us could do is to press ahead with our plans in a blinkered way and ignore what is going on in the wider world.' He paused for a moment, apparently to let them all dwell upon that thought, before looking down at his next agenda item. 'Report on new initiatives introduced last year.'

A rather nervous voice said, 'Yes. That's me. I have the figures to hand.' This was Sarah Vaughan, Director of Research and Development, at thirty-three the youngest person in the room. She had long blonde hair and the sort of delicate, pretty, brittle-looking features which often seem to go with fair colouring. Sarah had a Business Studies degree and some years of experience in the retail trade with a big supermarket chain. She helped to run the shop on the site, but also had the brief to initiate new means of developing the full commercial potential of Abbey Vineyards. She was normally self-confident and energetic, but she found herself a little overawed to be included today in this formal

19

meeting of the six people who were the driving force in what was now a large company and a considerable local employer.

Sarah shuffled the papers which had been ready on the table in front of her since the meeting began. 'The gift vouchers continue to enjoy a steady sale, but they are hardly a new or original idea. I think we can say that the guided tours we developed into a regular programme last year have been a success. It's a difficult thing to measure, because we're talking about the public's goodwill – there are no directly measurable effects from the tours. But in my opinion the indirect effects have been valuable.'

'I'll vouch for that.' The words came from a stocky figure, with the build of a prop forward and the face of one of the swarthy Welsh miners who had dominated the valleys fifty miles to the south of here in the not-so-distant past. Gerry Davies was the shop manager. He oversaw the sales of wines and the multiple associated products which had been the heartbeat of the enterprise since the earliest days of Abbey Vineyards. 'And I'd say there are direct results. We sell considerable quantities of wine to the people who have been on the guided tours. More now than when we started. In my opinion they're well worthwhile.'

The chairman nodded thoughtfully. 'You think these sales result directly from the tours?'

'Almost invariably. I'd say most people who go on one of Sarah's walks buy at least one bottle of wine. Quite often someone will buy a

20

case. I can say that with conviction, because I've seen the improvement since we've had a regular programme of tours.'

'And why would that be?'

'I've no idea.' He shrugged his big shoulders and looked interrogatively at Sarah Vaughan.

'I think I know why,' said Sarah Vaughan slowly, 'but I'm glad to hear that you think things have improved.' She looked round the table, as if checking that she had a receptive audience. 'You get better at anything by doing it. I noticed that I was getting more relaxed and confident myself, and I could sense that my talk was going better, that I had a better rapport with my audience as we went round the different areas. They began asking me more questions, for one thing, which I took as a sign of interest. So I didn't just work on my own little talks, I watched to see who else went down well. When we began the tours we used anyone who was free at the time. Now I assign them as far as possible to three people: Gerry, myself and Joe Logan, who works three days a week in the shop but seems to have a gift for communication with the public. I feel the tours are more interesting as a result. I'm glad it's paying concrete dividends in the shape of sales.'

There was a little murmur of approval from her fellow workers. Martin Beaumont said rather stiffly, 'It's good to hear that people like you are thinking about the job and how it might best be done, Sarah. This is the sort of initiative we'll all need to show in the testing two or three years ahead. How is the "Adopt a Vine" scheme going?'

'It's really too early to say. This is probably the time of year when we should sell most memberships. We've only sold seven so far this year but we've had quite a lot of interest expressed. The scheme has the disadvantage that you lay out £25 and wait for quite some time before you get anything back for your money, so take-up is probably going to be confined to real wine enthusiasts.'

The 'Adopt a Vine' scheme was one of Martin's own, which he had brought back from a vineyards convention. He would have preferred to hear that there was a more enthusiastic take-up, but he had no idea how that might be achieved. He was more concerned to get his own ideas across than to listen to those of other people, more conscious of his own reactions to items than of those of the other five people in the room. He said abruptly, 'Item Four. Shop Sales.'

There was a moment of tension. Everyone knew that it was the sales in the shop, and above all else the sales of wines, which drove the whole enterprise. It was a long process planting the long rows of vines, then tending them for years until they reached commercial production levels. Those years had been endured some time ago and Abbey Vineyards was now a prosperous business. But it needed perpetual vigilance, awareness and industry to keep it so. There was still much scepticism among the public about

English wines; there were still yearly battles, first to bring in a worthwhile grape harvest and then to sell the steadily increasing wine yield.

Gerry Davies took his time and spoke calmly. 'So far, we seem to be immune from the worst effects of the recession. We are a specialist market with niche sales, which we all hope may not suffer the worst troughs of the economy. We shall know by the end of this year whether this is indeed so. Sales of our white wines have increased again, as they have done every year in the last ten – as in fact they need to do, since we are producing more dry and medium-dry whites every year. This remains the core of our business.'

Beaumont nodded slowly. 'It does, but we are also producing more red each year. There seems to be a steady demand for it: a higher percentage of red wine from all sources is drunk in Britain each year, so we need to take account of that trend.'

Gerry Davies nodded. 'So far, we are selling all the red we produce. However, we have to push the "rough but fruity and characterful" aspect rather more than I like to do, and we take a smaller mark-up on the reds than the whites. We could do with something to rival the Australian Shiraz. But no one as far north as us has come up with a vine to rival them so far.'

'We should get some economies of scale on our reds from this year onwards,' said Beaumont. 'I calculate that we should increase our production of them substantially over each of the next five years.'

'Economies of scale will depend on us shifting everything we produce,' pointed out Davies. 'We've had to work very hard to clear all the reds in the last couple of years.'

There was a tension between him and Beaumont which everyone in the room could feel. Beaumont was a man who didn't like to be challenged too openly or too far, whilst Davies for his part was not prepared to let anything go which might cause him trouble in the future. The Welshman now said, as though making a concession, 'The new sparkling wines have gone quite well. Quality and flavour don't seem to be too important with sparkling wines.' He glanced up at the faces in the quiet room, wanting to see their reactions. 'A lot of the people who drink sparkling wines don't seem to be wine drinkers at all, you see. It's used mainly to celebrate family or group achievements, and everyone has a glass or two.'

Beaumont knew that their latest champagne-type wines were better than that, but decided that he would not be insulted. 'So long as we sell whatever we produce in the way of sparkling wines, we need not concern ourselves too much with what motivates the drinkers,' he said affably. 'How is the beer we agreed to stock selling in the shop?'

'The Dog's Whiskers pump? Surprisingly well.' Davies spoke eagerly, as if he too were anxious to move on from controversial ground. 'The brewery gave us an astonishingly good

24

margin because they were so anxious to get in here, so we couldn't really lose on it. Nevertheless, it's sold well. There are still quite a lot of real ale enthusiasts who come in here to buy our wines.'

Beaumont nodded. 'We are talking about the heartbeat of our business when we discuss shop sales. Everything else is driven by the profits from the shop. Are there any comments from our financial director?'

Alistair Morton had spoken not a word throughout the meeting, confident that his expert view would be demanded if he bided his time. For better or worse, accountants controlled the finances and thus the policies of many businesses nowadays. He cleared his throat and said, 'I think it's time we began to distinguish between the retail activities of the shop and the mail-order business, which is increasingly important. It may be a better indication of the way we should plan for the future than the changing week-to-week takings in the shop. In my view, it is the orders we secure for many cases of wines at our discount rates which are a better reflection of our progress than anything else.

'There is now a steady take-up on our products from restaurants – not all of them local – and some of the specialist wine shops. As our production expands over the next few years, it is this wholesale trade which is essential to ensure that we sell in the quantities required.'

It was a long speech and a prepared one, but none the worse for that. People listened carefully because they expected considered, not spontaneous, views from people who advised about finance. Even dullness was allowed, if it made commercial sense; indeed, to some people, dullness was almost a guarantee of accounting respectability and reliability.

Beaumont nodded his agreement. 'And what do you foresee for us in the next two or three years, Alistair? There are plenty of prophets of gloom and doom about, but I think we are better placed than most to come through a recession.'

Alistair Morton took his time. 'No one can make reliable forecasts, because no one knows yet how deep or prolonged this slump is going to be. There are two key factors for us, as for any business: turnover and margins. As with any other agricultural crop, we have to be certain that each year we can grow and market a good harvest. Assuming we can do that, our success or otherwise will then depend on what profit margins we can maintain on those products. So far, we have managed to maintain our overall net profit margin at eleven to twelve per cent. Whether we can do that during the next two or three winters remains to be seen.'

Gerry Davies said a little mischievously, 'But it's your view that we can do that?'

'There are too many imponderables for me to say that. We shall have to see whether demand remains buoyant when most people haven't as much to spend on luxuries. Despite our increasing turnover, all the evidence is that English wines are regarded as luxury spending.'

Morton glanced at Beaumont at the head of the table. 'So far, we have managed to keep a healthy margin on all of our wine sales. We shall have increased supply again this year – probably twenty to thirty per cent more in the reds and ten per cent in the whites, if we have a decent harvest. Whether we can continue to increase demand and keep sales buoyant during the biggest recession on record will be the great question for all of us in the next two years.'

Beaumont said, 'I don't think times are going to be as bad as that, as far as spending power goes. We are a much richer nation now than in the thirties.'

Alistair Morton decided that as the supposed expert on the economy he would offer a little comfort. 'That is certainly true. And the world seems to be determined to be less passive about this slump than the one in the thirties. More important, we are a completely new industry, which didn't exist in the thirties. We should be able to think on our feet and devise solutions for ourselves. I am encouraged to hear talk of economies of scale. It might be possible to reduce our prices per bottle over the coming decade, whilst keeping our overall profit margins the same.'

Beaumont nodded. 'That should be our overriding thought, I think. It is something which none of us can achieve alone, but which we should be working for as a team. Unless anyone has any other urgent thoughts, I think we should leave it at that for this morning.'

He hastened to close the meeting on an upbeat comment. 'I'd like you to reassure all our staff that no one's job is in danger at the moment. We have a good workforce. I want to keep it intact if I possibly can.'

Martin Beaumont sat for a while in his office after everyone had left. The meeting had gone well, he thought. No one had raised anything that was particularly embarrassing. He thought he'd succeeded in putting some important people on their toes for the year ahead.

He was much better at estimating his own performance than other people's reaction to it.

# THREE

Detective Sergeant Bert Hook was not usually nervous. The roughest young thugs of Gloucestershire and Herefordshire had often found that out the hard way when they had thought to intimidate him. Proficient batsmen in the Minor Counties competitions had found themselves hopping about on the back foot when they had underestimated his pace as an opening bowler.

Yet today Bert was uncharacteristically uncertain. He turned the white foolscap envelope over and over between his short, strong fingers. He decided several times to slit its flap decisively with his paperknife, yet each time desisted and went back to looking at his neatly typed name and address on the address label. He knew whence this missive had come and knew its purpose. Yet he could not bring himself to meet its simple message. It was one of those letters where you dearly wanted to discover the contents, yet at the same time feared to know them. If the human brain is a complex thing, the human mind is even less predictable.

'It's come, then.'

He leaped at the sound of the familiar voice, as though detected in some criminal act. 'I didn't know you were there,' he said accusingly.

His wife Eleanor smiled down at him as he sat at the kitchen table. 'I do live here. And I didn't creep up on you. It's just that you were miles away.'

Bert resumed turning the letter between his fingers, as if he had been interrupted in some ancient and essential preliminary routine. 'I knew it was coming, didn't I? Now that it's here, I almost wish it hadn't come. It's like being a child again. It brings back the Barnardo's home and having to open the letter with my GCE results.'

'This will be as positive as they were.'

For a moment Hook was back in that boyhood world, at the long table in the office of the institution's principal, fingering that other envelope. 'I enjoyed that day. They told me at the home that I'd done well enough to get into the police, if I could meet the other criteria. I felt as if I'd won the lottery, getting myself a job – any sort

29

of job.' He could hear again the cut-glass tones of that well-meaning lady who had chaired the governors of the home, telling him on the day that he left that he had done well for himself, that he should continue to give thanks for the grace of the good Lord, who had seen fit to reward him for his rectitude.

At length he said abruptly, 'I don't want to open this. I know it's silly and I wouldn't confess it to anyone else, but as long as I don't open it I can't have failed, can I?'

'You haven't failed, you great lummox.'

It was a long time since Eleanor Hook had left her native north, but she retained the occasional colourful dialect word. There was a bump on the ceiling and the sound of childish admonishment from above. She said, 'The lads will be down any second. Better to get it over without that sort of audience, don't you think?'

'You know how to produce the ultimate threat,' said her husband glumly. Bert picked up the paperknife, slit the envelope decisively, and carefully drew out the single sheet within it.

Eleanor could divine nothing from his weather-beaten, impassive features. Only she knew how much effort he had put into his studies over the last six years. She was probably the one person to whom he would have admitted how much this meant to him, but marriage meant that these things did not have to be spoken. He stared for a long time at the notepaper with the Open University crest at the top of it. Then he looked at his wife and felt the smile creeping over his face. He handed her the paper. Eleanor read as unemotionally as she could: 'Herbert James Hook is awarded the degree of Bachelor of Arts, with second class honours, division one.'

She paused for just a moment, to let the joy flood into her own face, then threw her arms round Bert. The kiss had relaxed into a hug and she was murmuring words of congratulation into his ear when a voice from the doorway said, 'They're at it again, Jack!' and the two of them sprang automatically apart.

A noise as of approaching thunder from the stairs announced the precipitate arrival of their elder son, who studied the tableau before him, shook his head sadly, then announced to thirteen-year-old Luke, 'You'd think they could control themselves, at their age and at this time in the morning.'

'And in front of innocent children at an impressionable age, too,' said Luke with the despairing shake of his head which he had spent some time developing in front of his bedroom mirror.

'There's nothing innocent about you two,' said Bert Hook sadly. 'And you're about as impressionable as Genghis Khan. Sit down and eat your breakfast.'

They hastened to obey. 'God knows what it's doing to us, being exposed to shenanigans like this at this time in the morning,' said Jack.

'You wouldn't recognize a shenanigan if it got up and bit you,' said his father with feeling. 'Do

31

you want toast?'

'Two slices, please, if you two can tear yourselves away from each other.'

'That's enough of that,' said his mother, with all the sternness she could muster.

'That's what we thought,' said Jack, with a benign smile at no one in particular.

'Your father has some news for you,' said Eleanor seriously.

They caught a hint of her seriousness, and looked up expectantly from their cereals at Bert, who drew in a deep breath and said, 'I've got my degree – the one I've been studying for over the last few years.'

Luke's thirteen-year-old eyes widened. 'Who's a clever boy, then?' he said with his head on one side.

Like many a boy of his age, he did not quite know how to react when confronted with some serious issue in his parents' lives. It was left to his fifteen-year-old brother to say simply, 'Well done, Dad!' Jack got up and came round the table and shook his father's hand, awkwardly but firmly. It was at once touching and slightly ridiculous, like a parody of adult congratulation, and it became more so when Luke followed him and solemnly repeated the exercise.

Eleanor, who was suddenly very much moved by the sight of the trio, said stoutly, 'That's a very good degree, you know. And he's done it part time, whilst making sure we're all safe in our homes. I hope you realize now that your father is a man of many talents.'

32

'We know that, Mum,' said Luke. 'Billy Singh, our opening bat, has the top average in the whole league, and Dad bowled him middle stump in the nets last summer, didn't he, Jack?'

'Yes. Got him out twice in five balls. Billy says Dad should never have retired. Should still be playing for Herefordshire, he says.'

Eleanor smiled. 'Well, even a man of Dad's amazing talents has to give up some time. And he might never have had time to get this magnificent degree if he'd gone on playing cricket.'

Luke obviously thought such academic distinction a poor consolation for eschewing triumphs on the sports field, but he did his best to look impressed. The boys demolished large bowls of cereal and two slices of toast in swift succession.

It was not until Jack was alone in the hall with his mother that he said, looking determinedly at the carpet, 'He's a bit special, our dad, isn't he, Mum?'

On the day after the meeting at Abbey Vineyards, Vanda North cornered Martin Beaumont in his office.

'We need to talk.'

'If you say so.' Martin looked at her coolly as she sat opposite him on the other side of his desk. The table which had been brought in for the meeting on the previous day had been removed immediately after it. With the lack of ornaments and the single picture of the Malvern Hills on the wall, the room had resumed its normal rather bleak spaciousness. He looked at Vanda's short, expertly cut dark-gold hair, then down at her slim, small-breasted figure and the long legs in the fawn linen trousers. She had always been striking rather than pretty, but she was still a handsome woman at forty-six, he decided.

When a woman had been your mistress, you were surely entitled to have an opinion on such matters.

He wasn't good at assessing other people's reactions to his words and attitudes. That was probably just as well, for Ms North was wondering for her part why she had ever been enticed into his bed. She was well aware by now that sexual attraction often paid little heed to matters of character, but now she couldn't even see the physical attraction which had once driven her to this man.

Beaumont was ten years older than her, and he wasn't ageing well. The face which she had seen as handsome was now florid, developing jowls and the suggestion of a double chin beneath them. No man could successfully combat thinning hair, but as he drew the ever-scarcer strands which were left obstinately across his pate, he risked looking ridiculous. Well-cut suits could disguise an insistent embonpoint only up to a certain point, a point which her critical eye insisted had now been passed.

He was a powerful man; she had no delusions about that. And she had long ago accepted the old saw that power was the greatest aphrodisiac.

34

You wanted to investigate men who had power. You wanted to discover how they had acquired it and how they thought of the people whose lives they controlled. It gave them an extra and highly important dimension. It was very easy to persuade yourself that men who exercised power had greater intelligence and greater depth to their personalities than was in fact the case.

With the benefit of hindsight and that pitiless objectivity with which one examines past sexual mistakes, she saw now that she had invested Martin Beaumont with this kind of mystique. There was really nothing very complex or intriguing about either his power or the way he exercised it. He was a man on the make, with a sharp eye for the main chance, and there wasn't a lot more to it than that. He had acquired a certain amount of money early in life – she had never found out exactly how – and he had used cunning and ruthlessness to make a lot more. There was no reason to see him as more incisive or more gifted than he was, but she had tended to do that.

Like many a disillusioned ex-lover, Vanda went too far in her reactions. Martin Beaumont had in fact inherited a certain amount of money as a young man, but he had been shrewd and capable in his use of it. Moreover, he had had both a vision and the courage and the determination to pursue it. When he had conceived the idea of a vineyard in Gloucestershire, it had been both an original and a high-risk notion. He had to produce figures to convince his bankers that it was a commercial proposition, rather than an enthusiast's indulgence, a hobby which would eventually ruin him.

Martin had worked very hard in the early years, had ploughed back every penny of the meagre profits into developing the business. Gradually, he had acquired and developed more and more land for viniculture. A sceptical public in what was essentially a rural area had gradually accepted that the vineyard was here to stay. Indeed, the more enlightened locals had eventually conceded that, with all the problems of both arable and livestock farming in the area and the yearly evidence of global warming, there might just be a future for Abbey Vineyards.

The outbreak of foot-and-mouth disease and its sombre consequences in the early years of the new century had reinforced that view. What most had seen as a gimmick might just have a future. As the monstrous piles of burning cattle carcasses clouded the skies with their dark smoke and darker smells, viniculture seemed not only possible but desirable, even glamorous. Discreet advertising helped to reinforce the impression that Abbey Vineyards was a more innocent use of the land than dairy farming, or even the sheep farming which was suffering intense competition from overseas.

Vanda North had put all the money she had into Abbey Vineyards ten years earlier, when she had been more besotted with Beaumont than she had realized at the time. It should have been a good investment – perhaps would have been, if she had taken more care over the terms on which she had entered the concern, instead of letting Martin draw up the junior partnership deal. She realized now that she needed some income, that what might be a promising deal on the face of it did not suit her needs. Income was ploughed back each year into new developments, and she was committed for an indefinite period. She had no right to sell her holding without the approval of the senior partner, and Martin was never going to give it.

She was determined to assert herself, but she was uncharacteristically uncertain about how to do that. As if he read her mind and saw her dilemma, Martin Beaumont said suddenly, 'We need to go on expanding.'

This assertion, the very opposite of what she wanted to hear, freed her tongue at last. 'On the contrary, all the signs are that we need a period of retrenchment. No firm can afford to ignore this recession. No one is going to be immune to its effects.'

'You heard the feeling of the meeting yesterday. We are not a typical industry. You need to realize that what is going to be a difficult time for others may well be a time of opportunity for us.'

'No, I didn't hear the feeling of the meeting. What I did hear was you asserting these things, in the face of what other people were saying about the need for caution.'

She could see him pausing to control himself before he spoke. What had seemed an impressive ruthlessness in the early days of their association now struck her as an autocratic cruelty. 'I repeat what I said. We need to expand.'

'That is flying in the face of the facts.'

'On the contrary, it is perfectly logical, Vanda. For a start, if others around us suffer, the price of land will come down. We should take advantage of that.'

She felt her anger rising, her hands beginning to tremble. The very things she had been determined to avoid when she came in here were beginning to happen. 'You can do whatever you like. I want out.'

He smiled, unaware how obnoxious that made him seem to her. 'Not possible, I'm afraid, Vanda. The terms of our agreement prevent that. The terms you signed up to quite willingly.'

'You took advantage of me. You know I didn't read any of it very carefully at the time.'

'Forgive me if this sounds ungallant, Vanda, but you weren't some young ingénue ten years ago. You were a mature woman of thirty-six who knew exactly what she was doing.'

'If you're saying I was a fool, at least that's one thing we can agree on. I was a fool to trust you.'

'I'm sorry you should feel that. I was putting you into an excellent investment.'

'On terms which prevented me from realizing it for twenty-five years, unless one of us died in the meantime.'

'Perfectly normal practice, when one is developing a new business. Partners have to commit themselves. If those terms didn't suit you, you shouldn't have signed up to them.'

She wanted to step forward and slap him hard across his smug face. 'I've never been a proper partner. I want my money out. It's all I've got and I need it.'

'Not possible, I'm afraid. It's tied up in a developing business. It will be an excellent investment, in the long run.'

Vanda felt now that she had always known this would be the outcome. She had put herself through a humiliation which was pointless. How could she ever have found this man desirable? 'You know as well as I do that you gave me all sorts of assurances that I could have my money out whenever I wanted, given a couple of months' notice.'

'I don't remember any such promises. I'm afraid that verbal agreements have no standing unless both parties agree on what was said.' He was enjoying the familiar feeling of exercising power over another being's future, of knowing that he held all the cards in this particular game. 'It wasn't a large sum you invested, but I'm afraid it's impossible to return it at this moment, much as I should like to.'

'And that's your last word?'

'I'm afraid it has to be.'

'I shall take legal advice on this.'

'You'll be wasting your money if you do. I'm sorry, but there it is.' He didn't look at all sorry as she flung back her chair and left his office.

Vanda North's hands were shaking as she

gripped the wheel of her car. She had to force herself to concentrate on the simple business of driving as she turned out of the car park and on to the B road outside. She caught a glimpse of Beaumont's face at the window of his office as she went. He still had that supercilious smile he had worn for most of their exchanges. She put a mile between herself and the vineyards, then drove into the parking lay-by she had been aiming for and stopped.

Her face was in her hands for what seemed to her a long time. As far as she could see, there was no solution to this. Well, only one. And that surely wasn't possible, was it?

Jason Knight was used to working under pressure. It is a necessary skill for any chef in charge of a busy kitchen.

This was a different sort of pressure and he wasn't coping anything like as well. Playing golf against the club champion in the third round of the singles knockout competition was proving more testing of his temperament than he had expected. It was ridiculous to take the random bounces and rolls of a small white golf ball quite so seriously, he told himself, but the thought did not help him.

Jason was thirty-eight and in his golfing prime, in his opinion. He had played the game intermittently since he was a boy, and regularly since he had come to this area and joined the Ross-on-Wye Golf Club. He had a handicap of eight, which he considered generous, whereas

40

his opponent played off scratch. Jason was receiving eight shots in this match. When discussing his chances with other members beforehand, he had discounted his chances against the young man with what he hoped was a becoming modesty. Privately, he had thought his progress to the next round highly probable.

Now, after eleven holes, he was one down and five of his shots were gone – squandered, for the most part, in his view. On the short twelfth, he was standing over a putt three feet above the hole for a half. It should have been a doddle, with his normal calm putting technique. He stood over the ball for what was probably a little too long, jerked his putter convulsively at it, and watched it shoot over the right edge of the hole.

Two down.

'Bad luck!' said his opponent sympathetically, before he moved away gratefully towards the thirteenth tee. Both of them knew that it was bad play rather than bad luck, but the polite golfing fiction was observed.

The thirteenth at Ross is a shortish but very tight par four, where any errant tee shot will leave you baulked by trees from a second shot to the green. Most good players take a fairway wood or even an iron from the tee, to place the ball safely on the fairway; Jason was delighted to see his opponent reaching for his driver. The arrogance of youth, he thought happily, and stood silently waiting for the appropriate punishment to befall this tall and gifted young man.

Sometimes talent subdues justice. The young Titan hit the ball long and very straight indeed, and it seemed to Jason to go on bouncing for a disagreeably long time. It came to rest over three hundred yards from them, and it looked to Jason to be no more than fifteen yards from the green. 'Good shot, Tom!' he said through clenched teeth.

His own much more puny effort was also straight and he managed to put a six-iron second into the middle of the green. Tom in turn chipped his short shot on to the green and watched it run perhaps six feet past the hole. There followed an illustration of what some enthusiasts call 'the glorious unpredictability of golf', and what its victims call something much more vulgar.

Jason Knight holed his curling putt of perhaps twenty-two feet up a sharp slope, then watched his opponent's six-footer lip the hole and stay out, to give him the hole. 'Bad luck, Tom! No justice!' said Jason, trying and failing to keep the elation out of his voice.

Buoyed by this unexpected success, he holed another decent putt to win the difficult fourteenth, where he had a shot. He managed to halve the next two short but tricky par fours, where Tom Bowles was unlucky not to make at least one birdie. He received his last shot on the long, difficult seventeenth, where he could not reach the green in two but managed to hole his tricky curling putt for a four and the win. For the first time in the afternoon, he was ahead. A half at the eighteenth would give him the match.

He got on to the green in two, but his ball ran to the back, leaving him a long putt to the hole. His rather tentative effort stopped a tantalizing four feet short. He studied the line he knew perfectly well for a long time before he could make himself hit the ball, then watched it run right round the rim of the hole before it dropped in. Tom was thrusting his hand out in congratulation almost before Jason could appreciate that he had won a famous victory.

Jason had a pint waiting for his opponent when he came into the bar. He had never even spoken to Tom Bowles before, but the tall young athlete now confirmed the impression Jason had formed of him on the course: he was a pleasant and friendly young man. Both of them were well aware that Jason would have been heavily defeated in a straight contest without handicaps, so that Tom was not much cast down by his defeat. He had more serious matters to contend with: a county match at the weekend to start with, and after that a move to London and a new job. He had already been proposed for membership at the prestigious Sunningdale Golf Club, a fact which much impressed Jason Knight.

'You're doing well to get in there so quickly,' he said. 'I suppose being scratch must help.'

'And being a lawyer doesn't do any harm. There's a strong legal element at Sunningdale, and a couple of them have proposed me.'

'What sort of a lawyer are you?' said Jason, trying not to sound too interested.

'The dull sort. Company law is my speciality.

It's nothing like as glamorous as criminal law, but pleasingly lucrative, so far.'

Jason Knight took a long pull at his pint, trying to disguise the fact that he was thinking furiously. This bright young man knew he was a chef, but nothing more than that. Like many bright lads of his age, Bowles was preoccupied with his own concerns and his own progress in life. He was leaving the area and going off to a new job in London very shortly; the probability was that Jason would never see him again. He said slowly, 'I expect being a lawyer must be like being a doctor – as soon as you say what you do people start asking for advice.'

'Not really, no. Company law isn't the most riveting subject. As a matter of fact, I'm still wet enough behind the ears to find it quite flattering when people think my opinion is worth having.'

'Really? Well, a pal of mine has a problem, actually. He's an important person in the firm, a key to its success, and he feels he should have more say in how the business is being run.'

'Which is understandable. Unfortunately, the fact that he's central to the firm's success doesn't give him any legal standing. Is he any more than a salaried employee?'

'No. He would like to be.'

Tom shook his head, transformed for a second or two into the dullest of family solicitors. 'Is it a public company? Could he buy shares?'

'No. It's a private limited company. There's just the owner and one very junior partner involved. In effect, it's a one-man band, with the owner making all the important decisions.'

Each of them was well aware by now that Knight was talking about himself, but it suited both to preserve the fiction of the mysterious friend, so as to keep the exchange at a less personal level. Tom Bowles said, 'Is there any chance of your friend becoming a partner?'

'How would he do that?'

Tom pursed his lips, shook his head sadly, and again looked for a moment like a much older man. 'Difficult, without the willing acceptance of the big cheese. He could offer to put up capital, when he sees the firm is short.'

Jason shook his head decisively. 'He couldn't do that. The firm is in perpetual need of capital, but he isn't in a position to provide it.'

'Then his only option seems to be to persuade the owner that he is so integral to the firm's development that he deserves greater recognition, in the form of a partnership.'

'And if that doesn't work?'

Tom Bowles grinned. 'He could try twisting his employer's arm. Tell the boss that he'd take his valuable labour elsewhere unless he got more recognition, in the shape of a share of the ownership. But he'd need to be very confident he was indispensable before he risked that. A friend of mine tried it and was looking for a new job the next day.'

'I'll pass on what you say,' said Jason glumly.

'I must be on my way,' said Tom Bowles with a glance at his watch. 'All the best in the next round of the knockout.'

'Thanks, Tom. And all the best in the new job and at Sunningdale.'

The bar was quiet at this time. Jason Knight bought himself another drink and sat quietly for a while, digesting the results of their discussion. He told himself not to be disappointed – this was surely what he had expected to hear. He had already known in his heart of hearts what the harsh facts of the situation were.

Martin Beaumont wasn't an owner prepared to listen to reason, to share his power with the man who was steadily building it up for him. If Jason was going to get the share of the business he wanted, he was going to have to use more than mere reason. Something much harsher would be needed.

# FOUR

Tom Ogden's family had farmed this land for almost four hundred years – since the area had been rent by the civil war which had resulted in the death of Charles I and the brief rule of Lord Protector Cromwell.

Tom had watched the spread of Abbey Vineyards beside him with interest – farmers are conservative folk, and a completely new use of land always seems more risky to them than to anyone else. That interest changed first into a

46

vague feeling of unease; this was rapidly followed by the outright apprehension which a small landowner always feels with the spread of a bigger and more prosperous neighbour. Yet Ogden had been glad to sell the highest and least productive part of his land to Martin Beaumont in the early days of the vineyard. The money had enabled Tom to convert the fertile lowland area of his farm to intensive cultivation. He had opted for a new life of his own which to him seemed quite daring enough.

Tom Ogden was now a strawberry farmer, with long rows of plastic cloches stretching away across his fields and an influx of foreign pickers at the height of the season. Both of these developments had brought opposition from different sectors of the local population. This opposition had been accorded full voice in the Gloucester *Citizen*, which had many pages to fill each evening and was delighted to fan local controversy. The issue had then been taken up by local radio, and had even featured on Central Television news. Tom Ogden had been uncomfortable in the face of such publicity, but had affected to treat it with the sturdy indifference farmers customarily accorded to aesthetes and townies.

Tom now had half his fields converted to the increasingly popular 'Pick Your Own' option for his strawberries. People came out from the towns and villages of Herefordshire and Gloucestershire to pick his produce, often treating the expedition as a family outing. They had caused a little damage at first with their clumsy fingers and clumsier feet, but Tom had soon learned to limit that. The important thing was that they paid almost as much for his strawberries as the retail price in the shops, and far more than he could get from the markets or supermarkets. Children in particular tended to eat energetically whilst they picked, but Tom treated that as a necessary but minor evil, to be set against the lower overheads of selling on site. He was delighted with his profits, whilst his customers enjoyed the warm glow brought by physical exertion and then the flavour of strawberries which could not have been fresher.

On this bright April day, Tom Ogden was looking over the bent backs of his workers, as they weeded the rows and nourished the promising green fruits with a little fertilizer. He imagined the summer scene here, when he would be listening to children's shrill cries to their parents, and congratulating himself on taking what had seemed an adventurous step into this new area of farming.

Ogden went out into the field and exchanged a few words with 'Spot' Wheeler, his foreman. No one, not even the man himself, was sure how he had acquired his soubriquet. He was Henry on his birth certificate, but he had answered to Spot for so long that no one knew any other forename for him. Spot had rarely ventured outside Herefordshire and had an accent far stronger than even Tom's very noticeable one, so that any Englishman from more than fifty miles away found his speech difficult to follow. Yet, in some strange combination of sign and sound argot, which perhaps even he could not have explained, Spot managed to communicate effectively with the variety of mainly Eastern European workers who came each year to work in the strawberry fields.

Tom Ogden always enjoyed talking to Spot, feeling an affinity with a man who had the same roots as he had, whose family had worked the land as his had for hundreds of years. Though neither of them would have acknowledged it or voiced it, the bond between them was sealed by a sense of rank. Spot Wheeler accepted his lower station as labourer and now supervisor of labour as unthinkingly as Tom accepted his role as owner of the land and thus master of his workers' destiny.

Spot gave his employer a brief report on the progress of cultivation and directed two of his newest workers to a new area with a series of guttural sounds; they nodded and bent anew to their work with the forks. Tom scratched his head, then shook it once again in happy wonderment at his foreman's ability to communicate with his workforce.

It was at that moment that a cloud fell across his world. It was a metaphorical cloud, for the day was golden still with a steady sun, but a cloud nonetheless. Spot Wheeler said suddenly, 'That chap be 'ere again, Mr Ogden,' and Tom turned to see a figure outlined against the sun at the entrance to his fields. It looked to him for a moment like some great bird of prey, black and ominous against the sky.

'I don't know why. I've told him often enough there's nothing for him here,' said Ogden, turning his steps reluctantly towards the interloper.

'Wonderful day, Tom!' said Martin Beaumont, when Ogden got within ten yards of him. He forced the farmer to fall into step with him, turning his path along the edge of the strawberry fields. Tom had been intending to lead him quickly back to the exit and his car. 'At least the sun and this southerly wind are fine for vineyards. I expect you'd like a little more rain to swell your strawberries. Temperamental crop, I believe. I shouldn't like to rely on them for a living.'

Ogden resisted the farmer's temptation to agree about the weather. It was one of the modern jokes that no season was ever exactly right for the farmer, but he did not wish to agree anything with this man. He said gruffly, 'Nothing like as temperamental as vines, I should think.'

'Oh, they're much less difficult than most people imagine, once you get the hang of viniculture. Everyone else is moaning about global warning, but it's helping us. And we've diversified as we've developed, you see, Tom. We've got quite a variety of grapes now, so that something's pretty well bound to do well, even in a difficult season. One of the secrets of success in the agricultural industry, diversification. Now that I've got used to diversity, I shouldn't like to be dependent on a single crop for my livelihood.' He looked sideways over the long rows of plastic cloches and the bent backs of workers in the open areas beyond them. 'Must be pretty labour-intensive, strawberries. Not a good thing, nowadays, with men likely to let you down the moment they get a better offer.'

'We've got autumn raspberries as well as strawberries. And I don't have difficulties with labour. The recession's made people glad of a job. It's true it was difficult to get workers, a couple of years ago, but I can pick and choose a bit now.'

'Really?' Beaumont let his elaborate surprise slide into a grin. 'Better not let the *Citizen* know that, eh, Tom? They'll be saying you should get rid of these cheap-labour foreigners and employ local labour!'

'If they do, I'll know where their information's come from, won't I?'

Beaumont made an elaborate show of looking hurt. 'Oh, it wouldn't be me, Tom. I'm your friendly neighbour, aren't I? But there are always plenty of people ready to make trouble for us chaps who provide the work, aren't there?'

'These men work hard all day and earn their money. I've no complaints about them.'

'I'll bet you haven't. Slave labour without union rates. We'd all like a bit of that!'

'They're not slaves and they're properly paid. It's none of your business, anyway, Beaumont.'

'Could be, Tom. Could be. In a roundabout

sort of way, of course. I'm still willing to pay a good price for your land, you see. Should be music in your ears, that, with the worst recession for eighty years gathering pace, and the price of agricultural land steadily dropping.'

'The recession's helping my business. More people are prepared to pick their own, in a recession.' Tom felt himself being drawn into an argument he had never intended to have.

'You'd get a higher price from me than from anyone else, Tom. You're lucky in that your land would fit neatly into my estate, as I've explained to you before. Our vineyards could span the valley nicely, if we took this little tongue of land in, so I'm still prepared to offer you the price I offered last year. That might not be the case for much longer, though.'

Ogden glanced from right to left. Beyond his land, all he could see was Abbey vineyards. His strawberry farm was an obstinate, alien wedge in Beaumont's empire. 'My family were farming this land for centuries before Abbey bloody Vineyards was even thought of, Beaumont! And we'll be here long after you've gone.'

Martin allowed himself a leisurely snigger, well aware that his derision was only increasing Ogden's fury. 'Oh, I doubt that, Tom, I really do! In fact, I doubt it so much that I'm prepared to say definitely here and now that it won't happen.'

'If you get your hands on these fields, it will be over my dead body!'

'Oh, let's not get all dramatic about it, Tom.

We're talking as two friendly neighbours. At the moment, I'm prepared to do you a favour and take over your land at an excellent price. I should hate it if that situation had to change.'

'I've said all I've got to say. You're wasting your time here, Beaumont, and I don't want to see you again!'

'Spreading alarm among the workers, am I?' Martin took a leisurely look towards the distant, diligent men in the valley below them, and saw Spot Wheeler watching them curiously. 'Perhaps some of them are a little more realistic about the situation than their employer.'

'They're no more interested in you and your schemes than I am.' Ogden turned his back ostentatiously upon his unwelcome visitor.

'I just hope no one causes trouble for you, Tom. Be a shame if they did.'

Ogden whirled back to face him, his weather-beaten face puce now with rage. 'And what the hell do you mean by that?'

'I was just thinking this would be a bad time for some mischief-maker to start moaning to the *Citizen* again about you employing foreign labour when Englishmen are losing their jobs all over the locality. Just as we move towards the height of your season, I mean. It would be a real shame if some person like that encouraged people to boycott your fields, now that you've made yourself dependent upon the pick-your-own clientele.'

'If that happens, I'll know where to come looking for the culprit.'

53

'Oh, it wouldn't come from me, Tom, anything like that. I'm hurt that you should think it might. I'm a friendly neighbour, remember. But you can't prevent people talking, and once someone like the *Citizen* or Radio Gloucester chooses to offer those voices a wider public, it's surprising how things can build up. Mass hysteria, someone called it to me the other day. Still, we'll hope it doesn't come to that, won't we? It would be such a shame if you had to sell your land on a falling market.'

Tom Ogden wanted to seize him by the throat, to wipe that silly, gloating smile off his face and see panic there instead. He thrust his hands deep into the pockets of his trousers, felt the fists already formed and trembling. 'Get off my land, Beaumont! Get off before I throw you off!'

'I'll go, I'll go!' The viniculturist held up his hands in mock horror. 'I can see you're not in the mood to listen to reason, Tom. That's a pity, from your point of view as well as mine.'

Beaumont left his words hanging as a threat in the soft spring sunshine and walked unhurriedly towards his Jaguar. He looked over his neighbour's land as he went and smiled an anticipatory smile.

# FIVE

It was a quiet Monday morning in Oldford police station. There had been the usual drunken brawls in the centre of Gloucester on Saturday night and the usual half-dozen 'domestics', involving more personal violence. The usual number of youngsters between thirteen and eighteen had left home without any notice of their plans or destination; they would now become official Missing Persons and be added to that melancholy register of misery.

There was nothing of great interest to CID here, and certainly nothing to excite the attention of Detective Chief Superintendent John Lambert, who was in danger of becoming bored. He had made his usual report to the chief constable. He had written up his comments on CID officers who were due for their career assessments. He had even made out a detailed case to those faceless financial controllers for the maintenance of his overtime budget, which had not been fully used in the last quarter.

He was fully up to date with his paperwork, a situation which the experienced members of his team recognized as a dangerous one: a bored Lambert asked the questions which a busy one thought far too petty for him. He was roaming the CID area and taking an unhealthy interest in detail. He had even approached Detective Inspector Chris Rushton for instructions in the mysteries of computer science, bravely asserting that old police dogs needed to learn new tricks, if they were to keep abreast with the criminals of the modern technological world.

Rushton found that the chief superintendent knew more than he admitted about the possibilities of the computer, which was a little disturbing. Chris was happier with his picture of the chief as a dinosaur in the modern police world, the chief super who was not happy as others were to direct the investigation of serious crime from behind his desk. The senior man who still insisted on getting out to confront those nearest to the offence and make his own judgements upon them. Yet this morning Lambert was filing away useful information from his discussions with Rushton on how best to use HOLMES, the national police file on serious crime and serious criminals.

Lambert also gave Rushton an item for the station news bulletin:

Detective Sergeant Bert Hook has graduated as BA with second class honours (division one) in the Open University degree for which he has been studying in his own time for the last six years. He deserves our heartiest congratulations on this very considerable achievement. Bert has informed his senior officers that it is

56

not his intention to look for accelerated promotion through the graduate recruitment scheme!

Chris Rushton smiled at the idea of stolid, reliable Bert Hook joining the fresh-faced and eager young graduates on the accelerated promotion scheme. He was prepared to agree now that Bert knew more about police work than most of these youngsters would ever learn. It had not always been so: Chris had felt at a moral disadvantage with Bert because he knew the older man had turned down the prospect of promotion to inspector years ago, because he preferred his work as a detective sergeant at the crime-face. It is almost unknown for policemen to turn down the chance of higher rank, and although Bert never broadcast the fact, and few people were aware of it, the considerably younger and newly promoted Chris Rushton had felt uncomfortable in the face of such integrity.

Hook himself had been in court that morning, sturdily resisting the attempts of a clever young defence barrister to trip him up and cast doubt upon his evidence. The Crown Prosecution Service had secured its conviction and Bert was back in the police canteen at lunch. He found himself much more embarrassed than he had been in court by the police banter about this new Einstein within their midst. Policemen, even sometimes quite senior policemen, feel more threatened by intellectuals than those in any other calling. When, as in Bert's case, a degree was accompanied almost uniquely by many years of solid work and achievement in feeling collars and putting dangerous men and the occasional woman behind bars, they did not know quite how to react. There was genuine admiration behind all the routine banter and the comments on this new professor in the Oldford ranks.

Lambert seized him during the afternoon and took him into his own office, where he produced the bottle of whisky which rarely left the bottom drawer of his filing cabinet and insisted upon a celebratory toast with his old colleague and friend. 'I never doubted you could do it intellectually, Bert. I just wondered whether your resolution would hold, with the crazy hours we sometimes work and a family growing up around you.'

'The boys have been a stimulus really, I suppose,' said Bert. 'Once I'd started, I could hardly give up, in the face of all their comments. And of course, Eleanor's been marvellous. I couldn't have done it without her looking after the kids for long hours on her own, as well as encouraging me whenever it seemed too high a cliff to scale. I expect it's Eleanor who's blown the gaff on me now. I didn't expect to come into a station which was throbbing with the news.'

'You can blame me for that. I'm the one who told Chris to put it in the station information bulletin. The grapevine then relays it pretty quickly, especially on a quiet Monday like this. You might as well bask in a little glory whilst it's there to be had. You know it will be the centre of gossip for about two days, until something more salacious like an officer's divorce takes over.'

'I suppose I have Eleanor to thank for you knowing about it.'

'Christine asked her outright over the weekend. You know what wives are like. You would not have wanted Eleanor to lie, would you?'

'I suppose not. And as you say, it's probably better to get all the jokes out of the way at once. It won't last.'

'We could do with a good juicy murder to get everyone's attention back on the things that matter. Not that one wishes ill upon any of the honest citizens who pay our wages, of course.' Despite this routine denial, both of them felt the familiar CID men's lust for a crime that would fully occupy their predatory minds.

On the Thursday of that week, Sarah Vaughan had an attentive audience and was riding upon the adrenalin which came from it. These people were enthusiasts for wine and the work of producing it, anxious to hear what she had to say about the short history of the industry here and the grapes which had been most successful.

This was the second tour she had led this week and probably about her sixteenth during the year. She was confident enough now to take the pulse of an audience. She no longer spoke too quickly in her nervousness, as she was sure she had done when she had begun this work. She hadn't watched her audience's faces as she spoke in those early days. Now she not only smiled back in response to their friendliness, but even made the odd joke which she knew had succeeded before. The trick was to make the joke seem spontaneous, not carefully calculated or rehearsed.

There were a lot of questions at the end of the tour, which she took to be a sign of its success. When she was answering questions about the new reds, she let it drop that they had high hopes of the grape in question and that they were taking a low mark-up on last year's vintage to get the brand established. Two bargain-conscious wine-fanciers among her audience promptly went into the shop and bought cases of red, under the approving eye of Gerry Davies.

It was four thirty when she finished the tour. As usual, she found herself quite tired once the audience had gone and she was alone in her small office. There was a lot of nervous tension involved in being on show before a live audience. She was learning to enjoy the tension, to relish the need to be on her toes in the face of a constantly changing clientele, but it was tiring nonetheless. She had done practice presentations years ago as part of her Business Studies degree, but it was not until this last year that she had undertaken the real thing. It gave her a kick to find that she was reasonably proficient as a communicator, and getting better with practice. She smiled to herself: that was the kind of verdict she might have had from her tutor on the degree all those years ago.

There wasn't much of the working day left. Sarah decided she might allow herself the luxury of an early departure, then remembered that she had taken her car in for a service that morning. She rang the garage and found that the Honda was ready for collection. Gerry Davies would give her a lift into Ross-on-Wye to pick it up, though it would be a good hour yet before he would be ready to leave. But she'd better go across to the shop and tell him that she needed a lift.

She was halfway across the little courtyard when a vehicle drew up at her side, so silently that it made her start with surprise. A glance sideways reassured her; it was Martin Beaumont's 3.8 blue Jaguar. The window beside her slid softly down and her boss said, 'Can I give you a lift anywhere? I see your car isn't here today.'

'No, it's in for service at Ross. But Gerry Davies will give me a lift – it's almost on his route home.'

'No need to bother him – he won't be off for another hour, will he, whereas I can take you now.'

She wondered whether to say that she had work to do, couldn't leave early. It was such an obvious tactic to impress the boss with her work ethic that someone as shrewd as Martin Beaumont would surely see through it. So she said, 'If you're sure it's no trouble,' and slid gratefully on to the leather passenger seat beside the owner of Abbey Vineyards.

He'd seen her making the tour, had noted the animation of her audience, and now commented approvingly upon it. He didn't miss much, the boss, as she'd quickly realized when she came here to work for him. He said suddenly, 'It's good to see you in a skirt for a change. All the attractive women seem to wear trousers nowadays.'

'I usually wear a skirt or a dress for the tours, unless it's cold and blustery. The public seem to like it.'

'I'm sure they do, when they see legs as attractive as yours, Sarah.'

She was mildly shocked and a little amused. Employers weren't supposed to make comments like that to their female staff nowadays, though she supposed she should regard herself as out of the working environment at this stage of the day.

As if he read her thoughts, Beaumont said, 'Of course, I wouldn't pass compliments like that at work, but we've finished for the day now, haven't we? And they are very attractive legs!'

She couldn't think of a suitable light-hearted rejoinder. She was willing him not to deliver any more clichés. She resisted the temptation to pull her skirt down a little further over the fifteen denier tights beneath it and said, 'You won't say that in a few years, when the varicose veins begin to take over.'

They both laughed at that and he said gallantly, 'I can't imagine you with varicose veins, Sarah Vaughan!'

'Age catches up with all of us, in the end,

doesn't it?' She had learned to bandy clichés with the best of them, she thought wryly. 'I'm thirty-three already, and I expect the next ten years will fly past even more quickly than the last.' It seemed to her a good moment to remind him that she was not some inexperienced ingénue who would be flattered by the attention of the boss, even though he was probably only engaging in a little harmless flirting.

'No one would think you were in your thirties,' he said gallantly, swinging the Jaguar round a long left-hand bend. 'Every time I see you I think what an attractive woman you are.'

'I think we should change the subject now,' she said firmly. For the first time, she felt a vague fear, not that anything dire was going to happen, but that she was going to have an embarrassing few minutes. He had taken the B road, she noticed, the old road into Ross rather than the M50. Nothing wrong with that; it was the shorter, if not the quicker, way. But she would rather have been on a route which carried more traffic; this road was hardly used at all since the motorway had become available.

Beaumont said nothing for a full two minutes, so that she hoped he had seen there was nothing in this for him; hopefully, he was thinking, as she was, about being mildly embarrassed when they met at work the next day.

Then, abruptly, he swung the big car into the deserted parking space beside the old road. 'It's time we had a little talk,' he said.

'Just drive me into Ross as you promised to

do, please,' Sarah said primly.

The speed of his movement caught her by surprise. He flung himself suddenly across her. His hand clutched her shoulder and he kissed her clumsily, holding her lips against his until she managed to twist her mouth away from him. His breath was hot and damp in her ear. 'You must be able to see what you do to a man, you little minx,' he muttered. 'Parading yourself up and down at the vineyard, twitching your hips as though you don't know what you're doing.'

She felt as though she had got herself involved in a bad play. He surely could not be saying these things. She felt the panic of claustrophobia which she had known when she was a child, pinned to the floor by other children. Her seat belt was still fastened, and there was no way she could release it with this great bear of a man leaning on her like this. She tried to bring her knee up between his legs, to slam it into his balls the way the self-defence manuals taught you to resist, but his leg was splayed across her, pinning her own thighs to the seat. 'Let me go! Get your fucking hands off me!' she shouted into his face.

She did not know where the word had come from: it was one she hadn't used in years. Her voice, harsh and grating with panic, seemed to have come from someone else. The smell of his aftershave crammed itself into her nose and her mouth, making her want to retch. Past the edge of his head, she could see a low wall, a field, bright green beneath the still steady sun and dotted with black and white cows, an innocent world which seemed to exist but be far beyond her reach.

His hand was on her knee now, trying to lift her skirt, the thick fingers sliding higher even as she tried to prise them off. 'You're not as innocent and wide-eyed as you pretend you are, young Sarah. You're a mature woman, like you said. You know what life's about and you're up for it really, however much you try to come the nun.'

Sarah managed at last to get her left arm free from under him, to bring it up and get a handful of the hair at the back of his head. She twisted her fingers to secure her grip, then tugged as hard as she could, bringing a scream and a clutch of obscenities from the mouth that was now six inches above her face and full of pain as well as lust. She was sure afterwards that it was the sight of that pain which gave her strength. She twisted abruptly sideways, brought the knee which still had his hand upon it up between his legs, bringing a new gasp of pain from him as he yelled, 'You bitch! You crazy bitch!'

She had the door of the car open as he clutched himself, but she was not quick enough with the unfamiliar catch on the safety belt. She was still fumbling with it when he clutched her arm with both of his hands, shouting, 'Stay where you are! If you don't want it, don't have it, you bitch! I'll drop you off at the garage in Ross as promised. You can keep your hand on your precious halfpenny!'

He reached across her, pulled shut the door she had managed to open. Sarah was still fumbling with the wretched safety-belt clasp. He restarted the engine, revving it furiously in his confusion, then moved out of the lay-by and back on to the road. They had ridden a good mile before his breathing steadied and he spoke. 'You can't blame me for trying. You're an attractive woman, Sarah.'

'I can blame you for forcing yourself upon me, when I quite plainly didn't want it.'

'Sometimes women like to play hard to get. Sometimes a little resistance is just part of the game.'

'I don't believe that. I certainly don't accept that I didn't make my feelings very plain to you.'

He didn't come back with any reply to that. Perhaps he knew that she was right. They were off the old road, running into the outskirts of Ross now, and there was other traffic around them. She reached for her bag, fumbled for her comb. He reached up and pulled down the sun visor in front of her, said with an attempt at his normal voice, 'There's a mirror on the back of that.'

She ran the comb through her hair, resisted the temptation to reach for her lipstick and restore her make-up. Somehow that would have been condoning his action, accepting it as no more than a harmless romantic sally rather than the ugly attack it had been.

As if Martin Beaumont sensed what was in her

mind, he said, 'It was just a pass at you that failed, that's all, Sarah. You must have dealt with a lot of those in your time. Don't make it more than it was.'

He was telling her not to make the mistake of taking this further, that this would be his story and that she had no witnesses to help her to establish that it had been anything more than that. Sarah Vaughan wanted to tell him that it had been something much bigger and much uglier than a simple pass. Passes were something callow young men did when they were seeking a kiss; not attacks mounted by an ageing roué who was trying to assert the power of company ownership. All this flashed through her mind, though she was not able to put it into words until much later.

They were running into the forecourt of the garage where her car awaited her now, so she said nothing at all. She did not even look at him again, but slid quickly from the Jaguar's leather and moved into the office area of the garage without a backward glance.

# SIX

Alistair Morton hadn't given up the idea of murder. Indeed, every time that Martin Beaumont denied him the share in the business he had promised, it seemed a more attractive option. It was true that in the cold light of day murder didn't seem as easy a proposition as it did when you dreamed of it alone in your armchair in the hour after midnight, but he was still convinced that if you planned it properly the crime was eminently possible.

Sometimes you needed to fan the flames of your hatred, to convince yourself anew of how badly the man was treating you. At the end of April, two months after he had first entertained the delicious notion of ridding the world of Martin Beaumont, Alistair elected to set his grievances before the boss again. You couldn't be fairer than that, surely? Giving the man a final chance to redeem himself before you proceeded with your plans against him was more than fair.

Had Alistair not been a secretive sort of man, he might have shared his thoughts with someone else. But Morton had a wife who lived her own life and no children. There was no one to tell him that his thinking might be a little unbalanced.

He presented himself at precisely ten o'clock for the meeting he had arranged with the owner of Abbey Vineyards. Exactly on time as usual, as Beaumont observed with a slightly mocking smile. Alistair accepted the boss's offer to sit in the chair in front of the big desk. He didn't see how he could do anything else, though he really wanted to stand toe to toe and challenge the man, not go through the rituals of a polite exchange.

'What can I do for you, Alistair?' Beaumont had that formal smile which Morton now saw as very false.

'You can honour your promises!' said Alistair. He had wanted it to be the harshest of challenges, cutting through the fripperies of polite exchanges. Somehow it sounded rather feeble in this large, quiet room, with its big framed photograph of the Malvern Hills, which always seemed to remind him of man's impermanence in this ancient landscape.

'And what would you mean by that?' Beaumont hadn't lost his surface affability; the meaningless smile remained glued to his face. But he was on his guard now, Alistair had no doubt about that. He looked beyond Morton, out through the big window to where Sarah Vaughan had just driven her Honda into the car park. Beaumont was glad to note her arrival; he had feared when she was not here at nine o'clock as usual that she might be planning

69

some retribution for yesterday's little incident.

Alistair glanced at the photograph of Beaumont standing alone beside their first tractor, hoping that the man in the big, round-backed leather chair would follow his look and his thoughts. 'I worked for practically nothing for you in the early days.'

Beaumont raised his eyebrows. This was familiar ground to him, but he had prepared his tactics. He would pretend that Morton's renewed accusations were a disappointment to him, a revival of an argument he thought he'd already settled. 'We all worked hard to get things off the ground. We can all look back to the sacrifices we had to make to get the show on the road. And equally, we can all be proud of the progress we have made since those early days.' They were the opening words of a press handout he had given to one of the glossy magazines three months ago, but he doubted whether this man would have read that article.

Morton wished the big man would just shut up and let him state his case. He followed the movement of Beaumont's lips, but as the man went on with his bluster he heard less and less of what he said. Eventually he interrupted him. 'I worked for almost nothing for you for five years at the beginning. Found and exploited every loophole which a new business could exploit, got you allowances you'd never have dreamed of for yourself. Even cut one or two corners for you, to make sure that every penny could be ploughed back into development.'

Beaumont grinned, happy to show how little he was affected by the man's earnestness. 'Careful now, Alistair. We wouldn't want you to go admitting to any little peccadilloes that might get you struck off, would we? Do they unfrock accountants, or is that just randy vicars?'

Alistair found his voice rising to a shout in the face of this derision. 'Just shut up, will you, and listen to what I'm saying. I worked for peanuts for at least the first five years when we started this. That was on the clear understanding that I would eventually become a partner and a director of the enterprise.'

'Not my recollection, I'm afraid. I seem to remember we've had this discussion before. I was hoping we'd agreed to differ and get on with our different tasks. Not good for any business to be running a divided ship, is it? Or am I mixing my metaphors there?' Beaumont frowned and shook his head, as if a proper literary style was at that moment pre-eminent among his objectives.

'You know as well as I do what was agreed. I was to become a partner in the business as soon as it proved itself a going concern.'

'Let other people take all the risks until the business was a guaranteed success, you mean? That hardly seems a likely arrangement for a businessman like me to make, does it?'

There was an awful sort of logic about that. Alistair could see him arguing that line with a third party and sounding very convincing. He said doggedly, 'You know and I know what was

71

agreed.'

Martin Beaumont raised the bushy eyebrows on his wide face as high as they would go, making him look to Morton like a caricature of outraged innocence. 'It seems we remember things rather differently, Alistair, which is a great pity. Have you anything in writing to support this strange recollection of our relationship during the early years of the company?'

'You know damned well I haven't!' Alistair sought hopelessly for some external evidence to endorse him. 'My wife remembers it. I gave more and more of my time to your affairs, as the vineyard got off the ground. Worked day and night, sometimes. The other work I scraped together as a freelancer scarcely provided a living wage. We depended on her work as a secretary to survive.'

That oily, ridiculous smile was back on Beaumont's hated features. 'Scarcely the most objective of witnesses, a wife. I'm sure that as an experienced financial man you'd readily agree with that, Alistair.'

Morton leaned forward, planting his fingers desperately on the edge of the big desk in front of him. 'We didn't think we needed anything in writing, in those early, enthusiastic days. Leastways, you didn't. And I was foolish enough to let you convince me that we didn't.'

Beaumont looked at the fingers clasping the other side of his desk for a moment, as if studying with interest the movements of some small mammal. Then he said, 'It doesn't really sound

72

like the conduct of a man trained in finance, does it, Alistair? A trained accountant, whose first watchword must surely be prudence? I can't think that anyone like that would have been party to some wildcat scheme which involved him giving his valuable time and labour for nothing, in exchange for some vague promise of jam in the future. I ask you, does it sound likely behaviour for an accountant, even to you? Do you think you've made out the sort of case which would convince any kind of mediator we might choose to bring in to resolve the issue? I don't think so, and neither will you if you give the matter some sober reflection.'

'It's over twenty years ago. I was a young man then, and you had enthusiasm and the gift of the gab. You sold me the notion of developing our own firm, of being our own bosses. You had a certain amount of capital to set up the company, I had the necessary financial skills to set it on the right lines and guide it through the early years. You know and I know what we agreed. I'm simply giving you the chance to honour that agreement, even at this belated stage.'

'I'm afraid we must agree to differ on this one, Alistair. I think you would agree that you are handsomely paid for your present services to the company. I suppose we might stretch to another thousand or so, if it would resolve your difficulties.'

'I'm not arguing about my present remuneration. I'm telling you that I shouldn't be on a salary at all. I should be taking my part in

73

formulating the policies of the company and receiving my share of the profits.'

'Cloud cuckoo land, I'm afraid, Alistair. Somewhere along the line – somewhere well in the past now – you've picked up the idea that I made silly promises to you about the future of my company. The sooner you dispense with that idea, the better for you as well as for everyone else concerned. I'm happy with the way you advise on the present financial status and problems of the company, and am content to pay you well for that. I should hate it if I had to look for a new head of finance. If you persist with these unreal ideas, I may be left with no alternative but to do that.' He made an elaborate ploy of looking at his watch. 'And now, unless you have any more relevant ideas for me to consider, I think we should both get on with our working days.'

Alistair Morton offered him a look of molten anger, which lost all meaning when he found he was being coolly ignored in favour of the contents of a folder on Beaumont's desk. He left without another word and put the 'Engaged' sign up on the door of his own, smaller office.

There he sat alone with his humiliation for a good twenty minutes. He had gone into the man's office with the intention of issuing an ultimatum. Both of them had known perfectly well what Beaumont had promised in those early, pioneering days. But the older man had chosen once again to refuse him, to patronize him, not only to deny him justice but to reject

74

him with contempt. He had even closed with a threat about his present post.

Well, he had given Martin Beaumont his final chance to offer him justice. It was surely now time to consider how he might translate his idea of murder into a practical plan of action.

Had Alistair Morton but known it, there was another person, not at present on the site of Abbey Vineyards, who felt almost as violently towards its owner as he did.

Vanda North was wondering what her next move against Beaumont should be. She wasn't going to confront him again and risk more humiliation. It was clear to her that he was not going to relent. She had taken all the relevant papers to her lawyer a week ago and this morning she was going to consult him. She parked her car in the multi-storey car park in Gloucester and forced her unwilling steps towards the lawyer's office in Westgate.

Lawyers were not among Vanda's favourite people. She preferred callings more adventurous, less cautious, less pessimistic about the human condition and the way it made people behave. Lawyers, and solicitors in particular, were in Vanda North's view a necessary evil rather than people she would willingly consort with. But she had to admit that there were some situations in which they and their professional opinions were very necessary.

James Dolby complied with all her notions about the legal profession. He was approaching sixty; his straight grey hair was cut short at back and sides and immaculately parted. He was smartly dressed in an extremely conservative way, with the creases in his pinstriped trousers complemented by an immaculate white shirt and a dark blue tie. As he rose and greeted her with old-fashioned politeness, he looked to Vanda like a man who had never taken a chance in his life. The next twenty minutes were to reinforce that view, as James Dolby made it eminently clear that he saw the primary function of lawyers as being to protect their clients from undertaking any sort of risk.

Dolby had the copy of the agreement his client had signed twelve years ago with Martin Beaumont. He waited until Vanda was seated opposite him and the door of his private office was closed, then looked down with unconcealed distaste at the document. 'May I ask who was your legal adviser when this agreement was drawn up, Ms North?'

Vanda felt like an impulsive sixth-former called before the headmistress as she said, 'I don't think I had any legal advice at all on the terms of the agreement.' She watched him nod sadly several times, then felt she must break the silence with which he reinforced his disapproval of such wanton rashness. 'I realize now that I was rather foolish not to have it vetted.'

Dolby renewed his nodding at this. He turned over first one page and then a second, winced a little at what he saw there and said at last, 'Rather foolish is putting it mildly I'm afraid,

76

Ms North.'

'I was too trusting of the major partner in the business. I realize that now.'

He nodded his agreement, almost eagerly, she thought.

'I'm afraid our wide experience of human conduct makes us lawyers rather cynical, Ms North. It's a sad thing, but we have to advise people against being too trusting.'

'Yes. I understand now that I should have tempered trust with a little healthy suspicion.'

He winced a little at the aggression of the word. 'We wouldn't see it as suspicion, of course. We would prefer to use the term discretion.'

Vanda shrugged her shoulders hopelessly. How could she explain to a man like this the excesses induced by an overwhelming sexual attraction? She had signed this hideous tract at the height of her passion for Martin Beaumont, very probably after an intense session between the sheets. It was a lover's concession, a lover's declaration of trust, a lover's assurance to a man who held her in thrall that she trusted him with the rest of her life, that she did not need dry legal agreements when she was throwing in her lot with him. How could she ever make this dry stick of a man, this Dickensian caricature of legal caution, understand a vulnerability which at this distance she could no longer understand herself?

She reminded herself sternly that she was paying this man handsomely for his services, that there was really no reason why she should slip into the role of chastened schoolgirl. 'I realize now that I should have taken legal advice at the time, that I was very foolish not to do so. What I want to know is whether I have left myself any room at all for manoeuvre.'

James Dolby nodded his acknowledgement of the query, then looked once again at the brief document and shook his head sadly. 'Very little room at all, I fear. May I ask how good your present relationship with the senior partner in this enterprise is?' He made a great show of turning back to the beginning of the document, though she was certain he knew perfectly well by this time the name he was seeking. 'This Martin Beaumont.'

She suddenly wanted to shock this paragon of respectability, this moving statue of decorum. 'At the time when this agreement was drawn up, I was sleeping with Martin Beaumont. He was rogering me daily and I was thoroughly enjoying it, Mr Dolby. I'm afraid my feelings at the time affected my judgement, as you can see all too easily from what is in front of you.'

He was disappointingly unruffled. He raised the grey legal eyebrow the merest fraction, then nodded his head. 'I wondered if something of the kind was involved. You did not strike me as the sort of woman who would normally tolerate something like this.'

Vanda supposed that was meant as a compliment. He knew more about the way life worked than she had given him credit for. She had a

78

distressing image of a pinkly naked James Dolby, standing with a lascivious smile at the foot of her bed and launching himself upon her with a most unlawyerlike bellow of 'Geronimo!'. It was most disconcerting. She told herself sternly that she must banish this most unsuitable of pictures, but it was vivid enough to rear its unwelcome head at various moments during the rest of her day. She said as steadily as she could, 'I acknowledge now that I was a fool, and I don't want you to pull any punches to save my feelings. What I need to know is whether this agreement is of any use to me at all at this moment.'

'Do I take it that your feelings for this gentleman are no longer so ... er, warm?'

'You do indeed. I would willingly put a gun to his head, if I thought I could get away with it.'

Dolby held up a restraining hand. 'You should not voice such thoughts, Ms North, even in jest.' But a tiny smile played about the edge of his mouth as he spoke the words, and Vanda apprehended for the first time that he was quite enjoying the rituals of this little exchange. She had no idea whether she was pleased or outraged by this realization. Dolby enquired innocently, 'And am I right in presuming that Mr Beaumont no longer retains intense and intimate feelings for you?'

'We haven't slept together for at least eight years. And you can see from what is in front of you that he never entertained intense feelings for me. I was infatuated with him and I persuaded myself that he felt the same way about me. I know now that that was wishful thinking, mere self-deception. The proof of that is in those pages you have in front of you.'

'I'm afraid it is indeed, Ms North. Everything in this document is overwhelmingly to Mr Beaumont's advantage. I can only assume that he prepared the agreement himself, with his own interests pre-eminent throughout.'

'I agree. What I want to know from you is whether I have any hope of overturning some of those provisions which so obviously favour him.'

This time he looked genuinely rather than merely professionally disappointed for her. But perhaps that was just one of the skills lawyers developed to justify their fees, she thought. Dolby leaned forward earnestly and said, 'My only hope was that the other party in this was favourably disposed towards you. Now that you have assured me that that is not the case, I'm afraid I have little comfort to offer you. You put £80,000 into Abbey Vineyards with no clear guarantee of any return. You own one sixth of the business, but with such strings attached that it is a highly illiquid asset. You cannot dispose of your share of the business, nor even withdraw your capital, without the full consent of the major partner.'

'Which he steadfastly refuses to give me. Beaumont claims that under the terms of this agreement, my investment is made in perpetuity.'

'Which it clearly is, in the terms agreed by you in this document. It is an eminently one-sided and unfair agreement, in my view, and we could go to law and challenge it on those grounds. The trouble is that you signed your full consent to all these clauses at that time, almost like a wife eager to support her husband's enterprise. I fear that a plea of sexual infatuation is not one that is readily acceptable in English law. We might win, but I could not guarantee it and it would in any case be a costly business. If we lost, you see, the considerable legal costs of his defence might well be awarded to Mr Beaumont. In these circumstances, I could not recommend you to take this matter to court.'

'That is what I feared you would say.' Vanda flicked her short fair hair back over her forehead, resisting a sudden, unexpected wish to cry.

'In my view, you are probably correct in your assumption that Mr Beaumont drafted this very unfair document himself. It does not have the stamp of a professional legal mind. In particular, it makes no mention of what happens to the business in the event of the demise of either partner, which is a most unusual omission.'

'And what do you think might happen in such an event?'

He pursed his professional lips, a move which seemed to take considerably longer than the pursing of mere lay lips like Vanda's. 'I really couldn't say. It would have the makings of a most interesting exploration by industrial lawyers. There are only two partners, and although you are much the junior one, I feel that in the event of either partner's death, the other one would have a strong case for taking over the direction of the business, probably in conjunction with the heirs of the deceased.'

'That is an interesting thought.'

James Dolby gave her his most genuine smile of the morning. 'It is indeed. And in view of that, Ms North, I would urge you most strongly not to repeat publicly your sentiments about putting a gun to the gentleman's head.'

# SEVEN

Eleanor Hook put the official-looking envelope beside the box of cereal and waited patiently for her husband's reaction. Bert slit the envelope with his knife, studied the single sheet of contents with an impassive face, then cast it aside. He said decisively, 'Well, I shan't be attending *that*.'

Eleanor picked up the discarded sheet and quickly digested its contents. She said with ominous, wifely certainty, 'I think you should.'

'It's not my kind of thing. You know I don't like being on show.'

'This is one occasion when you should be. It's a recognition of your achievement. A chance for your family to share in your triumph.'

'You're getting this out of proportion. It's an Open University BA. That's not a triumph. It's a decent achievement, alongside hundreds of other people.'

'It is a triumph,' said Eleanor firmly. 'Considering how you've had to study, fitting it in around a variable load of CID work, never being certain when you'd have time to work at this and when you wouldn't, it's a terrific achievement. I know that. The boys know that, for all their joking. We want to see the formal recognition of what you've achieved.'

As if responding to a cue, Jack and Luke made a robust entry at this point, sounding as usual like a regiment descending the stairs. 'It's all right for you to read that!' said Eleanor, as her elder son seized on the letter, which had drifted to the floor.

'Open University Graduation Ceremony, May the thirteenth,' Jack announced to his brother.

'Oh, great, Dad!' said Luke enthusiastically. 'Will we be able to photograph you wearing one of those daft hats?'

'If you're thinking of that comedian receiving an honorary doctorate at the University of Northampton,' said his father testily, 'I'm afraid I don't qualify for anything so lofty or so freakish. I'm merely a Bachelor of Arts, not a doctor.'

'A distinction which you have thoroughly earned, rather than one awarded for no academic achievement whatsoever,' said Eleanor stoutly.

'No daft hat?' said Luke in undisguised

disappointment.

'No daft hat,' said his father firmly.

'Most of the graduates I've seen in pictures seem to have mortar boards,' said Jack thoughtfully. 'I think a mortar board on you might look quite daft enough for us.'

'Not as good as bright green with a big tassel, though.' Luke refused to be consoled. 'Any chance of you going on to become a doctor, do you think, Dad?'

'None whatsoever. The next graduates in this family will be you and Jack.'

'Don't rely on it, Dad. I fancy being an interesting drop-out,' said Jack provocatively. 'Stripped to the waist with a guitar, I should think. Driven to new heights of performance by banned substances.' He eyed his mother surreptitiously, but for once she refused to be drawn by his lurid provocation.

'If you want any breakfast, you'd better cease these ridiculous imaginings and get on with real life,' Eleanor said firmly.

'The local press will be interested in this,' said young Luke with relish. 'Sort of "Dull copper reveals hidden depths of scholarship" line.'

Jack's eyes lit up. 'You're right, Luke. "Sherlock lurks within the village bobby" stuff. I'm sure you and I will get together some interesting copy for the media if we give our minds to it tonight. You got any plans to retire to the south coast and keep bees, Dad?'

'None whatsoever. I'm going in to the station now to continue the task of keeping crime off our streets. Of making them safe for cheeky young scoundrels like you two!'

Jack nodded his fifteen-year-old approval. 'Good on yer, Dad! You'd better think what you're going to say to local radio, though. They're sure to want an interview, after Luke and I have finished as your PR men. I should think television and the national press will be on to it pretty quickly, after we've made our first releases.'

'If I hear that you've said a word to anyone, there'll be trouble!' said Bert, with as much menace as he could muster.

Eleanor followed him out to his car. 'You've got to go to the graduation ceremony,' she said firmly. 'I know they like ribbing you, but those two lads will be as proud as Punch to see you get your degree.'

Gerry Davies was happy to see the Abbey Vineyards shop crowded with people on a Saturday morning. Weekends were usually their busiest time, as you would expect, but it was good to see that there was as yet little sign that the recession was affecting either the number of visitors or their rate of spending.

There had been almost from the start a pleasing mutual support between the shop and the restaurant, which now carried two AA Rosettes. People who bought wines and other offerings in the shop became aware of the restaurant, with its pleasantly spacious rooms and its splendid outlook over the slopes of vines and the wilder

85

and more dramatic outlines of the Malvern Hills in the distance. It was difficult to imagine dining anywhere in the area with a better view, a point emphasized by the colour postcards they displayed and sold in the shop.

Equally, there was now substantial evidence that those who enjoyed their meal and its accompanying wines in the restaurant often returned to the shop in the weeks which followed, keen to buy the wines they had sampled and enjoyed with their excellent food. Gerry Davies had no culinary skills himself, but that made him only more appreciative of those of Jason Knight. They were two very different men, but they had worked well together from the outset. And, to Gerry's secret surprise, they not only respected each other but enjoyed each other's company.

Gerry's father had been a Welsh miner in the Rhondda Valley in the years before Thatcher's government had decided that Britain no longer needed its pits. Gerry had enjoyed the mixed benefits of a comprehensive education, then left school at sixteen to work in a steel works which had closed down when he was thirty-two. The closure had proved a blessing in disguise. After six weeks of the misery of unemployment and supporting a wife and two children on social security, he had obtained employment in a supermarket.

Initially he earned little more than he had been paid 'on the social'. But Gerry had not only recovered his self-respect but revealed a talent for

86

the retail trade hitherto unsuspected by himself as well as the world at large. Tesco had recognized this swiftly, and he had enjoyed three promotions before becoming manager of one of its new smaller outlets on a garage site. When thirteen years ago Martin Beaumont had been looking for a manager to expand the sales and the range of activities at the shop at Abbey Vineyards, he had shrewdly recognized in Davies a man of forty-four who had both achievement and further potential.

The entrepreneur who was the driving force behind Abbey Vineyards and the man who felt he still had something to prove had struck up an immediate, instinctive and productive relationship. Each was anxious to prove to a sceptical world that English wine had a bright and exciting future. In their different ways, both men were proving themselves. Both were therefore prepared not to count the hours they spent in pursuit of the development of the company into a more profitable enterprise.

There had been no destructive rivalry between them. Beaumont had been the entrepreneur content to make his savings, his working hours, his whole life dependent upon the success and prosperity of this enterprise. Davies had never aspired to be more than a trusted employee. He had devoted his loyalty and all of his newly discovered and newly recognized retail talents towards the commercial exploitation of British wine. Gerry Davies relished his confounding of a job market which had once deemed him unfit for employment. It gave him additional satisfaction to be making a successful career by steadily expanding the distribution of English wine. This was a product which more distinguished business heads than his had once dismissed as frivolous and thus unsaleable.

In a different way from those of Detective Sergeant Bert Hook, the wife and two boys of Gerry Davies were also at once surprised and delighted by the achievements of the head of the family. Gerry's children were much older than Bert's. They had gone to university and were carving out careers of their own, but they became steadily more admiring of their father's achievements.

Gerry Davies had the ability to work productively and to mix socially with men with very different backgrounds from his own, and that too had been part of his continuing success at Abbey Vineyards. Jason Knight, the chef behind the success of the restaurant, was a very different man from Davies. Unusually among those of his calling, he had an excellent education, including a university degree. He was also well travelled and had an interest in business practice, which gave him very different thoughts about the future of Abbey Vineyards from those of Gerry Davies.

Yet the two men had got on well from the start. They had formed an excellent working relationship, being prepared to exchange ideas quite frankly and to heed and learn from the other's very different experiences and expertise. From this had grown a genuine friendship, a relish of each other's company and a concern for their interests and happiness. They moved easily within each other's areas without either feeling in any way threatened.

Thus Gerry Davies was delighted to see Jason Knight come into the shop area, even at eleven thirty, the busiest time on a busy Saturday morning. The younger man waited patiently whilst Gerry helped an overworked assistant at the Dog's Whiskers beer pump. Then he said quietly, 'I'd like a word with you, Gerry.'

'Sure. I'll make myself free in a moment.'

'A rather longer word. Want to run one or two ideas past you.'

Gerry was pleased to hear the jargon. He still found it difficult to believe that his working ideas could be considered valuable by senior and successful people like Jason Knight. But Jason didn't do bullshit. He must genuinely have something to discuss; he wouldn't just go through the motions to be tactful. 'OK. When do you suggest?'

'Can you do a late lunch in my little den? Say two o'clock?' Jason had insisted on having his own small private retreat at the end of the kitchens away from the restaurant, where he could escape to save his sanity and keep his temper in those trying times which beset every chef, and Martin Beaumont had sensibly granted it to him.

The older man grinned. 'Sure I can. I'll let my staff have their breaks at civilized times. They'll think I'm being unselfish, waiting until two.'

Gerry spent the next part of his morning persuading a hesitant lady in late middle age that she really would enjoy a bottle of their cheapest rosé. It took him slightly fewer minutes to organize the delivery of a dozen cases of their best current dry white to a fashionable restaurant in the Cotswolds. Only then did he have a moment to speculate about what it could be that was important enough to Jason for him to arrange such a meeting. Only the closest of friends or associates were ever invited into the den. Only something which was really engaging Jason's attention would dictate an exchange there in the middle of a busy day.

Sometimes Bert Hook quite liked being at the station on Saturday mornings. He couldn't admit to it at home, of course – he maintained the conventional attitude of the overworked and exploited public servant there – but he rather enjoyed being in Oldford nick with few people around, as was usual at a weekend, unless there was a major case to justify the overtime.

You could tidy up your paperwork without interruptions or, as he was doing on this occasion, utilize your developing computer knowledge to explore the Internet. He was consulting the Open University website, with particular reference to graduation ceremonies, when he found John Lambert looking over his shoulder.

Bert started a little guiltily and said grumpily, 'I'm going to have to waste a day's leave in

May. Eleanor and the boys are insisting on attending the OU graduation ceremony, to see me parading in fancy dress.'

'Quite right, too. I'll need to take a day of my leave, too. I'll have to confirm for myself that it's really happened and old Bert's made it at last.'

'"Old Bert" can give you ten years, John Lambert. "Old Bert" isn't operating on a special Home Office extension to his normal service.'

'And "Old Bert" has been energetic enough and determined enough to study for six years in his own limited spare time and get himself a degree. Quite a distinguished degree, in my opinion. So much so that I absolutely insist on being present at the official recognition of your labour of Hercules.'

'Bloody hell, John!' A very mild expletive by police standards, but strong words for Bert Hook, who had eschewed all intemperate language since the birth of his first son. 'This is getting out of hand.' A happy escape suddenly presented itself to him. 'I probably won't be able to get tickets for everyone. They said in the letter that there was normally heavy demand and the supply was almost certain to be restricted.'

'And it advises you here to make the earliest possible application for any extra tickets you might require.' Lambert indicated a line towards the bottom of the screen. 'Better get on with it, I'd say, Bert. Two extra tickets for Christine and myself. Try telling them an unbelieving chief superintendent needs to see the official confirmation of a copper's achievement with his own eyes.' He gazed into the middle distance. 'I suppose I could always offer to take charge of security if there were real difficulties about getting in.'

Gerry Davies was thoroughly intrigued by Jason Knight's mysterious summons. At two o'clock he proceeded cautiously to the chef's den at the far side of his kitchen.

The lunchtime rush was almost over and Knight's staff were winding down and preparing to close the restaurant and enjoy their own lunches. Jason had removed his chef's hat and combed his dark-blond hair, but was still wearing his white overalls as he came into the small room which was his private domain. 'Thanks for coming, Gerry. I know you'll keep this to yourself – it's not the sort of discussion either of us would want bandied about.'

'This gets more intriguing by the minute. What is it that we need to be so cloak and dagger about?'

Jason grinned in that beguiling, almost schoolboyish way which was so engaging. 'I take myself too seriously sometimes, don't I? But I still think this is important to both of us.'

'Then I've no doubt it is. I hope it's nothing too difficult for a simple thick Welsh boy from the Rhondda.'

'Don't undersell yourself, Gerry. You've nothing left to prove. The company is doing well. Agreed?'

'You're better equipped to judge that than I am, Jason. But I think so, yes. Martin said it was at last month's meeting, and from what I can see in the shop since then, we're going from strength to strength.'

'I would agree with that from what I see in the restaurant. But I think it's Martin's policy to keep us all a little in the dark about the success of the total enterprise. We each have a pretty good idea about what's going on in our own section of the empire, but only the haziest notion of the overall progress of Abbey Vineyards.'

'That's inevitable, surely. It's the nature of the beast.'

'It seems to be, at present. I think it's also policy on Martin's part.'

'But even if you're right, there isn't much we can do about it, is there? We could ask for a rise, I suppose, but if I'm honest I have to say that I think I'm already pretty well paid for what I do.'

'You're too modest for your own good, Gerry. I told you, you shouldn't underestimate yourself, or what you've achieved here.'

Gerry Davies wasn't sure whether he was pleased or disturbed by this. Bewildered was more the word, he decided: he couldn't see where the conversation was going. 'Jason, we know each other too well to piss about. What is it you're getting at?'

'I want to sound you out about an idea. In confidence, as I said at the outset. I haven't spoken to anyone else about this, except to take informal legal advice on the situation.' Jason supposed that a ten-minute discussion over a pint with an industrial lawyer in Ross-on-Wye Golf Club just about constituted that.

'Hadn't you better tell me straight out what's bothering you? I'm not much good at guessing games.'

'Sorry. Well, to put it at its simplest, I feel we should have a greater say than we have at present in company policy, and a greater share of the profits the company is going to make in the years to come.'

'And how do we get that? Perhaps it should be obvious, but I'm out of my depth here.'

'We should have shares in the company.'

'But it's a one-man band. Martin Beaumont set it up and took all the early risks.'

'No. Not quite. Vanda North is a junior partner. I don't know how junior, but she put money into the business in the early days.'

'When they were living together.'

'I presume so. I get the impression that she's very much a junior partner, without any real say in policy.'

'Perhaps she prefers it that way, whilst the company goes from strength to strength.'

'Perhaps. I didn't get that impression at last month's meeting, or on one or two other occasions. But as I say, apart from taking a little professional advice, you're the first person I've spoken to about this.'

'So what are you suggesting we do?'

'That's what I want to discuss. The first thing to establish was whether you felt the same about

94

the situation as I did.'

Gerry paused for several seconds. 'My first reaction is that I enjoy my work and like things the way they are. I feel that I'm doing a good job but that in return I am well paid for it.'

'I thought you might feel like that.' Jason Knight couldn't quite keep the disappointment out of his voice. 'I knew you'd be absolutely straight with me. But in turn I think I should urge you not to underestimate yourself. Martin Beaumont's success probably owes more to you than you imagine.'

'We all contribute to it. But that's what we're paid for. Martin took a chance on me when he gave me this job. I work hard partly because I love my job and partly because I want to repay him for his faith in me.'

'You're wrong about one thing in that. He didn't take a chance when he picked you, Gerry. You'd proved yourself with Tesco. They promote talent, but they're efficient and hard-headed about it. How many times did they promote you?'

'Three. From very humble beginnings.'

'I didn't know it was three. But that proves my point. Martin wasn't taking a chance when he chose you to run his shop and retail sales here: it was a hard-headed business decision. You were in charge of one of Tesco's new small stores and no doubt making a success of it. He chose the best candidate of those he interviewed to come here. He's a good picker – I'll give him that!'

'I think he was taking a chance. But even if you're right, he put me into a job I enjoy and he's paid me handsomely for doing it well. I don't see that he owes me any more than that.'

'Maybe not in the last industrial generation. The one where unions fought employers for whatever they could get and as often as not destroyed each other. But employee involvement is one of the modern trends. Even big companies are seeking to involve their workers in share schemes, to give them an ongoing interest in the prosperity of the company and reward them for good service. It's the modern way.'

Gerry Davies grinned, his teeth looking for an instant very white against his still thick and densely curly black hair. 'I don't deny I'm old-fashioned and content with things as they are. I'm fifty-seven now – perhaps too old a dog to learn new tricks, Jason. Probably out of the ark, in your terms.'

'I don't believe that and I don't think you do. All I'm asking you to do is to consider the situation here. We're part of a successful enterprise which promises to become bigger and better – principally through the efforts of no more than six people. Martin Beaumont himself, who should without question remain the major bene-ficiary of his original vision and input. Vanda North, because she is at present the only one with any official share in the company above that of wage-earner. Alistair Morton, who has handled the finances of the company since the beginning and should in my book be its financial director. Me, who should be in charge of the restaurant and possibly the allied area of residential accommodation. You, who should be the sales director. Sarah Vaughan, who has made a promising start and should probably be in charge of research and development.'

'You've obviously given this a lot of thought. But would these be anything more than grandiose titles?'

Jason Knight grinned. 'Indeed they would. What I'm proposing is that we should be involved in the formulation of policy. In historical terms, I believe we're still in the early stages of the development of a major company. We're key figures, who have already proved ourselves in different ways, and we deserve to have our roles in shaping what will become a much larger concern.'

Gerry Davies tried to take this in. It made sense, once you adjusted your viewpoint. 'You've got a wider vision of things than I have, Jason.'

'There's nothing wrong with that. And there's nothing wrong with being ambitious, is there?'

'No. No there isn't. But you're pushing me out beyond the boundaries of where I work and feel comfortable.'

'But not beyond where you would be competent. I'm pushing you – pushing all of us, if you like – to recognize what we're capable of. It might be a little uncomfortable, even a little frightening. But it's exciting as well.'

Gerry Davies thought hard about that, then suddenly smiled. 'You may well be right. I haven't got beyond uncomfortable at the moment.'

Jason Knight smiled in his turn, a little ruefully, a little at his own expense. 'I get carried away a bit, don't I?'

'You do a bit. But I'm not saying you're wrong. I'm just finding it difficult to adjust. In my terms, I've come a long way in a short time and I still sometimes go home and can't believe I'm so lucky. I don't say you're wrong, but it's a lot for me to take in.'

'I say it's not luck but talent and application which have put you where you are. But I appreciate what you say – taking on the idea of pushing for more power is a new concept. I'm not asking you to decide anything now. Give the matter some thought over the weekend and the next few days. Discuss it in confidence with your sons and see what they think. There's no immediate hurry, though I think the sooner we move the better it will be for us. I shan't say anything to anyone else until I have a reaction from you.'

Gerry stood up, then voiced a final thought. 'Martin Beaumont regards this as very much his company. He won't be easy to convince.'

Jason grinned at the older man. 'There you are, I told you that you had the potential. You're thinking like a strategist already, you see, not a mere employee. This is company politics among the senior staff, if you like. And you're right, of

98

course. Martin probably wouldn't listen to any one of us as an individual. He'd say no, and if we persisted he'd tell us to piss off and look for other employment. But if we went as a group and told him we wanted in, I don't believe he'd be willing to risk losing all of us at once. I'll be interested to hear whether you agree with that view when you've given the matter some extended thought.'

Gerry Davies was very busy in the shop area for the rest of the day. During the rare moments when he had time to think about his exchange with his friend in the restaurant, he found that he had already accepted one thing at least.

Taking over control of the firm was an exciting idea.

# EIGHT

Jane Beaumont was a sad figure. Although she was actually two years younger than her husband, she now looked a good five years older than him. When Martin had married her after a short courtship, she had been a tall, willowy girl, with flowing tennis ground strokes and two appearances at Wimbledon behind her. She had considerable ability in several other sports and a physique which reflected this. She had been a lively, pretty twenty-four-year-old, with perfect white teeth and a wide and frequent smile.

Jane Montague had had everything going for her, in that popular phrase of the seventies. She had been educated at Roedean and her teenage years had been carefully monitored by protective parents. A couple of generations earlier, she would have been that peculiarly British female phenomenon, a debutante. Her old-fashioned father sent her to a Swiss finishing school rather than a university. The company she kept was carefully selected for her. But this was the late seventies, not the thirties, and the dutiful daughter began to insist rather belatedly on choosing her own friends.

Then, within the space of eighteen months, Jane's father was killed in one of the fast cars he could never resist and her mother died of ovarian cancer. Three months later, the attractive young athlete Jane Montague was married to the handsome, articulate and eminently plausible Martin Beaumont. Thus was she cut off from the life she had just begun to explore.

Two of Jane's aunts had reluctantly assumed some sort of oversight of their niece after the unexpected deaths of her parents. They were disturbed by the sudden advent on the scene of this predatory young man, especially in view of Jane's newly acquired wealth. But they were no match for the energy and persuasiveness of Martin Beaumont.

Jane was old enough to make her own decisions, she told them. She was certainly legally well past the age when she needed to heed their reservations. If the aunts suspected that these arguments were articulated by the young man who stood to benefit from them, there was very little they could do about that. Jane Montague became Jane Beaumont and disappeared from their world.

Jane was very taken at first with the whole business of marriage. Because of her protected upbringing, sex was a later and more exciting discovery to her than it was to the vast majority of her contemporaries. But the children she had taken to be an inevitable consequence of union did not arrive. She was disturbed as well as puzzled by that, though her husband did not seem unduly worried. And during the first two years of her marriage, her allegiance to Martin was unquestioning and indeed unthinking.

At the end of that period, she realized that he had invested the whole of her inheritance in a new and exciting project he decided should be called Abbey Vineyards. It was done not without Jane's knowledge but without her real aware-ness. Martin assured her repeatedly in the long years which followed that this was no one's fault but her own. Because she had been com-pletely trusting or, as her husband put it, had shown no real interest, Martin had walled in her participation in his enterprise with all sorts of restrictive clauses from his lawyer. The implica-tion throughout the documents was that the capital which fed the firm had been provided by the man who drove and controlled it.

All this was of no matter, Martin assured Jane.

They had agreed marriage for better or for worse, hadn't they? What was his was hers, and vice versa, of course. That meant that when it emerged when she was thirty that Jane was suffering from bipolar disorder, there was no question of her long-suffering husband choosing to renounce the burden. If she had to be treated in specialist hospitals rather than at home during the periodic attacks which were part of her disorder, that was unavoidable and only showed his concern to do everything possible to alleviate her suffering.

The suggestions from Jane's few remaining friends that Martin had provoked and exacerbated this disturbing condition in his wife were both mischievous and ill-conceived. Surely anyone with even rudimentary medical knowledge knew that the condition was genetic? It had been there from birth, Martin reasoned, but had probably been disguised in childhood and adolescence by the obsessively sheltered upbringing which the then Jane Montague's parents had visited upon their only daughter.

Martin took his sexual pleasures elsewhere, of course. Some of his male acquaintances nodded their heads and said that was surely to be expected. The man was behaving like a saint in refusing to renounce his unfortunate wife, and there were bound to be a few consequences. A man had his needs, after all, they said. It was one of those vague clichés which are designed to keep people at a comfortable distance from suffering.

Jane Beaumont became more lonely and more desperate with the passing years, but very few people were aware of her plight.

On a still, cloudless evening in early May, Jane sat on the patio at the back of the house for a very long time. She heard her husband come into the hall, but he did not come through to greet her. It was an hour after this, as twilight moved into darkness, that Jane came into the house. She studied Martin without speaking for a moment and then said without preamble, 'I think we should get divorced.'

'No, Jane. We've discussed it before and it's not on.' He had the resigned air of a parent dealing kindly with a difficult child.

'Why? Because I might want my share of the loot?'

'There isn't any loot to be had, my dear. Everything is ploughed back into the business – it always has been. There'll be profits in the future, but not now.'

'I could make you sell the business.' It was the first time she'd threatened that, and it gave her the little thrill that came from unwonted aggression. Hit him where it hurts, she thought. That precious business is all the man cares about.

Martin didn't think she could make him sell, without his consent, not with the business legally protected from just such a move. But the last thing he could stand at the moment was the messy and expensive business of a protracted lawsuit, especially with all the unwelcome publicity that would bring to Abbey Vineyards. All he said aloud was, 'It would be a very bad time to try to sell any business, darling, at the height of a major recession.'

'I'm not your darling. I haven't been that for a long time. It's time we put an end to the sham. Are you frightened of the world finding out about your other women?'

'You're not yourself tonight, dear. Have you taken your pills today?'

'Don't fob me off with that. You think that if I'm an invalid I won't have the energy to challenge you, don't you?' Jane was voicing her own fear. Always in the end he was able to override her, because he had more energy and a fiercer will power than she had. But it mustn't be like that, if she was ever going to find a way out of this.

'No one is sorrier that you're an invalid than I am, Jane. In your more rational moments, I'm sure you can see that. But it's very hurtful to me when you say things like this, even when I know that it's really your illness that's speaking.'

'It's a long time since I was able to hurt you, Martin Beaumont. I want out. That way neither of us will complicate the other's life.'

'I think you must have one of your bad times coming on, Jane. Perhaps we should see what the medics make of your state of health at the moment.'

He made it sound like a threat, she thought. And indeed it was a threat, coming from him. It was the most potent weapon in the strange array he used against her. Jane wondered if she looked

104

as unkempt and uncontrolled as she felt. She was sure now that her long black hair was straggly and uncombed. She couldn't remember when she had last given it any attention. She didn't enjoy looking in mirrors nowadays.

She said as firmly as she could, 'This hasn't got anything to do with my health. I'm being perfectly rational about our future.'

Martin gave her the little mirthless chuckle which was the one of his reactions that most annoyed her. 'Oh, I doubt that, Jane.' He walked over to the drinks cabinet and mixed himself a whisky and soda with merciless deliberation. 'Perhaps we'll talk tomorrow, when you're in a more sensible frame of mind.'

He walked out of the room and into his study, shutting the door firmly behind him. He might have to do something about Jane if she went on in this vein, he thought. It would have surprised him to know that Jane Beaumont was thinking exactly the same about him.

Like quite a lot of head chefs, Jason Knight did not work on a Monday. It was the quietest day of the week in the restaurant. It was also the logical day for Jason to rest, after weekends that were usually successful but often hectic.

His absence had the happy effect of giving Gerry Davies an extra day to think about the proposition his friend had put to him on Saturday. Taking control of the firm was a radical step. It was also one which Gerry would never even have entertained, had Jason not

105

suggested it to him. He discussed it in confidence with each of his sons over the weekend, as Jason had suggested he should, but that made his decision more rather than less difficult. It was a good idea in principle, all three of them agreed, but the final decision would depend on the particular firm and the particular circumstances involved.

Only he could weigh all the facts in this particular instance. He must do that and make the decision which was right for him. All of which put the ball firmly back in Gerry's court. Wrong metaphor, he decided: the only kind of ball he had ever been happy to handle was a rugby ball, when he was in his physical prime. Thirty years ago, on the mudbaths of Llanelli or Treorchy, that greasy leather-clad ovoid had been difficult to handle, but it had been child's play compared with this.

He hadn't made his mind up what to do by Monday, so he was glad that Knight wasn't around to ask for his decision. He passed him a couple of times during the day on Tuesday, and thought the chef was looking at him quizzically, but that was probably just his imagination. Gerry waited until he saw Martin Beaumont drive his Jaguar out of its reserved parking space at five thirty before going across to the restaurant kitchen.

Jason nodded immediately towards the door of his den. Gerry Davies went into the little room and sat rather nervously for a couple of minutes until his friend joined him. Jason must have been a little on edge, for he said without any preliminaries, 'Well? Have you mulled over what we discussed?'

'I seem to have done nothing else for the last three days. I've discussed it with my sons as you suggested. They thought it a good idea, in many respects. They're more up to date, more forward-looking, than I am.'

'And?' Knight was too anxious to hear the words of support he wanted to allow any further delay.

'I'm afraid I can't go along with it, Jason. I don't feel I can challenge Martin to give us control of his company, in view of my present relationship with him. As you suggested, he wouldn't welcome the idea, and I'm afraid I should feel disloyal. He backed me to do a major job in this place, and he's paid me handsomely for my efforts. It would feel to me like kicking him in the teeth to say, "Well, loyalty only goes so far, Martin. You picked me up and backed me, but now that we're successful, I want more than just a wage from you." I'm sorry, Jason, but that's how it's come out. I've considered all the other arguments, but they don't override what I feel.'

'That's a pity.' Jason wanted to revive the arguments he'd put before, above all to point out that Beaumont hadn't picked up Davies out of the gutter but had backed a man who had already proved his ability. But he knew Gerry well enough to accept that he wouldn't change his mind once he'd made a decision. He thought of a new, more positive, argument, and fancied he heard the pulse of desperation entering his voice as he put it. 'The company might be all the stronger, you know, if we all had a say in its direction. The people we were talking about are all able people.'

Gerry Davies smiled ruefully. He felt much happier now that he had announced his decision, even though he knew he had disappointed his friend. 'You could well be right. I've never said what you want to do is wrong, have I? It's just that it wouldn't feel right for me, and I can't go against my instinct.'

'All right. I won't pester you again. And I respect what you say about having to do what's right for you. This won't affect our friendship.'

'Thank you. I didn't think it would, but I'm happy to hear you say that.' Gerry resisted an absurd impulse to get up and pump the younger man by the hand. He felt a need to offer him some sort of consolation. 'If you consult the other three you mentioned and they all feel as you do, then do come back to me. I've already told you that I might be wrong, that to an extent I'm acting on gut instinct rather than logic. If you all feel the same and want me in, then I'll reconsider at that point.'

It sounded as if he was trying to have the best of both worlds. But Jason Knight knew that it wasn't like that, that Davies merely needed the reassurance of knowing that other and different people shared his friend's views. The trouble was that Jason doubted whether he could enlist that support. He didn't know the others anything like as well as he knew Gerry and he didn't think they trusted him as Gerry did.

The financial expert Alistair Morton had been here longer than anyone. He was something of an introvert who always played his cards close to his chest; Jason didn't know how he would react to an assault on the boss's control. Jason had always been slightly in awe of Vanda North; he fancied that as an ex-mistress she knew far more about Beaumont than she was prepared to confide in him. He suspected also that she did not entirely trust him, that she saw him as a young man on the make, gifted perhaps, but not entirely to be relied upon. He liked Sarah Vaughan and thought she had the talent to contribute to the firm and its policies. But she was quite young, still relatively new to the job, and lightweight. She might follow the others into a challenge against Beaumont, but she'd hardly be the instigator alongside him.

Jason realized now how much he had been relying on going to the others with the sturdy Gerry Davies already beside him as an ally. The older man had the gravitas and the integrity which would be important if he was to make the others share his aspirations for power. He said, voicing a perfectly genuine dilemma, 'I shall have to consider where I go from here. I was rather relying on having you at my side to help persuade the others.'

'I'm sorry about that. But I don't see that I'm going to change my mind. Unless, as I say, I knew everyone felt the same, or there were new situations to consider.'

Jason Knight couldn't see how there was going to be any significant change, unless he could initiate it himself. He would have to think of other methods.

Sarah Vaughan had given herself a severe talking to, then got on with the job she knew and liked.

There was surely no reason why she should allow Martin Beaumont and his sexual harassment to interfere with her life. Because harassment was all it was, surely. And because that was all it was, a mature woman like her could put it into its proper perspective. She was thirty-three, not seventeen. It wasn't the first time a man had made a pass at her, and it wouldn't be the last. Like all attractive women, she had long ago learned how to brush off advances she did not want to encourage.

Why then had she been so upset on the night after Martin Beaumont had made his bid for her body in his car? Well, partly because it was exactly that: attempted rape. It wasn't a pass in the way she had always had to deal with them, a clumsy attempt at a kiss which left the perpetrator more embarrassed than the recipient. Her boss had been claiming something like *droit de seigneur.* He had wanted her body and he had been pretty determined about it. Attempted rape was not an exaggeration.

No doubt Martin would say that she was being

absurdly dramatic if she challenged him about it, would say that her imagination had translated an innocent bit of flirting into something more sinister. The old male lies would spring readily to his lips, she was sure. Indeed, he would have little alternative but to take a line like that: anything else would be admitting his guilt and inviting her to take whatever steps she wanted in retribution.

She realized something else as she woke from a troubled sleep on the morning after the incident. He might, indeed, deny it altogether. There were no witnesses, after all, and it was only her word against his. No doubt he would have more expensive lawyers at his command than she could ever employ. She had even heard of men bringing counter-suits for defamation of character, when the victim had had no witness to support her claims. Beaumont had an invalid wife, though no one seemed to know much about her; he would no doubt command the sympathy of a court, once some glib and experienced brief had put his case for him.

There was no use cutting off her nose to spite her face, Sarah Vaughan told herself firmly. She had a job she liked and good prospects, because everyone seemed very pleased with the start she had made at Abbey Vineyards. She was well paid for her work. A tiny voice she did not want to acknowledge told Sarah that she might in the future be even better paid as a result of Beaumont's clumsy assault. He would surely want to keep her quiet and compensate her for her discretion.

At midnight on the night after her mauling in the Jaguar, she had been determined to storm in the next morning, to give in her notice, to make Martin Beaumont pay for what he had done. By morning, she was not so sure. She would go to work, see whether Beaumont wanted to be conciliatory, hear what he had to say for himself, and then decide on her tactics. She had surely nothing to lose by doing that.

Sarah didn't want to acknowledge it, but she felt acutely the lack of anyone she could confide in. She was between boyfriends – had been for about six months, if she was honest about it. So there was no one to mount the white charger and challenge Sir Jasper on her behalf – she was already seeing Beaumont in that rather absurd Victorian role. Her mother was seventy now and simply wouldn't understand the issues: it wouldn't be fair to burden her with them. She had never really been close to her younger sister, and even less so since marriage had taken her up to Aberdeen. Her close university friend was married with two young kids in a London suburb. She would be highly indignant on Sarah's part, would be violently in favour of hitting the villain with everything they could muster. But that wasn't quite what her injured friend wanted to hear.

So Sarah Vaughan hugged her knowledge tight and told herself that as a modern woman she could certainly cope with this.

Beaumont had come into the shop when she

112

was helping behind the counter on the day after the incident. They did not acknowledge that they had even seen each other, but she knew that he had been eyeing her up, wondering what, if anything, she proposed to do. And she had taken note of his every movement, in case his body language might reveal what he was feeling. The whole thing was over in ninety seconds, without a word or a look exchanged.

Sarah found that she was trembling a little after he left the shop. She also had a strange feeling she had never anticipated, a small, exhilarating feeling of power. She had always been rather in awe of Martin Beaumont, as owner and driving force behind Abbey Vineyards. Now he had revealed his weakness and she had some sort of hold over him. She felt a small but definite surge of power, which she might at some time in the future be able to exploit.

There were several similar encounters in the days which followed, where they circled each other in the safe presence of others, like wary beasts in the wild. Five days after the incident, Martin acknowledged her with a smile and a nod. Seven days after it, he spoke to her, and she responded. It was no more than one of those meaningless greetings which help to grease the wheels of daily life, but it was a further stage in the restoration of a working relationship.

It was another week later that Beaumont called her into his office to receive her monthly report on her promotional activities. She found that her heart was beating absurdly fast as she went across the courtyard to the big room where he operated. This was just the sort of response she should have long since left behind, she told herself firmly. The man wouldn't attempt anything here, with his secretary in the outer office and numerous other people at hand. But he might be embarrassed, and if he were she would enjoy it.

Martin Beaumont gave no sign of being embarrassed. He listened to her report, asking her pertinent questions about the problems she saw and what she intended to do about them. One or two of his comments were even quite critical. She responded as sturdily as she could, though she found herself quite nettled that he seemed so little affected by what had happened between them.

Then, when she thought they were finished, he said quite suddenly, 'Car running all right now, is it?'

'Yes.'

'That's good, isn't it?'

It was his smile which did it. Complacent, when the least he should have been was penitent and conciliatory. She found herself voicing the speech she had rehearsed a few times in the privacy of her flat but had thought she would never deliver. 'I have decided to do nothing about what happened on that day. You may regard the incident as closed. I think you should consider yourself extremely fortunate, Martin, that I have resolved to take this no further.'

He looked at her steadily for a moment, his

face deliberately expressionless. 'I haven't the faintest idea what you're talking about.'

'I don't think you should take that line. I could make life very unpleasant for you, if I chose.'

'I don't for a moment think you could, my dear. And even if you felt inclined to pursue whatever absurd fantasy has beset you, you would of course be most unwise to do so. You have a promising career here, which is still in its early stages. I should hate to see you jeopardize it. In these uncertain times, being dismissed and denied any sort of reference would hardly help your future employment prospects.'

Sarah could hardly believe it. He, and not she, was being the aggressor. All her carefully weighed judgements flew from her like frightened swallows. 'A claim for sexual harassment, or something much worse, would hardly enhance your own reputation, Mr Beaumont.' She noticed that she had switched to the formal address and was pleased with that. It seemed to reinforce the threat she was offering to him.

But the man did not look as if he felt threatened. Indeed, he said nothing for a moment, as if to allow the smile which flooded his features its full effect. He must have been handsome in his day, which to her mind must have been at least twenty years ago. But the features which had no doubt then been smooth and sharp were heavy now. The cheeks had the first fine red lines of veining and jowls were beginning to form on the neck above the collar. When eventually Beaumont spoke, his words were slow and

115

deliberate, which added to their menace, 'I think you would be well advised to drop that tone right away, my dear. It shows your ignorance of life.'

'I'm not your "dear". And I'm not ignorant. I'm very clear about what you were trying to do to me. I'm very clear about the resistance I offered. I'm very clear about my rights.' But she was not clear that she would win any contest: the unpleasant spectre of an expensive lawyer ridiculing her protestations in court reared itself obstinately. It was a vision which undermined her attack.

He took his time again, probably aware that the more calm he appeared, the more she would be disconcerted. 'I spoke of your ignorance of life, Sarah. The world does not work in the way well-meaning people think it should work. You have a good job and I'm your employer. I shouldn't like you to lose that job, but I have it in my power to terminate your employment. Fact of life, you see. The kind of situation that can never be acknowledged in the law.'

'You conducted a sexual assault on me. Now you're threatening me with dismissal when you've no complaints about my work.'

'I think you should forget about this fiction of an assault you've dreamed up. And I haven't threatened you with dismissal. I've just pointed out some of the facts of real life to you.'

'You're saying that I should forget all about what happened two weeks ago and carry on as if nothing had happened.'

Once again the pause; once again that patronizing, infuriating smile. Didn't the man recognize that any charm he might once have possessed had long since left him? 'You should accept the situation, my dear – and I use that term because I am still fond of you, despite the attitude you have displayed this afternoon. The situation is that you are a young woman with a career to make and I am an employer, who at the moment is pleased with your work. I should hate that situation to change.'

'This is incredible!' She tried to force all the indignation she felt into the words, but she knew they were totally inadequate, in the face of his measured, confident attack. She couldn't work out why the words as they dripped from him sounded so astoundingly logical.

'I'm sorry you should find it so, my dear Sarah. I'm sure that given a little time for reflection, you will find it entirely credible. You would be well advised to review your position. Nothing has changed here, despite your preposterous allegations, which I shall charitably ignore. You are still a woman in her early thirties with an evolving career. I am still your employer and, because of that, in a position to strangle that career at birth. Or to give it a helping hand. Needless to say, I should prefer it to be the latter. The process would be considerably assisted if you could see your way to making certain ... accommodations.'

For a moment she couldn't believe her ears. 'You're asking me to sleep with you, even now?'

He smiled behind the big desk, then held his arms wide and opened the palms. 'I'm asking you to be open-minded, as one would expect every ambitious young executive to be. Your work, as I say, is generally satisfactory. You seem to have found in me a good and appreciative employer. All I'm saying is that work and the rest of life are related. I'm telling you gently that if, when the working day was over, you chose to make certain moves towards a more intimate friendship with your boss, they would be well received. Most women, I'm sure, would be pleased to hear that, pleased to know that such possibilities for career advancement existed.'

This time it was she who paused, but not as a tactic, as Beaumont had used his silences. She was simply taken aback by his effrontery, rendered temporarily speechless by it. She shut her eyes, because she had to shut out that grinning face, that thinning but perfectly groomed hair, before she could begin to think. Eventually she stuttered, 'You're – you're amazing!'

'Thank you, my dear! Even though I fear you did not mean that to be entirely complimentary, I shall take it as such. I hope I have been able to open your eyes to the reality of the situation. To the facts of working life, as I said.'

'I – I can't believe that you have the – the insolence to—'

He held up one of the large hands he had recently spread wide, projecting it palm forwards towards her. He looked for an absurd instant like a stern but benevolent traffic policeman. 'Don't say anything more at the moment, Sarah. I should hate you to say anything you might regret. I think you should go away and reflect on our little discussion before you say anything further.'

Sarah felt that Beaumont's secretary was looking at her curiously as she moved like a sleepwalker through the outer office. Moments later, she found herself not in her own office, as she had expected, but at the back of the shop, where Gerry Davies had shut the doors for the day and was preparing to be the last one to leave his empire.

She wanted to be the controlled young executive, prepared either to keep what had happened entirely to herself or to ridicule it with a mature cynicism as she told it to the man who had become rather a father figure to her. But he could see immediately that something was wrong and he said, 'Come and sit down for a minute. I'll make a cup of tea while you decide whether you want to tell me about it.'

But she did not sit down. Instead, the mature thirty-three-year-old executive found herself weeping uncontrollably, with her head against the older man's chest.

# NINE

Vanda North did not know what to make of the phone call, even an hour afterwards, when she had had time to think about it.

'This is Jane Beaumont. You don't really know me. We met once, ten years ago.' The delivery was even. The tone sounded brittle, as though the sense might disintegrate if the sentences the woman had prepared were challenged.

Vanda was scarcely calm herself. It was not usual to be contacted by the wife you had cheated on – certainly not in these measured tones and many years after the passion had died. She replied cautiously, 'I remember meeting you. It was a long time ago, as you say. What can I do for you, Mrs Beaumont?'

'I need to speak to you about a private matter. I cannot do it on the phone. I shall not make any trouble. By that I mean that I shall not make a scene or cause you embarrassment.'

'Is this about your husband, Mrs Beaumont?'

'It is. But I should prefer not to say any more on the phone.'

'Perhaps I should say that it is many years since I had any close ... association with him.'

120

Vanda was furious with herself because she had fumbled for the word. But she had never expected to be speaking in this situation.

A short pause. 'But you are a partner in his firm, are you not?'

'A very junior partner, yes. It is a status I would rather relinquish, as a matter of fact. But he apparently does not wish me to do that.'

Again a pause, longer this time. Was the woman weighing this, or simply trying to retain control of her emotions and her speech? There was an unexpected trace of irony in the tone as the voice eventually said, 'Then we have things in common, as I suspected. I think it would be in our interests to talk. But not here, please. I do not wish Martin to be aware that I have contacted you.'

Vanda thought for a moment about a neutral venue: it was usually easier to talk when neither of you felt the disadvantage of being on the other's ground. But she could not think of anywhere where they could rely on being able to talk freely. And in any case, why shouldn't she have the advantage? It was Jane Beaumont who wanted this meeting. If it was going to be embarrassing, as the circumstances said it must surely be, Vanda might as well have the territorial advantage. She said calmly, 'You can come here. Almost any time today or tomorrow would be possible for me.'

'Today, then. This afternoon. Three o'clock.'

'You'll need the address. It's—'

'I know the address.'

'You do?'

'It's in the phone book, Ms North.' There were traces of relaxation and amusement in the voice, now that she had what she wanted. 'I shan't need directions. I have a satnav in my car. Thank you for agreeing to meet me.'

'That's all right. May I ask—' But the click at the other end of the line told her that Jane Beaumont had put down her phone.

Gerry Davies was behaving irrationally and he knew it.

He was fifty-seven now. He had been happily married for thirty-six years; he was the father of two boys who were making sensible careers of their own. Even as a young man, his life had been grounded in the hard reality of the Rhondda Valley and Welsh mining, his leisure enacted amidst the slag-heaps and muddy playing fields of Pontypridd and the like. He hadn't gone off to university and torn up his roots, like some of the men he had grown up with. He was proud of his background, proud to assert the basis for life that it had given him. He had been disciplined in the realities of human existence for as long as he could remember.

And yet. And yet he'd never had a daughter, and that was making him vulnerable in a way he had never expected. Sarah Vaughan had come to him for advice ever since she had arrived at Abbey Vineyards three years ago. She had been able enough, but young for her years. She had lacked the confidence to assert herself, even when she knew she was right. Sarah had been very happy to adopt Gerry Davies as a father figure, and he had been pleased and a little flattered by her dependence. It was only when she had flung herself on his chest with the news of Martin Beaumont's sexual harassment that he realized how completely he had accepted that role. Accepted it almost eagerly, he acknowledged to himself ruefully.

There was nothing sexual in the bond between them. He had joked about it over the months with his wife. Sarah had sworn him to secrecy when she stopped weeping and recovered her self-control, or he would have told Bronwen now about Beaumont's predatory attentions. It was a pity he was not able to do that, for Bronwen would have given him a better perspective on the situation. She would have told him that Sarah was not a pretty and vulnerable girl, but a woman of thirty-three who was quite capable of looking after herself.

That was exactly what Sarah Vaughan herself told him, but it did not have the same effect coming from her. Gerry saw it as the brave attempt of a victim to assert her independence, in a situation where she was at the mercy of a predatory and experienced older man.

Gerry would have loved to discuss Sarah's predicament with his closest working colleague, Jason Knight, but her demand that the information should go no further meant that too was impossible. That again was a pity, because the chef would also have put a better perspective on the news than he could. Jason would, indeed, have been rather more cynical, not about Sarah's innocence and shock, but about the possibilities of turning the situation to her advantage. It might just have been to his advantage as well, of course, but that would have been no more than a happy coincidence.

As it was, the effect upon Gerry Davies of Sarah Vaughan's revelations was unfortunate. It upset his usually sound business judgement. It meant that he allowed personal and emotional considerations to impinge upon his working relationships, a thing he had always previously avoided. As he had told Knight, he respected Martin Beaumont as an efficient entrepreneur, a shrewd judge of markets and potential niches in them, a good picker of men and women to serve him, an excellent leader, and an employer who rewarded ability and hard work.

These were accurate judgements. They should not have been modified by the news of Beaumont's lubricious tendencies. He was not the first owner of a business who thought power and position entitled him to put his hand up skirts, and he certainly wouldn't be the last. Lust was a more dangerous weakness than it had been in the past, and that was surely a good thing. But it didn't make Martin Beaumont any less efficient at the things he did well as a business leader.

When it was much too late, Gerry Davies would see all of this. But on the day after Sarah Vaughan had arrived in his deserted shop in such a distressed state, he took a decision which

124

was to prove momentous for other people as well as him.

He went across to Jason Knight's kitchens at four o'clock, knowing that at that time he would find the chef resting in his den before he began directing the preparations for the evening's meals. Once the door was safely closed, Davies spoke abruptly, as though he feared that hesitation might affect his decision. 'I've changed my mind about what you said. I think we should challenge Beaumont about the future of the firm. I think we should have our say in the running of this place.'

Vanda North couldn't remember what Jane Beaumont looked like. A solitary meeting ten years ago had left no lasting impression. A tall, rather pretty, athletic woman, she thought. But she had only the vaguest memory of Martin's wife.

When she opened the door to her visitor, she was shocked by what she saw. She looked into a haggard, strained face. The high cheekbones must once have been striking, but now they were too prominent under the stretched grey skin to look anything but unhealthy. The deep-set dark eyes had probably been intriguing in this woman's youth; now the dark rings beneath them made them look haunted.

Vanda knew from her time with Martin that Jane Beaumont was two years younger than her husband, which would make her now fifty-four. Had she not known that, she would have taken her for over sixty. Vanda had expected to be embarrassed by this meeting. That might still happen, but she realized now that she would have to be careful not to show the pity and concern she felt for her visitor.

Jane Beaumont smiled. 'You have a nice place here. Charming and quite individual.' She sounded like a polite child who had been primed by her parents with the right things to say.

'Thank you. I like it, and most people seem to find it an intriguing old place. Please come inside. I have tea and biscuits waiting.' Vanda spoke as robustly as she could, thrusting aside the thought that she in turn was responding as if her visitor were a well brought-up youngster. Two minutes later, she carried a large tray into the sitting room where she had taken this unexpected guest. 'Old places have their disadvantages too, of course. I had to have the thatch on the roof renewed when I moved in here twelve years ago. Set me back a pretty penny at the time, that did. And buildings insurance can be prohibitive.'

Jane Beaumont gave her a wan smile. 'I want to talk to you about Martin.'

'I see. I doubt whether I can be of any help to you, but I'm prepared to listen to whatever you have to say.' Despite the embarrassment she felt was coming, Vanda was glad that the woman had dispensed with small talk. She had been wondering how to move beyond the meaningless preliminaries.

'You were Martin's mistress. I know that.'

126

'Yes. It sounds trite to say this now, and it's probably meaningless, but I regret any pain I caused you. Passion makes you selfish, makes you disregard the effects of your actions upon others. I know that's no excuse for—'

'Passion, yes. I suppose it was that. Perhaps I felt that myself at one time. I doubt if it was strong enough to merit the term passion, but it's too long ago for me to be certain of anything now.' She looked past Vanda, staring at a picture on the wall but seeing in her mind's eye something else entirely. She picked up a biscuit, took a small bite from it, then stared at it in her hand as if wondering how it had got there. 'It may be that now I have to hurt you. But I want you to help me.'

'I'll do that if I can. At this moment, I can't see anything I could do which might be useful to you.'

'I'm going to sue Martin for divorce.' Jane was quiet for a long time, sipping her tea and staring at the painting again. Vanda wondered whether she was going to offer any development of a statement she seemed to regard as self-explanatory.

At last, Jane looked at her host and smiled mirthlessly. 'He's going to resist. As you know him well, that won't surprise you. Martin fights hard against any rearrangement of the world he has set up for himself.'

Vanda was relieved to see signs of animation in the thin white face which had until now resembled a mask. 'That sounds like a very good summary of your husband. You may know that I am a junior partner in Abbey Vineyards. I have been trying to divest myself of that investment and take my money out of his firm. But I find that his lawyers hedged it about with so many clauses that it is proving almost impossible for me to do so.'

Again that thin smile. 'That does not surprise me, Ms North.'

'Vanda, please.'

'Vanda then. Probably he took care to act in his own interests, whereas you were trusting and heedless. That would be in the early part of your relationship with him – when passion ruled, perhaps.' There was just the faintest stress on her recall of Vanda's own word. But if she enjoyed turning the mistress's earlier excuse against her, it was not apparent in the taut face.

'That is exactly what happened.' It was quite bizarre, but in the intimate, low-ceilinged setting of this familiar room, Vanda felt a bond of sympathy extending itself between the two of them. 'I was totally trusting of Martin. I felt I could safely put my interests in his hands. It wasn't until later that I found everything in his life was totally subsumed in Abbey Vineyards. He had been quite ruthless in pouring my money into that and in making sure that I could never extract it.'

It was a relief to say it, to state openly what she had long since decided was the truth of the matter, but had been unable to confess to anyone else. Jane Beaumont was nodding almost

128

eagerly, showing for the first time a little pleasure, as she recognized this account of a husband she had grown to detest. 'That would be a fair summary of my marriage, Vanda. I was a rich woman at the outset of it. Martin used the fortune I had inherited to set up Abbey Vineyards. He also used his lawyers to make it virtually impossible for me either to extract my money or to exercise any degree of control over the enterprise which had been founded on my capital. Everything in his life revolves around the firm. Even his sex life, apparently.'

The last phrase should have been full of acid, but she said it almost sympathetically. They were sisters united by the man's inhumanity rather than women bitterly divided by being his bedfellows. Vanda said, 'We seem to be agreed on that. The scales have fallen from both our eyes when it is rather too late for us. But you said I could help you.'

Jane Beaumont paused to drain her cup. She was aware of her movements and her audience now, no longer the chilling automaton she had been when she first accepted a seat in this room. 'I came to warn you that I might have to hurt you. That you might be called upon to give evidence in a messy divorce. He's sure to contest it.'

'You are going to cite me as a co-respondent. As evidence of his adultery.'

'Yes. If those old-fashioned terms are still the correct ones.'

'You can do that, if it should be necessary. I

129

don't think I would have to appear in court. Our affair went on for several years, so he could scarcely deny it. He was supposed to be moving in with me, finishing with you and remarrying. It all seems quite unreal now, knowing him as I do.'

Vanda glanced at the wife Martin had said he was going to leave, then refilled her cup and offered her another biscuit, as if they were friends meeting happily after a long interval. 'I'm sorry to say that; I realize it must be hurtful. At the time, I was taking care to know nothing of you, to have no picture of you in my mind. I suppose I hoped such ignorance might mean that I was hurting you less. I realize now how cowardly that was. I was merely protecting myself.'

'It might have been hurtful, once. A long time ago. But not now. You were in a long-term relationship, as I was supposed to be. I feel we've suffered similar fates. You didn't have a piece of legal paper, as I had, but each of us was promised what she was never going to get.' Jane took another bite of biscuit, realized for the first time that she was enjoying the taste. She could not remember whether she had eaten today before coming here. 'It might not be necessary to involve you at all. No doubt there are other and more passing fancies of Martin's we could cite.'

'There certainly are. I could provide you with chapter and verse on some of them, if you would like it. It mattered to me at the time, though I don't give a damn whom he beds now.' Vanda could scarcely believe it, but the mistress and the wife he had cheated were working now as partners against a common enemy. 'He won't make divorce easy, if he doesn't want it.'

Jane smiled ruefully, but this time with a small, companionable humour. 'I'm well aware of that. He wouldn't mind losing me, but he can't afford a divorce. As things stand, it's very difficult for me to take anything out of Abbey Vineyards because of the way I passed everything over to him to invest, but any divorce settlement would surely give me rights I don't have at the moment. He might even be forced to sell the firm to pay me out.'

'I'm sure he would. And that might also mean that I could retrieve my investment and end the partnership. Look, let me have your telephone number and give me three or four days. I'm pretty sure I can get you quite recent evidence on some of his women. Martin's always been a goat – more fool us for not seeing that when we got involved with him, I suppose. That's not going to change. It's almost his only weakness.' Vanda thought for a moment, then spoke almost to herself. 'I shouldn't be surprised if he's had a go at Sarah Vaughan – I doubt whether he'd be able to resist it. Sorry, you don't know Sarah. She's a pretty woman in her early thirties who's one of the bright sparks at the vineyard. I'd be surprised if Martin hasn't tried to seduce her. I'm sorry, this must be distressing for you.'

'It isn't. Our marriage was over a long time

131

ago. Getting Martin to acknowledge that is the only thing that concerns me now.' Jane sipped her second cup of tea, set it carefully down in the saucer and stared at it for a long time. 'There's something you ought to know. I didn't expect to be telling you this, but if we're going to work together, you've a right to know it.'

Vanda wanted to reach across the low table and take the other woman's hand, to establish some sort of physical contact which would assure Jane of her support. But she knew that it was much too early for that, that this most unexpected liaison must be allowed time to develop. She said very quietly, 'Are you sure you want to tell me this now? I'm sure we shall be seeing each other again. Maybe the time—'

'No, I must tell you now. You have a right to know, if you're going to help me. I have a bipolar disorder. It's relatively mild, the doctors tell me. Most of the time I control it with drugs; occasionally I need treatment in a specialist unit for a few days. At present it isn't a problem, but you need to know that I have the condition, because Martin will use it. He fights dirty when he's under pressure; I suspect you already know that. If his back is against the wall, he'll make out in court that I'm a raving lunatic, or at best a highly disordered personality, whose evidence is totally unreliable.'

Vanda didn't want to admit that when her own judgement had been undermined by the excitement of sex, Martin had hinted something of the sort to her. She had accepted these vague hints of a wife like Mr Rochester's in *Jane Eyre*, probably because at the time it was what she wanted to hear. She said, 'He'll have two of us to contend with, if it comes to anything like that. We'll get our own medical evidence in, if we should need it.'

Jane Beaumont had been planning ahead, even to the extent of deciding upon the medical specialist she would call. But it gave her immense confidence to hear this sturdy woman of the world declaring her allegiance. Almost thirty years of marriage to Martin as well as her bipolar problems had ensured that she rarely felt confident. To have not only her resistance but her tactics endorsed by such a robust ally was more heartening for Jane than she could begin to express.

In their different ways, both of these women led lonely lives. Vanda's isolation was nothing like as desperate as Jane's, but she realized now how empty life had felt over the last year or two. How empty she had let it become, perhaps. Once they had what they wanted out of this situation, she would make the rest of her life altogether richer.

The two exchanged details of their lives outside Martin Beaumont, of their very different childhoods, of their preferences in books and art. And in television, that perpetual resort of the lonely. As she drove away from the thatched cottage on the edge of the village, Jane Beaumont was much more animated than she had been when she arrived.

Vanda North stood in the doorway of her ancient home until the car was quite out of sight. She went thoughtfully back into the house and sat down to revolve her thoughts on this new commitment. It was only when the clock chimed in the hall that she realized the visit she had so feared in prospect had lasted for three hours.

# TEN

Martin Beaumont was no fool. Even those who hated him knew that. It was what made opposition difficult. And those women who had more personal reasons to resent him, such as Jane Beaumont and Vanda North and Sarah Vaughan, realized when they thought coolly about it that he was a man who would not easily be defeated.

Beaumont was a shrewd and highly experienced operator. He sensed that there was going to be a challenge to his domination of the empire he had created at Abbey Vineyards. Not perhaps to his leadership, but to his position as the autocrat who determined every aspect of policy. He knew all about Vanda North's desire to end her powerless partnership and withdraw her funds, of course, but he was confident that his lawyers had tied that up for him years ago.

Nevertheless, if she became more than a lone voice of opposition, things might get difficult.

Beaumont sensed rather than knew that Jason Knight was considering how to strengthen his position. Knight was an ambitious and well-informed man as well as a highly proficient chef. Martin was keeping an eye upon him as the restaurant prospered and the chef's position within the firm strengthened. Knight had taken care that his sounding of Gerry Davies was unobserved by the owner, but Beaumont was well used to divining what was going on around him from the minimum of information.

Fiona Cooper was just the sort of personal assistant he needed. She was both discreet and intelligent: she gave away nothing, but vacuumed up the gossip around the place and passed it to her employer. And Beaumont himself noted the odd phrase which signified a change of attitude in Gerry Davies, a man too honest for his own good, too unused to the ways of dissimulation to adopt them when he needed them. Davies took care to say nothing about either his meetings with Jason Knight or his knowledge of what had passed between Beaumont and Sarah Vaughan. Nevertheless, Beaumont noted subtle changes in his speech and his bearing which suggested that his unthinking loyalty and admiration for the owner had been affected.

It was always Martin Beaumont's inclination to tackle opposition head on. If he was in a position of strength, he believed in exploiting it as quickly as possible, lest the situation changed. And he felt himself to be very much in a position of strength with Tom Ogden, that obstinate strawberry-grower whose land obtruded so inappropriately into his. When he sensed that he held all the cards, Martin liked to bully the opposition.

He acknowledged that openly to himself. He knew that he enjoyed a little bullying when he felt he could not lose – it was a release from the more subtle and patient manoeuvres which were so often necessary in the rest of his dealings.

On the morning of Tuesday, May the eleventh, Beaumont chose to bully Tom Ogden.

### PICK YOUR OWN STRAWBERRIES.

Ensure that you have the freshest fruit of all.
Bring the family and enjoy a day out.

Tom Ogden was inspecting the signs which had been newly prepared for this season's picking. There was a road junction near to the entrance to his fields which meant that traffic often had to stop. That gave drivers and passengers a chance to read more than if they had been passing at thirty or forty miles an hour. Last year's signs had been perfectly serviceable, but Tom had decided upon complete refurbishment.

The psychological effect of pristine paint was to assure the public that a new and exciting opportunity was now available; Tom's son assured him of this. And Tom, like many people of his age and background, affected to despise such nonsense, but felt secretly that there might just be something in it. No one ever went bankrupt by underestimating the intelligence of the public. Some rich American showman had said that, and Tom's experience bore it out.

Take all those idiots who poured into Abbey Vineyards next door, for instance. The supermarkets and the specialist wine stores were full of decent wines at decent prices. Yet people who should know better not only flocked in to eat in the expensive restaurant. They also bought the dubious English wines grown on the long lines of vines which had surrounded Tom's defiant fields over the last twenty years.

Tom Ogden did not pretend to be objective: he saw no need to sample the product before delivering his trenchant verdict.

When he turned from the new signs to find Martin Beaumont also inspecting them, Ogden's day took an immediate turn for the worse. He said harshly, 'You're not welcome here. You should know that by now.'

Beaumont gave him a leisured, mocking smile. 'Going to horsewhip me out of town, are you, Thomas?'

'Don't think I wouldn't, if I thought I could get away with it!'

'Ever the friendly neighbour, aren't you?'

'There's nothing for you here. How many times do you need telling?'

'I'm a persistent soul, Tom. Anyone who has had dealings with me will tell you that. I get my own way in the end. Always, and usually on my own terms. At the moment you're lucky, Tom. Very lucky, because I'm being patient. But don't rely on your luck lasting forever. Those same people who would tell you how persistent I am could also tell you that I am not noted for my patience.'

It was like a confrontation in the western films Tom Ogden had so relished as a young man. The small landowner was being threatened by the wealth and power of the land baron who wanted to consolidate his holding. At least there were no guns here, as yet. 'We've nothing to say to each other, Beaumont.'

'Not quite correct, that, Thomas. You don't have much to say to me, but in spite of your churlish attitude I am still prepared to talk to you. To say things which would be sweet music in your ears, if you weren't such a stubborn old mule.'

'My family's farmed this land for years, Beaumont. I don't intend to change that now to suit some johnny-come-lately like you.' It was an old argument that he had delivered before, but Ogden enjoyed repeating it, enjoyed the contempt he could put into his epithet for this unwelcome presence.

'Times change, Thomas, times change. Bigger people than you have ended up in the bankruptcy courts through failing to recognize that.'

'Get lost, Beaumont! Look at the evidence before your eyes!' He waved a wide arm towards the fields behind the man and his Jaguar, to where Spot Wheeler and his workers were assiduously tending the rows of his crop. 'We're going to have a bumper crop and a bumper year. We'll still be here when your bloody vines have been and gone!'

Beaumont's face darkened, as it always did when anyone directly insulted his enterprise. 'I hope you're right about your crop, Thomas. It would be a shame if anything happened to affect this bumper year.'

This was more than ever like a western. Tom Ogden felt he should have his gun belt slung low on his hips, with his hand hovering above the holster. 'If you're threatening me, Beaumont, you'd better watch out. That's a game two people can play.'

Martin knew he held all the cards here: God was always on the side of the big battalions. 'You shouldn't be hinting at violence, Thomas. Most inadvisable, for a man with your record.'

Tom Ogden whirled from a contemplation of his land and his workers. 'What do you mean by that?'

Beaumont tapped the side of his nose. 'No names, no pack drill, eh, Thomas? Let's just say that I have ways and means of finding out all I need to know about the people I do business with. And those ways and means tell me that you aren't a man who can afford to threaten anyone with violence.'

'Look, just get off my land, will you, before I treat you as a trespasser.'

'Very complicated, the law of trespass, Thomas. A study of it would tell you my rights as a bona fide visitor. A visitor who comes here in a neighbourly spirit.' He held up his hand as Ogden advanced towards him. 'As that spirit clearly isn't reciprocated by a man who seems to be under business pressures, I shall say what I came to say and depart. I wish you to know that my very generous offer for this small parcel of land still stands. No one else will match it, and it won't last for ever. It won't last longer than another month or two, I think. The best tactic for you – the *only* realistic tactic for you – is a prompt acceptance. I might even be prepared to cover your legal fees for the transfer, and set a date which allows you to have the takings from this year's crop, if you sign by the end of June.'

'I shan't be signing anything, Beaumont. I'm sick to death of telling you that.'

Martin had his hand on the driver's door of the Jaguar as he delivered his final thought. 'Sick to death, eh? I do hope it doesn't come to that, Thomas.'

'I've been watching Dad closely. He doesn't seem much different, as yet,' said thirteen-year-old Luke Hook magisterially to his brother.

'Maybe we shall have to wait until after this graduation ceremony we're being forced to attend,' said Jack gloomily. He took advantage of his two years of seniority to ask a more practical question across the family's evening meal. 'Will it mean promotion, Dad?'

'No, it certainly will not!' said Bert Hook.

140

'Your father could have been an inspector years ago,' said his mother sternly. 'He had all the exams, but he turned down the chance because he enjoyed the job he was doing.' Eleanor caught Bert's sharp look of surprise. She probably shouldn't have said that, but she was immensely proud of her husband's integrity, and felt that it was only right that the boys should know about it. They were at an age when they should be learning that there were more important considerations in life than money and rank.

'So we could be living in luxury, rather than leading a life of abject poverty,' said Jack soulfully.

'You two have never wanted for anything! Finish your dinner, if you want pudding.' Eleanor began to gather in the plates. 'Abject poverty, indeed!'

It was becoming almost too easy to wind up the old folks, especially Mum, reflected the precocious Luke. He dispatched the last of his roast potatoes with impressive speed and enquired innocently of his father, 'Will you be learning to play the violin and smoking coke now that you're an intellectual, Dad?' An enthusiastic form-master had lately introduced his charges to Conan Doyle's immortal creation. Luke pushed his empty plate towards his mother, leant back, and lit an imaginary pipe. 'This is almost certainly a three-pipe problem,' he informed his brother in an artificially deep voice.

'The only crime I am likely to indulge in is

infanticide,' said Bert Hook as sternly as he could. 'And you're both very welcome to miss Friday's graduation ceremony. I'd rather like to miss it myself.'

'No chance, Dad, with Mum and Mr Lambert on the job,' said Jack. 'And Luke and I aren't going to miss a day off school, are we?' His eyes lit up delightedly as apple pie and custard arrived upon the table. 'I expect you'll get a more interesting succession of cases, now that you're a graduate, Dad. When you have to pit your brains against the modern Moriarty, the Napoleon of crime, I might agree to chronicle your exploits, if you ask me nicely. I quite fancy being your Watson.'

Martin Beaumont was elated by his latest encounter with Tom Ogden. He had seen fear in the man's eyes. No one enjoyed the feeling that an enemy had the power to find out all about him, including those secrets he had kept hidden for years. It gave you a feeling of power over other people's lives, and Martin knew enough about himself to know that nothing excited him more.

Today was a day for action; he felt that he was definitely on some sort of a roll. That was no doubt why he decided it was time to have a word with Jason Knight and Gerry Davies. The two were conferring outside the entrance to the shop as he drove back into Abbey Vineyards. Martin lowered the window of the Jaguar and called, 'I'd like to see both of you for a short meeting.

In ten minutes?'

He didn't believe in giving people time for elaborate planning.

They came in nine minutes; he was still arranging the set-up of chairs he wanted in his room when he heard them talking to his PA in the outer office. He had pulled up the two armchairs in front of his desk, so that they would be looking into the light and lower than he would be on his seat behind the desk. Crude stuff, but it often worked, even now that more people were conscious of such things. If they realized that he had arranged things to give himself the advantage of position, that would be no bad thing. He decided against coffee.

He would sound them out, test whether they were moving to curb his power, as he suspected they might be. He wasn't paranoid about such things, but it was as well to be perpetually aware of the way your senior executives' minds were working. He would approach the matter obliquely, as was his way in these matters.

He said, 'This shouldn't take very long. I wanted your advice about something. Both of you have your fingers on the pulse of this place.' A little flattery never came amiss, so long as you did not lay it on so thickly as to sound false. He might quite enjoy this, if it went as he hoped it would.

Neither of them spoke. He sensed that they wanted to look at each other, but the configuration of the furniture he had set up did not allow that without it being a sign of weakness. He asked each of them conventional questions. Gerry Davies reported that there was as yet no discernible decline of spending in the shop as a result of the recession which was hitting other Gloucestershire businesses hard. Jason Knight reminded him that there was usually a falling away in the number of restaurant bookings in spring and early summer, as the lighter evenings offered other options and the tourists were not yet around in great numbers. However, he had compared April bookings with those for the same month last year and found that they were marginally up.

It was all a little cautious and stilted, as if they were waiting for something more important. Martin cleared his throat and said, 'We must continue to expand. I regard you two as the most forward-looking and experienced of my senior staff. That means I shall need your support.'

There was a pause before Jason Knight said, 'Are you thinking about something which was not discussed at our general meeting in March? If you are, perhaps we should convene—'

'It's nothing very radical. Merely a continuation of the expansion we have pursued successfully over the years.'

Gerry, feeling the unease of the man beside him and wanting to support him, said, 'We're only talking about a meeting of six people, Martin, with you in the chair as usual. It's easy enough to arrange. Even if it was only an informal meeting, you would then be aware of everyone's opinion.'

Martin Beaumont hadn't expected opposition from this quarter: Davies had always been the most stalwart of his supporters. And this was opposition, despite the reasonable tone used to clothe it. It seemed that he was justified in his suspicions: Knight had been marshalling support. It was just as well he'd detected this now, whilst there was still time to nip it in the bud. He gave them what he hoped was a disarming smile. 'As I said, there is no radical departure from previous policy involved. I am merely keeping you in the picture. I propose to buy out the strawberry farmer next door and incorporate his land into ours.'

They were feeling their way as he was, but it was he who held the map. He knew where he was going; no doubt they would follow him when they saw his plans clearly. Jason Knight said cautiously, 'It's a logical development. His land would consolidate our control of the area.'

'I knew you'd see that. It would make future planning much easier if we got rid of the hedges and allowed our machinery full scope over the whole area.'

It was Gerry Davies who said, 'Has Tom Ogden accepted your proposal?'

Martin smiled as if they were discussing the best way to deal with a recalcitrant child. 'Ogden's a pig-headed soul. He doesn't see the realities of the situation. I've made him a very good offer. He hasn't yet accepted it, but I'm sure he will, before the summer's out.'

'His family's farmed that land for a long time.'

145

'So he keeps telling me. That doesn't alter the realities of economic life, Gerry. Times change, and Ogden must be made to recognize that.'

Jason Knight knew Ogden because he was a member of Ross Golf Club. He was well aware of the farmer's bitter resentment of his more powerful neighbour. He said, 'Tom's a stubborn old bugger, as you say. Is there any way you could offer him some sort of junior partnership in Abbey Vineyards, rather than just money? That would allow him to continue an association with the land he feels he cannot relinquish.'

Martin frowned. 'I wouldn't want Ogden anywhere near this firm. He's looking backwards, not forwards. We don't need people like that.'

Gerry Davies said, 'He's capable of taking new ideas on board. Look how he's converted his land from mixed farming to a specialization in strawberries and hooked on to the pick-your-own market.'

Martin frowned. He had only introduced the subject to sound out the thinking of these two. Ogden and his strawberry fields were not really up for discussion. 'You can leave Ogden to me. I'm confident I can make him see sense.' He certainly wasn't going to tell them exactly how he proposed to do that.

This time Jason Knight did glance sideways at the man next to him before he spoke. It was instinctive, but significant. With the autocrat's paranoid sensitivity to any sign of dissent, Beaumont divined in that instant that these two had been plotting against him. 'This is, as you

146

indicated at the outset, a policy matter, Martin. And Gerry and I have been thinking for some time that we – that is to say the five of us who are most involved in forward planning in the firm – should have a greater say in policy.'

It was out at last. But this was exactly the situation that Jason had been trying to avoid when he spoke to Gerry about a united front. He had wanted to come here with Vanda North and Sarah Vaughan and Alistair Morton and present a unified group, instead of being anticipated by Beaumont and pinned down like this. At least he had Gerry Davies to support him, but he would have preferred that they and not Beaumont had taken the initiative and chosen the moment.

The silence seemed to the two men in the easy chairs to stretch for a long time, though it was probably no more than a few seconds. Martin Beaumont finally said with ominous calm, 'I built this firm up from nothing. I brought us to where we are at the moment. Neither of you would hold the jobs you have without my efforts.'

Gerry felt that he must support his friend, though neither words nor resistance came easily to him. 'I don't think any of us would dispute that, Martin. We are well aware of what you have done for the firm, and indirectly for us. It's just that as it gets bigger and bigger, Jason feels – well I feel as well, and I think we all feel, really – that the senior people should have a greater say in policy matters.'

Martin stared hard at him whilst he thought

furiously. They weren't organized yet, but they were moving against him: he had been right to suspect that. And the man behind it was Jason Knight, as he had known it would be. He said firmly and with ominous calm, 'This firm is a one-man band. It has been from the outset and that is the secret of its success. If you don't like that, you should think seriously about other employment.'

Jason smiled and tried to simulate a relaxation he could not feel. 'There's room for manoeuvre here, surely, Martin. I don't mean – none of us means – to challenge your leadership. It's just that as things move on and development becomes more complex, a different sort of organization might benefit us all.'

'You've taken everyone's opinion, have you, Jason? Gone behind my back without saying a word to me in order to organize opinion against me, have you? I don't like what I'm hearing, Jason.'

Gerry Davies tried desperately to mitigate a confrontation he had never envisaged. 'We haven't talked to anyone else, Martin. All we've done is exchange a few ideas on the best way to go forward. Jason was able to convince me that we should look at new ways of running things. Surely it's in everyone's interest that we should keep open minds as—'

'So you two have been making your little plans to take over, have you? Without even having the decency to take me into your confidence. How long would it have been before you came

148

out with these ideas if I hadn't brought you in here today?'

Gerry said miserably, 'It isn't like that. There isn't a plot against you.'

Martin Beaumont had the knowledge he wanted now. The others weren't in on this, but only because he'd nipped it in the bud at this stage. And the man behind the challenge to his authority was Knight, as he had suspected it would be. He'd intervened at the right time, though, before Jason had been able to unite the others against him. Divide and rule was the answer. That maxim had always served him well in the past. Leave Knight isolated, then attack him. He didn't want to lose him, if it could be avoided. He was a brilliant chef, and the restaurant was a healthy profit-maker on the back of the reputation he had built there. Send him away chastened, but still prepared to work as hard as ever.

He shook his head sadly at Gerry Davies. 'I'm sorry to find this disloyalty coming from you, Gerry. You've done well here, so far, very well. I've had no complaints about your work or your attitude, until today. I have to say I'm disappointed, after the chance I took in giving you a key job.'

Jason Knight said, 'You shouldn't take it like this, Martin. And you shouldn't blame Gerry. He simply listened to what he saw as reasonable arguments. We'd all benefit if there were greater inputs, from Vanda North and Sarah Vaughan and Alistair Morton, as well as from Gerry and

149

me.'

'These arguments came from you, I suppose, Jason. Well, you're a good chef, but not irreplaceable. Perhaps you should look for work in a different environment, where the organization might suit you better.'

'It shouldn't come to that, Martin. All we wanted to do was to bounce around a few ideas, with you involved in the discussion. I thought it might benefit us all to debate whether power-sharing might be possible, even desirable, from the company's point of view.'

'Did you, indeed? Well, as I say, my initial reaction is that it might be better for all of us to have a chef in our restaurant who doesn't get too big for his boots.'

'You won't get a better chef than Jason,' said Gerry Davies, desperately trying to support his friend as the situation rocketed away from them.

'That's hardly the issue, is it, Gerry? I might get one who is perfectly efficient, without spreading dissent among hitherto loyal staff.' Divide and rule, that was the answer. Jason was now isolated and he knew it. Martin felt elation coursing like a drug through his veins. 'Whether Jason would find it easy to secure a similar post with a reference which questioned his loyalty is another matter entirely. But a matter for him alone to consider, not any of the rest of us.'

'You're taking this the wrong way, Martin.' Jason heard the note of desperation in his own voice. 'I didn't intend to be in any way critical of you or your management. I think we're all aware that there wouldn't even be an Abbey Vineyards without your initiative and drive. It's just that I – we – thought that as things move on and the enterprise gets bigger and more prosperous, it might be appropriate to adopt a slightly modified structure. I wasn't intending to be at all critical of the way you have led us or continue to lead us.'

'I'm glad to hear it.' Martin allowed himself a slow smile as he felt his triumph complete. 'In view of these assurances, I am prepared to forget today's exchange, to move forward as if no opposition had been voiced. I think it only fair that I should add that if there is any future challenge to my authority, I shall be well aware of the likely source of it.'

Beaumont watched them leave his office without another word. They looked like two penitent school prefects who had been checked for a serious breach of the rules, he thought.

That was entirely satisfactory.

# ELEVEN

In one respect, the Open University graduation day at Hereford surprised Chief Superintendent John Lambert, who was able to enjoy it purely as a spectator, proud of his friend's achievement.

It was surprisingly like a conventional degree ceremony at any university. He had somehow expected these grizzled professionals of various ages and callings to be quite different from the youngsters concluding three years of full-time student life. But today they were surprisingly similar. There was the same sense of joyous achievement, the same slightly surprised air that they were now the holders of degrees.

In one sense, he was surprised to be here himself. You were always warned about making close friends in the police service. It might affect your judgement in crisis situations. It might force rash acts of schoolboy heroism which went against all the rules, when you stared into the barrels of a shotgun held by a violent man forced into a corner.

Such situations were still mercifully rare. More often, a sense of comradeship made officers cover up acts of villainy or weakness in colleagues they had grown to like. Mistaken loyalties had undoubtedly aided the spread of corruption in the Metropolitan Police in the sixties and seventies. More trivially, camaraderie might make you cover up minor omissions of timekeeping or short cuts in procedure in your colleagues, and thus affect the efficiency and reliability of the service and its reputation with the public.

Lambert was not exactly a law unto himself, but his seniority and reputation had secured him certain privileges. He had been able to retain Bert Hook as his detective sergeant for much longer than would normally have been the case. The situation had been consolidated by Hook's surprising refusal to accept the inspector status which could undoubtedly have been his, in favour of retaining the work he enjoyed as Lambert's assistant. It had never been openly stated, but each of them clearly understood and respected the fact that their virtues complemented each other's.

One of Bert Hook's advantages was that the criminals and others he came into contact with in CID work consistently underestimated him. They accepted too easily the stolid village-bobby exterior and manner as the reality of the man, and missed the shrewd intelligence which his manner and appearance concealed. That was useful to Lambert in his work, but he was delighted to be here today to witness the formal recognition of Hook's intelligence and application in the conferral of an excellent degree, achieved by part-time study in conditions which would have defeated lesser men.

Eleanor Hook and Christine Lambert had awarded themselves new dresses to celebrate this joyous occasion. Jack and Luke Hook, who had known Lambert as 'Uncle John' since their early childhoods, were a little awkward with him now, as befitted their teenage status. In truth, they were rather in awe of his local fame as a solver of serious crimes, including the murders which always dominated the headlines. However, being fifteen and thirteen meant that they could not really acknowledge their awe of anyone, except the pop stars and top sportsmen they would never have to meet. But they were immensely proud of their father, though of course they could not demonstrate that in his presence. But there would be no more enthusiastic applause in the hall than theirs, when Bert eventually went forward for his degree.

The person least at ease in the group was Bert Hook himself, sweltering in his best suit beneath the blue and gold gown of the soon-to-be graduate. He had enjoyed his studies, in literature and history particularly, far more than he had expected to, but the formal reception of his degree was less to his taste. 'This is like a school speech day,' he said gloomily, looking round at the plethora of gowns like his. He grinned weakly at John Lambert. 'Do you think Lord Wotsisname will ask if we can have a half-holiday?'

'They don't have school speech days any

154

more. Mrs Fisher says they're elitist because they single out the most able,' said Luke Hook piously.

'Your Mrs Fisher has a lot to answer for,' said his mother darkly.

'She doesn't approve of Open University degrees. She says they're too easy because you can pick them off in modules.'

'That young lady talks too much about things she doesn't know anything about,' said Eleanor Hook. Then, thinking that she might be undermining the teacher's position, she added guiltily, 'Not that she doesn't know her own subject and teach it very well.'

'She's a ... a bit of an idiot, really,' said Jack. He blushed furiously, because he'd only just prevented himself from saying 'tosser' and shocking the delicate sensibilities of these adults. 'She doesn't think sport should be on the timetable and wants playing fields sold to build affordable housing.'

'You'll be able to tell her she's an idiot at the parents' evening, Mum,' said Luke cheerfully. He turned to his father. 'Perhaps now that you're going to have time on your hands, you could come along in your gown to argue with her about the OU, Dad.'

'This is the one and only day you'll see me in this thing,' said Bert Hook firmly, raising his arms beneath the gown and then letting them fall helplessly to his sides. 'It's hired at a ridiculous fee for this occasion and this occasion alone.'

155

'Then I'd better take your picture whilst we have the opportunity,' said Christine Lambert cheerfully, producing her digital camera determinedly from her handbag. She set the group beneath an aged oak tree and took several photographs of various combinations, including one of Bert Hook smiling shyly with an arm round each of his sons, which would later turn out to be unexpectedly impressive. 'And now the one to be framed and put on the mantelpiece,' she said, when Bert thought she had finished. He refused all requests for a picture wearing his mortar board, but she eventually persuaded him to sit alone in his gown with the offending headgear in his lap, in the conventional pose of the newly recognized graduate.

Twenty minutes later, he walked across the stage, with that rolling gait he had used so many thousands of times to walk back to his bowling mark, before making the best amateur batsmen in the country hop about a bit. Then the announcer told the audience that Herbert James Hook was a policeman, and there was surprised applause from the public to support the more raucous enthusiasm from his own group of determined supporters.

When the assemblage of proud relatives and friends emerged blinking from the hall into the sunlight, Bert was sent off to renew acquaintance with the group he had met with regularly over the last year. And this group of mature men and women laughed their delighted recall of incidents during their studies, for all the world

156

as if they were twenty-one-year-olds giggling their delight and relief on this day of triumph. When they had set out so diffidently on this academic journey, this day had seemed distant, even impossible, to all of them. The day and the ceremony were all the sweeter for that. Both seemed afterwards to have passed very quickly.

The women said they would drive home, in view of the bottle of champagne which had concluded events at Hereford. Bert and the boys were surprised when Eleanor turned off the road five miles outside the ancient cathedral city, following Christine Lambert as the two had arranged. They were even more surprised to find that a table had been booked for the six of them, with gleaming cutlery and glasses laid out in readiness. 'My treat,' explained John Lambert shortly. 'In recognition of your efforts over six years, and the pleasure you have given us over one day in gown and mortar board.'

The meal was a great success. Jack and Luke were allowed a minimal quantity of alcohol, the ladies a responsible small glass of white wine each, whilst the two men sank rather a lot over the two hours' traffic of the meal. Well, they weren't driving, were they, and if you can't in-dulge yourself when a detective sergeant is awarded a 2:1 honours degree, when can you?

The two boys had never seen Dad and Uncle John, the great detective, so relaxed before. They were delighted by the experience. They didn't use the word 'relaxed', of course. But as their mother told them in the car as she drove

157

carefully home, the word 'pissed' was very rude, as well as a gross exaggeration.

Throughout the long bright day of DS Hook's graduation ceremony, the blue Jaguar of Martin Beaumont stood still and undisturbed. In the quiet wooded area where it was parked, there were few people about on an ordinary Thursday morning. As the long day passed, no one noted that the big car had now been there for many hours.

The twelve-mile long ridge of the Malvern Hills runs from north to south. It is not ranked among the country's major mountain ranges, but its dominance of the local landscape is far more dramatic than that of many greater elevations. Its flanks rise very steeply from only three hundred feet or so above sea level, making it the commanding feature for many miles around. The rivers Severn and Wye rise almost within hailing distance of each other in the Welsh hills, but run through very different country on opposite sides of the Malvern ridge. From the wide flat valley of the Severn on one side and the less regular country of the Wye Valley on the other, the spectacular outline of the Malverns is visible at most points, defining the limits of the visible landscape.

For those who care to walk the ridge, a modest effort is rewarded by extensive views over some of England's most historic country. Here were fought the decisive battles in the two internal struggles which rent the country, the Wars of the

Roses and the English Civil War. Ridge walking is always enjoyable, with views available on both sides as one moves along the backbone of the height. The northern extremity of the ridge, with Malvern itself immediately below it and the ancient city of Worcester faintly visible to the north east, is the most frequently walked.

The southern extremity of the Malverns, the last of the sharp rises which constitute the ridge, is the lower height known as Chase End Hill. This is much less frequented than the greater heights to the north, though its sides rise with the characteristic Malvern sharpness on its western and eastern slopes.

A small lane skirts the western side of the hill, and the lowest of its slopes are wooded. The blue Jaguar was just off this road, on an unpaved track which ran beneath the fresh foliage of forest trees. It was just visible from the lane, but probably only to pedestrians or passengers, because drivers would be too busy peering towards the next bend on their winding route to spot the patch of blue metal in the shade beneath the huge chestnut.

And so for all of the long May day the big car stood unremarked. As the sun dropped away to the west, it caught the side windows of the vehicle, which sparkled brilliantly for a few minutes. But there were no eyes there to notice the car, or to speculate on why it had not moved for so long. Twilight, then dusk, and then the full darkness of the warm spring night, enveloped the quiet scene.

There were insects in the car, though all the windows were tightly closed. Insects always find their way in, in circumstances like this. Busy insects, concentrating on the blackening blood which had brought them there.

Martin Beaumont lay where he had lain now for many hours, slumped sideways in the driver's seat, with the left half of his head shattered by the bullet which had ended his eventful life.

# TWELVE

On Friday morning, Bert Hook was pleased that he had had the foresight to take two days of his leave for his graduation ceremony rather than the one he had originally planned.

As a young man, he had prided himself upon his capacity for beer drinking. But he wasn't used to champagne and white wine and red wine in yesterday's quantities, and the final brandy had definitely been a mistake. It must be because he wasn't used to such things that he had a thick head this morning. It couldn't possibly be anything to do with the advent of middle age now that he was past forty.

He was glad that this was a school day for the boys. He loved them dearly, but this wasn't the morning for their boisterous jocularity. He

160

listened to the agreeably distant sounds of domestic contest between Eleanor and the boys and left it as late as he could to join them at the breakfast table.

Jack glanced at his father as he came into the kitchen in his dressing gown. He winked at his younger brother before giving the paternal countenance more prolonged and delighted study. 'A little the worse for wear are we this morning, Dad?'

Luke glanced towards the door of the utility room, where his mother was loading the washing machine, and decided she was safely out of earshot. 'I told you he was pissed!' he insisted delightedly to Jack.

'Get on with your breakfast, or you'll be late for school.' Bert reached for the cereal, poured a helping from the newly opened packet, and found surplus corn flakes dancing across the table.

Jack reached across the table and swept the surplus expertly into his own dish. 'Drink's bound to have more of an effect at your age, Dad,' he said sympathetically. Then, much too loudly, he yelled almost in the paternal ear, 'Mum? I think we're going to need the Alka-Seltzer in here!'

His mother entered abruptly and ordered him to look to his own needs. 'You'll be at the last minute for that bus as usual, the pair of you.' She chased them up to their rooms to gather their gear for the day, and came back into the kitchen to catch her husband wincing at the sound of the thundering hooves upon the stairs.

'Jack might have a point,' she said with a sigh. Moments later, a fizzing glass was planted beneath Bert's nose. The sound of bursting bubbles was deafening in his ears. He downed it, stifled a burp and managed his first smile of the day, half relieved and half apologetic.

'You all right?' he said.

'Of course I am. I wasn't able to drink, was I? I had to drive the family safely home, if you remember. Which of course you may not.'

'I do. But I overdid it a bit, didn't I? I'm sorry about that.'

She put an arm round his shoulders and hugged him gently, carefully avoiding his breath. 'You snored a bit more than usual, and I could not get you to turn over. But you're allowed to indulge yourself, on an occasion like that.'

The stampeding of the cattle resumed, more headlong this time, as the steers descended the stairs. 'So long, Dad. Hope the hangover improves,' called Jack solicitously.

'There's no hangover and you're going to miss that bus!' said Bert, reckless of the sharp agony which coursed through his forehead.

'So long, Dad. I won't tell Mrs Fisher you got pissed!' Luke called defiantly from the front doorway, and disappeared in a blur of grey flannel before his mother could tax him with the offending word.

'They're good lads, but sometimes even better in their absence,' said Bert Hook, as a blissful silence crept slowly back into the house.

162

Eleanor left him alone with his thoughts and his slowly diminishing headache. He munched a slice of toast and marmalade at half his usual speed, seeking to restore the world to normal through the steady rhythm of his jaws. He was on his second mug of tea when the phone rang behind him. He hesitated, unwilling to resume contact with the outside world; the ringing was offensive enough in his head to make him realize that his recovery was still at the fragile stage.

'The Hook residence. Bert speaking,' he said, in that snooty voice which was a parody of something he had now forgotten.

'It's DI Rushton, Bert.'

'I'm off duty, Chris. On official leave.'

'You might want to revise that, when you hear this. There's been a suspicious death. A man shot through the head in his car.'

'Sounds pretty suspicious, that, right enough. Where?'

'Not that far from you. Near a hamlet called Howler's Heath, at the southern end of the Malverns.'

'Sounds vaguely appropriate.'

'Chief Superintendent Lambert said I was to let you know.' It was always safer to pass the buck upstairs, when you were interrupting a man's leave.

'Quite right, too. They don't pick their moments, do they, suspicious deaths? A man can't even have a peaceful day off.'

But as always, the CID man in him was

intrigued. It sounded as though a hunt was beginning, and Bert Hook didn't want to be left out of it. He drained his beaker at a single gulp and went to get dressed.

Hook was combing his hair in front of the mirror when John Lambert rang. He would pick him up in ten minutes.

At Abbey Vineyards, it was ten o'clock. Martin Beaumont's PA was wondering whether she should contact his home when the call which made all such considerations irrelevant came through.

Fiona Cooper was an experienced aide to senior executives and directors. She knew when to ask questions and when not to, when to be discreet and when to be forthcoming. But with the police, there was no room for diplomacy, let alone concealment. You had to be forthcoming.

When the cool, detached voice of the man who had announced himself as Inspector Rushton asked her if she knew of the whereabouts of her employer, she did not even think of evasion. 'I don't know. I was getting anxious about him myself. I had expected him to be here before now. He has an appointment in half an hour and he usually wishes to make sure that he is well briefed for such meetings.'

'You will need to cancel all his appointments, unless you think someone else can stand in for him.'

'Why? What's happened?'

There was silence at the other end of the phone

164

whilst Chris regrouped. It was a long time since he had done this. Normally he would have sent someone round to break the news of a death, as someone had indeed already been dispatched in search of the wife. But a junior officer might not get the right response and he was anxious to get as many basic facts as he could, as quickly as he could. 'I have to tell you that a body has been found. A body which we think is almost certainly that of Mr Beaumont. I should be glad if you would keep this information to yourself for the moment. I shall get in touch with you when we have more facts, probably later in the day.'

'Was this an accident?'

There had been a long pause from the PA, but no tears, no hysterics. Rushton was thankful for that. 'I am afraid that I am unable to reveal any further details at the moment, Mrs Cooper. Could you tell me when you last saw Mr Beaumont, please?'

She felt curiously without emotion. This was a man she had served for the last five years, and yet she felt nothing except a profound shock. Perhaps the other things like grief would come to her later. 'Late on Wednesday afternoon. He was still in his office when I left at five thirty. He told me to go and I think he was almost ready to leave himself.'

'That is over forty hours ago. Did you not think it strange that you did not see him for the whole of yesterday?'

'No. Mr Beaumont is the owner of this firm and its chief executive officer. It is his habit not

165

to arrange any appointments for Thursdays if they can possibly be avoided. That leaves him free to visit other parts of the country, other concerns. Perhaps to develop new lines of business. To do anything, in fact, to further the interests of the company.'

'Or perhaps to pursue more personal concerns?'

Her instinct was to be loyal to her employer. But this was a senior policeman, and a situation which was outside even her wide-ranging experience. She said as severely as she could, 'It was not my business or my concern to know where Mr Beaumont was and what he was doing for every minute of his day. All I can tell you is that a considerable amount of business has accrued over the years from his Thursday activities.'

'I see. So neither you nor presumably anyone at Abbey Vineyards would think it unusual that you have seen nothing of him since Wednesday evening?'

She picked her way carefully through this; it sounded as if her reply might be important at some future date. 'The junior staff would, I am sure, have no awareness of the pattern of Mr Beaumont's working week. He delighted in giving them the impression that he might turn up at any time and in any situation. It kept them on their toes, he said, as well as showing them that he was interested in people working at all levels in the firm.'

'But your senior staff would be aware of his

habit of leaving Thursdays free?'

'I think they would, yes. He made no secret of it.'

'And how many of those would there be, Mrs Cooper?'

'Five.' Fiona was surprised by the speed with which she had delivered a number. But Martin had regularly circularized these five with documents he thought appropriate only for them.

'Could you give me their names, please?'

Now, belatedly, she asked him a question, the way a good PA, operating for her boss and the firm, should surely be doing. She was glad she had followed her usual practice in jotting down the man's name and title at the beginning of all this. 'May I ask why you are requesting this information, Detective Inspector Rushton?'

This time it was Chris who paused. He could hardly tell her he wanted a list of potential suspects in a murder enquiry, as the people who had been closest to the dead man were likely to become. 'It is standard practice, Mrs Cooper. As yet we know very little about the way Mr Beaumont died. It is those who were nearest to him at work and at home who can best give us a picture of a dead man.' He had almost said 'victim'. That showed how long it was since he'd broken news like this, he thought ruefully. It was usually left to junior officers to make the first contact and convey the news of a death, but he realized now that everyone should do it occasionally, to keep himself aware of the problems.

Fiona said, conscious for the first time of a

quickening of her pulse, 'This is what you call a "suspicious death", isn't it, Inspector Rushton?'

'It is exactly that, Mrs Cooper. I cannot tell you any more at the moment. I know very little more myself. I am following standard police procedures, as I said just now.'

'I can give you the names and job descriptions of the five senior people I mentioned.'

'That will be most useful information.' He had been considering whether he should throw in Chief Superintendent Lambert's name. Most local people were aware of his name and reputation, and the glamour of celebrity often persuaded them to volunteer information they would otherwise have been reluctant to offer. But it was too early to use Lambert's name yet; time enough for that when this became officially a murder investigation. And this woman was being both efficient and cooperative, in DI Rushton's opinion, the best possible combination of virtues to offer to a police officer. 'If it causes you any embarrassment, we will not need to reveal whence this information came to us.' He liked that last phrase; he had heard Lambert use it years ago, and filed it away for his own use.

'There will be no need for secrecy, Inspector,' came the prim response from the other end of the line. 'I shall give you these names in no particular order of importance. Our finance director is Alistair Morton, aged forty-four. Our shop manager and retail sales director is Gerald Davies, aged fifty-seven. Our manager and

168

director of residential accommodation is Vanda North, aged forty-six, who is also a junior partner in the firm. Our head chef and restaurant director is Jason Knight, aged thirty-eight. Our research and development director is Sarah Vaughan, aged thirty-three.'

Fiona wondered why she had reeled off their ages as well as their names. Probably because she was reading from the employment records and the dates of birth followed the names, she thought. Or was it just the bitchy desire to indicate that pretty young Miss Vaughan was the youngest, most recently arrived, and thus most junior of these people who earned more than she did? She added a little guiltily, 'Mr Beaumont always stresses that we are a small and dynamic organization, so that these roles are not definitive and inevitably overlap from time to time.'

Rushton finished writing and said rather breathlessly, 'Thank you. This will be most useful information, I am sure. Should it prove necessary to talk to any of these people, I or someone else here will contact you again, probably later today.'

Fiona Cooper set down the phone and sat like a statue for several minutes. She was looking through the open door of the office at the round-backed chair which her late employer had so recently occupied. She had spoken of him throughout in the present tense, she now realized, though she had been told at the outset that he was dead. Not very efficient, really, for a PA, though the police must be used to it.

They would already be contacting the people she had just named.

Howler's Heath was indeed no more than the tiniest of hamlets, as Rushton had told Bert Hook. As Lambert drove up the lane beyond it, the scene of the crime was soon apparent by the unwonted activity which surrounded it.

The scene beneath the huge chestnuts was already cordoned off with the plastic ribbons proclaiming 'Do not enter', which always define the environs of a serious crime scene. Not that there was much danger in this remote spot of the curious crowds who often gather round the site of a murder in a town or suburb, at once attracted and repelled by the macabre glamour of the most serious of all crimes, the wanton termination of another being's life.

There were already two police cars at the point where the unpaved track left the lane. Lambert parked behind them; to drive on to the track itself might contaminate important evidence left by other vehicles. The civilians who now constitute most SOCO teams were already busily at work. The photographer announced as they arrived that he had finished his business, but would wait around in case the man in charge of the investigation required any further shots. His manner proclaimed that this was most unlikely.

Two of the others were on all fours, systematically retrieving and bagging in plastic any items which might have a human connection, any detritus which might at a much later date

170

become an important exhibit in a court case. Every calling has its dreams, and it was the aspiration of these worthy seekers to retrieve a piece of jewellery, an accidentally dropped pen or pencil, even at a pinch a soiled tissue, which would secure the conviction of a killer. It very rarely happened, of course. Evidence collected was usually cumulative and supplementary to other findings in building up a case. But very occasionally it did happen, and the hope of it sustained workers in what was essentially a boring task. Because of that, the dream was rarely disparaged by the Scene of Crime Officer or the senior detective in charge of the case.

One of the men with tweezers in hand, a retired police constable who was now operating as a civilian, gestured towards the cigarette end he had recently bagged, which might have been a precious find in the right circumstances, and shook his head glumly. 'Almost certainly pre-dates this crime, sir. I've bagged it to be on the safe side, but I'd say it's at least a week old, possibly more.'

Lambert nodded his sympathy and moved towards the big blue car. Although the site was remote, you could get to it easily enough by car, and for those who were aware of that it would afford an almost certain privacy. A perfect site for lovers who, for whatever reason, wanted to conceal conversations, clumsy gropings or more serious couplings, for instance. As if the thought had provoked the discovery, the woman at the other extremity of the site now produced with a despairing groan a used condom. She lifted it with tweezers, held it at arm's length, and deposited it within her polythene container with a gargoyle moue of distaste.

Lambert walked across and bent over the car, opening the driver's door gingerly with gloved hand. What remained of Martin Beaumont was slumped away from the door, hunched over the gap between the two front seats. It was the left temple which had been targeted, but there was no exit wound.

The voice of the SOCO behind him said quietly, 'He's been here for some time, sir. The pathologist said rigor mortis had been and gone, but he wouldn't commit himself to a time of death.'

'More than twenty-four hours, though?'

'It looks like it. He said he'd treat the post mortem as urgent and give you his report asap.' He looked past the superintendent at the gory remnants of what had been a man. 'It looks as though the bullet is lodged within the skull, sir. He seems to have hit the door and bounced back towards the centre of the car.'

'Not a Smith and Wesson then. That would have blown most of the head away.' The right eye and most of the face were undamaged. Even the left side of the features might clean up after the post mortem, so that the body could be presented as decently as possible to whatever relative had to undergo the formality of identification. 'Any sign of the murder weapon?'

But even as he spoke, he knew there wouldn't

be. Any prize trophy of that sort would have been triumphantly volunteered to the man in charge of the case as soon as he arrived on the scene. The SOCO said, 'No. I should be very surprised if you ever see it again.'

Lambert nodded sourly. Probably in the muddy depths of the Severn or one of its tributaries by now. Murderers were rarely so co-operative as to leave such key evidence around. And he was already sure that this was murder. The faint possibility of suicide had disappeared with the absence of the weapon. 'Did you get anything from the car?'

'A few fibres from the front passenger seat; one or two more from the rear seats and carpets. Impossible to tell how long they've been there. Forensic and their labs might find something more, when their boys and girls are released on to it.'

Lambert looked again at that blank, unseeing right eye. How easy it would be for policemen if the old myth about the cornea retaining the image of what it had last seen had any truth in it. He waved a hand in futile dismissal of the flies, which would return within seconds to the blackening wound which had ended what had once been a man. 'If the pathologist's taken what he wants from here, you might as well have the meat-wagon in to remove the corpse.' He said to the photographer, 'You'd better stay until then, and take a shot of whatever's underneath him.'

Hook had been looking hard at the unpaved

173

track whilst Lambert studied the car and its grisly contents. 'You found any tyre tracks here?' he asked the man who had been inspecting the ground.

'Nothing which looks significant as yet. We'll give it a detailed examination before we leave, but it's been very dry over the last couple of days.' The officer had the pessimism which was characteristic of such workers. They were reluctant to offer much hope to those conducting the case, fearful of being reviled as the producers of false dawns.

Hook nodded, thinking of the bright scenes at his graduation yesterday, of the sun beating down on those happy, noisy, celebrating hordes of people from all sorts of backgrounds. The Jaguar and its ghastly contents had been here beneath these green trees through those same hours, silent and unremarked, save for the heedless singing birds and the flies which scented food.

He was beset in that moment by an illogical guilt, as if his heedless rejoicing had in some way contributed to the fact that this corpse had been undiscovered through the vital first day of its existence. Lambert rejoined him and they removed from their shoes the plastic coverings used to avoid contamination of the crime scene, then picked their way slowly back along the grass verge at the edge of the track to Lambert's old Vauxhall Senator car.

When they looked back a hundred yards to the scene beneath the trees, two men were unloading the plastic body shell from the van the police called the 'meat wagon' and were preparing to lever their blood-spattered cargo from the big blue Jaguar.

And still the sun blazed steadily over the quiet scene, as if to remind them how tiny within the cosmos were the petty affairs of men.

# THIRTEEN

It was a big house, as they would have expected of the man who had owned Abbey Vineyards. The grounds were tidy enough. A gardener in overalls glanced curiously at the police vehicle, then continued planting long lines of bedding plants alongside the drive. An impressive oak front door stood between the pillars which framed it in the mock-Georgian frontage. The exterior woodwork of the house looked as if it had been recently repainted.

Nevertheless, the house itself looked curiously unloved and uncared for. The curtains of the room to the left of the door had been pulled back untidily and those in the room on the first floor above them were tightly drawn. The end of a newspaper protruded still from the letter box, though it was now two o'clock on this sunny Friday afternoon. They rang the doorbell twice. It was some time after the second effort that their ringing was answered.

'Sorry. Mrs Forshaw comes in to clean on Tuesdays and Thursdays, but she isn't here today.'

The woman had straight black hair which fell almost to her shoulders. Her paleness was stark. It was accentuated by the loose-fitting black dress and shoes she wore. Her deep-set eyes must once have been an intriguing feature of the face, but now the rings beneath them made them look haunted, fearful of what might be at hand. Her thin nose seemed pinched, whereas within a healthier setting it would have been attractive. When Lambert announced himself and Hook with their ranks, she smiled and said, 'Yes. I was told to expect you.' Her teeth were regular and attractive. As that single smile briefly lit up the face, they had a glimpse of the woman she had been thirty years ago.

She took them into a large, well-furnished sitting room, which somehow seemed too big a setting for this wan, uneasy figure. Lambert was seeking to ease his way into the interview with the bereaved spouse, which was usually the most difficult of those to follow a suspicious death. He said, 'You know why we're here then, Mrs Beaumont?'

'Yes. The two young women in uniform told me this morning that Martin was dead. I'm afraid they had to get me out of bed, even though it wasn't very early. I often don't sleep very well.'

'I'm sorry we have to intrude at a time like

176

this, Mrs Beaumont, and we'll be as brief as we can. But we have to follow certain procedures.'

'Was he killed? Did someone murder Martin?'

'That is yet to be formally confirmed, but we very much fear he was killed, yes. Forgive me, but you sound as though you were expecting that.'

'You'll need someone to do a formal identification, won't you?'

'We will need that, in due course, yes. But if you don't feel up to it, I'm sure that we can—'

'I'll do it. No problem, Superintendent, I'll do it. How did he die?'

Lambert smiled at her, seeking to mask the rebuke in what he had to say. 'Mrs Beaumont, you are understandably rather on edge at the moment, as we all would be in these circumstances. But the idea of this meeting is that we ask the questions and you answer them, to the best of your ability.'

'Sorry. I'm jumping the gun, aren't I? I tend to do that, I think.'

He watched her carefully to see whether she would recognize her unfortunate choice of metaphor, but she looked only like a woman on edge. It was an effect which was to persist throughout the interview.

Hook flicked open his notebook and said, 'When did you last see Mr Beaumont?'

She looked at him as if registering his presence for the first time, though she had nodded to him politely enough when Lambert had introduced him. 'Wednesday morning. He spoke to

177

me before he went out to work.'

Bert registered a puzzlement he scarcely felt upon his homely features, persuading his listener as usual towards the notion that he was less intelligent, and thus less threatening, than was the reality. 'That is a full forty-eight hours before his body was found. Did you not wonder where he might have got to, or feel any anxiety on his behalf during those hours, Mrs Beaumont?'

'No.' She seemed to think for a moment that it was an odd notion that she should be worried about her husband. Then she said, 'I was used to him being away at nights, you see. I expect he was at Abbey Vineyards on Wednesday. And on Thursdays he was always away. Drumming up new business, he said. I expect that he was, some of the time.'

She caught a glance between the sergeant and his grave-faced superior. What did that mean? Vanda had told her to play the grieving wife, when she'd phoned to say they were coming. That way, they won't get much from you, she'd said. It was curious how close she and Vanda had become, in just a few days. It seemed odd now that she'd been full of such apprehension when she'd gone to meet Martin's ex-mistress in her own home. It was because of Vanda's advice that she'd put on this black dress she hadn't worn for years. It was a little creased, but it was the right colour.

It was the older man who now asked her, 'Did he give you any idea of where he was proposing to go on this particular Thursday?'

She stared down at the carpet and frowned, giving the question the concentration of a dutiful schoolgirl. 'No, I'm afraid he didn't. Is that when he was killed? Sorry, I'm asking you questions again, aren't I?'

'That's all right. We don't know yet exactly when Mr Beaumont died. We expect to have a better idea within twenty-four hours.' He didn't mention post-mortems if he could avoid it. The thought of the body of a loved one being severely cut and mutilated upset many people, though he suspected this rather abstracted woman would have accepted it without much emotion. 'We need you and everyone else to assist us as much as possible as we try to fill in the story of his last hours. Murder is one of the few crimes where the victim cannot speak for himself. We shall need to find out what sort of man he was, what kind of appointments he might have made. We shall assemble that information not only from such facts as we can gather but from the thoughts of you and of others.'

'Am I allowed to know how he died?'

She was brittle, unpredictable. But hardly likely to collapse into hysterics, Lambert judged. He watched her closely as he said, 'He was shot through the head whilst sitting in the driver's seat of his car.'

Jane Beaumont seemed neither surprised nor shaken. Whether that was because she knew these facts already or not, he found it impossible to judge. She was silent for a moment, nodding slowly, as if lost in her own thoughts. Then she said, 'You don't know about us, do you?'

Lambert smiled encouragingly at her, trying to get her to concentrate on him rather than the wall behind him. 'We don't know very much about anything concerned with your husband at present, Mrs Beaumont. We need to know much more, and we need the help of people like you.'

'I see.' She nodded slowly, as if she was having some difficulty in assimilating the simple idea he had put to her.

She didn't seem inclined to offer anything by way of response. It was Hook who eventually prompted gently, 'Mrs Beaumont, you said just now, "You don't know about us, do you?" That is very true, and we need to know. We're asking you to help us, though we realize this is a difficult time for you.'

'Difficult, yes.' She took a deep breath and frowned, as if striving hard to give the matter her full attention. 'We weren't close, Martin and I.' She nodded again, perhaps congratulating herself upon the precision of her grammar. 'We hadn't been close for years. Maybe some of that was my fault – he always said it was.'

Hook said hastily, 'There is no need for you to speculate about the reasons why you were no longer as close as you once were. What would be useful to us is the most precise summary you can give us of the state of your relationship at the time of Mr Beaumont's death.'

'Yes, I see. Well, I wanted a divorce. He wasn't going to give me one. But we were going to fight him about that.'

'We?'

'Oh, a friend of mine. A female friend. No one can really resist divorce permanently nowadays, if you can prove the irretrievable breakdown of a marriage.' She spoke carefully, as if she was repeating phrases which might be new to them. Then she suddenly brightened, looking at Hook for the first time as if conducting a genuine conversation. 'I was going to fight him for my divorce. I won't need to do that any more, will I?'

'No, you won't, Mrs Beaumont. Is it because you no longer felt close to your husband that you seem to know so little about his movements since Wednesday morning?'

'Yes, that would be it, wouldn't it? I haven't known much about his movements on any particular day for quite a long time, now. For many years, I suppose.' Her brow puckered again, and for a moment she was like an adolescent determined to be fair to an errant boyfriend. 'I haven't wanted to know. I suppose I could have found out more about what he was up to, but it's a long time since I was interested.'

'I see. Well, this is useful information for us. We shall probably be able to get a good idea of his movements on Wednesday from his staff at Abbey Vineyards. I appreciate that you have no certain knowledge of what he was planning to do on Wednesday night or Thursday, but have you any thoughts on where he might have been then?'

Jane Beaumont gave the question that dutiful, rather touching, attention she had given to all of his queries. 'No. I'm sorry. I wasn't very interested. I was more concerned with my plans for divorce, so I was quite happy that Martin wasn't around.' She watched Hook make a brief note and added apologetically, 'I'm sorry. I'm not being very helpful, am I?'

Bert gave her an encouraging smile. 'I think you're being honest, Mrs Beaumont, and that is the most we can ask of anyone we talk to. It may be that something will occur to you over the next few hours, when you've had time to accustom yourself to the shock of this. Please get in touch with us immediately at this number with anything at all you think might be useful. Even the smallest things can turn out to be significant, sometimes.'

She took the card and studied it for a moment, as if she had been handed some strange and technical artefact. Then she nodded. 'I'll ring you immediately, if I think of anything. I'm afraid all I can think of at the moment is things to ask you, which is the wrong way round, as Mr Lambert pointed out.'

Lambert said hastily, 'You've been very honest with us, Mrs Beaumont. If there are questions we are able to answer, we will certainly do that.'

'Yes, I see. You told me how he died, didn't you, Mr Lambert?'

He looked at her, deciding that there was a strange and sturdy strength beneath her abstracted air. She seemed to have more rather than less control of herself and her emotions as she had accustomed herself to the idea of this death. Lambert watched her closely as he said quietly, 'I told you that he was shot through the head in his car, Mrs Beaumont.'

She winced slightly, then nodded. She did not seem to be disturbed by the picture. 'He didn't shoot himself, did he?'

It sounded more a statement than a question, but he answered, 'No, we're already certain he didn't do that. We're sure in fact that he was killed by person or persons unknown, as the law has it.'

'The law, yes. But you're going to find out who that person or persons are, aren't you?'

'Yes, I hope so, Mrs Beaumont. That is our job.'

'He didn't use his own pistol, then.' She nodded to herself again, as if that was a reassuring thought.

Lambert, who had been preparing to take his leave, sat down again quickly. 'Your husband had a firearm?'

'A pistol, yes. That's what you have to call it, he said. Not a gun.' She smiled a small, private smile at her satisfaction in recalling that.

'Do you know the make?'

'No. I don't know anything about it, I'm afraid, except that it was a pistol. The thing frightened me. I didn't like having it in the house, but he said he needed it to protect himself.'

'And you think he might have had it with him when he was killed?'

She gave the query careful attention in that curiously touching, diligent way again. 'I think he probably did. I think he carried it about with him in the car. I haven't seen the pistol in the house for years. Didn't you find it there?'

'No, we didn't, Mrs Beaumont. But this is useful information. This is the sort of thing Detective Sergeant Hook meant when he said that if you think of anything that might be useful you should let us know.'

She smiled. It seemed in simple delight that she had been able to help them, though her cheeks remained as white as ever. 'I'll certainly phone if I think of anything else. I hope you find who did this. I didn't want him killed, did I, even though I wanted to be rid of him?'

It was a question which rang in their heads for a long time as they drove away from the big, neglected house.

# FOURTEEN

Whilst Lambert and Hook were conducting their rather strange interview with the newly bereaved Mrs Beaumont, DI Rushton rang the dead man's PA, as he had promised her that morning he would.

'I can confirm for you that we are indeed treating Mr Beaumont's death as murder. There are not many more details available as yet, but I can tell you that Mr Beaumont's body was found in his own car, near a hamlet called Howler's Heath.'

Fiona Cooper was making notes on the pad in front of her. 'I don't know where that is.'

'No. Very few people would – it's a tiny place, just a farm and one or two cottages, I believe. I had to look it up on a large-scale map myself. It's in a valley at the southern end of the Malverns. The car wasn't in the place itself, but some way beyond it, under a copse of trees. It was because it was so isolated that the crime wasn't discovered for some time after it happened.'

'When can I let people know about this? They are all wondering exactly what's happened. I had to cancel all Mr Beaumont's appointments.'

'You can release the news now. That is why I rang you. The bare facts of what I have just told you will be embodied in a press release, which will be carried by the evening papers and by radio and television.'

'Thank you. I'll let the senior staff know immediately.'

'You can let everyone know, Mrs Cooper. You could also make it clear that Detective Chief Superintendent Lambert will be taking charge of the case, and that he and his staff would be delighted to hear from anyone who knows anything at all which they think might have a bearing on this death.' Throw in the local hero now: John Lambert's name was likely to elicit more contacts than that of some anonymous inspector.

'I'll do that. It won't take long for the news to spread.'

'No. Bad news always spreads quickly. And sensational bad news such as violent murder spreads quickest of all.'

'Well, you'd know more about that than I would, Detective Inspector Rushton,' Fiona said primly. She felt a sudden need to distance herself from this awful thing. The vision of the blue Jaguar with its driver dead at the wheel was for the first time appallingly vivid to her. She had worked closely and happily with this man for the last five years. And someone she knew here, one of these people she greeted each day as a friend, might be involved in this, might even have committed murder.

She gave Rushton the extension and home telephone numbers of the five senior people she had named to him earlier in the day, so that he might set up meetings with them.

Fiona sat for a few minutes to compose herself after she had put down the phone, deciding exactly how she would phrase this sensational disclosure for the rest of the staff on the site. It was whilst she was deciding upon the correct form of words that Vanda North tapped briefly on her door and came into the office.

The director of residential accommodation looked very animated. A few strands of her shortish fair hair, usually so tightly disciplined, flew free on the right of her head, creating an effect which was quite attractive. Her blue eyes glittered with life and her cheeks had more colour than Fiona could remember them ever having before. Miss North looked perhaps five years younger than her forty-six as she asked, 'Is there any news yet on how this happened?'

Fiona took her through the sparse facts which Rushton had just released to her. She could not understand why she felt so disturbed, why she was delivering her information as though on automatic pilot. By the time she concluded her brief bulletin, she realized what it was that was so alarming. Vanda North should have known nothing about this death, yet her opening enquiry had shown quite plainly that she did. And her reaction to the facts Fiona had just given her was unsurprised, even a little impatient.

187

Had she unearthed her employer's killer at the outset, simply through this woman's disclosure of knowledge she should not have had? Fiona Cooper said, through a throat which now felt very tight, 'You knew about this, didn't you? But I've only just found out some of these facts myself, only just been given police permission to release them.'

Vanda North looked at her for a moment as if she could not understand the accusation behind the words. Then she laughed abruptly, the unexpected sound shrill and loud in the quiet room. She realized the reason for the apprehension she had seen for a moment in the woman behind the desk. 'Of course, you wouldn't know, would you? I spoke to Jane Beaumont this morning. She told me about it – two policewomen had been round quite early to break the news of Martin's death to her.'

Fiona hoped that the horror she had felt for a moment had not shown on her face. She dropped into her PA's efficient, non-committal voice. 'I knew it must be something like that.'

The house of the finance director of Abbey Vineyards was altogether less grand than that of the company's late owner.

It was a pleasant, rather boxy, detached house in a cul-de-sac of identical buildings on the outskirts of Tewkesbury. It would have been more impressive if allowed more space, but the developer had followed the modern trend in building the maximum number of residences the local authority planning committee would allow him to erect on the site. The land had once been the gardens of the two late-Victorian houses he had demolished to allow this project. There were now fourteen residences here, so that the houses were nothing like as elegant as the artist's impression on the front of the brochure. They had built-in garages and were set in pocket-handkerchief gardens.

Alistair Morton himself opened the door to Lambert and Hook. The room into which he led them was square and well lit by its single broad window in the front wall of the house. The dining-room set of table and six chairs and matching long sideboard made it seem quite small. The three oil paintings of what seemed to be Scottish Highland scenes combined with a few ornaments to make the decor seem almost fussy.

Perhaps Morton noticed them taking note of the room, in the calm, unhurried way which is common in CID officers anxious to pick up every informative detail from the living spaces of those they interview. He said nervously, 'This is a dining room, but we don't use it much for that. I needed it for a study and a place to do freelance work, until I was fully established and provided with my own facilities at Abbey Vineyards.'

Lambert turned his attention with a polite smile to the human being at the centre of this room. Morton was slightly built, his thinness making him seem a little taller than he was. He

189

had straight black hair, neatly parted in the style of a previous generation and closely cut at the back and sides of his head. 'Have you been with Abbey Vineyards for a long time, Mr Morton?'

'Very nearly since the outset. I came to Mr Beaumont as a newly qualified chartered accountant, doing his books in my spare time in the early days. Even when I decided to throw in my lot with him, I still did other work on a freelance basis, because he couldn't afford to pay me much at the beginning.'

Lambert nodded. 'I remember the vineyard beginning as a very modest concern. Most people thought the notion of English wine rather ridiculous at the time, or at best as no more than a novelty. You must have had faith in the idea.'

'I suppose I did. Or rather, faith in Martin Beaumont, if I'm honest. I knew nothing about English wine and very little about wine in general. But Martin was an enthusiast. He carried people along with him.'

'Nevertheless, you showed a lot of faith, to throw in your lot with him when he was dependent on what was then a largely untried idea.'

Alistair hadn't anticipated this. He had expected to be defensive, to have to devote all his resources to concealing the fact that he had been thinking for months of the means by which he might dispose of the employer he had come to hate. Yet this grey, lined, experienced face seemed to understand his situation, to appreciate what he had risked in those early days. He was tempted for a moment to disclose his real relationship with Beaumont, to say exactly what sort of man he had been and how treacherously he had reneged on those early promises of partnership. But that would surely be folly, with Beaumont on a slab with a bullet through his head and these men looking hard for a killer.

Alistair went back to the words he had prepared. 'I was young. I had a wife working. I felt I could take a chance to pursue an exciting idea. We didn't have any children – we still don't have. I was a qualified chartered accountant. It wouldn't have been the end of the world if Abbey Vineyards had failed. I'd have found other employment easily enough.'

It all made sense. But Morton was picking his words very carefully for a man with nothing to hide, thought Lambert. 'You will appreciate that at present we know almost nothing about a man who has been a victim of violent homicide. We've already spoken to Mr Beaumont's widow. Apart from her, you have probably known him longer than anyone else we shall talk to. Would you tell us what sort of man he was, please?'

Alistair wasn't ready for so direct a challenge. Any frank appraisal of the man was plainly dangerous ground for him. He didn't want to say what he really thought, but he couldn't afford to come across to them as evasive. He played for time by rising and going across to the sideboard and sliding open one of its bottom drawers. After searching for a moment through a sheaf of documents, he produced a small leaflet and handed it to Lambert.

'That is the first brochure we produced at Abbey Vineyards. That is a picture of Martin as he was then.'

It was a modest advertising venture, pushing the notion of English wines, reminding the reader that the Romans had grown vines here. It gave brief accounts of soil analysis and the writer's views on why the gentle, south-facing Gloucestershire slopes where the first plantings had taken place were going to produce viable commercial yields. Its only printing extravagance was a full-length picture of the man behind the venture, probably taken a year or two before it was used here. Martin Beaumont was a handsome man, slim in his well-cut suit, with an open face and flowing, carefully cut, dark-gold hair. The features exuded confidence and enthusiasm, as was obviously their purpose in the brochure.

John Lambert studied the photograph for a few seconds, as Morton obviously intended him to do. The Martin Beaumont of those years looked a winning figure, who could easily imbue others with the enthusiasm and conviction he felt for his ideas. He wondered for a moment whether there might have been a sexual attraction between the two men, but immediately dismissed the notion. He was almost sure Morton was not gay, and he certainly didn't present the shaken figure of a man who had lost a lover, whether current or former. More likely there had been an attraction of opposites, a bond between the handsome entrepreneur with his visions of commercial glory and this introverted and cautious figure, excited by an unexpectedly adventurous outlet for his accountancy skills.

Lambert said, 'So you were in at the beginning. It must have been an intoxicating ride.'

Alistair weighed the word carefully. He would have used other, less complimentary words, but it would pay him to accept this view. 'It was. There wasn't much money around at all for a year or two, because Martin insisted on ploughing every penny that was made back into the firm.'

'But no doubt you approved of that, in view of the progress you have seen since then.'

Was it a straightforward comment, or was he being led on to confess something he would rather conceal? These two were experienced at this interview game, whereas he was a novice, whatever he had decided in advance. Alistair said carefully, 'I did, I suppose. It's difficult to recall all the details now, but I remember that Martin could certainly inspire other people with his enthusiasm.' And with promises he never intended to fulfil! But he mustn't tell them that. 'There wasn't much money available for anyone in those early days, including me. But I supplemented what there was with a little freelance work in my spare time. And my wife was bringing in a secretarial salary.'

'You didn't think of going so far as to take a direct stake in the business, rather than just

193

receiving what you admit was a very small salary in the early years?'

It was almost as though this man Lambert knew all about Beaumont's failure to deliver on his promises of partnership. But he couldn't possibly know, could he? He'd given nothing away himself and the only other man who could have told them anything about it was Martin himself, who certainly wouldn't have left any details of that sort around in his papers. Alistair forced a little laugh at his own expense. 'Put it down to an accountant's natural caution, if you like. No one except Martin was certain we were going to be a success, at the outset. Once the early days were past and the business was even a modest success, I'd have liked to be a part-owner, of course, but Martin didn't want that. He was always very much a one-man band, you know.'

'No, we didn't know that, Mr Morton. That's the kind of information we're here to gather, as I explained earlier.'

'Well, he was. And what he really needed in the early days was capital, which I hadn't got. I contributed only my financial expertise. Eventually, when the firm was fully established, I was appointed formally as its financial director. I have no quarrel with the salary I have been paid in that post.'

'I see. And other senior staff are salaried employees in a similar way, are they? None of them has any say in the policies of the company?'

'I understand that Miss North, our director of

194

residential accommodation, is a junior partner in the company. You should ask her if you wish to know the details of exactly how junior. She put in some money ten years or so ago.'

But as the financial director and compiler of the annual accounts, you must know all the details of exactly how far she and anyone else is involved, thought Lambert. Are you just being professionally cagey about financial matters, in a typically British way, or are you really trying to conceal something significant here? 'Abbey Vineyards is now a large and apparently prosperous industrial concern. Is it not unusual that, apart from what you say is a minor involvement by Miss North, it should still at this stage of its development be so much a one-man band?'

'It is probably unusual, but by no means unique. It is – was – part of Martin's temperament to control what he had set up and developed. That is a common trait of many successful entrepreneurs. He didn't operate as a complete autocrat. We had regular meetings, where the five senior staff were allowed their say. Some of us expressed our views on policy pretty forcefully at times.'

'And no doubt the chairman listened to them, and then went ahead with exactly what he had planned from the outset.'

Alistair allowed himself a smile. 'It was a little like that at times, I confess. But that is one of the things you have to accept with a strong-willed leader like Martin. You get rapid progress and success, but less power than in a more democratic set-up. If you don't like it, you go some-where more congenial.'

Lambert gave him an answering smile, showing his understanding, inviting revelations. 'As Mr Beaumont no doubt didn't hesitate to inform any dissenters.'

'It happened, from time to time, I'm sure,' said Morton stiffly.

'But you were perfectly happy with this set-up yourself.'

It was almost as if he was trying to trip him up, thought Alistair. But he mustn't become para-noid: the man couldn't possibly know anything. He must pick his words carefully if he was to avoid showing his resentment. 'On balance, I was happy, yes. There were times when I felt I'd like to have a little more direct involvement, and been able to influence policy more, but as I say I am well paid for my services, so I accept the rewards of the set-up alongside its small limita-tions.'

Lambert regarded him steadily for so long that Alistair thought he was going to pursue the matter. But eventually he said, 'A man like Mr Beaumont must inevitably have made many enemies. Do you know of anyone who might have wished him serious ill? I need hardly say that any thoughts you have on the matter will remain entirely confidential.'

It was an opportunity to divert suspicion away from himself. But he mustn't be too eager to accept the invitation, or it would become obvi-ous what he was about. Alistair said with an air

196

of reluctance, 'I think Miss North would have liked to withdraw her money, to realize the benefits of her stake in the company. But you would need to ask her about that. And I'm certainly not suggesting that she felt strongly enough about it to undertake murder. That would be ridiculous.'

'Murder appears ridiculous to most of us, Mr Morton. But there is one person to whom, at the time at least, it seemed a logical action, even an inevitable action. We shall isolate that person or persons, in due course. In the meantime, who else do you know who was a declared enemy of Mr Beaumont's?'

'There's a strawberry farmer just down the road from us. Martin has bought up various properties over the years as we've expanded. This man's farm is now a tongue of land which cuts right into the vineyards.'

'Name?' said Bert Hook. It was the first time he had spoken, though Alistair had been conscious of him making notes.

'Tom Ogden. He's around sixty, I should think, and he says his family have farmed that land for hundreds of years. I know Martin offered him a good price for it ten years and more ago. He's upped the offer several times as the years have passed and he's acquired the other land around that farm, but Ogden has always refused to sell. Tom's a determined old sod, but so was Martin. He was also used to getting his own way, so he didn't take very kindly to Ogden's refusals. I'm not saying Tom would have killed him, mind. But you asked me about Martin's enemies, and Tom Ogden would certainly admit to being one of those. He'd probably claim it rather proudly, as a matter of fact.'

Alistair thought he'd managed that rather well. He hadn't offered the name until it was prised out of him. He watched Hook completing his entry on Ogden before he said, 'Anyone else?'

'I'm sure there are lots of people. As Superintendent Lambert suggested, it's almost impossible to grow a business the way Martin has grown this one without upsetting a lot of people on the way. And even those of us who worked happily for him found him an abrasive character at times. That doesn't mean that we killed him, does it?'

Hook left that rhetorical question hanging in the air. 'Where were you on Wednesday night, Mr Morton?'

'I was here at home. I did an hour or so in the garden after our evening meal. During the latter part of the evening I was watching television, I expect, like most of the rest of the populace.'

'And overnight?'

'Here. I didn't go out on Wednesday after I came home from work.'

'Is there anyone who can confirm this for us?'

'Just my wife. As I think I said earlier, we do not have any children.' He'd read or heard that they didn't like spouse alibis. But if they could not disprove them, they had to accept them. He wondered if they'd go straight to Amy now and ask her to confirm it, but Hook merely made a note. Lambert said he was to get in touch if he thought of anything else which might help them, and then they were gone.

He sat in the empty dining room and reviewed the meeting. It had certainly gone as well as could be expected, he decided, and perhaps even a little better than that. He went through into the kitchen, where Amy was stirring the beans into the chilli con carne.

He went over and stood behind her, sliding his arms round her waist. 'That was fine, I think. Just routine stuff about the work I do at the firm and so on. The police may not speak to you at all. If they do, just remember that I was here for the whole of Wednesday evening.'

# FIFTEEN

The CID section in the police station at Oldford was unusually busy for a Saturday morning. Murder investigations have that effect. Even overtime budgets are treated flexibly, when chief constables are haunted by the fear of tabloid headlines about unsolved mysteries and police incompetence.

Lambert, Rushton and Hook were gathered around the computer on which the DI recorded the mass of information generated by a murder case. He was about to enter the limited information offered by the post mortem report, much of which they already knew or expected. Powder burns around the temple indicated that Martin Beaumont had been shot at a range of no more than an inch or two by a .38 calibre pistol. The cartridge had now been retrieved, but the weapon had not been found at the site.

The body had in all probability not been touched after the single fatal shot was fired. Beaumont had certainly died in the car where he was discovered and the car had not been driven after his death. He had been in good health for a man of his years at the time of his death. He had died not less than twenty-four and not more than forty-eight hours before the body was found, and probably but not certainly between thirty and forty-two hours before that time.

Stomach contents indicated that a substantial meal had been consumed several hours before death. 'Several' in this case probably meant three to five, but it would be impossible to swear to anything so precise in a court of law. A little alcohol was evident, probably imbibed at the same time as the food, but the blood milligram level was well below the legal limit for driving.

The detection team wanted as always a time of death, which would give them a starting point and pinpoint the enquiries of the large team of officers who were doing the dull but necessary work of house-to-house and local motorist enquiries. Rushton had been computerizing such information as it came in: there were already surprisingly substantial files on his computer.

He said, 'The last sighting of Beaumont to date is at half past five in his office at Abbey Vineyards, by his PA Fiona Cooper. She thought he was almost ready to leave. If we assume he ate an evening meal shortly after that, he probably drove out to the spot where he was killed late that evening.'

'Probably towards midnight.' Lambert nodded glumly. 'He died in a very quiet place at almost the quietest time of day.'

'He may have driven his killer with him to Howler's Heath,' said Rushton. 'It's early days, but there are so far no other sightings reported of another vehicle parked near the scene. But we have as yet no report of a taxi having been summoned to anywhere in that area in the late hours of Wednesday or early hours of Thursday. We've covered the major firms in Gloucester and Tewkesbury, but not all the smaller and individual operators as yet.' He consulted a note he had made. 'The only one of his executive workers who lives near enough to have made his way home on foot from the site of the death is Alistair Morton, who I compute lives some six or seven miles from there.'

'Morton assured us yesterday that he was tucked up at home throughout the evening and overnight,' said Lambert dryly. 'We shouldn't dismiss the possibility that Beaumont might have driven his killer out there with him; it's possible, if we assume an accomplice, who could have picked up the killer at or near the scene after the murder. But the probability is that Beaumont was fulfilling an assignation with the person who killed him. Whether the place and time were selected by Beaumont or by his killer, we cannot know at this stage.'

Hook said, 'It would have been quite possible for the killer to park on the lane, somewhere near where we parked when we went out there, and walk the hundred yards or so to the Jaguar under the trees.'

'It's also possible that in that place and at that time no one noticed a parked vehicle, especially if it wasn't there for very long,' said Rushton grimly. 'I'll tell our officers they should now concentrate on a time an hour before or after midnight.'

'Have forensic come up with anything?'

'They're still working on the car, but I don't expect it to produce anything significant. They've got various fibres from the front seat, but whether any of them were left on the night of the killing is another matter. In any case, they'd only be any use much later, probably not until we can match them with the clothing of someone we've arrested for this.' Rushton paused, looking at what he had already entered from Hook's reports on the interviews already conducted. 'Has the widow got her own car?'

Lambert smiled. 'She has. And she made no great pretence of being devastated by her husband's death. She'd dressed herself in black to meet us, but grief didn't seem to go any deeper than that. The first thought is that it's a pretty obscure place to meet a husband whom you could confront at home at any time. But of course, it would divert suspicion away from her to kill him out there, at what looks like a secret meeting. Jane Beaumont admitted that she knew he had a pistol. According to her, she knew nothing definite about where he kept it and wasn't interested. But for all we know at this stage, she might have had easy access to it.'

Rushton nodded. Then, as if reluctant to raise the possibility, he said, 'Presumably Mrs Beaumont has the resources to pay a contract killer to do this for her, if she'd wanted to do that.'

Lambert nodded. 'That had crossed my mind. It would apply to others too, presumably. By definition, all of the people we are considering as likely suspects are well paid, or in Ogden's case prosperous in his own right. Any one of them might have paid someone else to do their dirty work.'

The three of them looked dolefully from the PM report to Rushton's computer files. It wasn't a welcome possibility. Professional killers who operated for a third party were the hardest of all homicides to bring to book. Lambert said determinedly, 'It's early days yet.'

'Saturday's a busy day. I hope this won't take too long.'

Jason Knight was on his own ground and feeling confident. He had taken the CID men into the tight, almost claustrophobic confines of his private den, behind the kitchens where he ruled supreme.

Lambert smiled the experienced smile of the man who knew his own world better than any outsider could, who had met and dealt with every attitude known to man in the course of nearly thirty years of detection work. He glanced round the bare cream walls of the little room, then said almost affably, 'It will take as long as it needs, Mr Knight. This is a murder investigation.'

'I'm sorry. I didn't mean to sound insensitive.'

'What sort of man was Mr Beaumont, in your view?'

Jason tried not to look shaken. He'd asked them to be brisk and not to waste time on the social niceties; they'd certainly taken him at his word. 'He was a good employer. As long as he was satisfied that you were good at your job and knew what you were doing, he let you get on with it without much interference.'

'And you've got on with it to good effect. I'm aware that your restaurant has an excellent reputation. Would you agree that it's been a key factor in the successful growth of Abbey Vineyards?'

Jason, like most people of his calling, was never averse to words of praise. But he was also shrewd enough to wonder where this was going. He tried not to sound like his late employer in one of his publicity pamphlets as he said, 'The restaurant is one factor, certainly. But it's a team effort here. There are many other areas and many other people involved in the prosperous business which has been developed over the

years. There are the people who plant and culti-
vate and harvest the vines, for a start. Without
them, there would be nothing. The raison d'être
of this place and the centre of everything we do
here is English wine.'

'Yes. I seem to remember Mr Beaumont saying something very like that when he was alive.
Would you now describe your relationship with
him, please?'

Jason told himself not to react badly to this
brusqueness. He couldn't afford to get annoyed;
the plain fact was that he was a suspect. He
needed to deal with that. He tried to take his
time, to ignore the long, quizzical face and the
grey eyes, which seemed to be striving to peer
into his very soul. 'Martin was a good employer,
as I said. He respected your skills and he paid
you well for what you did.'

'So you'd say your professional relationship
was good?'

'Yes. I'd go as far as very good.'

'And your personal relationship?'

'Good also. I liked Martin. He cut out most of
the fripperies. He didn't give himself airs and
graces.' Jason felt he was scraping the barrel
here. He wanted the phrases to sound spontaneous and genuine, but they weren't doing that.
'Some of the other people have said to me that
you always had to do things his way, but that
didn't apply to me. Martin made it clear that he
knew very little about both cooking and the
organization of work in a busy kitchen. He was
happy to leave it all to me, the more so once he

saw that I knew what I was doing and was achieving results.'

'I see. So you didn't feel in any way frustrated.'

Jason wondered what the others had said or were going to say. He realized for the first time that you couldn't just prepare what you wanted to tell the police and deliver it. You wouldn't get away with that, because they were going to compare it with what others said, about you as well as about Beaumont. As far as he knew, these top CID men hadn't spoken to Gerry Davies yet, but they would do, and he wasn't confident that honest Gerry wouldn't let things out in spite of himself.

Jason would need to give them a little of what he had really felt. 'I suppose everyone feels a little frustrated from time to time, when things don't go exactly as planned. Martin was used to getting his own way. He was very successful, so that it was difficult to argue with him, even when you felt that you had a good idea to put forward.'

Lambert smiled at him, pleased to see him struggling. 'You've just said that he didn't interfere with you in your kitchens or the restaurant. You'd better make it clear exactly what you're telling me now.'

'Yes. Well, it's difficult to be specific, but I think other people felt it as well as me. I'm about twenty years younger than Martin was, and I suppose I felt sometimes that he wasn't always open to new ideas.'

206

'You will need to be specific, however difficult you find that, Mr Knight.'

'Well, I suppose I'm saying I'd have liked more of a say in policy matters. I think we all would – all the senior people, I mean.'

'You wanted to be more than mere employees.'

'Yes. I'm not sure how far other people shared this view, of course. You'd need to speak to them to find out that.'

'Which we shall be doing, in due course. At the moment I'm trying to establish how much you resented Mr Beaumont's autocratic way of running a business.'

'Oh, our relationship was amiable enough. We'd agreed to differ, for the moment. I expect there'd have been ongoing discussions as time went on, if Martin hadn't been removed from us.'

'I see. You didn't accept that Mr Beaumont's attitude was immovable on issues affecting his control of the business? Mr Morton gave us the impression that there wasn't room for manoeuvre on this sort of issue.'

Jason's heart jumped at this. He hadn't expected them to be so direct. It was forcing him to move off the ground he had been prepared to fight on. He forced a smile. 'Alistair Morton and I have different temperaments, I think. Not that I feel I know him really well, even after years of working here. He's very efficient about matters of finance, but something of an introvert. He isn't an easy man to get to know. Perhaps

Alistair accepted Martin's decisions as final, whereas I tend to think that there is always the possibility of change. It was my view that as the business grew bigger and bigger, Martin would eventually have had to compromise a little, to allow other people a greater input on decisions of policy. Unfortunately, we'll now never be able to see whether I was right or whether I was too optimistic. I must admit I always tend to look on the bright side of things.'

'Perhaps someone else didn't share your view. Perhaps that someone saw Beaumont's death as the only way of changing things.'

'I suppose that is a possibility. I must confess that I had assumed that Martin's death was unconnected with the business. I'd presumed that it was likely to have stemmed from his private life.'

'And what reason do you have for thinking that?'

'None, I suppose. I just thought violent death must have come from violent emotion.'

'It often does. Do you have a particular reason for thinking violent emotion prompted this crime?'

This Lambert man wasn't letting him get away with anything. He had planned to offer them a bland, stonewalling performance and send them away feeling he had nothing to offer. But everything he suggested seemed to be treated as if he had special knowledge. He said carefully, 'No, I've no real reason to think this was a killing prompted by private passion. I've no idea what

208

motive Martin's killer had. But when you know a man had a fairly turbulent personal life, you inevitably think his death might be connected with that.'

This time Lambert offered him a nod of agreement. 'You'd better tell us about this turbulence in Mr Beaumont's personal life, hadn't you?'

'I don't know any details.' Jason was immediately and instinctively defensive; he could hear it in his own voice. He knew he needed to offer them something. 'I do know that Martin wasn't particularly close to his wife. He produced her about once a year, usually on a formal occasion like dinner in the restaurant, but otherwise we never saw her. I've been told that she has some sort of mental illness, but I couldn't give you any details of that.'

Lambert smiled a rueful acknowledgement. He should have expected sex to rear its multi-coloured head. It invariably complicated murder investigations, and unfortunately it was rarely absent from them. 'What you're telling me is that Beaumont had other women in his life.'

'Yes. But I don't—'

'And other men?'

'No.' Jason permitted himself a smile at the thought. 'I'd be confident that Martin was thoroughly heterosexual in his tastes.'

'And by "thoroughly" you would mean extensively.'

'I think I would, yes. But I can't give you any details. It's all hearsay as far as I'm concerned.'

'But well-informed hearsay, no doubt.'

209

Jason felt no threat here; on the contrary, it was an opportunity to divert suspicion away from himself and into the murky world of Beaumont's couplings. He relaxed his language as well as his attitude. 'Martin was a big personality, as you've no doubt gathered already. He dominated this firm and he liked it that way. There was bound to be a lot of gossip about what he got up to when he was away from the work which was his main passion. Some of it was probably no more than salacious rumour, but I'm sure Martin was a red-blooded male who needed his sexual release. Don't they say that autocrats are the worst? I read that Mussolini used to pop out of meetings for a quick bit of how's-your-father and then be back for the next agenda item. I'm not suggesting that Martin was anything like that, but I'm sure he had an active and varied sex life.'

'Are you, indeed? And yet you can't give us any details of these activities.'

Jason contrived to look a little hurt. 'I'm just trying to be honest, Chief Superintendent. I'm sure these things happened, but I didn't want to know the details. They weren't my business and Martin wouldn't have been pleased if he'd found me prying into his private life.'

That certainly made sense. They already had this picture of the murder victim as a despot who would not welcome such interest. A benevolent despot, perhaps, so long as no one opposed his formidable will. Rewarding to work for, as Jason Knight had told them at the outset, so long as you were prepared to accept his every decision unquestioningly.

Lambert said, 'You have been very successful here, as you mentioned. I'm sure you have ideas of your own about how not only the restaurant wing but the whole of the business might best be developed. Did you not find Mr Beaumont's dictatorial attitude frustrating?'

It was so nearly a summary of the way his thinking had evolved that Jason wondered for a moment of panic whether they knew all about the very things he had set out to conceal. But they couldn't know: this could only be speculation. He paused, smiled, said, 'You're quite right, of course. When you feel you have good ideas, you like to see them implemented. But you were allowed your say. Sometimes you found that your good ideas were being implemented as though they were Martin's own a few months later.'

Lambert nodded. He'd seen plenty of that in the police service over the years. Your good ideas could sometimes be implemented, as long as you were content to let them emerge as someone else's bright proposals. 'Nevertheless, that is a rather dubious way of making progress. You strike me as the sort of man who would like a more direct input and a more direct recognition.'

Jason nodded a gracious acceptance of what he took as a compliment. He had an answer ready for this. 'I am still developing my restaurant here, both in terms of the quality we offer and the numbers we serve. That is satisfaction

211

enough. If in due course I'd felt the sort of frustration you mention, no doubt I would have moved on to pastures new.'

But chefs more than others were reluctant to abandon what they had built up from scratch, thought Lambert. They might develop and extend, open new branches, but they were usually reluctant to abandon the place where they had built a reputation. It was as though that place contained a part of themselves which they could not readily relinquish. He nodded to Hook, who said quietly, 'Where were you on Wednesday evening, Mr Knight?'

'At the golf club at Ross-on-Wye. I saw you on the course there.' Jason tried not to sound too pleased with himself.

Bert Hook disappointed him by nodding impassively. 'You weren't working?'

'No. Normally I would have been, but this is a quiet time of the year for us. My deputy is quite capable of handling the numbers we had on Wednesday. Good experience for him to be in charge.'

'What time did you leave the golf club?'

'It must have been at around eight o'clock.'

'And where did you spend the rest of the evening?'

'I went home. Watched a little television. Dozed off in front of it, I expect, after the fresh air and exercise and a couple of drinks.'

Jason wondered if they would ask him about the programmes, but Hook merely made a note and said, 'Is there anyone who can confirm this for us?'

'No. I live alone, since I was divorced three years ago. Is it important?'

'It's a routine question. We should like to eliminate you from the enquiry, if it were possible.'

'If I think of anyone who rang me on that night, I'll let you know.'

'Thank you. That would be useful.' But Jason had the feeling that both of them knew he wasn't going to be able to come up with anyone.

Lambert didn't speak until Hook had piloted the police Mondeo out of the crowded car park at Abbey Vineyards and on to the road outside. 'What did you make of him?'

'I felt he had most of his answers ready for us – not that that's always significant. I also thought he was being evasive.'

'Interesting. So did I. No doubt we shall need to speak again with Mr Knight.'

Saturday afternoon was busy in the strawberry farm down the road, far too busy for Tom Ogden to notice the police car as it passed the entrance.

Half an hour later, after several minutes hesitating over the decision, he picked up the phone and rang his wife. 'It's me, Enid. I'm almost finished here. I'll be with you in an hour or so.' The farmhouse was only a few hundred yards away, at the other end of his land.

'All right. I'll have the meal ready. And a beer, seeing as it's Saturday, so long as you're prompt.'

213

'The police are coming to see me about Beaumont. About his murder.' He'd planned to wrap it up a little, to deliver it more casually. But as usual he was no good at needless words. And he'd never been able to keep anything from Enid.

There was a tense little pause before she said, 'Why's that?'

'I don't know. Routine enquiries, the woman who arranged it said. I suppose someone's told them I hated the sod. I don't expect it's anything to worry about.'

'No. You might be as well not to tell them what you told me this morning about how glad you were that the bastard was dead.'

'No.' Tom knew she was joking, but he wished she'd actually laughed at the idea. 'And there's one thing I thought of. I think we should both say we were at the cinema on Wednesday night. Just to be on the safe side.'

'Even though that was on Thursday.'

'Yes. According to the papers, Wednesday night is when he was killed, you see.'

'All right.'

'Just to be on the safe side, as I said.' He wondered why he wanted so much to do this on the phone, not face to face.

'And I said all right, Tom. If you think it best.'

Enid Ogden put down the phone and stared at it for a long time, wondering where her man had actually been on Wednesday night.

# SIXTEEN

'There's a picture of Dad in the local rag,' Jack Hook informed his mother with satisfaction. 'He looks like the cat that pinched the cream.'

Eleanor knew she ought to discourage him, but she was too curious not to come out from the kitchen and look at the news sheet he had spread out across the table. The photograph had been taken as Bert descended the steps after the award of his degree. The reporter had caught him off guard, no doubt commanded him to smile, and had been rewarded with an obedient, meaningless smirk. The caption described him as 'Detective Sergeant James Herbert Hook, delighted with the award of his BA with honours, after six years of unremitting part-time study'. Eleanor shuddered in anticipation; her husband never used his first name of James and hated the Herbert, which was a regular source of tiresome police-canteen humour.

'Don't upset your father,' she admonished her sons; Luke had appeared mysteriously and silently at his elder brother's side, in response to Jack's discovery of the article in the free local weekly.

It was Luke who sought out the gems in the

accompanying copy and delivered himself of an unseemly guffaw. 'They call Dad Jim, Mum. It says here: "The well-known Herefordshire detective Jim Hook is now the proud holder of a distinguished honours degree." Then it goes back to that stuff it always prints about cricket and how he got Geoff Boycott out in the days of prehistory.'

His father, who had entered the room in time to hear this last sentence, said a little wearily, 'Anything before you were born is "prehistory", is it, Luke? It was a mere fourteen years ago, you know.'

'When you were in your pomp and King Boycott was well past his, then,' said his elder son, with a crushingly accurate knowledge of the game he now loved with the same passion as his father.

'Indeed it was,' Bert admitted with his habitual modesty. It was not without a tinge of regret that he added, 'It was in a benefit match, when the great Geoffrey had retired. He'd already compiled over fifty runs.'

Eleanor Hook said loftily, 'If you know as much about the game as you claim, Jack, you will be aware that Mr Boycott was renowned for never giving his wicket away. At any time and in any circumstances.'

'Well done, Mum,' said Luke. 'I bet it was one of Dad's good 'uns, like you say. You know, Jack, he was a great bowler, our dad, long before he was a professor.'

'Can we eat as soon as possible, please, love?

I have to go out again tonight,' was all that modest luminary said in response to this unwonted filial admiration.

Luke was not going to let him off so easily. After perusing the print beneath the picture carefully, he read with his finger fastened triumphantly on the passage, stressing the forename whenever it occurred. 'It says here, "Whilst his colleagues were anxious to assure us that *Jim* Hook was not allowing his academic distinction to go to his head, the great man himself was not available for comment. It seems that conscientious detective *Jim* was too busy with his work to speak to us. We understand that he is currently engaged on the case of the sensational and as yet unsolved murder of Martin Beaumont, the well-loved local businessman who owned and ran Abbey Vineyards. At the time we went to print, a source described the police as baffled by the crime."' Luke looked up with delighted innocence. 'I don't think they should call Dad "baffled", now that he's a graduate. Do you, Mum?'

'Dinner's ready. Get the cutlery out and set the table,' ordered his mother sternly. Bert forbade all discussion of both degrees and detection for the duration of the meal.

Jack Hook had a parting shot for his father as he left the house and hurried to his car. 'Best of luck with the detecting, Jim!'

Tom Ogden lived with his wife in a long, low, two-hundred-year-old farmhouse, built in the attractive amber-coloured local stone. The barn alongside it was in good repair but now disused. It had already elicited several enquiries from local property developers, who had been told firmly that it was not for sale in Tom's lifetime. The other, smaller outbuildings housed the compact modern machinery used in the cultivation of the strawberry fields.

Hook, who was used to the convenience and confinements of modern suburbia, said with genuine appreciation what an attractive place this was to live. Ogden led them across a wide, stone-flagged hall and into a room which comfortably accommodated several easy chairs alongside the old, oak dining-room furniture which denoted its main use.

Tom Ogden looked genuinely pleased with Hook's compliment. 'We rattle around a little, now that the children have gone. Enid says we should go for a modern bungalow, but my family's been here for centuries – I can't see myself living anywhere else. Besides, there are advantages in living on site, even now, when there are no beasts to milk and we operate like a vast smallholding.' He delivered the last phrase with a practised contempt, so that they caught a little of the nostalgia for a vanished way of life they often saw in countrymen of his age.

Hook, who was seeking to get a flavour of the man before they began formal questioning, saw the odd but attractive mixture of openness and shrewdness he often found in people who owned and worked the land. He had played cricket with men like this, who had been veterans of the game when he had arrived as a raw but promising teenager, a police cadet newly released from the Barnardo's home where he had spent his boyhood. He had been a green lad in those days, knowing little of life outside the home and anxious to pick up whatever he could from every experience. He had learned much from men like this.

Ogden had the weather-beaten skin, the tanned face and hands of a man who had spent the bulk of his life in the open air, who had worked outside in all weathers and come through the worst of the heat and the cold, labouring as hard and as long as the men he had eventually employed. At sixty-three, he was a picture of healthy vigour, bulky yet sinewy, an excellent representative of the yeoman stock which had bred him. He was also an intelligent man, who had reacted to the changing demands of farming in the new century.

As if he read those thoughts, Tom looked round the low-ceilinged room and said, 'I can remember having over thirty people in here for the Sunday tea my mother made, when I was a nipper in the fifties and we had everyone out for the haymaking.'

'You've seen the world of farming change a lot in your working lifetime,' agreed Bert Hook.

'Ay. But at the moment I'm wondering what you're doing here.' He said it with a smile, but with the air of a man who was used to directness in himself and in others. You wouldn't get away with much, if you worked for this man, but he would treat you fairly, if you were honest with him.

Lambert said, 'It's routine in a murder case. Anyone who was close to the victim is interviewed in case he can provide useful information.'

'Not on Saturday night, they're not. And not by the man in charge, the celebrated John Lambert.' The smile was still there, but this time there was an edge to the words. 'If this was no more than routine, you'd have sent a copper round, maybe a DC. I wouldn't have been honoured with a chief superintendent and a detective sergeant.'

Lambert answered the smile, but did not hurry his reply. There was nothing wrong with letting a man who was used to being in control see that you were assessing him. 'I see you have some knowledge of police procedure, Mr Ogden.' He waited until he saw the man's face cloud with anger, then went on briskly, 'I think you have enough common sense to have expected this visit. Physically, your land is close to Abbey Vineyards. Very nearly surrounded by their vines, in fact. And I don't think you would expect the fact that you have had what one might call "ongoing discussions" with Mr Beaumont over the years to have escaped us.'

'All right. So we didn't see eye to eye and never would have. Doesn't mean I killed the man, does it?'

'Indeed it doesn't, Mr Ogden. But could you

220

now tell us about the source of your disagreements, please?'

'You already know it. You only have to look at a map. Beaumont wanted my land, but he wasn't going to have it.'

'I can certainly see that he would want it. It would have consolidated his holding, made a natural completion of the land he held.'

'Yes. I've watched him swallow up the land of everyone else who held fields adjacent to his, over the years. He was never going to get mine.'

'You make it sound as if you weren't friendly neighbours.'

'I hated his guts. I'm sure he felt the same way about me.'

'You hadn't agreed to differ?'

Ogden smiled sourly. 'You didn't know Beaumont, or you wouldn't be asking that. He wasn't used to being refused things. He warned me years ago that he wouldn't take no for an answer. But that's what he got and what he'd always have got. He didn't like it. He was used to getting his own way and he turned nasty when he didn't.'

Bert Hook looked up from his notes. 'How nasty, Mr Ogden?'

Tom Ogden looked from the notebook into the rugged face above it. For some reason he could not quite fathom, he felt an affinity with this burly man with the countryman's face and the Herefordshire accent. He made a real attempt to explain how things had been with his more affluent neighbour. 'Beaumont first came to me

221

over ten years ago. He made me what would have been a fair offer, if I'd wanted to sell. A very fair offer – the fairness has never been a matter of dispute. Over the years, he's been back half a dozen times, each time waving a better price under my nose. I've told him the same thing every time: I'm not interested in selling, and the price makes no difference. He didn't seem to understand that. At any rate, he never accepted it.'

Hook nodded, made another note. 'And when did he make the last of these offers?'

Tom wanted to distance himself from this crime, to tell them that he hadn't seen the man for many months. But that wouldn't be safe; for all he knew, they had already learned how recently he had clashed with the man whose death had been so convenient for him. 'He'd been round to the farm twice in the last couple of months. He always came during the day. I think he wanted my workers to see him, to be unsettled and think that their jobs might be at stake. He was that sort of man.'

'When was the last time you saw him?'

'Last week. He came round with an even bigger offer than he'd made in April.'

'Which you rejected.'

'As I'd rejected all the others. It was more than a fair price, but that wasn't the issue. Beaumont didn't seem to understand that. He never learned that there were more important things than money.'

Hook nodded, seeming to Tom to understand

222

how it had been, even to sympathize with his point of view. 'And how did he take it when you rejected his latest offer?'

'He didn't like it. Like I said, he was a man used to getting his own way and to pressurizing you when he didn't. He turned nasty.'

'How nasty, Mr Ogden?'

Despite his agitation, Ogden wanted to tell the sergeant to call him Tom, when he'd never have asked the tall bloke to do that. But he sensed he should keep this formal. 'He threatened me. He said that this was his final offer and it would be all the worse for me if I didn't take it.'

'And what did you take that to mean?'

'That he'd send people in to ruin my crops – soft fruit is very vulnerable and he knew that as well as I did. And that if that didn't work he'd send people in to attend to me.'

'You mean that he was threatening you with physical violence.'

'Yes. I'd seen how he compelled another farmer to sell to him, eight years ago. He'd wrecked his machinery during the night, then sprayed his newly planted crops with weedkiller. The man sold out to him the following week.'

'So exactly how did he threaten you, Mr Ogden?'

'I'd told him the farm was doing well and that I was expecting a bumper crop this year. He said it would be a shame if anything happened to ruin that crop.'

'And how did you react to that?'

Ogden hesitated. He recalled the conversation

223

quite vividly, having been over it in his mind many times since it happened. But he couldn't recount the full details to these men without compromising his position. 'I told him that two could play at that game. He said I couldn't afford to threaten him.'

'And why was that?'

Tom stared at the Indian carpet which covered the middle of the room; he couldn't bring himself to look at either of the CID men. 'I don't know. I suppose he meant that he could play things far dirtier than I could, if it came to it. He was certainly right about that. God – or in Beaumont's case, the devil – is always on the side of the big battalions, isn't he?'

There was a long pause, but Tom knew now that he'd already said too much. It was Lambert who said, 'If Beaumont is the kind of man you say he was, I expect he'd done his homework on you. I expect he knew that you had a record of previous violence. A criminal record.'

Tom Ogden glared at him resentfully. 'Beaumont wasn't the only one who'd done his damned homework, was he?'

Lambert smiled grimly at him. 'I have people to check these things for me, Mr Ogden. A murder enquiry warrants a big team of officers. It's automatic that we check on known enemies of the victim to see if they have criminal records.'

'So it's once a villain always a villain, is it? It's a hell of a long time since that happened. I'm not the young fool I was then.'

Lambert nodded. 'Thirty-seven years, Mr

Ogden. But you were then twenty-six, not sixteen. Certainly not an easily led teenager. And Grievous Bodily Harm is a serious charge, to which you pleaded guilty.'

'Because I was guilty. I hadn't meant to injure the man seriously, but I did. So I admitted it and took my medicine.'

'In the form of a hefty fine and a suspended sentence. You must have had a good brief, to get away without a custodial sentence.'

'I did. My dad got the best man for me, when he'd finished reading me the riot act. I pleaded guilty and it was my first offence. I've never been in trouble with the law before or since. It's years since anyone's even mentioned this. I didn't expect it would ever be flung in my face again.'

'Murder awakens all kinds of sleeping dogs, Mr Ogden. You may think that incident is now irrelevant, but it's got to interest us. It shows a man with a quick temper and an immediate use of violence as retaliation. The kind of man, in fact, who might see murder as a solution when he was pressed too far.'

'I didn't murder Beaumont. I don't deny that I'd have liked to, but I didn't kill him.' Tom looked from the long, grave face of Lambert to the rounder, more sympathetic one of Hook and added defiantly, 'But I'm bloody glad the bastard's dead and I'm sure whoever killed him had good reason for it.'

He felt himself trembling with the vehemence of his emotion in the seconds which followed.

225

Then Hook said quietly, 'Where were you on Wednesday night, Mr Ogden?'

'I was at the cinema with my wife. Enid will confirm that for you. We don't go very often, but she wanted to see *The Duchess*. I think she'd read the book. We'd missed it the first time. Personally, I didn't think much of it.' He was aware that he was talking too much, sounding nervous and defensive, filling the silence with irrelevant detail when he was normally sparing with words. He stopped abruptly, looking at Lambert for a reaction.

The chief superintendent studied him for a moment, in which Tom thought he read these thoughts, and said impassively, 'Then who do you think did kill Martin Beaumont, Mr Ogden?'

'I don't know. One of his women, or one of their husbands? The gossip is that he put it about a bit. Someone who worked with him? I don't know anyone at Abbey Vineyards except Beaumont, and I wish I hadn't known him.' It sounded rather desperate, but he ended defiantly, 'I probably wouldn't tell you if I did know. I'm delighted the bugger's dead!'

'You would be most unwise to withhold any information which could lead to an arrest, Mr Ogden. It would make you an accessory after the fact and lead to very serious charges.'

The two big men were on their feet, leaving the farmer to follow them to the door with a surge of relief that this was over. Lambert paused at the entrance to the handsome old building.

'We may well need to speak to you again, when we know more of the details of this death.'

The words rang like a threat in Tom Ogden's mind through the evening which followed.

# SEVENTEEN

There is a popular misconception that the team never takes time off during a murder investigation. A moment's consideration exposes this as the myth it is. Investigations often last for weeks or months, and officers would remain fresh in neither body nor mind if they worked incessantly on them. Indeed, there have been some high-profile failures when senior officers became so obsessed with a case that it took over their lives. Judgements are then impaired, and attention to detail becomes worse, not better, when people drive themselves too hard.

Detectives were too close to the cases and the suspects involved to spot the obvious in two of the most notorious cases of recent years. Peter Sutcliffe, the notorious Yorkshire Ripper, eventually found guilty of thirteen murders and seven attempted murders, was interviewed and released several times by the police in the course of that enquiry. The awful Fred West, who buried several young female victims beneath the concrete of his house and its surrounding area in

Gloucester, was a known petty criminal who was deemed to be incapable of such monstrous crimes.

John Lambert had often come near to obsession in his early CID days, to the extent that his preoccupation with detection had endangered the marriage which most of his juniors now saw as a model alliance in a difficult profession. He was aware of the dangers now, and he watched for the signs of fixation in those around him as well as himself.

Sunday morning was not a good time for interviews or any other kind of progress in a case like this one. Lambert made a move which he would once never have made. He arranged that Hook and he would present themselves bright and early on Sunday morning at Ross-on-Wye Golf Club and find themselves a game. Golf would blow away the cobwebs, he assured Bert conventionally. His DS was not convinced. Lambert had played the game for thirty years and more; he played to a handicap of eight and kept his temper on the course. Hook, who had taken up the game only three years previously at his chief's insistence, was not persuaded that Sunday-morning golf would provide him with the healthy release his senior confidently predicted.

The possibilities of disaster were increased by the opposition John Lambert secured for them. He lined them up against the only scratch player in the club, Tom Bowles. 'Only a friendly. A chance for us to watch and learn,' he assured a fearful Bert Hook. Tom had moved to the

London area now, but he was down for the weekend with a friend of his who played off four at his new club at Sunningdale. Bert, fearing the slice which made even his modest handicap of sixteen optimistic, was filled with sporting apprehension.

In the event, things worked out pretty well. Bert Hook disappeared into the woods on two holes, but elsewhere produced some sensible and occasionally outstanding golf to take advantage of his handicap strokes. John Lambert was his usual steady self and the pair fitted their scores together to stay alongside the experts to the very end of the game. On the eighteenth hole, with the match all square, Tom Bowles followed an excellent drive with a seven-iron to eight feet. He then directed a curling putt into the heart of the hole, to secure a splendid win for the young tigers and an honourable defeat for the CID pair.

Tom Bowles's partner made his excuses and left, casting a longing eye at the drinks Lambert was carrying from the bar for the others. He explained that he had to go and eat a dutiful Sunday lunch with his aunt and uncle, who lived in Monmouth. He made them sound ancient; Lambert reflected that they were probably in their fifties and about the age of Christine and himself.

Tom Bowles took an appreciative pull at his pint and said, 'I expect you've cracked the case of the murdered vineyard owner by now.'

Lambert gave him the quiet, unrevealing smile

229

of long practice and prepared to change the subject. But before he could speak, Bowles added reflectively, 'I played a match in the first round of the knockout against someone from there – Jason Knight, who runs the restaurant. He put it across me on the eighteenth, rather as I did to you two today.'

'I played Jason last year. He beat me very comfortably,' said Bert Hook. He didn't even need to look at John Lambert. Both of them knew the rules here without even thinking about it. If anyone asked you about the case, you gave them nothing, politely putting up the confidential shutters. If, on the other hand, anyone chose to speak to you about people involved in the case, you let him talk. Nine times out of ten it was no more than extraneous gossip; on the tenth you picked up something useful.

Bowles nodded. 'He's done wonders for the place. I've eaten there a couple of times, and the food's very good. Jason was telling me they've trebled the number of tables since he started there. I wonder how the death of the owner is going to affect him.' He took another swallow of his bitter, whilst Lambert and Hook remained reflectively silent. 'Perhaps he'll be able to get the say in policy he wants, now that Martin Beaumont's gone.'

'Too early to say yet what's going to happen to Abbey Vineyards,' said Lambert. 'Not our problem, I'm happy to say.'

'No, I suppose not. Jason will be anxious to know, though. He's ambitious, as well as being

230

an excellent chef. I wouldn't mind betting that he'll be having a big influence on the future of Abbey Vineyards.'

'I expect you're right there,' said Bert Hook, studiously non-committal. He sensed that murder was as usual exercising its ghoulish glamour. This pleasant young man, whether he was conscious of it or not, didn't want to relinquish the subject and his tenuous connection with it.

Tom said, 'Jason wouldn't have got very far whilst Beaumont controlled things, as far as I could see. I told him that.'

'You did?'

Tom Bowles nodded, moving into the anecdote he realized now that he had always been anxious to offer them. 'I'm an industrial lawyer. Pretty dull stuff, as far as most people are concerned. But Jason was anxious to pick my brains after our match was over. He said he was asking for advice on behalf of a friend, but I suspect both of us knew perfectly well that it was his own situation he was talking about.'

'We have the same problems as policemen, sometimes,' said Lambert gnomically. 'People tend to think we're experts on all aspects of the law, when we're often as ignorant as they are. At least you had the benefit of having professional knowledge to draw upon.'

'Yes. I couldn't offer much hope to Jason Knight, though. As a key member of the team at the vineyards, he was anxious to get more power for himself, to have a greater share in policy. I told him that he could perhaps buy his way in,

231

but he hadn't the capital for that. And from what he said, Martin Beaumont had control of the business neatly tied up – I couldn't see how Jason was going to get the say in things he wanted, unless his employer was willing to give it to him.'

'Which people tell us he wasn't,' said Bert Hook, taking a drink and shaking his head sadly over the obstinacy of autocrats.

'No. I wonder what Jason would have done about that. He was certainly pretty keen to get more of a say in things. Perhaps he'll get what he wanted without needing to do anything, now. Another drink, gentlemen?'

'Sorry, I think we need to be on our way,' said John Lambert quickly.

Even in this ancient part of England, there are not many thatched cottages left. This one had been little altered externally since it was built in the seventeenth century. Inside, its nooks and crannies retained the essence of its quaintness, but accommodated the fittings now considered essential for modern living.

Vanda North said, 'I made a pot of tea when I saw you reversing the car into the drive. You need some compensation for having to work on a Sunday afternoon.' There were biscuits which looked home-made on a china plate beside the teapot. Vanda North did not look to Bert Hook like the sort of lady who made her own biscuits, and Bert was something of an expert on such things. Probably, though, a lady with good taste,

232

who knew where to get the best things in life. Her fair hair was short and expertly cut. Her blue eyes, above a nose which was just a little too prominent, were observant, despite her conventional phrases. He had no doubt that she was measuring them as intensely as they were assessing her.

He flicked open his notebook and retreated into the conventional first question. 'How long had you known Mr Beaumont, Ms North?'

'I use Miss. I find the Ms clumsy to pronounce and tiresome to operate. I'd known Martin for just over fourteen years in all.'

Lambert took over the questioning as Hook made his first note. 'Then obviously you knew him very well. Would you say you were a friend of his as well as a working colleague?'

She smiled at him with her head a little on one side, apparently not at all disturbed to be questioned by the chief superintendent in charge of a murder enquiry. 'I would, yes. But there's something you should be aware of from the start. I knew Martin better than most people. I was his mistress for several years.'

She looked at him to see how her little bombshell would be received, but she could not tell from his reactions whether he had already known it. Probably he had, she thought; it was their business to find out such things and someone would surely have told them about it, even though Jane said she hadn't mentioned it when she'd spoken to the police. It was strange how she now thought of the Mrs Beaumont she had feared to meet as Jane and a friend. Life was very unpredictable.

Lambert's long, grave face told her nothing. He said, 'Thank you for being so frank, Miss North. Obviously honesty is helpful to us. The people we talk to normally find that complete openness is the best policy for them too. How long ago did this close relationship end?'

She smiled at his use of that anodyne phrase. 'You mean when did I stop going to bed with Martin? Eight years ago now. When I was past forty and he decided that I was getting a little long in the tooth. Men like young flesh between the sheets, when they can get it, don't they?' She heard her bitterness come out in the question. Before they arrived she had been determined to be cool and detached, so as to distance herself from this killing. That hadn't lasted very long – perhaps it was something to do with Lambert's congratulating her on her honesty. She had better treat this man with his reputation as the Great Detective with due care, if she was not to make herself even more of a suspect.

'You're telling us that Mr Beaumont had other women, which confirms what others have suggested. Was there someone particularly close to him at the time of his death?'

'I don't know. I've made it my business over the last few years to know as little as possible of his private life. It seemed the best policy once I had recognized that our affair was over and that I had been no more than one of a series of bits on the side for Martin over the years.' She heard

234

again the asperity she had been resolved to conceal. 'Incidentally, I have no wish to emerge to you as an expert on sexual matters. I did not take Martin into my bed casually, and it is not in my nature to flit from one man to another.'

'Thank you, but it is no part of our brief to take moral stances in these things. We need the facts, but in the main we confine ourselves to those.'

'Of course you do. But it was also no part of my brief to come over to you as a high-class tart.'

She grimaced a little on her last phrase, and Lambert felt a sudden sympathy for the spirit and courage of the woman. He said quietly, 'I'm surprised you stayed around to work with Mr Beaumont over the last few years, in view of the circumstances.'

He was studiously polite, but he wasn't going to let her get away with anything. Vanda found herself warming unexpectedly to this grave-faced opponent, enjoying the excitement of the contest a little despite herself. 'You're asking the question I've asked myself a few times over the years, though not recently. There are practical considerations, Chief Superintendent. All my capital is tied up in Abbey Vineyards. It was in my interests to see that the company succeeded, as Martin was often pleased to remind me. Over the last few years, the development and the management of residential accommodation at the vineyard has been in my hands, and we have been very successful.'

'Nevertheless, there must have been a time

eight years ago when you felt like withdrawing your investment and leaving Beaumont to it.'

She gave him that knowing smile again, partly to conceal her irritation at his probing of this area and partly out of respect for his intelligence in fastening upon it. 'There were indeed. There are two reasons why I am still around at Abbey Vineyards. The first is that Martin had tied things up legally so that it proved very difficult for me to withdraw my capital from his company. I only have about a fifth of what he has invested in the company, and my junior partnership was drawn up very much on his terms. I could not withdraw my funds, or even sell on my share in the company to someone else, without his permission. I do not need anyone now to tell me that these are very foolish terms to accept. I signed all the agreements when I was completely infatuated with Martin, in the early stages of our relationship. I trusted him to look after my interests. He took very good care to look after his own.'

'You've investigated the possibilities of withdrawal?'

'Indeed I have. The latest occasion was only last month. The lawyers tut-tutted and told me as lawyers delight in doing that I should never have signed such documents without their expert advice. The legal expertise was all Martin's; the stupidity in trusting him to safeguard my interests was all mine. That left me in a situation where I couldn't afford to take on a legal case with no guarantee of success and with Martin able to employ the best lawyers. It was his habit to ensure that he had the big artillery on his side. He was usually at pains to let his opponents know that.'

Lambert let her bitterness hang in the quiet, low-ceilinged room like a tangible thing, making sure that all three of them appreciated the strength of her motive to murder. It was Hook who eventually looked up from his notes and reminded her, 'You said there were two reasons why you had continued to work with Martin Beaumont. What was the second one, Miss North?'

Vanda measured her reply carefully. It was important to her that she should convince them of this. 'I do not think I am without ability, but I have no formal qualifications to speak of, other than a secretarial diploma acquired a long time ago in another life.' She was silent for a moment, as if contemplating the person she had been in those vanished years. 'I have enjoyed developing the residential wing at Abbey Vineyards. I think I have a skill in recognizing what the people who stay with us want and how much they are prepared to pay for it. I enjoy managing the staff involved, who are even more vital to success in residential work than in other fields, and I think they are happy with the way I handle things. To use a phrase that now seems to be overworked, I have job satisfaction. I also have a generous salary, which I could certainly not command if I moved away from the company. So long as he remained in control of things,

Martin always recognized efficiency and was prepared to pay for it. I think the other senior staff at Abbey Vineyards would agree with that.'

Hook nodded, then without any change in his quiet tone, asked, 'Where were you last Wednesday night, Miss North?'

She smiled as she set her cup and saucer back on the tray, as if it were important to show them how unruffled she was at this key point. 'I expected you to ask that, of course I did. I am not the only one with a motive, but I clearly stand to gain by having Martin out of the way. There would be a better chance of withdrawing my stake in the firm, if I wished to. The irony is that with Martin off the scene I may not wish to do that.' She looked from Hook's reassuringly ordinary face into the intense grey eyes of Lambert. 'The answer to your question is embarrassing. No, not embarrassing – I'll change that to surprising. I was with Jane Beaumont. The woman I had gravely wronged during the years when I was Martin's mistress.'

If she had expected amazement, she was disappointed. Hook's expression changed not a muscle as he made a careful note of the fact in his round, surprisingly swift hand. Lambert's eyebrows lifted the merest fraction before he said, 'I take it, then, that the two of you are now friends.'

She weighed the word with a small smile, her face softening a little with the thought. 'We are. If you think that an unlikely situation, I can only say that a month ago the notion would have

238

surprised me too.'

'This is a recent development, then?'

'Very recent. Jane came to see me two and a half weeks ago.' She stopped for an instant, wondering why it mattered to her that she should be so precise about this. 'She wanted to warn me that she was proposing to sue Martin for divorce and that I might find myself cited as a co-respondent.'

'That must have given you a shock.'

'It did. But it was fair enough. I'd hardly thought about his wife during the years I was with Martin. It seems quite odd now, but I was besotted with him at the time.' She shook her head, as if the recollection of that time still amazed her. 'Jane and I had scarcely seen each other, and I suspect scarcely thought about each other, until she came to see me here. We got on well, which must have been a surprise to her as well as to me. I said she could cite me if she needed to – I could scarcely have denied it – but that I could probably provide her with evidence of more recent women, if she wanted it. I've seen her a few times since then. Last Wednesday night, she was a little upset and I agreed to stay the night with her.'

'A fortunate decision for both of you, as it turned out,' said Lambert dryly.

He didn't pull any punches, this man. But Vanda didn't resent his comment. She felt again the thrill of the contest, the excitement of pitting her wits against this seasoned campaigner. That elation was a warning to her to be careful, however. 'I suppose in the light of what happened to Martin, it was indeed a fortunate decision. Neither of us could have seen it as that at the time.'

'You say Mrs Beaumont was upset. In what way was that?'

It sounded impertinent, but she knew it wasn't. He had to ask about the time when Martin was killed, and it was important to Jane and to her that she got this right. 'Jane has a bipolar disorder. I don't know whether your police machine has yet discovered that. It is one of the reasons why even those who have seen the firm develop over the years have never seen much of the boss's wife.'

'And it was affecting her on Wednesday?'

'I'm no medical expert, Chief Superintendent Lambert. I wouldn't pretend to understand the condition, though I've read up a little about it in the last few days. All I know is that Jane was jumpy and unpredictable on Wednesday. I offered to stay the night with her and she seemed very grateful. She accepted immediately.'

Lambert nodded. It seemed to Vanda that his eyes never blinked as he studied her. 'And you didn't think that she was simulating this distress?'

'No, I'm sure she wasn't. Jane was jumpy and unable to concentrate – unpredictable in what she would say next, as though her mind was flitting from subject to subject. Why on earth should she be pretending that?'

'This is a murder investigation, or I wouldn't

240

be questioning you in this detail, Miss North. If Mrs Beaumont knew that her husband was going to die – if, for instance, she had employed the services of a professional killer to dispose of him – she might well have been anxious to establish an alibi for herself. You are the only one who can confirm for us that she was many miles from him at the moment of his death.'

'But if she'd used a hit man, she wouldn't need to establish that, surely?'

'Without your presence in the house over-night, we could not be certain that either one of you wasn't in the car with Beaumont when he died.'

He seemed to her to have put just a little emphasis on that 'either one of you'. Perhaps she was becoming too sensitive to his changes of tone. She took care not to react to the phrase. 'I know enough of Jane Beaumont to be quite certain that she wasn't involved in his death. But I understand that you have to make your own mind up in these things, that you have to assume that we're all liars until you know for certain that we're not.'

Lambert was not at all put out. He smiled grimly. 'Not everyone involved will be lying, Miss North. But one person will be quite deter-mined to deceive us. Have you any idea who that person might be?'

She was used to his directness now. 'I've thought about that a lot in the last couple of days. I'm happy to say that others have motives as well as me. But I can't imagine that any of us

241

would have killed Martin. It would be wrong if he came across to you as a monster. He had an obsession with his company and his direction of it, but apart from that he had a lot of good qualities. He could be a good friend, and he was a fair and generous employer. And I have got to know the people I work with pretty well over the last few years. We all have our strengths and our weaknesses, but I can't imagine that any of them is capable of murder.'

Just when she had got used to fencing with Lambert, to parrying his thrusts and preserving her position with him, it was Hook who now took up the attack. He said quietly, 'You said earlier that you might have been able to provide evidence of further and more recent sexual adventures to assist Mrs Beaumont in her divorce petition. You will appreciate that such information has to be of interest to us.'

She smiled at his open, rubicund face. 'Sex and money. They're the great motivators to murder, aren't they? And hatred, I suppose – but I've just told you that there wasn't much of that around. Well, both Jane and I are sure Martin was still putting it about, if you'll excuse the crudity. He isn't the man he was, of course, in looks at least. You might not believe it now, but there was a touch of the Greek god about him when I first knew him.' She paused for a moment, her mind abstracted for an instant to that time long ago. 'I'm sorry, I'm trying to explain away my conduct from all those years ago, when it has no relevance whatever to this

242

death. What was it you wanted from me again?'

Lambert wondered if she had really forgotten the question. Perhaps she had; she had seemed embarrassed from the outset by her conduct as an intelligent woman in becoming so helplessly infatuated with the younger Beaumont. He reminded her tersely, 'DS Hook was asking you if you could give us the details of any recent liaisons of Mr Beaumont's.'

'Of course he was. But I have to disappoint you. As I said, I am quite sure that Martin has other women, and probably frequently. But I cannot give you details. All I said to Jane was that I would ask around and try to find out more. I confess that I had a selfish motive in offering that. I would have preferred to keep myself out of any divorce proceedings by providing more recent and thus more relevant evidence. As I think I pointed out to Jane, Martin's lawyers would have been certain to query why she had known all about my affair at the time and done nothing about it until many years later.'

'So there are no names you can give us?'

'No. I suspect that his alliances recently had been much more casual and short term. I had no interest in whom he was currently bedding, but I think I should have known if there'd been any serious long-term affair.' She paused, weighing a last idea on the subject, wondering whether to offer it to them and what the consequences might be for her. She didn't see it could do her any harm; it could only divert their thoughts further away from her. 'You could try Sarah

Vaughan, I suppose. She's the most recent and the youngest of our senior staff. She strikes me as a capable young woman, with far too much sense to get involved with Martin, but she might know a little more than I do about his current preferences.'

Lambert stood up. He had enjoyed pitting his wits against this alert and intelligent woman, but he suspected she had told them exactly what she had planned to do before they set foot in this comfortable old cottage. Quite possibly that was all she knew and she was being as helpful as she could, but he would like to have thrown her off balance a little more, to have seen how she behaved when she was disconcerted.

'If you think of any other detail which might be helpful to us, however small, please get in touch immediately, Miss North. We may well need to speak to you again to clarify certain issues, when we are further into this enquiry.'

It was standard stuff. At the moment, he couldn't think what those issues might be. Vanda North seemed to know that and be perfectly confident about the future. She conducted them quietly to the low door of the cottage, warning him that he might need to stoop a little. But she had the composed air of a woman who had fulfilled her duty and did not expect to see them again.

# EIGHTEEN

Gerry Davies went across to Jason Knight's den early on Monday morning. He went as soon as he received the phone call, while the shop was still quiet and before any of the catering staff were due on duty. A week ago, he wouldn't have considered such discretion necessary. He threaded his way through the deserted kitchen area to the little private room and watched his friend shut the door carefully behind him.

'Did anyone see you coming in here?' Jason asked.

'I don't think so. My own staff will notice I'm missing if I'm away for any length of time. Does it matter?'

'Probably not. I just felt that the fewer people who saw us getting together the better. They might think we're plotting.'

'As we are.'

Jason looked at him sharply. 'I wouldn't call it that. I'd say we were thinking about the new situation and how it might affect us.'

Both of them were silent for a moment, assessing the accuracy of this. Gerry wondered if Jason was thinking, as he was, that last week neither of them would have worried about

245

people noting their movements. Murder brought suspicion with it. It made people watch the actions of others and question what they were up to. It made them watch what they said, sometimes even with people they regarded as friends.

Jason brought him abruptly out of his reverie. 'Have they interviewed you yet?'

'No. They're seeing me this afternoon.'

'Good.' Jason wondered why he said that; it had been automatic, probably relief that others as well as him were being questioned. 'It's good that they've left you until now, I suppose. It probably means they don't have you high on their list of suspects. They saw me on Saturday morning.'

'I hadn't really thought of myself as a suspect.'

'You should get used to the idea. They'll be investigating everyone who was close to Martin. I'm sure they've given his wife the third degree. If and when they decide it isn't a domestic, we're all in the frame.'

'You seem to know a lot about it.' A week ago, the words would have been said jokingly; today they rang deadly serious.

Jason Knight hastened to lighten things. He managed a rather brittle little laugh. 'I watch too many cop series on the box, I suppose.'

Gerry didn't think Jason saw much television. As head chef, he was usually working six nights a week. He said as casually as he could, 'Give you a good going over, did they, the CID men?'

'They're professionals, Gerry. The police use

the best they have, on a murder case. Until they have a prime suspect – which isn't yet, as far as I can see – we're all in the frame. It will pay you to watch what you say this afternoon.'

'If I tell them the truth, I've nothing to fear.' Gerry knew that at fifty-seven he was sounding like a priggish schoolboy. 'If I didn't do it, I've surely nothing to fear.'

Jason didn't laugh at the absurdity of the notion that Gerry might have killed Martin. 'Murder is big, for the media as well as the police. If they don't make an arrest in the next few days, they'll have the press on their backs. And the radio and television won't be far behind the papers; they pick up ideas from the press and run with them, when they're short of news. The CID will want to arrest someone as quickly as possible. I think we should make sure it isn't either of us.'

Gerry didn't know what to say to that. 'I believe they've got the famous John Lambert on the case.'

'They have. He questioned me on Saturday morning. I didn't tell them about us.'

'About us?' said Gerry stupidly. He knew what Jason meant; he couldn't think why he was pretending that he didn't. This was the sort of distrust a murder enquiry fostered, he supposed.

Jason said with a trace of impatience, like an old sweat instructing a green recruit, 'I meant our discussion about the future of the company, about how we were going to get ourselves more control of policy.'

247

Gerry wanted to say that that idea and all the drive behind it had come from Jason; he wanted to dissociate himself from anything which might leave any sort of cloud over himself. 'Didn't you say anything about it when they spoke to you?'

'No, of course I didn't.' Jason was suddenly impatient with this man who was a generation older than him and yet still so naive. 'I didn't lie. You don't have to lie. You simply don't mention it. You show them that you're as mystified about this death as everyone else is pretending to be.'

'I might have to lie to conceal it. In any case, isn't not telling them like a lie?'

Jason wondered for the first time whether this was all a front, whether Gerry Davies had long since realized the danger and was conducting this elaborate charade of guilelessness when he actually proposed to look after his own skin, at whatever cost to others. Like his companion, he felt murder driving a wedge between them; this distrust would have been impossible last week. 'I didn't say anything about it. You must realize how bad it would make me look if you now blab about it to them.'

'All right. I'll do my best to keep off the subject.'

'You might have to be prepared to do a little more than that, Gerry. I should think they're quite likely to ask you why you didn't want more of a say in the way things were being run.'

'So what do I say to that?'

'I can't put words into your mouth, Gerry.

248

They'd spot them if I did. Your best policy would be to follow the line you took with me at first. Tell them you're quite happy with the salary you're being paid. You could give them all that modesty stuff, about how Martin gave you your chance in the first place and encouraged you to go on from there, but I wouldn't make a meal of that.'

Gerry Davies stared disconsolately at the table between them, where once he would have looked at his friend. 'Be better if we hadn't talked to Martin about it last Monday, wouldn't it? Especially as he turned us down flat.'

Jason sighed. 'It would indeed. It seems much more than a week ago now, doesn't it? But there's no reason why they should know anything about that meeting. What took place there was just between us and Martin. There won't be any record of it. If neither of us mentions it, there's no way they can know that it took place.' He'd only just prevented himself from saying that dead men tell no tales.

'I suppose not.' Gerry looked thoroughly miserable.

'Cheer up, Gerry! It won't be as bad as you seem to think. Try not to be nervous. After all, neither of us killed the bugger!'

But neither of them laughed, as Jason Knight had intended them to.

The two big men made the room seem even smaller, Sarah Vaughan thought. She said, 'I have the smallest office here, as the last of the executive staff to be appointed. It's quite big enough for my needs, though.'

They looked round unhurriedly at the small desk with its PC, at the swivel chair behind it in which she sat, at the two upright chairs which barely fitted into the space in front of it. They took in the single filing cabinet, the pictures of Provence and the portrait of an eminent nineteenth-century French vineyard owner on the walls.

Lambert folded his long legs carefully into the limited space between him and the front of her desk. With Hook accommodating himself equally carefully, shifting his chair three inches sideways so that he was not actually touching that of the chief superintendent, Sarah felt hemmed in. Their faces were too close to hers for comfort, and the grey, all-seeing eyes of Lambert seemed to be boring into her mind and soul as their exchange developed.

He began conventionally enough. 'Could you tell us a little about your role here please, Miss Vaughan?'

'I'm responsible for Research and Development.' She spoke it with the capital letters which she hoped would give her a little more standing, then immediately threw a little of that away. 'Mr Beaumont does – sorry, did – a lot of the research himself. He went to the French vineyards almost every year and the German and Italian ones every two or three years to find how the newer grapes are doing there and check on the production of the long-established brands. Of course, wine production for export is a much more worldwide industry now than it was fifty, even thirty, years ago, but we research other areas from here. Not even Martin could go everywhere.' She gave a little laugh to show that was a joke, wondering how much of what she used in her talks to the public she could feed in here. It was safe ground for her, this stuff.

'I see. You have quite a few competitors in the English wine industry nowadays. Does your research work take any account of that?'

'Indeed it does. You have to keep your eye on your competitors, as Martin always reminded us. I keep a record of the volumes sold and prices charged, as comprehensive as I can achieve. It's usually about a year out of date, as you would expect. Martin used to get out and about and do a little incognito investigation into how well the bigger English producers were doing, in relation to us.'

'A little industrial espionage.'

She wondered whether to take this as a tease and respond in that spirit, but decided she had better not do that. 'There's nothing to prevent you going incognito into retail shops and even wholesale outlets. It's surprising what some people will tell you about the way their year is going, if you can fasten on the right person to talk to.'

She wondered quite what truncated version of this the detective sergeant was making in his notes. As if he divined that her attention was on him, Hook now looked up and said, 'So much for research. What about the development side of your work?'

'Well, I'm rather proud of my work in pushing some of our new lines. I suggested that we should supply beer and cider in our shop here, when other people thought it would militate against wine sales. It didn't, and Martin got us an excellent deal with the brewery. We now make a very good profit on our beer sales in particular. And whilst it's impossible to be definite about this, I'm sure that our wine sales have benefited too, because of the extra customers we have attracted into the shop. Mr Davies, the shop manager, certainly supports that view. And whilst we're very much a team here, I'd say that I was mainly responsible for the development of our sparkling wines. We do a surprisingly good English champagne here – we can't call it that of course – which I think we shall be able to retail at £7.99 a bottle this year. I recommend it to you: I think you'll find it surprisingly good.'

She smiled nervously into the encouraging face of Bert Hook, wondering if she was lapsing too much into the commercial chat with which she concluded her talks to the public. But he said, 'Thank you. We have a clearer picture of your role here now. Is there anything else you do?'

'You're right to ask that. We're still quite a small organization, though our turnover increases each year. I help in the shop when they're busy. And I do little tours of the vine-

252

yard, in which I talk on the history of wine-making and of Abbey Vineyards. The abbey part's a bit of a con, actually. We don't think there was ever an abbey here, though there may at one time have been a Saxon church. I think Martin thought it would give the right ring to the name when he started. It suggests an ancient lineage for the place, I suppose, which is a bit more glamorous than farmland to most people. I don't disillusion them unless anyone asks. I think my talks have been going well this year – I've got bigger audiences, even though I'm doing them more frequently.'

'They're very interesting, from what I've heard,' said Hook.

'I hope so. It's like anything else, one improves with practice. And I don't try to disguise the fact that like everything else we do the tours are directed towards bringing in a profit, even if that's indirect and long term.'

'And you think they do that?'

'I do. They're getting more orders in the shop at the conclusion of my little talks, quite often for full cases. Of course, I can't prove that these people weren't planning to buy in any case, but Gerry Davies, our shop manager, says a lot of the sales come directly from what I've been saying. I speak quite honestly about our best wines and our best years for them. And Martin wouldn't have increased the frequency of the tours if he hadn't thought that. He was a very shrewd commercial operator.'

'So everyone tells us,' agreed Lambert. 'And

the evidence is all around us in the growth of this place. How did you get on with him?'

She was rather thrown off her guard by the abruptness of this, after she had been encouraged to talk so much about herself. 'I'd say very well. He was very successful, which always helps. A successful ship is usually a happy ship.' The phrase came back to her from a course during her Business Studies degree. She hoped it wasn't the cliché to them that it was to her.

'You found him a good employer?'

She made herself take her time, knowing now that they were coming to the heart of the interview, where she was most at risk. 'He was a good boss, as long as you did things his way. And I was earning more than I'd ever earned before, with the prospect of it rising year by year.'

'But how would you describe your relationship with Mr Beaumont?'

'Good. He paid well and he was fair. You had to toe the line, as he made clear when he interviewed me, but as long as you did that you earned good money.'

'You didn't feel once you were well-established here that you wanted a say in future policy? Research and development are all about the future, after all.'

'No. I'm still only thirty-three and making my way. Martin was a generation older and had much more experience.' She paused, then was unable to resist the opportunity to divert their attention to others and thus take some of the heat off herself. 'I think some of the executives who've been here longer than me were chafing a little about Martin's dominance, but you'd have to ask them about that.'

Lambert afforded her a smile which made her uncomfortable, as if he knew very well what she was about. She wondered if her face was colouring; she knew that her fair skin and delicate features often revealed more than they should. She was very conscious of how close those gimlet grey eyes were to hers as he said, 'Everything you've said has been related to your working relationship with Mr Beaumont. We're grateful for that information. But what about your personal relationship with your employer? You're a small team here, as you've told us yourself, and no one works all the time. How did you get on with Mr Beaumont outside your working relationship?'

'Perfectly well. Martin was wrapped up in the business: it was his whole life. He has a wife, I believe, but I've never seen her. I was perfectly content with my social life. I think I've indicated that our working relationship was a good one.'

'Miss Vaughan, we have had indications from several sources that whilst Mr Beaumont ran his business as an autocrat and built his life around it, it was not as you claim "his whole life". We have it on good authority, indeed, that he had involved himself over the years with quite a stream of women.'

She wanted to tell him to go back to that good

255

authority and get his information there. But that source, whoever it was, might tell them about her. She was suddenly not sure how much the people who worked here knew about her, how much they might try to incriminate her in a situation like this. She said dully, 'I've heard that, too. About the other women, I mean. He said his wife was an invalid, but some people say he exaggerates that to get sympathy. I can't help you. I don't know any details about these other women. Maybe they were all in the past, for all I know. He was late fifties, wasn't he? Perhaps he'd given up that sort of thing.'

'Perhaps,' said Lambert. His tone on the single word seemed to convey how easily deceived she was, how little she knew of life compared with the two men opposite her, whose work had left them with few illusions. 'He didn't make any suggestions to you that you might like to see him away from work, then?'

If only it had been as polite and civilized as that, Sarah thought bitterly. She was tempted for a moment to tell them about those terrifying minutes in the big blue Jaguar. But her resolution held. She mustn't even hint that she'd had any sort of motive for disposing of him. The quickest way to send the CID away was to distance yourself as far as possible from the victim. 'No. I didn't see any evidence of the womanizing I heard people gossip about. For all I know, that was all it was – gossip.'

She sounded like a prim twenty-year-old rather than a woman of thirty-three who had seen much of the world and was making her way steadily in it. But at least she would have the sense not to try to change that with more words. If they thought of her as unworldly and in-experienced, they would be less likely to think of her as a murderer.

Hook, his wide brown eyes seeming now as searching as those intense grey ones of Lambert, said calmly, 'Where were you last Wednesday night, Miss Vaughan?'

'I was here until about six. Then I was at home. I cooked myself a lasagne I'd picked up from Waitrose and curled up on the sofa to watch the telly.'

'Is there anyone who can confirm this for us?'

'No. No one spent the night with me and I didn't go out again, once I'd got home and garaged the car. A couple of friends rang me during the evening.'

It had all come very promptly, but that was fair enough; the time of the death was public now, and you would expect an intelligent woman to have thought about how she was going to account for herself. 'Can you recall the time when you received these calls?'

'I can't pinpoint the times exactly. But I think both of them were between eight and nine.' She'd been tempted to say they were much later than that, but they would check them out with the callers. And if they found her lying about one thing, they'd suspect everything else she'd said.

Lambert studied her face for a moment. It was

anxious, pale, taut, looking a little older and more worn than when they had begun the interview. He said, 'You've had some time to think about this death now. Have you any views on who might have killed Martin Beaumont?'

'No.' It had come too promptly, almost before he had finished the question. Sarah had thought about many things before they came, but had not realized that even the timing of her replies might seem significant. 'As you suggest, I've thought about it a lot over the weekend. I don't even know Mrs Beaumont. And I can think of motives for most of the people here. But I can't imagine that any one of them would have killed Martin. None of them seems like a murderer.'

'That is a sentiment we hear often, Miss Vaughan. Our experience tells us that even the unlikeliest person can commit murder, given the right set of circumstances. You say you can think of motives. Let us into that thinking, please.'

An invitation to divert the attention away from herself, to suggest more rewarding targets for their efforts. But she mustn't seem too eager or go too far. She forced a smile. 'You mention the unlikeliest person to commit murder. In my opinion, that would be Gerry Davies, our shop and sales manager. He's liked by everyone here, including Martin when he was alive. He's been a good friend to me, as I've found my feet here, and I'm sure to lots of other people as well. As for the others, well, I sense that most of them would have liked more say in the future of the company, as it becomes more and more successful. That's natural: there's a general feeling that two or more heads are better than one, that a growing firm needs to take account of all the ideas available if it is to grow successfully.'

For a moment, she was back again in one of her essays for the Business Studies degree, throwing out the phrases she had used successfully there. She hoped these grave-faced men did not recognize them as the glib clichés they now seemed to her. Apparently they didn't, for Lambert said as he stood up, 'We shall be seeing Mr Davies later today. We shall bear in mind your glowing opinion of him, though of course we shall not retail it to him. Like other things you and other people have volunteered to us, it will remain confidential. If you have any further thoughts, please get in touch with the Oldford CID section immediately – ask for Detective Inspector Rushton.' He set a card carefully upon her desk.

Sarah saw them out, then shut the door firmly and slumped thankfully into her chair. It hadn't gone too badly, she decided. They'd seemed happy enough with what she had been able to tell them, and she hadn't revealed what she was most anxious to conceal.

Sarah Vaughan would have been less sanguine if she had heard the conversation in the police Mondeo as Hook drove it towards the station. They had travelled a mile and more before Lambert said, 'What did you think of pretty young Miss Vaughan?'

259

Hook grinned. 'She isn't a girl, John. You're getting older. But there were moments in the interview when she'd have been happy if we thought of her as at least ten years younger and very gauche. She's concealing something.'

'I agree. Whether it's significant or not remains to be seen. But I think we shall need to see the glamorous Miss Vaughan again, in due course.'

'Life has its consolations, if you work at it,' said Bert Hook, his attention studiously upon the road ahead.

# NINETEEN

Lambert glared at the television set resentfully. 'It's far too early for them to be playing one-day cricket internationals. We're scarcely into spring yet.'

Christine set his sandwich in front of him and smiled tolerantly. 'It's May the eighteenth and the longest day is in five weeks. You're just annoyed because you won't see much of it. If I know you, you'll be off out again in half an hour. How long is it since you were last home for lunch?'

'I don't know. A few weeks, I suppose. Everything seems to fly past too quickly, nowadays. I suppose you're going to tell me I'm getting old.'

'I wasn't, but you are. You must learn how to wind down. You're better than you were at relaxing, but there's still room for improvement.' Then, running against her own advice but sensing that he wanted her to ask, Christine said, 'How's the case going?'

'That's why I'm here, if I'm honest. To get away from the string of pressmen ringing in and wanting a quote from John Lambert about the progress of the case. You can't even digest what you've learned properly at the station, with people buzzing around your ears all the time.'

'I heard you'd talked to Tom Ogden.'

He grinned resignedly, where once he might have been annoyed. 'Local grapevine in operation, I suppose. I expect no less.'

'I saw his wife in Tesco's. She didn't seem put out – they'd expected it. Their farm cuts right into the vineyard's land, doesn't it? And Tom was apparently no friend of Martin Beaumont's.'

'That he wasn't. He didn't try to disguise it.' He grinned at the memory of Ogden's honest avowal of his feelings. 'He has a decent alibi, though. He was at the cinema with his wife on the night of the murder and she's confirmed that he went straight home with her afterwards.' John watched another England batsman sky a catch straight to the man on the boundary and gratefully accepted a large beaker of tea from his spouse.

Christine Lambert had taught in the area for

over twenty years, although since a serious illness three years ago she now only did part time. She knew many of their contemporaries as parents and many of the younger generation as former pupils. John had come to regard her now as a source of information rather than an unwelcome intruder into his affairs. She was pleased that he was letting her into this corner of his working life, which he would never have done at one time. She said as casually as she could, 'Have you got a prime suspect yet?'

'No. I'd say we have several leading suspects, at the moment. We've eliminated the more peripheral figures, but not his wife or any of the people who worked closely with him.'

'Does that include Sarah Vaughan?'

He looked up sharply. 'We saw her this morning. She's in charge of research and development at Abbey Vineyards.'

Christine laughed. 'And I remember her as a little girl with flying blonde pigtails and a brace on her teeth! Too small for the netball team, but desperately keen to get into it.'

'She's thirty-three and quite a looker now. Blonde, blue-eyed and pretty, with long legs and a bust that got Bert Hook's attention. No fool, though. She certainly isn't the conventional dumb blonde.'

'Married?'

'No. And hasn't been, though she's thirty-three now. Heterosexual but no serious boyfriend in tow, our research suggests.'

'And your research will no doubt have been

262

meticulous on such a delicious subject. If she's still unmarried at thirty-three with looks like that, she's clearly got brains.'

John decided to ignore this slur upon his sex. 'She conducts tours of the vineyard and talks about the history of winemaking. Apparently they're very successful, so she learned something from you.'

'If she impressed you and Bert Hook with her looks and her brains, she must also have impressed her employer. He clearly rated her, to give her the job she has.'

Food for thought, John Lambert concluded, as he drove back to resume the hunt.

Gerry Davies lived in the 1950s semi-detached house on the outskirts of Monmouth in which he had spent the last twenty-eight of his thirty-five years of married life.

The purchase had been a great leap forward at the time, when he had two young children. He had undertaken a mortgage which had then seemed huge. In his boyhood, miners in the Rhondda Valley had lived in rented cottages. The notion of going into debt to acquire a house of your own had seemed a dangerous extravagance to his parents; the mortgage would in his father's view prove 'a millstone around your neck'. For a short, nightmare period when he had been unemployed, it had seemed as if his father might be right. His parents hadn't lived to see him pay off the mortgage and secure the prosperity he now enjoyed. That was a matter of lasting regret for Gerry. To have seen their grandchildren attending university would have been an impossible dream for them.

He could afford a more expensive house now – perhaps even a detached bungalow with a spacious garden, now that the boys had left home. All in good time, Gerry told Bronwen. The truth was that even after thirteen years of success at Abbey Vineyards, even when he looked at the substantial sum which went into his bank account every month, he could not quite believe in his success. To move to a more expensive residence would not only be presumptuous, but also an invitation to the Fates to put him in his proper place by removing his job and the source of his comfortable income. He did not voice this view and there was not a single fact to support it. But instincts nourished in youth can be stronger than logic.

He was glad that the CID men had offered to come here to interview him, rather than to his office at work. The less you were seen with policemen the better, in Gerry's view. It was another thought rooted in the misty distance of his youth, when young men drank too much after rugby and the Saturday night rozzers were not always sympathetic to brawny young forwards from the long terraces of cottages. There had been some hairy moments, especially in strange towns after muscular away victories.

Gerry took the officers into the rather cramped front room, which had seemed a luxurious extra space when they had moved into the house.

Nowadays, they used this dining room only when the boys were down with their wives. Gerry had never been comfortable at the dinner parties which most of the other people in the road seemed to enjoy. He was still happiest in clubs, usually in an all-male setting, but he and Bronwen threw a boisterous and very successful party once a year for their many friends, when all the downstairs rooms of the house were crowded and noisy.

The two men who came to see him looked with interest at the rugby photographs which lined the walls. There was one of the great Welsh side of the fifties, with Cliff Morgan holding a ball in the centre, another with the greatest of all teams of a generation later, with Barry John and Gareth Edwards and JPR Williams. The rest were of teams just below that national level, in which Gerry Davies himself had figured.

The CID visitors sat on upright chairs beside each other and confronted the man whose presence dominated this room across his dining table. 'We've been a long time getting to you, Mr Davies,' said John Lambert. Gerry wasn't sure whether that sounded apologetic or ominous. 'We've learned quite a lot about Mr Beaumont and a little about the way he died. Now we'd like your views.'

'I'm sure I won't have a lot to add. Martin was a good employer and I liked him. But other people will have told you that.'

No one previously had said openly that they

liked the man. There had been a little nostalgic recollection of the younger man and his attractions from Vanda North, and much respect for what he had achieved in his business, but his other close associates had been guarded. No one, not even his wife, had previously professed an unqualified liking for the man. In the perverse influence murder exercised over such declarations, it might mean exactly the opposite of what was said. But Gerry Davies, in the comfort of his pleasant, slightly old-fashioned home certainly looked genuine enough, with his square, open face, his burly frame, his still plentiful frizzy black hair, now slightly tinged with silver.

Lambert said, 'Tell us a little about what you do at Abbey Vineyards, please.'

'I run the shop. We sell a lot of wine, as you'd expect, plus beer and cider and associated products. Increasingly over the last few years, I've also taken on the work of wholesale information and supply. We sell a large number of cases to restaurants now, and our sparkling wines are particularly in demand at weddings.' Gerry hoped he did not sound too much like their publicity brochures. 'Martin said that I should describe myself as the sales director on correspondence and invoices, but I only bother to do that with the big customers. He thought it was important to show the big buyers that we aren't some tinpot little concern, but are used to meeting large orders.'

'I see. Were you happy in this work?'

266

'Very happy.' Gerry saw an opportunity to show his respect for Beaumont, as well as a chance to assert his own innocence. 'Martin ran a happy ship as well as a successful one. He was very easy to approach. He gave me a lot of encouragement and guidance in my early years with the firm. It's only in the last year or two that I got used to calling him Martin. I still took care to call him Mr Beaumont when there were customers around.' Gerry didn't know why he'd told them that – it said more about him than his late employer.

But the tall man with the intense grey eyes didn't seem to think it out of place. He said with a little smile, 'We operate a similar system with ranks in the CID team, Mr Davies. Detective chief superintendent is a mouthful which gets in the way of things. And I don't like being continually "sirred". But someone didn't like Martin Beaumont. Someone either hated him enough or found him obstructive enough to kill him in cold blood. Who do you think might have done that?'

The challenge was very abrupt, after the pleasantries which had preceded it. Gerry wondered whether those had been a deliberate tactic to soften him up. He must stick to his plans, whatever form of attack they used. 'I've thought about that a lot since we got the news on Friday, but I haven't come up with anything. Some of us had our differences with Martin, but I can't think that anyone would have killed him. I think it must be someone from outside.'

The familiar, entirely understandable, plea from those who had worked close to a murder victim. 'We've considered that, Mr Davies. We haven't ruled it out completely, but we now think it very unlikely. I think you should enlarge on these "differences" which people had with Mr Beaumont.'

He was on dangerous ground, but he mustn't show them that he felt that. 'It was nothing very serious. Martin operated very much as a one-man business. It was understandable, because he'd built the firm up from very small beginnings. And I must say that it suited me. I was very happy to have my own job clearly defined for me and to consult Martin whenever I felt there was a big decision to be made. I didn't want to stray outside my limits. For me, his methods worked very well.'

'But not for everyone. We need every detail of this that you can give us, Mr Davies: this is a murder enquiry.'

Gerry felt his pulses racing, though he told himself that he had known all along that this moment would come. He tried not to remember how Bronwen always found him transparent if ever he tried to lie to her; this was far more important than any little domestic deceit. He delivered the words he had prepared for this moment. 'I'm the oldest of the senior staff at Abbey Vineyards. I was grateful to Martin for giving me my chance in a senior post. I expect that has continued to influence me even many years later. The other executives are younger.

They are all better educated than I am and most of them have a broader work experience, despite my age. I can't speak for all of them, but I think some of them chafed a little at the system Martin had always used and was continuing to operate. They felt that now that the business was large and prosperous, they wanted rather more say in policy decisions than he was prepared to allow them.'

He'd got it all out without interruption. He wondered how it sounded to them. Lambert was watching him keenly. For a moment which seemed to Gerry to stretch agonizingly, he did not speak. Then he said quietly, 'You must see that in these circumstances we must have the names of these people who were not content.'

'I know nothing definite. It's just a feeling I've picked up from things said.' Gerry knew he had spoken too quickly, almost anticipating Lambert's instruction, instead of being surprised by it. 'At our company meeting in March – that involved just the five senior staff and Martin – there were various suggestions about how we should develop things, where we should go from here. Martin took them on board, but made it very clear that it would be he and not any of us who made the final decisions. That was fine as far as I was concerned; it's worked well in the past and I couldn't see any reason why we shouldn't carry on a successful system. If it ain't broke, don't fix it, as they say.'

'But other people weren't happy to leave it at that?'

Gerry Davies looked and felt uncomfortable as he was pressed. 'I don't really know. They may not have been happy with the system, but I've no evidence that they did anything about it. Only Martin would know that.'

'I see. And we can't ask him, can we?'

Gerry found himself shifting on his seat, feeling those all-seeing grey eyes much too close to him across the table. 'No. You'll need to ask the individuals concerned about it.'

'At the moment, I'm asking you, Mr Davies. Are you quite sure there's nothing else you can recall on the matter?'

'Yes. If you think it's important, you'll need to pursue it with the others.'

Without taking his eyes off his quarry's face, Lambert gave the slightest of nods to his detective sergeant. Hook made a play of consulting his notes. 'A week ago today, only two days before he died, Mr Beaumont conducted a meeting with you and Jason Knight, his head chef. What was that meeting about?'

Gerry Davies was shocked and he failed to conceal it. Perhaps he should have anticipated that they would know of the meeting, but he hadn't done that. He stumbled into inadequate phrases. 'I can't remember much about it now. It was nothing very important. That's why I didn't mention it.'

Hook smiled an understanding smile, a smile which said that he sympathized, but Gerry had been caught out, that he had much better cut his losses now and be honest. 'This is barely a week

270

ago, Mr Davies. Fiona Cooper, Mr Beaumont's PA, took us through his diary of appointments in the weeks before his death. She remembers voices being raised behind the door of her boss's office. Mrs Cooper thought the meeting was important. Mr Beaumont arranged it, she said, and he certainly thought it was important.'

Hook had picked up Davies's word 'important' and repeated it, until it seemed in Gerry's ears to have now an ironic, mocking ring. He had a thoroughly miserable air as he said, 'Martin seemed to think we had been stirring up trouble, trying to undermine him. He was wrong about that and we told him so.'

'And did he accept what you said?'

Gerry looked at the table. 'Yes, I think so. It was all a misunderstanding, really.'

Lambert, who had continued to watch him intently through this interlude with Hook, said sternly, 'All arguments which take place days before a man is killed have to be of interest to us. You must see that, Mr Davies.'

'Yes, I do. You're blowing this out of proportion, though.'

'Are we, indeed? Well, maybe Mr Knight will prove to have a clearer memory of the exchanges than you have managed to retain. I do hope so.'

Hook said in his more informal, persuasive way, 'One of the things we have learned about Mr Beaumont in the days since his death is that he had an eye for the ladies. More than an eye, in fact. When passions are aroused, violence is

271

rarely far away, in our experience. No doubt having worked with him for thirteen years and got to know him very well, you will be able to tell us more about this.'

Gerry was confused now. As a naturally honest man, he felt thoroughly ragged after the questioning about last Tuesday's meeting. He could not think straight, could think only of Sarah Vaughan weeping on his chest in her distress over Beaumont's attentions. They'd interviewed her in her office at the vineyard this morning. What had she told them about this? He couldn't afford to be tripped up again, or they wouldn't believe another word he said. 'I don't know any of the details of Martin's love life. You'll need to ask Sarah herself about this.'

He shouldn't have used that word 'herself'. It was, in some way he couldn't immediately grasp, a complete giveaway. Hook was studiously low-key as he said, 'Beaumont was conducting a relationship with Miss Vaughan, was he?'

'Not a relationship. You'll need to ask her, won't you? And Miss North, of course. Vanda used to be his mistress, you know.'

'Yes, we do know, Mr Davies. And we shall be seeing both these ladies again. Is there anything you think we should ask them?'

'No. I wasn't interested in Martin's love life.' He looked desperately around the room with its array of rugby photographs, then at the door which concealed Bronwen and the rest of his orderly house, as if he hoped that the happy rectitude of his own life could convince them of his ignorance about the restless lechery of Beaumont. 'He was a good employer to me and I shall remember that.'

Lambert said tersely, 'And if we find that you have concealed things from us, we shall be forced to remember that, and investigate the reasons why. Where were you last Wednesday night, Mr Davies?'

'I was here. I came home from work at about six twenty and I didn't go out again until Thursday morning.'

'And is there someone who can confirm that for us?'

Gerry glanced again like a caged animal at the firmly closed door of the room. Bronwen was out there somewhere, minding her own business as usual, confident as she had been from the first of his innocence of this awful thing. He hadn't asked her to lie for him; he would never ask Bronwen to lie – indeed, he was proud of the fact that she wouldn't be any good at lying. 'No, I don't think there is. Bronwen was in the Rhondda, in the house where she grew up. Her mother's still alive but she's ill. She phoned me to tell me that she was worried about her ma and I said she should stay the night.'

Bert Hook said quietly, 'Do you recall the time of that call?'

'It was some time between seven and seven thirty. I was just enjoying the cottage pie she'd left ready for me to heat. That's too early to clear me, isn't it?'

Hook's weather-beaten, outdoor face relaxed again into the smile which said that all might yet be well. 'If you mean that Mr Beaumont was killed much later in the evening, yes it is. Did you have any other calls on that night?'

'No. I'm in the frame for this, aren't I?'

Lambert said with a hint of impatience, 'If you've told us the truth, you've nothing to fear. We don't fit people up, Mr Davies, whatever the more lurid television series suggest. If you wish to revise or add to what you've told us, you should get in touch with us immediately at this number.'

He did not speak again as Gerry Davies showed them out, keeping them away from his invisible wife as if the contact would somehow soil her. At all costs, he wanted to keep Bronwen out of this.

# TWENTY

'My gran still doesn't approve of me staying here overnight,' said Anne Jackson. It was one of those inconsequential lines you delivered when you were still not fully conscious and attuned to the demands of the day.

DI Chris Rushton eyed her contours thoughtfully from the breakfast table as she stood beside the toaster. He still found it mystifying

274

that she could curve so attractively beneath a dressing gown, a garment he had always regarded as a necessary evil rather than a fashion item. 'Even though you're now an engaged person?' he asked dreamily.

'I don't think that makes any difference to her generation. She doesn't make a big thing of it. I can just tell that she doesn't really approve.'

'Remind me to steer clear of her at the wedding. A divorced bridegroom who is ten years older than you isn't going to get her stamp of approval.'

'It won't if you keep thrusting those facts into her face as you do with me.' The toast clicked up and she transferred it swiftly to her plate and came over to the table. She didn't sit down but came and stood behind Chris, resting her hands lightly for a moment on his chest, then raising them to softly massage his neck. 'Why do you make such a big thing of the age gap? I never even think of it except when you remind me of it – which is far too frequently.'

'I suppose I still can't quite believe that you've taken on an old wreck like me.' He lifted his own hands from the beaker and rested them for a moment on hers.

'You're not an old wreck. You're a mature man of thirty-four who has put childish things behind him and used his hard-won experience to make an intelligent choice of bride.' She looked down with love at the head she now pressed lightly against her stomach. 'A man without a grey hair to be seen among the black, a man who even from this angle hasn't yet got a bald spot. A man whom I might even describe as handsome, if I didn't think it would be bad for his soul.'

Chris stared dreamily across the warm little kitchen of his flat, reviewing fondly but silently the night that was gone. Then, characteristically, he recalled himself firmly to the real world. 'Kirstie will be coming over on Saturday. You won't be able to escape my past then. Just when you'll be feeling like a break from children.'

'I enjoy Kirstie – she's a good kid. And entertaining one child is very different from teaching thirty, you know.'

'I don't, but I'll take your word for it. All I know is that she's got far more energy than should ever be contained in one small body and that you're very good with her.' His face clouded for a moment. 'I hope we've cracked this case by then. I don't want to leave you to entertain Kirstie on your own all day.'

'The Abbey Vineyards' owner? How's it going? Or am I not allowed to know?'

'No sign of a solution. We're still gathering information. We know a lot more about the people close to him than we did four days ago, but so far, it's tended to obscure rather than illuminate.' He was surprised to find himself coming out with that phrase; it was the one John Lambert had used. 'The widow's still pretty mysterious, and too many people who worked with the victim have motives and no alibis.'

'Including Tom Ogden, I believe.' She was

276

studiously low-key, not sure yet how far Chris wanted her to enquire into his work, or indeed how much she herself wanted to know.

'You know Ogden?' He was suddenly alert, the CID inspector ready to gather information from any and every source.

She grinned at his intensity, as she often did, half in surprise and half in admiration. 'My dad's known him for years. Tom might be a year or two older, but I think they went to school together. He didn't like Martin Beaumont, did he?' She watched Chris with amusement as he struggled for the right reply. 'Don't worry, he's never made a secret of it. Beaumont had been trying for years to swallow up his farm, and Tom didn't like it. Tom Ogden's not one to disguise his feelings, Dad says.'

'That's more or less what John Lambert and Bert Hook reported. They interviewed him on Saturday. I haven't actually spoken to him.'

'We saw him at the cinema on Thursday night, actually, with his wife. They were the couple I waved to in the interval when I went for the ice creams.'

'You waved to so many and spoke to so many that I was bewildered.' He was still surprised how many people in this rural area had lived all their lives there, how those lives interwove and touched each other, even now, when people followed very different career paths. Now that Anne had come back from university to teach in the district where she had been born and bred, there would be another network, spreading over

277

parents and eventually grandparents, if she stayed in the area. Sometimes he thought it narrowed people's horizons, but he found that more often he liked the support and security it seemed to offer.

He mentioned the senior people Beaumont had employed to see if Anne knew anything about them. It seemed they had all moved into the area in the last twenty years or so, for she knew little of them, though she had eaten in the Abbey Vineyards restaurant and enjoyed it. 'Possible place for our reception after the nuptials,' she said lightly, before she left the house to start her day and disappeared towards her school and he towards the station at Oldford. Chris wasn't sure whether that was a bright idea or a threat.

Nine thirty on Tuesday morning. They'd suggested the time and she hadn't objected. Now she wished that she had.

Jane Beaumont wasn't at her best in the mornings. It was not until today that she had registered that nine thirty was still early for her. She had been up before eight, but it took her much longer to do things, nowadays. After she had showered and dressed, she'd barely had time for a bowl of cereal and a cup of coffee before the appointed time was at hand.

She had remembered to spend some time in front of her dressing-table mirror, as Vanda had told her that she must. She hadn't bothered with much make-up – she felt out of practice and

278

afraid of overdoing things. She didn't want the CID to put her down as a tart who didn't give a damn about her husband's death. But she brushed her hair carefully and applied a pale rose shade of lipstick. When these men had gone, she'd perhaps telephone to arrange to have her hair cut later in the week, as her new friend had suggested she should.

Before she was really ready for them, she saw the police car turn into the drive. She watched Detective Chief Superintendent Lambert climb rather stiffly from the passenger seat and look up at the front of her house. They came most carefully upon their hour. That was a quotation, she thought. The opening of *Hamlet*, if she remembered it right. That recognition gave her a tiny thrill of pleasure; perhaps Vanda was right and she could afford to cut down on the tablets. Martin had been so insistent, and she realized now that she had got out of the habit of resistance to him. It would be good if she could manage with less medication, perhaps eventually with none at all. Things were going to be different now. Different and better. She still had a lot of her life left to live, hadn't she?

Both Lambert and Hook were surprised by the change in Jane Beaumont's appearance. She seemed to have got younger by several years in four days. A nice trick if you could manage it, and one which would make you a swift and certain fortune if you could market it.

Lambert was emboldened to say, 'You seem much better today, Mrs Beaumont. Perhaps you were still in shock from your husband's death when we saw you on Friday. That would be entirely understandable.'

Entirely understandable, but neither of them really thought it was just the passage of time. Jane gave him a tight smile to show that they were at one in this. She said, 'I'm glad that I seem healthier to you. I suppose I am, but I doubt whether I shall be able to add much to what I told you on Friday. I expect I shall have to make funeral arrangements for Martin quite soon, won't I?'

It was always a moment of embarrassment, this. But this woman didn't look as if it would add anything to whatever grief she was feeling. 'I am afraid it will not be possible to release the body for burial or cremation at the moment, Mrs Beaumont. The law does not allow us to do that.'

'No. My friend told me that and I should have remembered it. It's because it's murder, isn't it? When you eventually charge someone, the defence has a right to a second post-mortem. Is that right?'

'That is exactly right, Mrs Beaumont.' She seemed so little distressed that he felt he should really give her a little formal bow to acknowledge her knowledge.

As if she read his thoughts, she said abruptly, 'I identified him, you know.'

'I did know, yes. It must have been quite an ordeal for you.' She gave him no reaction to this, but sat composed as a Renaissance madonna,

280

with the trace of a smile upon her lips. 'You are no doubt aware that the coroner's inquest returned a verdict of Murder by Person or Persons Unknown.'

'Yes. They said there was no need for me to attend the coroner's court unless I wished to. I didn't see any point.' She looked at him with her first sign of real interest. 'Are you any nearer to turning this Person Unknown into a person known?'

Her evident enjoyment of this little play on words reinforced Lambert's view that there was no need for him to treat Jane Beaumont with the kid gloves he normally donned for a grieving widow. 'Neither DS Hook nor I was aware that you had a long-term illness when we spoke to you last week. I apologize if we were insensitive because of our ignorance.'

'No. I don't think you were insensitive. I do not recall all the details of our conversation, but I'm sure both you and your sergeant behaved impeccably.' She nodded an acknowledgement towards Hook, much as Queen Victoria might have acknowledged a competent manservant. 'As a matter of fact, I rather think my condition has been much exaggerated in the past.'

'That is good to hear. As I say, there is no way in which we could have been aware of this on Friday.'

Jane afforded him a more generous and genuine smile. 'There is no reason why you should pussyfoot your way around this, Mr Lambert. I have what is usually called a bipolar disorder. Martin was always anxious that I should take all the latest drugs, and occasionally incarcerate myself in medical institutions, when the condition was at its worst. I went along with his wishes. I resisted him less over the years, as my energy declined. I now feel that I might have been wrong to do so.'

Lambert wanted to arrest this flow of medical speculation, to tell her that he was grateful for her frankness but didn't need to know anything more. He said stiffly, 'It's good to hear that you're feeling better.'

'I am indeed. I told you last week that I was planning to divorce Martin, so I feel that I do not need to pretend to any great grief for his death. Frankly, I feel better already. I now believe that he added to rather than alleviated the degree of mental suffering I have endured over the last few years.'

'Thank you for your honesty. But whatever your feelings about your husband, you no doubt wish us to arrest and charge the person responsible for his death.'

Jane Beaumont seemed to weigh the proposal for a moment before she answered. 'I cannot deny that his death has given me a feeling of release, because that has become more pronounced with each passing day. But the good citizen within me says that the law must be upheld and his killer brought to book.'

Her colour had risen. She seemed to be positively enjoying herself now. It appeared that the shaping of her replies and the declaration of her new-found health were giving her pleasure. Perhaps it was a feature of her condition, but she seemed to be almost surfing the wave of her own excitement now, to be waiting eagerly to discover what they might raise next for her in this novel situation.

Lambert was ill at ease with this unnatural reaction in a newly bereaved widow. He said rather desperately, 'You mentioned a friend earlier, who advised you that you would need to delay the funeral. It is good that you have someone to help you in this situation.'

He was fishing, and she knew it immediately. But she was not at all put out. 'There is no reason why you should not know the identity of my new friend. It will probably surprise you almost as much as it does me, Mr Lambert. It is the woman whom, until a fortnight ago, I was proposing to cite as Martin's co-respondent in my divorce proceedings. It is Vanda North.' She paused for a moment and seemed delighted by their reactions. 'It isn't a likely combination, is it? But Vanda and I hit it off from the first. I should perhaps add that it is many years since she had anything other than a business relationship with Martin. I fear we both felt the same about him by the time of his death. He could be charming and attractive in the early stages of a relationship, particularly when he was younger. But both of us had long since had our eyes opened to his vices.'

Jane wondered whether she was talking too much, whether she should be speaking so openly about her friendship with Vanda. But she was so cheered by it that she wanted to tell others about it, wanted to be open and cheerful about this startling new presence in her life. It wasn't startling any more, not to her. She was amazed by how quickly she had come to accept it and she felt that Vanda was too.

Lambert was certainly surprised by the depth of her feelings, though training and long experience had taught him to show no more than he wished to reveal. There was something a little febrile in her happiness. He would also have been less than human and a poorer detective if he hadn't wanted to shake this new-found confidence in someone who was still a suspect. He said calmly, 'Are there any revisions you would like to make to what you told us on Friday, Mrs Beaumont? It would be understandable if you were confused by the shock of this sudden death.'

Jane tried to be cool, literally as well as figuratively. She could feel the heat on her skin which excitement had brought to her face. 'To be honest, I can't recall in any detail what I told you on Friday. I wasn't trying to be obstructive, but if I said anything which wasn't correct I apologize for it.'

'All we wanted then and all we want now is the truth, Mrs Beaumont. We didn't ask you directly where you were when Mr Beaumont was killed. That was partly because we knew you'd be upset in the hours after you'd heard of Mr Beaumont's death, and partly because we already had the information. I believe you told the officer who came on that morning to break the news of your husband's death that you were alone in this house throughout last Wednesday evening and the night which followed.'

'Did I? Well if the young lady says I told her that, I've no doubt that I did. I wasn't long out of bed and I think I was still affected by the drugs I'd taken the night before. I was still trying to take in the news of Martin's death when she was asking me questions. It's quite possible I made mistakes, don't you think?'

'I do, and I am giving you the opportunity to put things right. I'm not asking you whether you intended to deceive us or not. I'm trying to get the facts of the matter right. They could be very important.'

Jane felt him watching her intently, but she wasn't unduly worried by that. She must get this right, but she was confident she could do it. 'If I did tell that young policewoman I was alone, I got it wrong. Vanda was here with me overnight. She stayed because she thought I needed her help.'

Hook looked up from his notes and said kindly, 'We'd better have the full facts of this, Mrs Beaumont. Better get it right once and for all, so that our records aren't confused. That could be important to others as well as yourself.'

'Yes, I can see that.' She frowned in concentration, anxious to show them that she was now giving the matter the attention its significance deserved. 'I'm afraid I can't give you the exact time when Vanda arrived. Early evening, I think, because she didn't want anything to eat. It was still daylight, because I showed her some of the rhododendrons in the garden. The sun was still well up then. It must have been about seven o'clock, I should think.'

'Thank you. That is helpful.'

She watched him making a note of the time in his round, clear hand. 'Vanda hadn't intended to stay the night. I had to lend her a nightdress and a toothbrush.' She looked very pleased with her recall of these details. 'She only stayed because she could see I wasn't very well. Martin and I had argued about the divorce the night before and I'd taken a lot of my pills before he left in the morning – he always wanted me to do that, when we'd quarrelled. I must have taken more than I should have, because Vanda could see that I was falling asleep as we talked to each other in the sitting room. I said that it didn't look as though Martin was going to be back and she said she didn't want to leave me on my own. So I put her in a spare room. We've plenty of those available, but Martin said we couldn't entertain people, because of my illness.'

'So Miss North was here overnight.'

'Yes.' It seemed strange to hear this stolid, friendly fellow calling her Miss North, when she'd got so used to Vanda.

'And what time did she leave on Thursday morning?'

'Oh, I couldn't be sure of that. You'd need to ask her.' Realization dawned. 'But perhaps you

286

already have. That's why Mr Lambert said I might want to amend things I'd said on Friday, isn't it?'

Hook smiled but did not answer her question. 'After breakfast, was it, when Miss North left?'

'Oh, yes. She brought me a tray in bed. It was probably about nine o'clock when she left, because she made sure I was up and feeling better. But she'd gone before Mrs Forshaw arrived – she's my cleaner, who comes on Tuesdays and Thursdays. She arrives here at half past nine.'

Hook made another note and said 'Thank you, Mrs Beaumont. That is much clearer. We previously had the impression that you'd been alone overnight, and of course that is what you'd led our officers to believe.'

'I'm sorry about that. I wasn't quite myself last week, as Mr Lambert was kind enough to say earlier. Martin would have had a harsher expression for it, but there's no need to go into that any more, is there?'

'Indeed there isn't. And of course we're happy that you're feeling so much better than you were. So do you have any idea who killed Martin?'

He dropped this hand grenade on the tail of his politeness with an inviting smile. That made it even more shocking. She again felt as if her cheeks were colouring, a sensation she had not endured for years. 'No. I've thought a lot about it, as you'd expect. I think I'm going to be a lot better off without Martin. But I'd tell you if I knew anything about how he'd died.'

# TWENTY-ONE

Lambert had briefed the full team of twenty-two officers involved in the murder case first thing on Tuesday morning, emphasizing the need to find local witnesses to events at Howler's Heath on the night of Wednesday, the thirteenth of May. 'Above all, we need to find someone who has seen a vehicle other than Beaumont's Jaguar near the scene in the late evening – any time between ten and midnight. There is definitely no record of anyone using a taxi in that area, so there must surely have been a private vehicle around, whether it belonged to the murderer or an accomplice taking him or her away from the scene.'

Later in the morning, when he and Hook returned from their second interview with Jane Beaumont, he called DI Rushton into his office so that the three of them could review all the information gathered thus far. Hook, snatching a quick coffee in the canteen, found himself still the butt of colleagues who envied him his degree and the unexpected academic distinction it had brought to him. A young female DC who should have known better said, 'Meeting the chief superintendent and Chris Rushton, are you, prof? I suppose they'll be expecting you to conduct this morning's seminar for them!'

'Just you get out on the house-to-house and find us a witness. Find us someone who spotted that car the chief was on about and justify your overtime!' growled Hook in reply. No respect for their elders, today's young officers.

In Lambert's office, Chris Rushton was putting the revisions to Jane Beaumont's account into his laptop and awaiting the moment when he could announce the solution to this mystery. Lambert always stressed the need for facts rather than speculation, and Chris had a fact which would make the old dinosaur sit up and take notice. Chris would listen to what the others had to say, as the rules of the game demanded, but Detective Inspector Rushton was pretty certain that he could provide them with a piece of evidence more telling than anything they would be able to offer him.

Lambert said, 'Let's begin with the grieving widow, who from the start has made little secret of the fact that she isn't grieving very hard. Jane Beaumont has a history of illness. She has a bipolar disorder which was first diagnosed around the time when she married Beaumont. The doctors and medical records confirm that this is genuine and that it has become more pronounced in recent years.'

'I get the impression that Beaumont, whilst pretending to be very concerned about her illness, actually aggravated her troubles,' said Bert Hook. 'Whether that was wittingly or unwittingly, we can hardly investigate now. But she seems to me to be better off without him, from a health point of view, as well as being rid of a loveless marriage. She was much more in touch with reality when we saw her this morning than she was last Friday, but I doubt that she'd have been capable of planning and executing a murder such as this one.'

Sometimes not having seen a suspect can be an advantage, in making you more objective, thought Rushton. He looked at his computer and said, 'Mrs Beaumont's changed her story since Friday. She now claims she wasn't at home alone but that Vanda North was there, thus providing herself neatly with an alibi.'

'And the capable Miss North with one also, as she confirms it,' said Lambert thoughtfully. 'For what it's worth, I did believe Jane Beaumont when she spoke to us today. For a start, someone who'd driven out and killed Beaumont would probably have had her alibi ready from the start, rather than producing it at a second meeting. And secondly, her tale of being drugged up to the eyeballs on the night of Wednesday and Thursday tallies both with Vanda North's assessment of her and with our first impressions of her when we saw her on Friday. She was certainly much sharper and more in touch with life today. And her changed account tallies with what Miss North had already told us, both about her presence there on Wednesday night and Jane Beaumont's condition at the time.'

'There is still the possibility of a pact between the two to see off Beaumont whilst providing each other with alibis,' Rushton pointed out. 'Though I must say that this alliance of wife and former mistress seems a most unlikely one.'

'Unlikely but genuine, as far as we could see,' said the usually sceptical Lambert. 'Miss North's affection for Beaumont is long gone, and Jane Beaumont has for many years been a lonely and isolated woman – largely as a result of her husband's efforts, it seems. It's quite a recent association, and both women say they were surprised by it. They appear to have been bonded by a mutual hatred of Beaumont's actions towards them over the last few years. We'll interview Vanda North again, though, and see whether that impression is confirmed.'

Rushton flicked the North file on his monitor. 'What about Miss North as a suspect?'

'She appears to be in the clear with Jane Beaumont, if we accept that they were in the Beaumont house together overnight at the time of the murder. She's cool and intelligent, and the fact that she's a former mistress of the victim gives an obvious motive. But if this was a crime of passion, would she wait for all these years to commit it? She appears to have dealt with the break-up of her relationship with Beaumont and moved on – even to the extent of forming a friendship with her lover's wife. How genuine did that friendship seem to you, Bert?'

'Both of them seemed surprised and even slightly embarrassed by the way a bond had

291

formed between them and then strengthened so quickly. If they are acting this, then they are both very accomplished. And if I were a wife looking for some sort of alibi, I'd look for a more likely companion at the crucial time.'

Rushton nodded and moved on methodically. 'What about Alistair Morton? He's been with Beaumont since the start of Abbey Vineyards.'

Lambert nodded. 'And he's resolutely low-profile. That may be merely his personality, but I want to speak to him again, now that we know more about the case and the other people in it. I get the feeling that there was general discontent with the way Beaumont was running things as the firm got bigger and bigger. With his grasp of financial affairs, Morton would be the natural focus for any organized revolt.'

'I might have a little ammunition for you against the low-profile Mr Morton. The Inland Revenue conducted quite a prolonged investigation into the affairs of Abbey Vineyards in the early days. There was even a possibility of the Serious Fraud Squad being brought in at one point, but in the end the whole thing collapsed for lack of reliable evidence. As far as I could gather, the directorate of Abbey Vineyards consisted of Beaumont and Alistair Morton in those days. There were lots of employees on the land, but those two were the only ones who knew what was going on financially and they were the subjects of the investigation.'

'Interesting. Mr Morton presented himself as a pillar of financial respectability. We might be able to shake him up and find out a little more about both him and others, if we can use this when we see him again.' Lambert looked as if he relished that prospect. He enjoyed pinning down evasive witnesses almost as much as the lawyers all policemen affect to despise.

Hook grinned at John Lambert's intensity. 'We also have grounds to pursue Jason Knight. He's no doubt an excellent head chef, but he appears to have ideas which were above his station as far as Beaumont was concerned.'

When Rushton looked a question at his chief, Lambert said, 'Golf club tittle-tattle, Chris, expertly unearthed by one DS Hook. I told you the game would bring you unexpected rewards, Bert.'

Hook grinned at Rushton. 'John and I played with a young industrial lawyer on Sunday morning. He happened to tell us afterwards that Knight had been sounding him out about the possibilities of getting more say in policy and perhaps shares in the business only a week or two before Beaumont was killed.'

Rushton frowned. 'It's a long step from that to murder.'

'Agreed,' said Lambert. 'But our informant said he told Knight that Beaumont had things so well tied up legally that Knight had very little chance of breaking his monopoly of power and decision-making. I agree it's still a long way from there to shooting a man in cold blood, but it's got to interest us that Knight concealed these aspirations from us when we saw him.'

'Gerald Davies,' said Rushton rather abruptly. He was anxious to get through these lesser suspects and on to the one damning piece of evidence he had unearthed.

'Salt of the earth,' said Bert Hook, equally abruptly and decisively.

Lambert grinned. 'Bert likes him because he's a sportsman from a working-class background. We have to make allowances for the built-in prejudices of our Barnardo's boy. Of course, we now also have to take into account the intelligent insights of the new graduate.'

'I came in here to get away from all that bullshit,' protested Hook. 'All that I'm saying is that Davies seemed a genuine and decent man to me.'

'And all three of us in this room have seen enough violent crime to realize that decent men can quite easily become murderers in the right circumstances,' Lambert pointed out gently.

'Which are usually domestic,' responded Hook. 'Anyone can be driven beyond his or her limits of control in some domestic set-ups. This isn't one of those, unless the widow killed him, which we seem to have agreed is most unlikely.'

Lambert nodded. 'Davies was trying to conceal things. Ineffectively, in the case of Sarah Vaughan: he let out that Beaumont had made some sort of sexual advance to her. I agree that he isn't a natural deceiver, but that's all the better for us.'

'He has no alibi.' Rushton was looking at his screen. 'Highly inconvenient for him that his

294

wife was away at her mother's on the night in question. Or highly convenient, if he wanted to drive twenty-five miles to kill his employer. His residence is further from the scene of crime than those of all the other suspects.'

'That might appeal to a man like Davies,' said Lambert thoughtfully. 'He's the kind of man who'd want any act of violence on his part to be as far from his own patch as possible. And whilst that meeting must have been arranged beforehand, we shouldn't assume the murder itself was necessarily pre-planned. Jane Beaumont was pretty certain that Beaumont had his pistol in the car that night. The killing might have been on impulse. It might even have been in self-defence, if Beaumont had produced the weapon and threatened whoever met him that night.'

'We're unlikely to find the weapon. And we still don't know whether it was Beaumont or his killer who arranged the time and place of their meeting,' Rushton pointed out. 'Do you think what Davies told you about Sarah Vaughan is significant?'

Lambert pursed his lips. 'She concealed some sort of sexual advance by Beaumont when she spoke to us. I'm not sure how serious it was, but I'd be interested in why she thought it necessary to hide it. Davies clearly thought it had shaken her.'

Hook decided to show that a pretty face and shapely legs were irrelevant to a professional man like him. 'Ms Vaughan pretended to be more recently appointed to Abbey Vineyards and more gauche than she is. She's a capable woman of thirty-three, whatever her physical attractions. Beaumont wouldn't have appointed a dumb blonde. We now know that he had a wandering eye and wandering hands, but he rarely made a bad appointment. And everyone we've seen says that Abbey Vineyards was his first and most consistent love, to the point of obsession at times.'

Lambert said quietly, 'We also know that he demanded his own way and got it. Perhaps he thought that should apply in sexual encounters as well as business. If he arranged to meet Sarah Vaughan last Wednesday night and then went too far, she could well have panicked and shot him. We shall have to investigate that possibility with her. She has no alibi.'

Rushton nodded. 'Like most of the others. Including our last major suspect, Tom Ogden.' This time his normally staid exterior could not conceal his excitement.

The others both looked at him keenly before Lambert said, 'He was at the cinema with his wife last Wednesday night. I understood that she had confirmed it.'

'She did. She also stated that he went home with her afterwards and didn't go out again. But it was Thursday night when they went to the cinema, not Wednesday. I was there with Anne and we saw them. It's most unlikely that they went to the same place to see the same film on two successive nights.'

Lambert and Hook digested this, their brains registering again what Ogden had told them and how he had seemed at the time. Then Lambert said heavily, 'He didn't seem a natural liar to me, but that only makes this more significant. He has a record for violence, though admittedly a long time ago. But he more than anyone made no secret of his loathing for Beaumont and his relief that he was off the scene.'

'Do we get him in here and grill him?' said Rushton eagerly. As he was coordinating the investigation from the station, he was even more conscious than Lambert of the attention the press and other media were giving to this high-profile case. A man 'helping with enquiries' was always a useful placebo to produce for them.

Lambert shook his head. 'No. If Ogden is our killer, he's not a danger to anyone else. Let him think he's got away with his alibi at the moment, whilst we investigate one or two other deceptions.'

Rushton concealed his disappointment; Lambert's rank and record didn't permit him to press the matter further. 'You don't even want an officer to see his wife and find out whether she wishes to revise her statement?'

'No. That would alert Ogden himself, which I don't want to do at the moment. I think we'll start with a word with Jason Knight, after we've grabbed some lunch.'

Rushton didn't envy the director of catering at Abbey Vineyards his afternoon.

\* \* \*

Jason Knight, like many of his calling, looked most confident in the kitchen where he reigned supreme. For a moment, he did not notice the arrival of his CID visitors and they watched him directing his staff in the preparation of the food for the evening menu. He was quiet, confident, obviously both respected and liked by his workers. He was still only thirty-eight, and several of the staff were older than he was, but there was no sign of resentment in what seemed to be a contented group. Knight seemed not at all put out when he noticed Lambert and Hook waiting patiently for his attention near the entrance door.

Lambert remarked how quietly efficient the kitchen looked as Knight led them into the small private room which adjoined it. 'It gets more hectic when the customers are in and waiting for their food,' Jason admitted ruefully. 'But it's my belief that you rarely improve efficiency by shouting at people. As a result of carefully edited television coverage of one or two of our number, the public has the impression that your cuisine can't be good unless you're foul-mouthed and temperamental.'

'Rather as you have to have a drink problem and at least one broken marriage to be a television sleuth,' said Lambert wryly.

'Overall, I suppose we should be grateful for the publicity afforded to our calling,' said Jason. He was pleased with this informal introduction to a meeting he knew he had to handle smoothly if suspicions were to be removed.

His satisfaction did not last for very long.

Lambert glanced around the chef's den, which was scarcely larger than a police station interview room, and decided its bare walls had nothing new to tell him about its occupant. 'We've found out quite a lot more about Abbey Vineyards and its late owner since we last spoke to you.'

It sounded ominous, as it was meant to do. Jason stalled with the opening he had planned. 'I'm glad you now know more about the sort of man Martin was. Not everyone's cup of tea, though all of us here have done well out of his enterprise.'

'Well enough, no doubt. But some of you felt that it was high time the firm moved on. And apparently thought also that it couldn't do that with the system Mr Beaumont was operating.'

Jason Knight put his elbows on the small desk, steepled his fingers and smiled affably, trying to look thoroughly in control on his own territory. 'Nothing wrong with that, is there? A little healthy debate about the ways we might go forward was very much in the interests of the firm, I should have thought. Particularly as we are becoming an ever larger concern, as a result of our success.'

Lambert's tone was equally pleasant. The bullets were in the words. 'Nothing wrong at all, on the face of it, Mr Knight. But you chose to conceal not only that view but an acrimonious meeting with Mr Beaumont the day before his death. That is bound to interest officers conducting a murder enquiry. I think you should now tell us why you did that.'

Jason told himself not to get annoyed, not to show that they had troubled him. This must have come from Gerry Davies. He'd known the bloke was too naive for his own good, that these people would get things out of him which he himself had been able to conceal from them. Why hadn't Gerry told him, given him some warning that they knew? Too anxious to preserve his own skin, probably. Still, there was nothing to fear yet. They hadn't anything to tie him directly to this death, and they wouldn't find anything, if he handled this right. 'I thought when we spoke on Saturday that my views on the way things should be run here were irrelevant to Martin's murder. I still do. That is why I saw no reason to dwell on the subject when I talked to you then. I did agree with you at the end of our conversation that I had wanted a little more say in policy. I thought that would benefit the company as well as me personally.'

'Very altruistic of you, Mr Knight. What we have to ask ourselves is whether an innocent man would have chosen to conceal from us a meeting initiated by Mr Beaumont two days before his death. A meeting in which he seems to have taxed you with plotting against him.'

Jason nodded slowly. 'Perhaps I should have mentioned it. But when you know you didn't kill a man, you know also that it's irrelevant.'

Lambert's smile said that he found this very hollow. 'And you no doubt also thought it irrelevant that you had been enquiring about exactly

300

what legal means might be available to force the issue on this matter, only a week or two before Mr Beaumont became a murder victim.'

Jason forced himself to keep calm. He hadn't anticipated this. The way the man had put it made him look bad, like a man who had been plotting against the dead man. But there was no way that it proved he had killed him. 'I admire your research, Chief Superintendent Lambert. I wish our own research and development department had the personnel to produce this degree of detail. I merely took whatever advice I could gather. Martin Beaumont would have done exactly the same himself, in the same circumstances. He'd built the business up well, but he was a stubborn old sod. And a clever one, as I found out – he'd surrounded himself with all sorts of legal provisions which made it difficult to challenge the way he ran things.'

'So the only way forward was to remove him from your path.'

Knight ran a hand quickly through his fair, well-cut hair. It was his first visible manifestation of tension and he stilled it immediately. 'I suppose that some member of the senior staff might have felt that way. I should tell you that there are others as well as me who wanted more power. I have to accept the possibility, with Martin lying dead in the mortuary, that one of us killed him. I can only tell you that it wasn't me who thought murder was the solution. And whilst I see that extreme frustration with Martin's autocratic methods is a motive, it is not the

301

only motive.'

'What other motives do you see?'

He smiled, happy to have diverted them away for the moment at least from the immediate area of danger for him. 'This is surely your area of expertise and your business rather than mine, Chief Superintendent Lambert. It is common knowledge that Martin had treated his wife abominably for years. It is common knowledge that Vanda North was once his mistress; she also feels as I do that she should be more than a junior partner in the firm. I told you on Saturday that Martin pursued an active and varied sex life outside his marriage: he must have made enemies there. Alistair Morton and Gerry Davies feel as I do that Martin could not have gone on being the sole wielder of the reins of power. Even our most recent senior executive, Sarah Vaughan, believes that.'

Jason paused. He had expected to be interrupted before now, but Lambert was merely watching him attentively, his head a little on one side and the grey eyes unblinking, as if he was revealing more of himself than the people he spoke of. He sought desperately to seem not a denigrator of his friends but a person who had considered also the wider context. 'From what I have heard, in the early days of the company, long before I was on the scene, Martin used some very dubious business practices to develop the firm. He trod on some dangerous toes to bring Abbey Vineyards to its pre-eminent position in English wines. He was still doing so at

302

the time of his death. With your excellent research team at work, you no doubt by now know vastly more than I do about all of these things. I mention them only because you invited me to speculate.'

Lambert caught the irony, but chose not to react to it. 'Then speculate a little further, Mr Knight. Since you have plainly given the matter so much thought, let us now know the full extent of your thinking. It need go no further than this room. Who do you think put that bullet into Martin Beaumont's head?'

'I don't know. If I did, be assured that I would tell you. I don't find it pleasant being a suspect, which is plainly what I am. If you put me on the spot, I should have to opt for one of the people he has trampled on his way to success – perhaps quite recently, for all I know. Ethics went out of the window when he was acting for Abbey Vineyards. Martin regarded any action as justified if it benefited the firm.'

He was pointing them towards Tom Ogden, thought Lambert, but he did not take up the hint. Instead, it was Hook who looked up from his notes and said, 'You told us on Saturday that you had no one who could vouch for your whereabouts after you left Ross-on-Wye Golf Club at around eight o'clock last Wednesday night. Is that still the case?'

'I am a single man, DS Hook. I was at home, relaxing after a round of golf and a couple of drinks. I dozed in front of the telly and went to bed some time after eleven. Does that seem unreal to you?'

'Not at all, sir. If you had unearthed someone who could confirm that, it would have been useful for you. As you have just told us, it is very unpleasant to remain one of the suspects in a murder enquiry.'

# TWENTY-TWO

The sound of laughter rang clear and high in Vanda North's thatched cottage. Female laughter. A rare sound, because Vanda lived alone and in the last few years had done little entertaining. A rarer sound still, almost unique in the last decade, because it came from Jane Beaumont.

It was seven o'clock in the evening, and the two women were eating in the conservatory at the back of the house. The May sun was still reasonably high in a cloudless sky, stealing towards the Welsh hills and its descent behind them. 'Fine again tomorrow, set fair for the week,' said Jane happily, as she watched the sun gilding the fresh green leaves at the top of the tall beech tree, sixty yards away at the bottom of Vanda's back garden. She could not remember when she had last considered the weather. That was a banal thought, perhaps, but the fact was significant: she was sure of that now.

Vanda brought in the strawberries and cream. She too was pleasantly surprised. She had enjoyed preparing the meal, when for years now cooking had seemed little more than a tedious chore. When she had felt it necessary to entertain friends, she had usually done so at a restaurant, making the excuse that she was no cook and they should be grateful to be spared her efforts in the kitchen. Today she had turned back the clock and felt all the better for it.

'Better finish that red wine before we eat the strawberries,' she told her guest.

'I don't know when I last enjoyed a meal so much,' said Jane, running a finger reflectively round her empty glass as she put it back upon the table. 'Mind you, you haven't much competition: for months now, I've hardly noticed what I was eating. But I noticed everything tonight. And enjoyed everything.'

Vanda brought two Benedictine liqueurs with the coffee. At her suggestion, they left the small square table she had set up in the conservatory and went back into the sitting room. The sun was dipping behind the big oak tree now, and the light here seemed dim after the brightness of the conservatory. But she did not put on the light, sensing correctly that both middle age and the pleasant lassitude which was overtaking them would be better suited by the twilight of a perfect evening.

Jane subsided happily into the deep comfort of the sofa and said, 'I shouldn't drink this. I won't be fit to drive home.'

'You've passed that point already. You'll need to stay the night. It's no problem; the bed is already made up in the spare room.'

Jane Beaumont nodded. They were close enough now for there to be no need for the ritual protest. She felt now that she had always known she was going to stay. She looked at the green liqueur in the glass, then rolled it around a little, relishing the rich colour and the moment without sipping the drink. 'If anyone had told me a fortnight ago that I'd have been relaxing here after enjoying a meal with you, I'd have said they were crazy,' she mused.

Vanda nodded. 'I had a very anxious hour after that first phone call of yours, wondering whether you'd cosh me when you arrived.' She hesitated for a moment, then came and sank down beside her new friend on the deeply cushioned sofa. 'Here's to us!' she said, clinking her glass against Jane's and taking a ritual sip.

She slid her arm round Jane's shoulders and rested it on the bare flesh of the arm below the short-sleeved dress. She felt the body beside her stiffen for a moment, then slowly relax. She glanced sideways at the strong, newly animated features beneath the neat dark hair, then outwards again through the windows of the conservatory at the crimson sky behind the tree. 'Perhaps I should say that I have always been of a strictly heterosexual persuasion,' she said, after a full minute had passed in silence.

'So have I,' said Jane Beaumont softly. 'Though I can't say that the experience has been

306

either frequent or varied over the last few years.'

They giggled a little over that, then were silent again. They willed the companionable darkness to steal in softly around them, exquisitely content in their friendship, resolutely refusing to consider where it might go from here.

Alistair Morton's office at Abbey Vineyards was almost as anonymous as the man himself, Bert Hook thought.

There were five photographs on the walls, but they were all of the vineyard and its buildings at different stages of their development. They spanned a period of over twenty years and were interesting enough as a record of the place's history. But they told you nothing about the man who spent a lot of his life in this room. He only appeared in one of the photographs, the earliest one, in which a young Morton with precisely parted black hair stood just behind the more striking blond-haired figure of the young and handsome Martin Beaumont. The founder and owner of the vineyard beamed his confident, extrovert smile at the camera. The man behind his right shoulder looked more shyly at the lens, as if he could not wait to disappear back to his office and away from public view.

It was eight o'clock on Tuesday evening, and Lambert wondered why Morton had been so insistent that they should meet here rather than in his home, where they had conducted their first meeting. It would be quieter here, he had said. But his house was in a sleepy suburb and he had no children. Had he wanted to keep them away from his wife? Did he fear that she might let him down under pressure? Hook decided to take up that issue later, unless the man proved cooperative.

In the meantime, Lambert would set about piercing the carapace of privacy which this slight, self-effacing man had grown about himself. 'We know a lot more about Mr Beaumont and his senior staff than when we spoke to you on Friday. This in turn means that we need information from you, Mr Morton.'

'I shall be happy to help you, of course, as far as I am able to. I should perhaps warn you that I know little about the private lives of my colleagues.'

'It is your own life, business and private, which interests me most.' Lambert glanced through the window at the restaurant with its busy car park, at the now deserted offices and shop, at the fields of vines stretching away as far as the eye could see into the soft evening sunlight. 'You were involved in all this from the outset. You have helped it to grow from a small, risky venture into a prosperous business. I believe you know more about the business methods of our murder victim than any man alive. Particularly the ones he used in those early days. You have so far told us very little.'

Alistair had not been prepared for the directness of this challenge. He told himself firmly that he had known they would get on to this ground eventually, that he had answers ready for them. 'It is a long time since those early days. I cannot see that they have any bearing on Martin's death.'

'You cut some very dangerous corners in the years when you were establishing Abbey Vineyards.'

'Martin did that, not me. It was a difficult process, establishing an enterprise in a totally new field. We hadn't really enough capital, but you can't ask Martin about that now. He took a few risks – pretended at times that we had more money at our disposal than we had, claimed tax relief on a few items which may have been dubious.'

'Claimed tax relief on items which did not exist. And you were his financial adviser. You not only went along with his lies but devised many of them for him.'

It was strong stuff, much stronger than Alistair had anticipated. He hadn't expected this to be thrown at him again after all this time. 'That was never proved. The Inland Revenue investigated everything at the time and gave us a clean bill of health.'

Lambert smiled the smile of the man who had made his point and put his adversary on the back foot. 'You know as well as I do that it was very far from "a clean bill of health". My interpretation of their findings is that they knew very well you were at fault but decided not to prosecute for lack of evidence. Mr Morton, you may be relieved to hear that I have no wish to reopen old wounds. We are interested in charging a murderer, not pursuing an ancient fraud case.'

Alistair looked down. His thin, stricken face looking like that of a schoolboy determined to get out the words he had prepared for this. 'Martin did things which I advised him not to do and said things which I advised him not to say. We were very much a two-man band in the early days; I went along with these things at the time because I felt I had to support him. I would not do it again.'

'No doubt he told you that he would make it worth your while to do so.'

Whilst Hook marvelled anew at his chief's ability to make many bricks from little straw, Morton flashed an anguished glance at his questioner, then dropped his gaze again to his desk. 'He said that once we were established as a going concern and had put those perilous early days behind us, I would become a partner in the firm.'

'A promise which he failed to honour.'

'He denied he had ever made it. And I'd nothing in writing to challenge him with, as he reminded me whenever I raised the matter.' Alistair felt as if teeth were being drawn from him, without an anaesthetic. Even with the assurance that he would not be prosecuted, it was agony for an accountant to admit crimes of financial deceit to a policeman. And it had all been for nothing. He had been a cautious financial man for many years now; it was agony to admit to such ancient naivety.

'So you felt that Beaumont had led you into a

Serious Fraud Squad investigation, with the possibility of a prison sentence and the certain loss of your professional status, without paying the price that he had offered.'

It was a statement, not a question. Alistair Morton could see no way to deny it. He nodded miserably. 'It remained a bone of contention between us until he died.'

Lambert smiled at the mildness of the cliché. 'A little more than that, Mr Morton. Mr Beaumont's intransigence in failing to recognize your loyalty and the risks you had taken without reward became a motive for murder.'

Alistair found himself drawn irresistibly into greater confessions than he had ever intended. He said in a monotone which seemed to come from someone else, 'I thought about killing him. I don't deny that.' He stopped for a moment, remembering the long hours of the night he had spent considering the methods he might employ. Then, almost as an afterthought, he added, 'But I didn't kill him. Someone else did that for me.'

The CID men allowed the long silence to stretch as a tactic, so that this denial seemed increasingly feeble. It was into this atmosphere that DS Hook eased his first question. 'You said on Friday that you were at home on the night of this death. That you did a little gardening, watched television, and did not go out again until the next morning. Would you now care to revise that?'

'No. My wife confirmed that, didn't she?'

Hook shook his head sadly as he consulted his

notes. 'Mrs Morton was interviewed by a junior officer in uniform. He said she seemed a little unsure of the facts of the matter.'

Alistair was suddenly weary of this, of the years of deceit, of the years of alternately wooing and badgering the man who had refused to concede his rights. He could picture his naturally honest wife trying to do her best for him and failing to convince. He was soiled goods. He didn't want Amy to become soiled goods too, as a result of what he had asked her to do for him. He said dully, 'I went out again, late in the evening, on the edge of dark.'

'And where did you go, Mr Morton?'

'I came here. Went through my files whilst it was quiet, trying to find something to help me to challenge Martin. I know I could have done that during the day, but somehow I thought that if I had complete privacy I'd have a better chance of finding something.' He paused, hearing how lame that sounded. 'And all right, I hoped I'd be able to get into Martin's own files, to find something from years back that I could use against him to make him deliver at last. I had a key to his office, but I couldn't get at anything in there. Fiona Cooper is far too competent to allow access to her employer's private affairs.' Through his bitterness, there was a strain of reluctant admiration for the PA's efficiency.

'And what time did you return home, Mr Morton?' No one would have guessed from Bert Hook's quiet prompting that he was recording what might be the preamble to a confession of murder.

'I can't be precise. But it was definitely after midnight. There were no lights visible in the avenue and Amy was in bed and asleep.'

The three men in the room were silent, watching Hook's swift, round hand record the evidence that there might be a murderer amongst them.

The scene was an appealing mix of ancient and modern. The small block of flats was new and the orange of its bricks still a little brash, even in the twilight. But it was framed by tall oaks on either side which had been there since they were planted almost two hundred years ago, after the Napoleonic wars had denuded the area of timber for the ships of Nelson's fleet. The long reach of the Wye which ran softly sixty yards to the south had scarcely changed in two thousand years.

Gerry Davies wondered if the new red sweater he had donned as leisure wear was too bright. He looked over the darkening river through the first-floor window and said conventionally, 'You've got yourself a nice spot here, Sarah.' He turned away from the view at the window and sat down carefully on the black and white sofa, beside the low table with its single small silver ornament. He felt not exactly guilty but a little embarrassed to be alone in this minimalist environment with a pretty woman who was a full generation younger than him. Young enough to be his daughter, as an amused Bronwen had reminded him when he had told her he was coming here.

Sarah Vaughan brought in her gin and tonic and his beer, setting them carefully upon coasters on the table between them. The sage green of her top and the darker green of her trousers fitted with the muted taste of the decor. Slipping off her shoes and curling her feet beneath her on the chair opposite her visitor, she contrived to look more relaxed than she felt. 'I like it here. I probably paid an extra ten thousand for the position, but I felt I could afford it, once I'd got the salary at Abbey Vineyards.'

'Yes. Martin was never a bad payer, if you gave him what he needed. Work-wise, I mean!' Davies added hastily, and only made his unintended innuendo more pointed.

She grinned at Gerry and his embarrassment. His small gaffe had eased the tension, not added to it. 'I wanted to talk to you about this police investigation.'

'I'm sorry I let out what Martin had done to you. I didn't know you hadn't told them.'

'That's all right. I've got over it now. It wasn't your fault, anyway.' They'd had words about it earlier in the day when he'd revealed what he'd said, but she'd realized since then that she needed all the help she could get. 'You only saw them last night, after they'd talked to everyone else. I was wondering how much they'd found out about us all. Do you think they're near to an arrest?'

'I don't know. They gave me the impression of knowing an awful lot about us, without telling

314

me anything they didn't want to. I suppose they're experts at that.'

And you'd be putty in their hands, thought Sarah irritably; you're far too trusting for your own good. But that was unfair. It was no good resenting the very qualities in the man which had made her trust him and go to him for advice when she was new in her job. 'I've heard they're looking for people who might have seen a strange car in or near Howler's Heath last Wednesday night. Do you know if they've found anyone?'

'No. They didn't say. But they were on to the fact that we all wanted more of a say in the way things were being run at the vineyard. And they knew that Martin wasn't having any of it. I believe they think someone who wanted more say in policy might have killed him.'

'And what about other motives?'

He was quiet for a moment, sensing her anxiety, wanting to offer her something which might make up for his gaffe of the previous day. 'They said Martin had an eye for the ladies. That's when I let it out that he'd made a pass at you.'

'Rather more than a pass, Gerry. I could have dealt with a pass easily enough. Do you think they've found out much about his sex life?'

'I don't know. I couldn't tell them much. I told them Vanda used to be his mistress, but they already knew that.'

'They'll come back to me, you know. Do you think there's anything I should be prepared for?'

He thought hard, still searching for something to compensate for his mistake in revealing the attack she had previously concealed from them. 'No. They get as much as they can from you, without telling you much. I'm sorry.'

Gerry Davies stood up. He wanted suddenly to be away from here, to be within the walls of his shabbier and more comfortable house, with the photographs and the memories of children, who could never have lived in this tidy, aseptic place.

She had been about to bring him another beer, but she sensed his mood and shared it. Perhaps things would never be as they had been again between them. On an impulse, she stood on tiptoe and kissed him lightly on the forehead, without putting her arms around him. 'I never had a dad, you know. He left us when I was two. Sent us money and all that, but I never saw him.'

He was at once embarrassed and pleased. 'And I never had a daughter. Two hulking sons, but no daughters!' He put his hands on her shoulders, pulled her lightly towards him and pressed his lips against her forehead as lightly as she had kissed his. 'Everything will be all right, you know,' he said at the door.

'Of course it will, Gerry!'

She stood for a long moment with her forehead against the door when she had shut it behind him, wondering if that could ever be so.

# TWENTY-THREE

Vanda North put the phone down and stared at it for a moment before turning back to Jane Beaumont. 'They're coming at ten. I think it would be better if you weren't here then.'

'Right. I can be on my way in twenty minutes.' Jane didn't question Vanda's judgement. Still less did she resent it. She had learned swiftly that her new friend knew more than she did about the world and the people who lived in it. Accepting Vanda's guidance had added to her confidence rather than diminished it. It was a long time since she had had a friend that she could rely on. She relished the feeling of trust which had grown up so quickly between them.

They had already finished their breakfast and the clock on the kitchen wall told her that it was two minutes past nine. Jane had nothing to pack, because she hadn't intended to stay the night. By twenty-five past nine, she was easing the grey Audi out of the narrow entrance to the old cottage and waving farewell to her friend. She enjoyed the drive home. The sun was already high above the fresh spring green of the trees and the Wye ran for a mile or two beside her, appearing and disappearing as the road rose and fell beside its winding course. She tried not to conjecture about where Vanda and she might be in six months' time, but it was too pleasant a speculation to stay out of her mind for long.

Back in the thatched cottage, Vanda North was busy removing all traces of her friend's presence. There was no reason why the police should not know that Jane had been here overnight, but neither was there any reason for them to know more of her private life than she chose to concede to them. Murder might allow them to open doors which in any other circumstances would have remained firmly shut, but there was no reason why they should learn any more than they had to.

She put the toothbrush she had lent to Jane carefully back in her bathroom cabinet and shut the door upon it. Then she went downstairs and stowed the dishes she had left draining in the kitchen cupboards. For no reason she could define, it was important to her to give her visitors the impression that she had breakfasted alone.

The two CID men came precisely at ten, as she had expected. The tall man with the grey eyes which seemed to see everything and his sergeant with the notebook and the deceptively friendly attitude; Vanda was determined not to underestimate them.

'We need to clarify certain issues, in the light of what we have learned from a variety of other sources,' said Lambert.

'I'm here to help you,' said Vanda with a

318

strained smile.

'What do you think will be the future of Abbey Vineyards?'

This was a tack she hadn't expected. 'I've really no idea.'

'You must have thought about it. You're a shareholder in the business. The only one still alive.'

'I presume Jane will inherit Martin's assets, including the business. I don't know yet how active a role she will choose to adopt.' She knew it sounded stiff and unyielding, but she saw no reason to confide the discussions she and Jane had had about the future. That was no one's business but their own. 'I can't see what this has to do with the investigation of a murder.'

'It has a connection. A week ago, you and several other people who occupy senior posts at Abbey Vineyards were interested in acquiring greater control of policy. The late owner was resisting you – successfully, it seems, for he had arranged things legally so that all the power was in his hands.'

'Yes. I told you as much when I spoke to you on Sunday.'

'You told us about your own situation, about how even your junior partnership in the firm had been defined by Mr Beaumont, so that it gave you no power to influence policy. We now know that several other senior staff were frustrated because they could neither acquire shares in the company nor have any say in its future development.'

'I am aware of that. Perhaps, as you say, they will now get that say. I hope so.'

'We have to consider the possibility that there may have been a conspiracy between two or more people to remove the man who stood in the way of such change.'

Vanda allowed herself a sour smile. They were floating theories; they didn't know anything for certain. 'I see the possibility. Therefore I shall tell you formally that I was not part of any such conspiracy; nor do I have any knowledge that any alliance of that sort existed. Chief Superintendent Lambert, I do not know who killed Martin Beaumont. Nor, if I am honest, do I care very much: Martin gave me ample reason to wish him out of my life. But that does not mean I will not give you every assistance I can in discovering his killer, because murder is not a solution of which I approve.'

No sign passed between the two men that Vanda could see, but the questioner suddenly became DS Hook. 'Could you tell us again where you were on the evening and night of last Wednesday, Ms North?'

She allowed herself a patient, understanding smile. 'Yes. That hasn't changed. I was where I told you I was on Sunday – at the house of Jane Beaumont.'

Hook nodded. 'The reason I ask you to confirm that is that Mrs Beaumont has changed her story. She originally told us that she was alone; she now says that you were in the house with her. You will realize, I'm sure, that this gives her

320

an alibi she did not previously possess for the time of her husband's death.'

'Then I am happy to provide it. I think I told you on Sunday that Jane was confused on that night, I think because of an excessive use of prescription drugs. I am happy if my presence in the house clears her of direct involvement in this crime. I am myself quite certain that she had no connection with it.'

'Thank you. You said just now that you would give us "every assistance". Will you now tell us in confidence who you think might have put that bullet into Martin Beaumont's skull, please?'

It was an unexpectedly blunt challenge from this quiet, considerate man. Shock tactics, perhaps. Well, it wouldn't shock her. Vanda North said, 'I've given that much thought, as I expect others also have. I have no name to offer you, I'm afraid.'

Tom Ogden did not immediately recognize his visitors. The two men stood awkwardly in the doorway of the old shippon which had become his administrative headquarters for the strawberry farm. He thought he had seen them before, but he was not sure where.

It was the younger man who introduced them. 'This is Alistair Morton and I'm Jason Knight. We're working neighbours of yours. We're from Abbey Vineyards.'

This man Knight spoke nervously, as Tom would have expected him to do. He had never made any secret of his dislike for his more powerful neighbour. But today something protected them from his immediate, open hostility. He needed to know how this murder investigation was going. Up the road at Abbey Vineyards, the staff were no doubt busy comparing notes, whereas he was isolated and alone, picking up none of the rumours about what the police might or might not now know. He said gruffly, 'You'd better come in and sit down.'

It was not really an office. There was a table but no desk, and four chairs in various stages of disrepair which did not match each other. Knight and Morton sat down gingerly on the two which looked most robust, whilst Ogden placed himself on the other side of the table. Tom was not a patient man. Instead of waiting for them to announce why they had come here, he launched into his most urgent query. 'Have they got anyone for killing Beaumont yet?'

Jason Knight's smile was bleak and humourless. 'All of us are wondering about that. Including the man who shot him, I presume.'

'They know it was a man, then?'

'No, I don't think they do. I was making an assumption.'

'But it needn't be a man, need it? A woman could have shot him just as easily.' Ogden was anxious for anything which would broaden the field of suspects; it sounded as though he was computing the odds against his own arrest. It was probably no more than a natural nervousness when you were a murder suspect, Jason decided. He said, 'We just wanted to discuss the

322

future with you, Mr Ogden.'

'It's Tom. And if you've come to persuade me to sell you this place, you've wasted your journey.' His jaw set in a firm line and he stared his visitor straight in the face for the first time, emboldened by the familiar instinct to protect his ground.

Alistair Morton said quietly, 'We're not here to offer you money, Tom. We couldn't do that, even if we wanted to. We don't know what the future of our firm is yet, nor even whether we'll have a part in it.'

Tom looked at him for a moment, then nodded brusquely. He liked the look of this older of the two men. Probably the first, subconscious reason was that he could have dealt with him easily in a fight. He was not conscious of any such reaction in himself, but when you worked with your hands in an environment where bodily strength and stamina were important qualities, you felt easier when you started with a physical advantage. Morton was older and slighter than Knight, and a direct contrast in appearance and manner to the blond, ebullient Martin Beaumont who had been his ogre over the years. Ogden said gruffly, 'What is it you want, then?'

'We have different ideas about the way our firm should go than Beaumont had. As our nearest neighbour, we'd like to know what you think of them.'

'How different?'

Alistair took a deep breath. Privately, though he had agreed they should come here, he had not

323

expected that they would even get a hearing from Tom Ogden. He decided the best introduction he could offer was to declare a dislike of his late employer. 'I'm the financial director at Abbey Vineyards. I'm also the oldest employee, now that the founder is dead. I was in the business from the start, and I don't mind telling you that Beaumont made some dodgy deals and did some hairy things, particularly in those early days. He also made certain promises to me about the future of the firm, on which he failed to deliver. To put it bluntly, he lied to me. He gave me his word on some important things and later denied it absolutely, because it suited him. I didn't like him any more than you did, Tom.'

'Fair enough. What difference does that make to either of us now?'

'Maybe none at all. Maybe quite a big one. That's what we're here to discuss.'

'I'm not going to sell out. You've wasted your time if you think I am.'

'That might well be so, Tom. We're not fools. We're not here to offer you the moon. We wouldn't propose anything that wasn't in our interests as well as yours. And as Jason says, we can't yet offer anything definite. It's just that if there was a measure of agreement amongst the three of us, that would strengthen our hands in whatever negotiations we may choose to undertake with other interested parties.'

Ogden was interested despite himself. Over twenty years and more, the situation with Beaumont had been black and white; he had never needed to think twice about his rejection of that odious man's proposals. But if he was going to have to deal with a group of people, perhaps making more subtle suggestions than Beaumont ever had, he would be at a disadvantage. He was an independent farmer, proud of his yeoman stock. He knew every yard of his land and he made his own decisions. But that meant he had little experience of negotiation.

Secretly, Tom Ogden feared being outsmarted. The kind of situation where you conceded one thing to gain another was foreign to him, and he felt he was too impulsive and excitable to handle it well. If he could indeed reach some agreement with these qualified, experienced men, he would feel much more confident in dealing with others. He said cautiously, 'I can see that we are all in a new situation. What is it you want to discuss with me?'

Alistair nodded appreciatively. They had already achieved more than he had expected. 'We hope that in future the system in our firm will be more democratic than it ever was under Beaumont. We hope that the five of us who have done most to run the place will have power, rather than just wages. We hope that we shall control policy in a way we have never been able to do in the past.'

'I keep hearing that word "hope". You're not in a position to make decisions or to come here making offers to me, are you?'

'Indeed we're not, Tom. Jason here told you that at the outset. We're not here to offer you lies or to make propositions we can't fulfil. All this is tentative, to see if we can establish some common ground between us.'

'That's all right then. Just so long as you don't expect any commitment from me today, I'm prepared to listen and to decide whether your plans are in my interests too.'

'That's good. Well, it's obvious to all of us that your land is in a particularly interesting position for us. The acquisitions made by Abbey Vineyards over the years mean that your strawberry farm is almost surrounded by our fields.'

'It's a prosperous concern. We're about to have our best year yet.'

'I don't doubt it. And Jason and I are not here to make you any cash offer for your land. We are not in a position to do anything of the sort. But let me tell you how we see the future of our firm, because that will obviously affect you as well, whatever happens. We see Abbey Vineyards as having a board of either five or six, depending on whether the widow of the late owner wishes to be involved. We know that you are not interested in a cash offer for your land and we understand why. But we thought that you might be interested in becoming the sixth or seventh director of the firm, in exchange for the absorption of your land into the vineyard.'

Tom Ogden, who had expected to reject these men as firmly as he had always rejected Beaumont, felt suddenly and unexpectedly exhilarated. His wife had been telling him for years that he needed to contemplate retirement; that he should be considering Beaumont's gold because he had no one to take over from him at the farm; that it was an inevitable fact of life that it would eventually become an anonymous chunk of Abbey Vineyards. This way he would not only get out with head held high, but would have a say in the future of his land, an interest in a thriving business which he could retain as long as he lived. He said guardedly, 'That would need a lot of discussion. A hell of a lot of discussion!'

'Of course it would, Tom. On both sides. And we can't even start on that yet, until all of us are clearer about the future. But you're not opposed to the idea in principle?'

'No. Not in principle. It's different from selling out. It would leave me with an interest in this land and how it was developed.'

'Of course it would. And from our point of view, it would make obvious sense. We'd like to be able to tell whoever else may be involved in the future of Abbey Vineyards that we've made contact with you and had a favourable response.' He saw the stirrings of dissent in the weather-beaten features opposite him and hastily modified his phrase. 'Or at any rate that you haven't turned us down flat, as you always did Beaumont. That we've talked about a very different sort of agreement, and that these discussions are ongoing. That would strengthen our hand too. There'd be three of us thinking along the same lines about the future policy for the firm.'

Tom Ogden didn't like some of the glib

modern phrases, but he'd already decided the general idea was acceptable. He stood up and offered his hand. 'I agree that what you have suggested might be possible, that I'm open to further discussion in due course. Let's hope none of us ends up behind bars because we saw off that bloody man Beaumont.'

He had tried to end on a light note, and all three men smiled. But none of them found the notion very amusing.

The flat which Gerry Davies had admired on the previous night seemed smaller, with these two large, threatening men within it. Sarah Vaughan asked them to sit down on the small black and white sofa, crushing them together a little, making their presence less dominating in her home. She sat opposite them on a chair which was a little higher, and gave Lambert a smile which he did not return.

She was used to people congratulating her on her taste and on the neat, minimalist interior of her dwelling, or at least on her securing of a picturesque site beside this quiet reach of the river Wye. This time there were none of those initial niceties. Instead, Lambert issued a direct challenge. 'Miss Vaughan, you lied to us when we spoke on Monday. You impeded the progress of a murder investigation.'

She felt a flash of anger at Gerry Davies and his clumsiness in revealing what she had sought to conceal, then guilt that she should cavil at this honesty in an honourable man. 'I didn't tell you

328

about Martin Beaumont's assault on me. Surely you can understand that. It was an embarrassment to me.'

'And a motive for murder. That is how we have to see it as detectives. Especially when someone takes elaborate steps to conceal it.'

'I just didn't tell you about it. I didn't lie to you.'

Lambert lifted an eyebrow at Hook, who turned back the pages of his notebook with what seemed to Sarah deliberate slowness. 'You said about Mr Beaumont, "I didn't see any evidence of the womanizing I heard people gossip about. For all I know, that's all it was – gossip." That seems a pretty definite denial.'

'All right. I didn't realize I'd been as emphatic as that. Martin made a pass at me. Well, a lot more than a pass, actually. It was an attempted rape, if you must know. He didn't accept my refusal. It was in his Jaguar and in broad daylight. He'd offered me a lift into Ross to collect my car. He pulled off the road and threw himself across me. Eventually, I managed to grab a handful of his hair and pull his head back, then get my knee into his balls.' She was breathing hard at the recollection of that afternoon, glaring at them accusingly. They were men, weren't they, and thus in some distant way to blame for this degradation?

Hook said quietly, 'When did this assault take place?'

'At the end of April. I can give you the date if you want it.'

329

'About a fortnight before Mr Beaumont was killed.'

'I suppose it was, yes.'

Lambert let the seconds stretch, encouraging her to make her own inferences about her hatred of Beaumont and what he had attempted. Then he said coolly, 'Did you take any action about this attack?'

She was suddenly furious with the man and his calmness. 'Get real, Detective Chief Superintendent Lambert! If I go to the police, he denies it, says I'm a silly young woman who's fantasizing about her boss. If I go to a solicitor, he wants evidence, which I can't provide. If Beaumont hears I've taken any action at all, I lose a job which I enjoy and earnings which I won't be able to match elsewhere. So I make sure that I don't give the man any opportunity to be with me alone and I get on with my life! That's the action I took.'

Lambert nodded several times, as if this time he accepted her account of things. 'Have you thought of anyone who can confirm that you were here at the time when Beaumont died?'

'No. There isn't anyone. I had telephone calls between eight and nine on that evening, but nothing after that.'

'Who do you think killed Martin Beaumont? We now think it was someone in his immediate circle, not an outsider.'

'I don't know. It's your business, not mine. It wasn't me. But you're not going to believe that just because I say it, are you?'

330

'Not just because you say it, no. The nature of our work does not allow that. You can see that you did not help yourself by concealing what you have now told us.'

'It's a motive; no more than that. I admit that I was quite pleased when I heard Beaumont was dead. But you must have other motives, as well as mine.'

They didn't respond to that. Sarah Vaughan was left staring bleakly through her window at the view which everyone found so attractive. She'd have to go in to work at the vineyard soon. She'd have to spend the rest of her day among the other suspects.

# TWENTY-FOUR

In Oldford police station, it was early afternoon. The sun was high, the CID section was almost empty, and the postprandial atmosphere was soporific.

Detective Inspector Rushton did not like that. He knew that the end of this day would mark a full week since Martin Beaumont had been shot through the head. His enthusiasm for data meant that he was well aware of one of the hoariest of police statistics: there was a sharp decline in successful conclusions to those murder hunts which had no arrest within seven days.

He wandered through to the front of the station, where his mood was not greatly improved by a conversation with the uniformed station sergeant. This corpulent veteran was due for retirement in three months and he wanted nothing more than an uneventful countdown to that date. Rushton wanted a sense of urgency, and he was not going to find one here. He enjoyed being at the centre of the investigation, correlating and cross-referencing the multitude of data as it accrued, but today he envied Lambert and Hook their more direct involvement with the people in this case.

Then, when he was telling himself that he would have to wait for any serious input until the pair arrived back at Oldford, he received an encouraging phone call. More than encouraging, in fact. Crucial, perhaps. A young probationary constable had unearthed a witness who had seen a car in Howler's Heath at eleven o'clock on the Wednesday night of the murder. A parked car, in fact. No number: you couldn't expect miracles of the ever-fallible public. But a colour and a make.

A colour and a make which tallied with the vehicle of one of the key suspects in the Beaumont case.

Two hours after Tom Ogden had finished his discussions with Jason Knight and Alistair Morton, he ushered Chief Superintendent Lambert and Detective Sergeant Hook into the same stone building.

He had set out the shabby furniture a little more formally, but he took the same chair behind the table, with the two CID men facing him across it. He met them as they climbed out of the police Mondeo, but they exchanged scarcely a word with him as he led them into the old byre. Once they had the privacy of the old stone walls around them, Ogden discovered why that was.

Even now, they did not speak, but looked at him expectantly. He said nervously, 'I trust you've made some progress. As I told you, I had no time for Beaumont, but I shall be interested to hear how—'

'You lied to us on Saturday night.' Lambert said bluntly.

The farmer's healthy outdoor complexion reddened visibly. In this place, he gave the orders and was obeyed without discussion. He was not used to being challenged. In addition, he was fighting the acute discomfort which affects the normally honest man when he has lied. 'I might have made some sort of mistake.'

'There was no mistake, Mr Ogden. DS Hook asked where you were last Wednesday night and you said you were at the cinema with your wife. That was a deliberate lie. You also asked your wife to lie on your account.'

Ogden was speechless. The justified allegation that he had forced Enid, the most honest and straightforward woman he knew, to lie on his behalf hit him hardest of all. As if he feared that the man might wander even further out of his depth, Bert Hook explained quietly, 'You and your wife were seen at the cinema on Thursday night. Not Wednesday, as you claimed to us on Saturday.'

'All right. I lied and I admit it. And I was stupid – as Enid said, with the size of the team you've got on the case, I was always likely to be rumbled.'

Bert hoped that Ogden was right in that assumption. He had an uncomfortable feeling that if Chris Rushton's fiancée hadn't recognized the Ogdens at the cinema on Thursday night, his story might have been accepted. Hook said heavily, 'You'd better tell us now where you really were on Wednesday night.'

'I was at home. Enid had had two sleepless nights with toothache and a visit to the dentist last Wednesday. She went to bed with painkillers at about half past nine. I'd no one to account for where I was after that.' Ogden spoke as if he was delivering words he had prepared for this moment, as he probably was. It made him sound as if he did not expect to be believed.

Lambert said curtly, 'In fact you went to Howler's Heath, where you met Martin Beaumont and shot him through the head with his own weapon.'

'No. I was at home. If you must know, I sat in a chair and worried myself about Beaumont's latest offer for my land, because Enid had said I should accept it.'

'Then why lie about the matter?'

Tom looked down at the deeply scratched

334

table, at the chip in the edge which had been there since his grandfather's time, when cattle had been milked in here. 'Because I hated Beaumont and everyone knew it. Because I had a police record of violence. I knew you'd bring that up. Because I'd have liked to kill the bastard, if I'd felt I could get away with it!'

They listened to the heavy, uneven sound of his breathing. It seemed to fill the room like the breathing of a heavy animal in pain. When it subsided a little and he glanced at them again, Hook spoke like a therapist. 'Did you kill him, Tom? It would be far better to tell us now, if you did.'

'No. I didn't stir from the house. But I can't expect you to believe that now, can I?'

'If you didn't kill the man, who did?'

'I don't know. I don't know what goes on at the vineyard. I've never wanted to know. That bugger must have had a lot of enemies, from what I saw of him.'

Lambert spoke more sternly, the complement to Hook's persuasion. 'It's your duty to tell us anything you know. If you didn't kill Beaumont, it's also very much in your own interest to speak out.'

Tom Ogden nodded. Having lied to them once, he had an urgent desire to tell them something, anything, which might persuade them that he was now telling the truth. 'Two of them came to see me this morning. From Abbey Vineyards, I mean. They've got plans for the future. They want me to join them.' It felt disloyal, but at the same time it felt the right thing to do. He didn't want to conceal things, not any longer. And a horrifying possibility had struck him only now, whilst the police stared at him across his table: one of his earlier visitors might have murdered to achieve what they wanted, what they were now inviting him to be part of. The two of them might even have done it together.

Lambert was studying the troubled face closely, as if he could read the workings of the mind behind it. All he said was: 'We'd better have the names of these people.'

Ogden dug his hand deep into his trouser pocket and produced the grubby scrap of paper on which he had written the names. 'Alistair Morton; I think he said he was the financial director up there. And Jason Knight; he runs the restaurant.' He watched Hook record the names, then added unnecessarily, 'They want me to become a director along with them. But nothing's definite yet. I said I'd need to think about it.'

Lambert nodded. 'They're not in a position to make offers, but they may be making plans. You would be well advised to mention this approach to no one else, until things become clearer.'

'I didn't intend to. I'm only telling you because I don't want to keep any more secrets from you.'

But he could tell Enid, he thought, as he watched them drive away. It would please her, if she thought he was planning to retire from the farm at last. And he owed her that, when he'd asked her to lie about the night they'd been at the cinema.

Lambert and Hook were silent for most of the six-mile journey back to Oldford. They had worked together for far too long now to talk for talking's sake. Moreover, the CID habit was to speak only about things which mattered and eschew small talk which meant nothing. An observer might have thought that they were merely appreciating the Gloucestershire countryside in spring, with the infinite range of greens offered by the burgeoning trees. A more experienced CID-watcher would have known that they were thinking hard about what they had heard, digesting what Ogden had said and weighing its merits. Silences between these two were never uneasy and often productive.

It was the driver, Hook, who eventually said, 'I believed Ogden. He's the most obvious candidate for murder, with his quick temper, his declared hatred of the victim, and his record of violence in his youth. But I don't think he's our man.'

Lambert smiled. That much had been evident to him whilst they were still with the farmer. 'For what it's worth, neither do I, Bert. I have a much better candidate, but very little proof as yet.'

They were turning into the police station car park as he said this. At the wheel of the vehicle immediately behind them was Chris Rushton, who could scarcely conceal his excitement until they reached the privacy of the CID section and his computer.

'I've been out to see a witness,' the detective inspector told them eagerly. 'The report came in from one of our youngest constables, so I thought I'd better check the statement out for myself. Especially as the person concerned may very well eventually become a witness in court.'

He was as animated as if he were a young officer himself. Lambert was both amused and delighted to see this zest in a thirty-four-year-old DI. 'Don't you think you'd better begin at the beginning with this one, Chris?'

'Yes. Sorry. I did try to get you on your mobile, but you were obviously with Tom Ogden at the time. We've found someone who saw a car in the right place at the right time. In Howler's Heath late last Wednesday night.'

'A reliable sighting?'

'Yes. That's what I wanted to check. Entirely reliable, I'd say.'

'It's taken this person a long time to come forward.'

'Yes. I'd say it was some pretty sustained burrowing by a young constable which unearthed this. It would be good if you could give him a pat on the back in due course. Youngsters get plenty of rockets when things go wrong. It's only right that they should get a bit of praise occasionally.'

For a few seconds, they were all back on the beat, considering the long hours of boring, repetitive work, the insensitivity of the public,

338

the contempt of old-sweat superiors who made out that today's beat work was a doddle compared with their time. Then Lambert said, 'I'll do that; let me have the young man's name. In fact, I'll do more: I'll make sure his sergeant and inspector know that he's produced a vital bit of information for us – always assuming that's what this proves to be.'

He looked interrogatively at Rushton, who said hastily, 'Details. A car was sighted at eleven o'clock last Wednesday night in Howler's Heath. It was seen by a young man of eighteen who was driving his father's car. He had his girlfriend with him and they were several miles from where they were supposed to be – hence his reluctance to come forward initially. Dad would not have been at all pleased to find his son driving his seventeen-year-old girlfriend out into the Malverns for a helping of nooky.'

'How sure is he about the time?'

'Very. The lad's prepared to swear it was within five minutes of eleven o'clock.'

'And the exact location?'

'He saw a stationary vehicle just off the road, within a hundred yards of the spot where Beaumont's Jaguar was parked.'

'Probably where we parked when we visited the scene of the crime,' acknowledged Hook as he made a note.

'The vehicle had no lights and the witness's impression is that it was empty at the time. He did point out that if people had been supine in the car, he would not have seen them as he drove

339

past – an idea no doubt deriving from his own activity a little while earlier.'

Hook smiled. 'Have we any idea how long this vehicle was parked there?'

'Not from this lad. But we have several people who say there was no car there at around half past ten and others who tell us there was nothing there from eleven twenty onwards.'

Lambert sensed that Rushton was happy to prolong the details, anxious to make this latest coup of his all the more dramatic. He said, 'What about the identity of this vehicle?'

It was Rushton's turn to smile. 'No registration number; that would be asking too much. But our man is confident of make and colour; like most young men, he's keen on cars. He spotted the rings on the bonnet as he went past. It was an Audi saloon, silver-grey metallic. He would swear to that in court, if necessary.'

'Do we have a match?'

Rushton flicked up the relevant file on his computer, though he knew well what he was going to say. It is part of the work of the most junior officers in a murder investigation to document all kinds of routine information, including the make of car driven by everyone who had been close to the victim. After six days of investigation, masses of detailed information had accrued, all of it dutifully documented on Chris Rushton's PC. Most of it remained tedious and useless. Occasionally, as on this occasion, the system threw up a nugget of gold.

Chris tried and failed to keep the excitement

340

out of his voice as he said, 'A silver-grey metallic Audi is driven by Mrs Jane Beaumont.' He glanced automatically for a reaction at the two older men. 'It looks as though, despite all the work we've put in on the people who worked with Beaumont, we have a domestic killing after all.'

# TWENTY-FIVE

With the afternoon sun high and wisps of white cloud seemingly stationary in the vivid blue sky, the thatched cottage and its neat gardens looked fit for a picture postcard. The scene reminded Lambert of Anne Hathaway's cottage, seventy miles away in Stratford-upon-Avon. As a boy, he had purchased a cheap print of that for his mother's birthday, and it had remained in a position of honour on the wall of her terraced house until the day she died.

The two big men stood looking at the outside of the cottage for a moment before they went to the door. There was no sign of life. But the oak door was answered quickly when they knocked. Vanda North said, 'I'm getting quite used to seeing you two. This is the second time today. I don't know whether I should be flattered or alarmed.'

Lambert said nothing until they were sitting in

341

the low-ceilinged lounge, with its comfortable sofas and the big television and hi-fi set in opposite corners. As always, his grey eyes fixed steadily upon his quarry. He waited until she was sitting motionless and looking at him before he said tersely, 'New evidence has come to light, Miss North. We need to know what you can tell us about it.'

'As ever, I am at your service, though I can't think of anything important that you haven't already had from me.' Beneath the routine politeness, the smiling confidence, she gave the impression that she relished their meetings not as exchanges of information but as intellectual contests.

'Tell us again where you were last Wednesday night, please.'

A little sigh, just the slightest suggestion that her patience was not inexhaustible. 'I thought we had cleared up any confusion about that. I was at Jane Beaumont's house, as I told you from the start. I know there was a little confusion on Jane's part, because Martin had her so drugged-up that she wasn't quite sure what she was doing. That had been going on for years and I shan't forgive him for it. I think everyone can see how much better she's beginning to look since he died. I'll tell you whatever you want to know about my colleagues at Abbey Vineyards, but when I see what he did to his wife, I can't regret that Martin's dead.'

She was saying too much, afraid of whatever challenge they had to offer, thought Lambert.

He didn't interrupt; there was always the possibility that even such an organized woman might let something slip if she was nervous. He was aware that if she denied him, if she took the obvious course which was open to her, even the police machine might find it difficult to amass the right evidence to bring her to court. But he didn't think she would do that.

Outside, beyond the conservatory, a blackbird was singing and a green woodpecker with a bright red head was exploring the lawn. He saw these things behind her without taking his eyes from her composed, intelligent face. And still neither of the men who sat so upright on the sofa spoke. Vanda North said, 'You said you had new evidence. Are you now going to acquaint me with it?'

'A car was seen parked near the scene of this killing at eleven o'clock last Wednesday night.'

'That is no more than circumstantial evidence, surely?'

Lambert smiled, recognizing the first concession in this macabre little endgame. 'It is a popular fallacy that no one is convicted on circumstantial evidence. It happens quite often, when the circumstantial evidence is strong enough.'

'Which hardly seems to be the case here.'

'As you may remember, we have details of the cars driven by all of the people who are involved in this investigation. In this case there is a match.'

Vanda North nodded and made her last bold

343

play to test their strength. 'I'm glad to hear it. When you have arrested the gentleman concerned, we shall all be able to get on with our lives again.'

'The car concerned is a silver-grey metallic Audi saloon. We believe it is the car owned by Mrs Jane Beaumont.'

Hook, studying her now as closely as Lambert, felt a reluctant admiration for the coolness of the woman. There was no obvious sign that she was forcing the smile she gave them as she said, 'What you believe and what is fact may be a long way apart. Jane Beaumont was at home in her bed at the time of the murder. I have already told you that. I am prepared to testify to it in court, if necessary.'

Lambert was inexorable, sensing now that he had her in a corner, that in the crisis she was not going to let her new friend suffer for her. 'Your testimony would not be worth very much, as you were not in the house at the time.'

'Jane will tell you that I was. I believe she has already told you so.'

'She was in bed and asleep at the time of her husband's death.'

'I'm glad that you admit that. The presence of a similar car to hers at the scene of the crime has no connection with Jane Beaumont.'

'It was Mrs Beaumont's Audi which was in Howler's Heath at the time of the killing. I said that she owned it. I did not say that she was driving it on this occasion.'

'This gets more outlandish by the minute. Do

I understand that you're now suggesting that some person unknown stole Jane's car and—'

'No!' Lambert's denial was like a gunshot in the quiet room. 'I'm stating, not suggesting, that, without Mrs Beaumont's knowledge, you drove out to an assignation with Martin Beaumont. That you shot him through the head with his own pistol.'

She looked him fiercely in the face for several seconds, in what had become a contest of wills. Then, with a sigh which was scarcely audible, she acknowledged that there was nowhere for her to go now. 'He'd arranged the meeting, not me. I didn't intend to kill him when I went there.'

They could hear the beginnings of a defence plea in court here, but that was not their concern. They wanted an arrest and a conclusion to their involvement. It was DS Hook, speaking as though he were neutral in this battle of opposing wills, who said softly, 'It's over, Miss North. You should tell us now about what happened last Wednesday night.'

She stared at him in surprise for a moment, as if she had forgotten his presence in the intensity of her duel with Lambert. Then she spoke in a steady monotone, like one under hypnosis. 'Martin asked me to meet him in that place and at that time. I asked him why he had to be so secretive about it, but he said he didn't want the rest of his staff at Abbey Vineyards to know about the meeting. I thought he was going to make some offer to me about the withdrawal of my capital from the firm. That's why the secrecy made sense. Martin regarded any concession as a mark of weakness, so I could understand that he wouldn't want others to know about it.'

She turned her head for a moment to look at the bright sunlight and the rich green of her lawn outside the house, as if realizing for the first time that these things were going to be denied to her. Then she resumed her trance-like monologue. 'Martin wasn't making any concessions at all. He wanted to warn me off any friendship with his wife, any attempt to rescue Jane from the prison without walls in which he held her. He said he wasn't going to buy me out of the company and he would make very sure that Jane didn't get her divorce.

'I think I said that he couldn't do that nowadays, that the laws of the land would allow Jane to escape him. That's when he reached for the pistol. I knew from my years with him that he always kept it in the driver's door of his car, hidden under a windscreen cloth, but for a moment I couldn't move: it felt as if someone had frozen my limbs. He waved the pistol in my face. He shouted at me that he wouldn't allow anything to threaten the future of Abbey Vineyards. He'd always been irrational about the business, almost as if it were a child of his, living and breathing. I believed him. I believe he was threatening that he would kill Jane or me if we damaged the firm. That was when I panicked. I grabbed at the gun and it went off.'

Beaumont had been shot very precisely

through the temple. Lambert wondered if that would have happened, in the sort of struggle she described. But that was for others to argue, months later and in the solemnity of a criminal court. Sinuous minds, well-versed in the law, would explore the plea of self-defence, perhaps the reduced charge of manslaughter, over days, maybe weeks.

That was not the concern here. Hook stepped forward and announced formally that Vanda North was being arrested for the murder of Martin Beaumont. She listened to the familiar words of arrest and the caution about prejudicing her defence if she withheld information, as if they fascinated her.

They led her to the door and the waiting police car. It was not until the door was opened for her that she stopped suddenly, as if she felt the need to explain her confession, 'I love Jane. I couldn't allow anything to happen to her, could I? We would have built a life together.'

Five minutes later, when she was sitting very upright in the back of the car with Lambert beside her, she said, as if there had been no pause, 'Maybe we still will, in a little while. Jane has a lot of life left to live, now that Martin's gone.'

# CIRCUS MAXIMUS

## The Economic Gamble Behind Hosting
the Olympics and the World Cup

ANDREW ZIMBALIST

BROOKINGS INSTITUTION PRESS
*Washington, D.C.*

The Brookings Institution is a private nonprofit organization devoted to
research, education, and publication on important issues of domestic
and foreign policy. Its principal purpose is to bring the highest quality
independent research and analysis to bear on current and
emerging policy problems. Interpretations or conclusions in Brookings
publications should be understood to be solely those of the authors.

*Library of Congress Cataloging-in-Publication data*
Zimbalist, Andrew S.
  Circus maximus : the economic gamble behind hosting the Olympics and the
World Cup / Andrew Zimbalist.
    pages   cm
  Includes bibliographical references and index.
  ISBN 978-0-8157-2651-7 (hardcover : alk. paper)
  1. Hosting of sporting events—Economic aspects. 2. Olympics—Economic
aspects. 3. Soccer—Economic aspects. I. Title.
  GV721.Z56  2015
  796.48—dc23                                                    2014038606


9 8 7 6 5 4 3 2 1


Printed on acid-free paper


Typeset in Sabon and Gotham Narrow


Composition by Cynthia Stock
Silver Spring, Maryland

# CIRCUS
## MAXIMUS

*To the memory of*
*Ellie Abend (1924–2014),*
*my loving mother-in-law*
*and intrepid copy editor*

# Contents

# Preface

When I received a call from Gerry Schoenfeld, chairman of the Shubert Organization, Broadway's oldest show producer, in 2003, I had been working in the field of sports economics for over a decade. Some of my work had explored the economic impact of sports teams on cities.[1] Independent scholarly investigation was virtually unanimous: stadiums and teams could not be expected to have a positive impact on a city's employment or output. Part of this conclusion rested on the fact that most of the money fans spent at an arena or stadium was leisure budget money that they would not spend at other entertainment venues within the city. Hence, spectator sport spending substituted for spending elsewhere in the local economy.

It seemed plausible that mega-sporting events (such as the Olympics, World Cup, or Super Bowl) would have a more positive impact. After all, a large share of the attendees came from out of the area or out of the country. They must be bringing new money, rather than recycled money, to town. Moreover, cities and countries were clamoring to host these events.

As it turns out, the substitution effect operates in a different way with mega-events, but it is still operative. Other factors as well conspire to render mega-events a dubious instrument to promote the local economy—except in special cases, with certain preconditions, and with very effective planning and implementation.

I wasn't fully aware of the lay of the mega-event land when Gerry Schoenfeld called in 2003. I did know that it was two years after the events of September 11, 2001, and that New York City had an urge to rebuild. Following the leadership of Dan Doctoroff, the city's deputy mayor for economic development under Mayor Michael Bloomberg, and with the support of the city's major construction companies and unions, a committee had already formed to bid for the right to host the 2012 Summer Olympic Games.

Schoenfeld and the Shubert Organization didn't like the Olympic plan. In part, they thought it was a waste of the city's thin financial resources and not the most rational way to use its scarce land, but in larger part they were concerned with the impact that hosting the games would have on Broadway. The keystone of the city's plan was a new Olympic stadium, to be built on land bounded by 31st and 33rd Streets and 10th and 11th Avenues. This six-square-block area houses the open train yards for the Long Island Railroad. Building an Olympic stadium on top of these yards would have first required putting a concrete slab over the yards. This six-square-block concrete slab alone would have cost an estimated $400 million (the construction of the stadium itself would have been an additional half billion dollars or more). The stadium would have had heavy use for the seventeen days of the games, and then, after some costly refitting renovations, it would have served as the home field for the NFL's New York Jets. The Jets would have played ten home games there each year (including two exhibition games). There may also have been a few concerts and perhaps a college football game, but it is not likely that the stadium would have been in use more than fifteen days a year. The slab and the stadium would have been paid for by the taxpayers.

I may not have fully understood mega-event economics at the time, but it was obvious to me that once a concrete slab covered six square blocks on the west side of mid-Manhattan overlooking the Hudson River, it would be one of the most valuable pieces of real estate in the country, if not the world. Using it for fewer than 5 percent of the days of the year made no sense whatsoever.

And it made even less sense to the Shubert Organization. The stadium would have been a few blocks away from Broadway's theaters. The Jets play most of their home games on Sunday afternoons—that's major traffic jamming the streets for Sunday matinees. A few evening contests wouldn't help either. If public funds were to be employed to spiff up mid-Manhattan entertainment options, the Shubert Organization wanted to ask, how about some money to help maintain and renovate Manhattan's most venerable entertainment, the theaters of Broadway?

Schoenfeld wanted me to do some economic analysis, some writing, and some public speaking. I gave myself a crash course in Olympic economics and decided that Dan Doctoroff was pushing an unrealistic plan. Fortunately for New York City, the International Olympic Committee (IOC) agreed. In 2005 the IOC announced its choice of London to host the 2012 Summer Games.

In the years that followed, I continued to study the economics of mega-events and was asked to consult for a few cities as they contemplated bidding and hosting. In 2012, I edited a book with the German economist and Olympic gold medalist Wolfgang Maennig, the *International Handbook on the Economics of Mega Sporting Events,* which provided a more academic, discursive, and technical treatment of the subject.

In February 2013, the United States Olympic Committee (USOC) sent out a letter to fifty U.S. cities inviting them to bid to host the 2024 Summer Olympic Games. Boston was one of the cities to receive the invitation. It was not until several months later, however, that Mitt Romney suggested to Massachusetts governor Deval Patrick that Boston bid to be the host city. Patrick took the matter to the state legislature, which in turn appropriated funds for a study to be performed by an eleven-member appointed commission.

After passing the appropriation, Massachusetts state senator and majority leader Stan Rosenberg e-mailed me to ask if I would be interested in serving on the commission. I responded affirmatively, depending on the timing and volume of the work involved. Senator Rosenberg thanked me and asked me to send him a résumé. He then sent my résumé with a cover letter to Deval Patrick, urging my appointment to the commission. Apparently, a similar interaction occurred between Victor Matheson, an economist at the College of the Holy Cross in Worcester, Massachusetts, and an expert on mega-event economics, and another state legislator. I also pointed out to Senator Rosenberg that Judith Grant Long, a well-respected expert on the effect of the Olympics and other sports mega-events on urban economies, taught at Harvard University.

As it turned out, Governor Patrick did not appoint any of us to the commission. Instead, eleven executives were appointed, all from the tourism industry and construction, the industry that had the most to gain if Boston were to host the games. After several months the commission concluded that the matter warranted further study. As of mid-July 2014, no decision had been made, although the USOC had selected Boston as a finalist among possible U.S. host cities.

With Governor Patrick's maneuver, my cynicism about our political process and what interests it serves reached an all-time high. Perhaps you can't fool all the people all the time, but many politicians certainly seemed to be trying. I decided it was time to take a cold, hard look at the economics of hosting the Olympics and World Cup that would be accessible to noneconomists. That is what I have set out to do with this book.

The book's title, *Circus Maximus,* refers to an ancient Roman chariot racing stadium and mass entertainment venue. The word "circus" today refers either to the traveling show of animals, high-wire acts, and clowns or, metaphorically, to a chaotic and busy situation. "Maximus," of course, means greatest or largest. I don't think there are better terms to describe what the Olympics and World Cup represent in 2014.

The *New York Times* editorial board member Serge Schmemann has referred to the World Cup as "the battle for global primacy in what

Americans insist upon calling soccer." As an American and an avid *New York Times* reader, I cannot make a liar out of Mr. Schmemann. Throughout this book I use the word "soccer" to denote "Association Football," to give the game its full title.[2] While "football" is the more common term used in the United Kingdom and most of the world, so as not to confuse it with American football, I demur. It is sometimes thought that the word "soccer" is an American invention for precisely this reason, but that is not the case. According to the *Oxford English Dictionary*, the first recorded use of the word "soccer" was in 1889 by an English writer (although using a variant spelling, "socca"). The word has been commonplace in England and elsewhere ever since. It is thought to be an abbreviation of "association," used originally to distinguish it from the game of "rugby football," also popular in England.[3] The Fédération Internationale de Football Association, or FIFA, is the governing body for international play in this arena.

I am indebted to many people who have assisted and supported me in researching and writing this book. First, I thank my colleagues Victor Matheson and Rob Baade. Initially our plan was to write jointly, but scheduling conflicts got in the way. We have discussed and shared a lot with each other. Second, I have learned much from the many colleagues I have worked with over the years on related projects, including Wolfgang Maennig, Roger Noll, John Siegfried, Brad Humphreys, Dennis Coates, and Stefan Szymanski. Third, several individuals were directly useful in sharing materials and their expertise and time with me: Luis Fernandes, Gavin Poynter, Paulo Esteves, Fernan Brunet, Ricardo Guerra, Don Fehr, Denis Oswald, Anita DeFrantz, Michael Leeds, Nancy Hogshead-Makar, Anne Power, Martin Church, Derek Shearer, David Goldblatt, Jules Boykoff, David Eades, Judith Grant Long, Sunil Gulati, James Easton, Phil Porter, Martin Müller, and Chris Gaffney. Finally, big gratitude and love to my family, Shelley, Alex, Ella, and Jeff and Mike (who are finishing their biopic on Pelé as I write) for supporting me throughout.

# CIRCUS
## MAXIMUS

# 1

# What's Wrong with the Olympics and the World Cup?

No city wanted to host the 1984 Olympic Games. Mexico City's games in 1968 were marred by violence and political protest. Munich's games in 1972 ended in wrenching tragedy as eleven Israeli athletes were killed by terrorists. Montreal's games in 1976 cost 9.2 times more than initially budgeted and yielded a debt that took the city thirty years to pay down.

There was no glory associated with hosting the Olympics back then, and the International Olympic Committee (IOC) was desperate to find a venue. With no competition, Los Angeles stepped forward and made a deal. The IOC would guarantee any losses suffered, and Los Angeles could basically get by with its existing sports infrastructure, part of which came from having hosted the 1932 Olympics.[1] This favorable deal, together with some clever and aggressive marketing of corporate sponsorships by Peter Ueberroth, led the L.A. Organizing Committee to realize a modest profit of $215 million.

The Los Angeles experience turned the tide. Shown the alluring path to possible profits, cities and countries now lined up for the honor of hosting the games. The competition to host the games became almost as intense as the athletic competition itself. Would-be hosts lavished more and more money on their bids; today, spending upward of $100 million on the bidding process alone is not unusual.

With each bidder trying to outdo all the others, expenditures on hosting the games rose to over $40 billion for the Beijing Summer Games in 2008 and reportedly topped $50 billion for the 2014 Sochi Winter Games. Developing economies have jumped into the bidding in recent years. They require more substantial investments owing to inadequate transportation, communications, energy, hospitality, and sporting infrastructure. Other sports mega-events have experienced similar cost escalations. The cost of hosting the FIFA World Cup, soccer's quadrennial showcase event, has risen from several hundred million in 1994, when the United States hosted the event, to $5–$6 billion in 2010 in South Africa and $15–$20 billion in Brazil in 2014. Qatar could shatter all records when it hosts the event in 2022, with some estimating the final price tag will come in at an eye-popping $200 billion.

But history might be repeating itself. Just as forces conspired to eliminate bidders in the late 1970s, by 2014 escalating costs had imposed a major financial burden on countries with meager resources and deficient public services. While promoters of the games made lofty claims about the economic benefits to be gained from hosting these sporting extravaganzas, the local populations seemed unimpressed. Not only were there no evident economic gains, there were social dislocations and resource diversions away from meeting basic needs. The games may benefit their wealthy promoters, but those at the middle and bottom of the income ladder appear to be picking up the tab— and increasingly, they don't like it.

In June 2013, before and during the Confederations Cup (a quadrennial international soccer competition that precedes the World Cup in the host country), more than a million Brazilians across the country took to the streets to protest the government's spending $15–$20 billion on new stadiums and infrastructure (much of which was never finished) to host the 2014 World Cup. Meanwhile, the Brazilian population faced woeful public transportation services, rising bus fares, deficient medical care, poor schools, and insufficient housing. Popular protests continued throughout 2013 and then reached a crescendo as the World Cup approached in June 2014. Strikes by police, teachers, and transport and airport workers erupted in many cities, and street demonstrations, though heavily repressed, accompanied the soccer competition.

Brazil is not alone in protesting government policies and priorities. People worldwide, from the United States (Occupy Wall Street) to the Middle East (the Arab Spring), Russia, Pakistan, Ukraine, Istanbul, South Africa, Chile, Bolivia, and China, have risen up to protest what they perceive to be unequal and unfair outcomes that are being aided and abetted by government policy. Globalization and the march of technology, together with market forces and a skewed distribution of market power, have conspired to widen economic inequality both among and within countries.

Of course, the members of the executive boards of FIFA and the IOC themselves belong to the economic elite. They travel first class, stay in the finest hotels, and rub elbows with the political and business leaders in the cities they visit. Sepp Blatter, the FIFA president, earns a salary in excess of $1 million on top of what seems like an unlimited expense account. Other FIFA executives earn compensation packages well into six figures.[2] Blatter had been giving the twenty-five members of the FIFA Executive Committee annual bonuses ranging from $75,000 to $200,000 a year on top of their salary of $100,000 for very part-time work. For appearances' sake, the practice of annual bonuses was ended in 2014, but FIFA's Sub-Committee on Compensation (an appointed body of Executive Committee members[3]) made up for the loss of bonuses by secretly voting to double their annual pay to $200,000, according to documents uncovered by London's *Sunday Times*. The *Times* also reported that Executive Committee members received a $700 per diem while doing FIFA work, traveled business class, and stayed in five-star hotels.[4] According to the FIFA ethics code, the twenty-seven Executive Committee members are not supposed to receive gifts that have more than symbolic value. In September 2014, however, it was revealed that in the hotel gift bags in Brazil for the 2014 World Cup there was a luxury Swiss Parmigiani watch worth $25,000. Twenty-four members of the Executive Committee, including Sepp Blatter, did not report this gift; three members, U.S. member Sunil Gulati, Australian member Moya Dodd, and Jordanian member Prince Ali bin Al Hussein, reported the violation to FIFA's Ethics Committee. Apparently, the plan was to gift two more watches, each worth over $42,000, to each Executive Committee member, until the first transgression was reported.[5] After this news became public in early September, FIFA's Ethics Committee took a stand and ordered the Executive Committee members to return their watches.[6]

The members of the IOC are unpaid, but the organization is populated by the rich, the famous, and others who seem as if they would be as comfortable in a ballroom or boardroom as on an athletic field. Royalty on the IOC include Prince Feisal bin Al Hussein of Jordan; Frederik, Crown Prince of Denmark; Princess Haya bint Al Hussein of Jordan (and sheikha of Dubai); Sheikh Tamim Bin Hamad Al Thani, emir of Qatar; Prince Nawaf Faisal Fahd Abdulaziz of Saudi Arabia;[7] Prince Ahmad Al-Fahad Al-Sabah of Kuwait; Anne, Princess Royal of Britain; and Prince Albert II and Princess Nora of Liechtenstein.[8]

Distributional concerns inevitably are more pressing in countries at earlier stages of economic development. In light of the recent trend for developing countries, in particular the BRICS (Brazil, Russia, India, China, and South Africa), to host the Olympics and World Cup—countries where resources are scarcer, the fiscal balance is more fragile, hosting costs are far greater, and the income distribution is more lopsided—the potential for explosive protests seems imminent. While hosting a sport mega-event is hardly a seminal force behind a country's inequality, there is little question that it contributes to and reinforces existing patterns of inequality. That the Olympics and World Cup are so heavily publicized and so visible only increases the likelihood that wasteful spending will catch the attention and scorn of the population.

With Olympics bidding, the typical pattern is for a country's National Olympic Committee (NOC) to call for bids from prospective host cities eleven years before the games. There ensues a competition among the interested cities to win their country's nod, which occurs nine years prior to the games. The selected cities at this stage are known as "applicants," and each pays the IOC $150,000 to be considered. The applicant cities are then whittled down to a group of usually three to five finalist or "candidate" cities. Each candidate city pays the IOC an additional $500,000 for the privilege of being considered as an Olympic host.

The bids by cities are driven by major private economic interests within the city's political economy, such as construction companies, construction unions, insurance companies, architectural firms, hotels, local media companies, investment bankers (who will float the bonds), and the lawyers who work for these groups.[9] These groups in turn hire a public relations firm and a consulting firm to generate interest and excitement around the hosting prospect and to make elaborate claims of the potential economic benefits to the city.

Except in special cases, however, the promised benefits are not forthcoming. Equally troublesome, to prepare for the games the host city often must clear land, which frequently means relocating communities and jobs; hire migrant labor; divert resources away from important social services; and borrow billions, encumbering future tax dollars. Along the way, local communities experience congestion and pollution in the name of constructing venues and infrastructure that may have little or no effective use after the games and that may charge admission prices well beyond the reach of the common person's budget.

Seven years before the games, after two years of competition among the candidate cities aimed to convince the IOC that they are the most worthy of the hosting honor, the IOC anoints a winner. A similar selection process occurs for the World Cup. With multiple bidders from around the globe and only one seller (the IOC or FIFA), it is almost unavoidable that the winning city or country will have overbid. This outcome is made even more likely because the groups pushing each city's bid are representing their own private interests, not the city's. And these groups will not have to pay the construction bills; rather, they will be the ones on the receiving end, getting the lucrative contracts. Economists believe the outcome of such a bidding process is likely to result in a "winner's curse"—an outcome in which the winner has bid above the object's true worth.

The problem for the IOC and FIFA is that rising popular protests are alerting politicians to the fact that hosting the Olympics and World Cup may not be such a good deal economically or politically. Fewer cities and countries are entering the bidding. Voters in Munich, Germany, in November 2013 and in Stockholm, Sweden, in January 2014 went to the polls and rejected their city's entering the bidding competition to host the 2022 Winter Games.[10] The new IOC president, Thomas Bach, spent much of December 2013 and January 2014 attempting to convince cities to bid for the 2024 Summer Games. At the pre–Olympic Games meeting in Sochi, Russia, in February 2014, trying to avert another downward bidding cycle similar to the late 1970s, Bach called for new approaches to the bidding process.

The chapters that follow take a closer look at all these issues. The next chapter considers the evolution of both the Olympics and the World Cup, how each came to be the Circus Maximus it is today, and the challenges each confronts. Chapter 3 discusses the short-term costs and benefits of hosting the Olympics and World Cup. Chapter 4 analyzes the long-run or legacy impacts of hosting. Chapter 5 presents the experiences of Barcelona with the 1992 Summer Games and Sochi with the 2014 Winter Games, while chapter 6 explores the experiences of Rio de Janeiro and Brazil with the 2014 World Cup and the upcoming 2016 Summer Olympics, and of London with the 2012 Summer Games. Chapter 7 offers an assessment of what works and what doesn't for host cities and countries, what problems FIFA and the IOC are facing, and what reforms they are considering or should consider.

# 2 | Setting the Stage

The modern Olympic Games began in Athens in 1896. They bear little resemblance to the ancient Greek games of more than two millennia ago.

## The Era of Amateurism

The French aristocrat, intellectual, and writer Pierre de Frédy, baron de Coubertin, studied the program of physical education at the Rugby School in England. Coubertin believed that the incorporation of physical education into the British educational system promoted the balanced development of mind and body and was a major reason for the expansion of British power during the nineteenth century. France, in contrast, was still reeling from its humiliating defeat in the Franco-Prussian War, and Coubertin saw educational reform as a key element in nation building.

Coubertin's effort at educational reform, however, found little success, and he soon turned his attentions to a new plan, also founded on some notion of the benefits of physical activity and athleticism: reviving the ancient Olympic Games of Greece.[1] Coubertin was wedded to two basic principles that he saw embodied in the ancient games: first, the competitors should be amateurs,[2] and second, the games should be a way to bring different cultures and antagonistic nations together, promoting better understanding and peace.

Historians question whether the ancient games were in fact characterized by amateurism and peace, as Coubertin imagined. While some historians hold that competitors in the Greek Olympics were always directly or indirectly paid, others maintain that the ancient games only became professionalized after 480 BCE. Whatever the reality, all historians understand that there was a class component to the notion of amateurism: only the upper class had the leisure time available to engage in sport. Coubertin's insistence on the modern games being for amateur athletes only was tantamount, in the late nineteenth century, to limiting participants to the upper class.

Coubertin's belief that the ancient games promoted peace was also suspect. The only recognizable peace ensued from an agreement among warring regions to allow athletes and religious pilgrims to pass safely through territories on their way to the games at Olympia. There appears to be no evidence that the games either ended existing hostilities or prevented new ones from arising.

## The New Olympic Movement

When the modern games began in Athens in the summer of 1896, however, it mattered not whether Coubertin had his history right or whether he was perpetrating myths. The intentions of the new Olympic Movement were enshrined in its charter, including these principles:

> Olympism is a philosophy of life, exalting and combining in a balanced whole the qualities of body, will and mind. Blending sport with culture and education. . . . The goal of Olympism is to place everywhere sport at the service of the harmonious development of man, with a view to encouraging the establishment of a peaceful society concerned with the preservation of human

dignity. . . . Any form of discrimination with regard to a country or person on grounds of race, religion, politics, gender or otherwise is incompatible with belonging to the Olympic Movement.[3]

The nondiscrimination principle was violated at the outset. No women athletes participated in the 1896 Athens Games. These first modern games were diminutive by current standards: 295 athletes from fourteen nations participated, competing in forty-three events. The Athens organizers had expected soccer teams from four countries to compete, but none showed up. The Athens games were funded jointly by private and public funds.

The next two Olympic Games were staged in Paris, in 1900, and St. Louis, in 1904, but were overshadowed by the coincident Paris Exposition in the former and the World's Fair in the latter. Nonetheless, the Paris games were notable because they marked the first time women participated, as well as the introduction of soccer competition. To be sure, the representation of women athletes was modest, but at least it was a start: Paris featured 1,066 male athletes but only eleven women. The St. Louis games were marked by the near absence of foreign participation—of the 650 athletes, 580 were from the United States.

London hosted the games in 1908, and Stockholm in 1912. The Stockholm Olympics are remembered for the legendary performance by the Native American Jim Thorpe, who won the gold medals in both the pentathlon and the decathlon competitions (and defeated the future IOC president Avery Brundage in each event).[4] After Thorpe admitted to playing a summer of professional baseball while a student at Carlisle Indian School, the IOC stripped him of his medals. Some critics raised questions about whether the IOC's action may have been tainted by racism.

Following a hiatus in 1916, when the Olympics were canceled because of World War I, the 1920 Games were held in Antwerp, Belgium. Although the Olympics were intended to be apolitical and to promote world peace, the Allied powers of World War I were not interested in having the Germans participate in the games, and Germany was unceremoniously excluded. The number of female athletes grew to 64, versus 2,527 male athletes.

## Money, Politics, and the Olympic Brand

The Belgian games exhibited a characteristic that was to become a hallmark for future hosting cities. In Antwerp, a group of wealthy sportsmen and businessmen initiated the drive to host the 1920 Games, along with a world's fair. They agreed to contribute 1 million Belgian francs, and asked for a contribution from the city of 800,000 francs. The intervention of World War I discombobulated the plans and prevented the original design from being implemented. Nonetheless, the promoters persisted, and a new plan emerged. The games were finally awarded to Antwerp in 1919, just sixteen months prior to the opening ceremony—which helps explain the unfinished stadium, the poor condition of the athletic tracks, and the inadequate accommodations.[5] The organizing committee ran commercial events for months leading up to the games to promote local businesses. In the end, the financial record showed the following: (1) the 1-million-franc private contribution had turned into a 1-million-franc loan, at 4 percent interest; (2) the public contribution from federal, provincial, and city coffers rose to 2.5 million francs; and (3) a bottom-line deficit of 626,000 francs remained at the end of the games. Meanwhile, the promoters from the local sporting and business elite benefited from new business and the modernization of the facilities of their sports club. Two Belgian historians concluded, "What is clear is that a small group of prominent citizens of large fortune had succeeded in using the Olympic Games for their own financial advantage and social prestige."[6]

The strict requirement of amateurism led to festering disagreements within the IOC. The IOC organized a special congress to debate the issue in Prague in May 1925. Was amateurism necessary? If so, could athletes' expenses be paid? Could an athlete receive "broken-time payments" to compensate for lost days of work? With some dissension, the policy going forward would be that athletes could receive expense reimbursement for up to fifteen days, but no compensation beyond that. The international soccer federation, however, broke ranks and declared it would allow its athletes to receive broken-time payments.[7]

Coubertin's intentions and exhortations to the contrary, political disputes were never far from the modern Olympics. If idealists did not acknowledge this before the 1930s, the staging of the 1936 Winter and Summer Games in Germany must have convinced even the most recalcitrant. Germany was awarded host status for the 1936 Games in May 1931, when Heinrich Bruning's centrist coalition was still in power. Hitler's rule was not to commence until January 1933, six days after the organizing committee for the games was formed.

Yet FIFA's new tournament, the World Cup, beat the IOC to the table in having its international competition hosted by a fascist government. FIFA was founded in 1904. By 1914, FIFA had been put in charge of organizing the soccer competition at the Olympics. But FIFA always regarded the Olympics as a second-rate soccer tournament because of the IOC's insistence on amateurism. FIFA had more clout than any other Olympic sport organizing body because soccer was an established and globally popular sport. In 1928, FIFA decided to have its own competition, unfettered by IOC rules. The first World Cup competition was held in Uruguay in 1930. Only thirteen countries sent teams to participate—seven from South America, four from Europe, and two from North America.[8] The rift between FIFA and the IOC grew deeper when the organizing committee for the 1932 Olympics, held in Los Angeles, opted not to include soccer, on the pretext that it was not a popular sport in the United States.[9]

The 1934 World Cup was hosted in Mussolini's Italy. Italy was selected over Sweden in 1932, primarily because of the impressive budget that Mussolini had proposed for new stadiums and infrastructure. Just as Germany saw the 1936 Olympics as a way to showcase its new government, Mussolini saw the World Cup as an opportunity to promote Italian fascism, but, unencumbered by the athletic embarrassments and eligibility battles that were to preoccupy the Germans, Mussolini's Italian team won the competition.

There was a strong lobbying effort in several countries to boycott the 1936 German Games. The primary concern was that Hitler would not allow Jews to participate on the German team. Based on nothing more than verbal assurances from the German government, Avery Brundage, a key figure on the American Olympics Committee and a future president of the IOC, persuaded the United States to participate.[10] In the end, no Jews were on the German team.[11] Brundage took his fawning one step further. So as not to irritate Hitler, Brundage seems also to have arranged for the only two Jews on the U.S. track and field team to be pulled from the relay race.[12]

The standout athlete at the games was the black American athlete Jesse Owens who, among other things, set the world record of 10.3 seconds in the 100-meter sprint, winning three gold medals and putting a dent in the claim of Aryan superiority. When the Korean Kitei Son won the marathon and Japanese swimmers took home four gold, two silver, and five bronze medals, Hitler's propaganda machine had to work overtime to claim victory.[13]

The 1936 Games were the first televised Olympics, though on a limited basis and only within Germany, and this pattern of limited transmission remained in place for a time. After the 1940 and 1944 Games were derailed by World War II, the next games took place in London in 1948 and were televised only within England. Similarly, the Melbourne Games of 1956 were broadcast only in Australia.[14] The 1960 Summer Games in Rome were the first televised live throughout Western Europe, with the broadcasts reaching a total of twenty-one countries.[15] CBS paid $660,000 for the right to fly film back to the United States for prime-time telecasts. Of this modest sum, the IOC kept only 5 percent, with 95 percent going to Italy's National Olympic Committee (NOC). The 1964 Summer Games in Tokyo were the first to be carried by satellite transmission and to be broadcast live around the world.[16]

**TABLE 2-1. Division of Television Rights Fees for Olympic Games, 1948–2010**

| Period | International Olympic Committee (%) | Organizing Committees for Olympic Games (%) |
|---|---|---|
| 1948–68 | 1–4 | 96–99 |
| 1972–80 | 10 | 90 |
| 1984–92 | 33 | 67 |
| 1996–2004 | 40 | 60 |
| 2006–2010 | 51 | 49 |

Source: Data kindly provided by Denis Oswald of the IOC Executive Committee.

For the 1968 Games, U.S. television rights jumped to $4.5 million. As the money became more substantial, conflict emerged among the IOC, the NOCs, the International Federations (IFs) of each sport, and the local organizing committees for the Olympic Games (OCOGs) over how to divide the loot.[17] A compromise was reached for the 1968 Games: the first million dollars would be divided equally among the IOC, the NOCs, and the IFs. Of the second million, one-third would go to the OCOGs and two-thirds would be split equally among the IOC, the NOCs, and the IFs; and the third million would go two-thirds to the OCOGs and one-third to the IOC, the NOCs, and the IFs.[18] The formula would be continually tweaked as the television rights fee grew and political tensions found new expression.[19] IOC money continues to be shared with the NOCs and IFs. The evolution of the division of television money between the IOC and the OCOGs is depicted in table 2-1.

The percentages given in table 2-1 functioned more as guidelines than as rules. As IOC television policy was being devised in the 1970s and 1980s, there were continual disputes between the OCOGs and the IOC, as well as among the IOC, the NOCs, and the IFs, over the distribution of revenues. One of the most contentious items was how to distinguish between the cash payments made by a network and the money the network would spend on "technical services" (for example, cameras, studios, technicians, telecommunications equipment, and so on). For instance, for the 1984 Summer Olympics in Los Angeles, ABC committed to $225 million for U.S. television rights. Of that sum, $100 million was paid in cash and the remaining $125 million was attributed to technical services. After much dickering and several international trips, the L.A. Organizing Committee was obligated to share one-third of the cash payment only, or $33 million, as opposed to one-third of the entire $225 million.[20] Disagreements also emerged over the split of television broadcasting rights payments from other continents (which were much lower, mostly owing to the presence of state television monopolies or negotiating cartels), and in those cases the IOC garnered closer to 25 percent.[21]

The 1968 Summer Games in Mexico City—the first Olympics to be held in a developing country—also introduced a new type of Olympian politics. There was the quadrennial squabble about whether or not apartheid South Africa should be allowed to participate. IOC president Avery Brundage (1952–72) stood again on the less moralistic side and espoused inviting the South African team. The IOC membership, however, voted not to invite the South Africans. Shortly after the vote, the UN Security Council condemned the white supremacist government of newly independent Rhodesia, and Mexico, ignoring instructions from Brundage, refused to grant entrance visas to the Rhodesian team.

Meanwhile, Mexican students were protesting the domestic policies of the hegemonic PRI (Partido Revolucionario Institucional) government.[22] The students saw an opportunity to attract world attention to their cause and established a theme that was to be repeated elsewhere, most recently in Brazil. When countries beset with social problems host the Olympics or World Cup, protesters seek to capitalize on the worldwide attention focused on their country.

The PRI government had other ideas. A few weeks before the games were to begin, the Mexican army was summoned to squash the student movement. According to some reports, more than 200 demonstrators were killed.

But other trouble was brewing. The IOC's waffling position on South Africa and Rhodesia and the assassination of Martin Luther King on April 4, 1968, almost led U.S. black athletes to boycott the Mexico City games. When black U.S. athlete Tommie Smith won the 200-meter race in a world-record time of 19.83 seconds and his teammate John Carlos finished third, they wore a black glove on their right hand on the medals podium and raised their fists in a Black Power salute during the playing of the U.S. national anthem. Smith and Carlos were summarily sent home.[23]

The 1972 Summer Games in Munich are infamous for a different political reason. Just after 4 a.m. on September 5, a group of Palestinian terrorists scaled the fence at the Olympic Village and entered the quarters of the Israeli squad.[24] The terrorists held the Israelis captive and demanded the release of 234 Palestinians detained in Israeli prisons. When the assault and negotiations ended, eleven Israelis lay dead, along with five terrorists and one German policeman. The Munich games, like those in Mexico City, are a vivid illustration of how the image of a host city can be tarnished rather than burnished. The brand of the Olympics also began to suffer.

IOC optics worsened once more in November 1972. At its Amsterdam meeting in 1970, the IOC awarded Denver the right to host the 1976 Winter Olympics. However, following a grassroots campaign that focused on escalating costs and environmental degradation, 60 percent of the voters in a public referendum objected to the use of public funds to finance the 1976 games. Denver had to withdraw as host city.

The Olympic brand took another hit with the 1976 Summer Games in Montreal. Several African nations boycotted the games over the IOC's refusal to ban New Zealand, whose rugby team had been touring in South Africa, and Canada's government, having recognized the People's Republic of China in 1970, refused to grant entrance visas to members of the Taiwanese team.

Montreal, with a bid estimate of C$120 million, had been awarded the games in May 1970 over rival bids from Moscow and Los Angeles. Not atypically, with poor management, industrial disputes, and problematic stadium and airport design, construction fell considerably behind schedule, and the provincial government of Quebec took over the Olympics works project.[25] Notwithstanding the notorious boast of Montreal's mayor, Jean Drapeau, that "the Olympics can no more have a deficit than a man can have a baby," the final tab exceeded C$1.6 billion, creating a debt that Montreal did not pay off for thirty years.[26]

The Montreal games were notable for one other feature—the rising dominance of East Germany's swimmers and track and field athletes. East Germany's Kornelia Ender set Olympic records in the 100-meter and 200-meter freestyle swimming events and the 100-meter butterfly, and then earned a fourth gold medal in the medley.[27] In track and field, East German women won nine events and finished first, second, and third in the pentathlon. Few observers were persuaded by East German denials about the use of anabolic steroids, and the IOC, which set up a drug commission in 1966, began to ban certain drugs in 1972, aggressively ramping up its enforcement against artificial performance enhancers. Under an IOC initiative and with IOC funding, the World Anti-Doping Agency (WADA) was eventually established in 1999.

In its bid to host the 1980 Summer Games, the Soviet Union showed some capitalist marketing flair. Beginning in 1970, Moscow set out to court the IOC. In 1973, thirty-two IOC members were invited to Moscow to be wined and dined. A year later all eighty members were VIP guests in Moscow, and in October 1974 the IOC anointed Moscow as the 1980 host. Although the ongoing cold war raised suspicions about the prospects for the Moscow games, all was progressing relatively smoothly until the Soviet Union invaded Afghanistan in December 1979. U.S. president Jimmy Carter issued an ultimatum three weeks later: if the Soviet Union did not withdraw from Afghanistan, the United States would boycott the Moscow Olympics. The Soviet Union stayed in Afghanistan for ten years, and first the U.S. Congress and then, threatened with the loss of government financial support, the USOC supported Carter's call for a boycott.[28] Carter then leaned on Prime Minister Margaret Thatcher to have England join the boycott.

Thatcher agreed and prevailed on the House of Commons to support the plan, which it did. The British NOC, however, in keeping with its tradition of political independence, voted 18-5 to send its athletes to Moscow. Over the ensuing months, the question of skipping the Moscow games was entertained by one country after another: West Germany chose to boycott, the rest of Europe opted to participate; Japan and China joined the boycott, and so it went. In the end, the athletes of sixty-two nations stayed home and those of eighty-one nations participated.

Following the political debacle in Mexico City, the horrific terrorist acts in Munich, the financial catastrophe in Montreal, and the extensive boycott of Moscow,[29] the Olympic brand was markedly diminished. The only candidate city to host the 1984 Summer Games was Los Angeles, and the L.A. bid did not come from the city but from a private group. IOC president Killanin at first insisted that, in accordance with the Olympic Charter, the bid come from the city and the city assume full financial responsibility. L.A. mayor Thomas Bradley responded that the city was not interested. Moreover, the L.A. city charter had recently been amended to prohibit public funding of the Olympic Games.[30] The executive board of the IOC relented and waived Rule 4, leaving Los Angeles without financial responsibility in the event of any operating losses.

It is noteworthy that despite the L.A. charter amendment proscribing the use of public funds, the city of Los Angeles agreed to collect a 0.5 percent hotel tax when the games were first awarded, and also to levy a municipal tax on tickets to Olympic competitions. The collected funds of approximately $19.3 million would go to help fund the games and their security. Of that sum, $15 million was budgeted for the Los Angeles Police Department, to be used as part of the games' security budget.[31] The notion that levying a tax on hotels or car rentals produces a free good for the local population has been promulgated by many cities when seeking to fund sports facilities. It makes little sense. The higher "tourist tax" will either discourage business travelers and leisure tourists by the higher prices or it won't.[32] To the extent it reduces tourism, it lowers demand and hurts the local economy. To the extent that it doesn't discourage travel (because tourists are not sensitive to a small increase in the price of visiting the city), then the tax could be levied even if the city did not host the Olympics, and then used to improve public services or to fund tax reductions. In either case, the local residents are paying.

In any event, the stop-loss precaution in L.A.'s agreement with the IOC proved to be unnecessary. Four ingredients made the L.A. games a financial success: one, television rights grew by almost $200 million above the fees paid for the Moscow games (and L.A.'s share grew accordingly); two, Peter Ueberroth, head of the L.A. Organizing Committee, followed an energetic and innovative marketing strategy, creating exclusive product categories[33] and raising another $130 million in corporate sponsorships; three, most of the athletic, transportation, and communications infrastructure was already in place; and four, the few new, smaller facilities that were built for the games were privately funded. In the end, it mattered little that the Soviet Union and most of its allies, along with the steroid-pumped athletes from the GDR, boycotted the games.

## The Rise of Commercialization and the End of Amateurism

The L.A. games marked a watershed for the Olympic Games. After sixteen years of a weakening reputation, the financial success of the L.A. games (which produced a $215 million operating surplus[34]) turned the IOC's fortunes around. That the L.A. games coincided with an explosion in television rights, a new corporate sponsorship strategy, and IOC president Juan Antonio Samaranch's move to professionalize the Olympics only made the uptick more pronounced. Despite all the positives that the L.A. games had going for them, Ueberroth still thinks that the surplus could have been a deficit had it not been for a run of good fortune: "We were lucky: Nothing happened—no massive security problems, no labor strikes, no transportation breakdowns, and no natural catastrophes."[35]

**TABLE 2-2.** Television Rights Fees for Olympic Games, 1960–2012

| Olympic Games | Broadcast revenue (millions of USD) | Olympic Games | Broadcast revenue (millions of USD) |
|---|---|---|---|
| *Summer Games* | | *Winter Games* | |
| 1960 Rome | 1.2 | 1960 Squaw Valley | 0.05 |
| 1964 Tokyo | 1.6 | 1964 Innsbruck | 0.94 |
| 1968 Mexico City | 9.8 | 1968 Grenoble | 2.6 |
| 1972 Munich | 17.8 | 1972 Sapporo | 8.5 |
| 1976 Montreal | 34.9 | 1976 Innsbruck | 11.6 |
| 1980 Moscow | 88.0 | 1980 Lake Placid | 20.7 |
| 1984 Los Angeles | 286.9 | 1984 Sarajevo | 102.7 |
| 1988 Seoul | 402.6 | 1988 Calgary | 324.9 |
| 1992 Barcelona | 636.1 | 1992 Albertville | 291.9 |
| 1996 Atlanta | 898.3 | 1994 Lillehammer | 352.9 |
| 2000 Sydney | 1,330.0 | 1998 Nagano | 513.5 |
| 2004 Athens | 1,490.0 | 2002 Salt Lake City | 738.0 |
| 2008 Beijing | 1,740.0 | 2006 Turin | 831.0 |
| 2012 London | 2,600.0 | 2010 Vancouver | 1,280.0 |

Source: IOC, *Olympic Marketing File*, 2014, p. 26. The figures apply to the total worldwide network commitment of rights fees, both the cash and the technical service components. In recent years the technical service component has been largely defrayed by the host city and the equipment has been paid for by the network and not included in the rights fee payments. The figures also do not distinguish the timing of the payments, parts of which can vary by months or by years.

Table 2-2 depicts the remarkable escalation in television rights fees. The largest percentage increase occurred between the Moscow and the Los Angeles games (and their Winter games counterparts, in Lake Placid and Sarajevo).[36] There was also a sizable jump in the number of countries receiving television coverage of the Olympics: from 111 countries for the Moscow games and 40 for Lake Placid in 1980 to 156 for Los Angeles and 100 for Sarajevo in 1984. In both 2010 and 2012, 220 nations received television distribution of the games.

The other substantial transformation that occurred at the time was the jettisoning of amateurism. Unlike his predecessors, the new IOC president, Juan Antonio Samaranch (1980–2001), sought to realize the Olympics' full commercial potential.[37] If that required allowing professional athletes to participate in the games, then so be it. Samaranch believed that the games should showcase the world's best and most famous athletes. Of course, the games' television partners saw matters exactly the same way, and this convergence of views helps explain the inflation of television rights fees with the L.A. games. The full sponsorship by the state of Olympic athletes in the Communist countries was another motivating force behind professionalization.

In 1984 the IOC voted to allow the IFs to set the eligibility rules for their sport, within some limits. In 1987 the IOC voted to permit professional tennis players to participate in the games, and in 1989 the IOC extended the welcome to all professional athletes. Finally, in 1991 the IOC lifted all restrictions on professionalism, a decision that was heralded by the U.S. Dream Team's competing in the 1992 Barcelona Games.[38] The Dream Team, which included Michael Jordan, Magic Johnson, Larry Bird, David Robinson, and Patrick Ewing, to no one's surprise, took the gold medal in basketball.

A final step toward commercialization was taken in 1992, when the IOC decided not to have the Winter and Summer Olympics in the same year. This way the take from business advertising expenditures could be maximized by not having to stretch corporate promotional budgets to cover two large competitions in the same year.[39] Henceforth the games would alternate every two years, commencing with the Winter Games in Lillehammer in 1994.

The Olympics were ascendant again, and aspiring host cities were springing up around the globe. The number of applicants went from one in the case of Los Angeles (to which the games were awarded in May 1978) and two in the case of Seoul (awarded in September 1981) to six in the case of Barcelona (awarded in October 1986), six in Atlanta (awarded in September 1990), eight in Sydney (awarded in September 1993), and eleven in Athens (awarded in September 1997).[40]

Thus, everything was turning up roses for the IOC—perhaps too many roses. All the media and corporate money and all the competition among bidding cities led to temptation. And IOC president Juan

Antonio Samaranch enjoyed every bit of what high demand had to offer. Samaranch, the son of a wealthy factory owner from Barcelona and longtime Francoist, set a new tone for the IOC when he began his reign in 1980. He insisted on being referred to as "His Excellency" and being treated like a head of state. Before Samaranch became president, IOC members had to pay their own way to cities bidding for the games. Within a few years they were getting not one but two first-class tickets, plus all expenses and lavish entertainment. Samaranch himself always insisted on limo service and the best suite in the fanciest hotel in any city. In Lausanne he had the IOC rent for his use a massive penthouse suite at the Palace Hotel for $500,000 a year. IOC members followed Samaranch's lead, and payoffs grew by leaps and bounds.[41]

Although isolated innuendos concerning payoffs and abuse of the IOC bidding process had reached the media before, the flood began on November 24, 1998.[42] The Salt Lake City television station KTVX reported that a 1996 letter in its possession revealed that the Salt Lake City bid committee had offered a college scholarship to the daughter of the IOC member from Cameroon. At the time, IOC regulations permitted members to receive gifts from bid committees, but only up to $150 in value. Subsequent testimony and written evidence showed that this limit was surpassed in spades. Relatives of IOC members had received approximately $400,000 in financial aid or scholarships in a program that began after 1991, when Salt Lake City lost its bid to host the 1998 Winter Olympics. Further evidence revealed that IOC members and their relatives had benefited from lavish gifts, hospitality, escort services, medical treatment, employment, shopping trips, holiday travel, and opulent accommodations.[43]

As the news about the Salt Lake City scandal was breaking, reporters approached the Nagano (1998 Winter Games host) bid committee to see its records. The journalists were told that the Nagano committee had ordered its ninety-volume accounting books to be burned.[44] A senior official with the bid committee, Sumikazu Yamaguchi, explained that the books were destroyed because they contained "secret information." There were many stories circulating about the unsavory, behind-the-scenes maneuvering during the Nagano bid. One concerns Samaranch's close adviser Artur Takacs's son, who was a lobbyist for Nagano's organizing committee and was being paid a salary of $363,000, plus a bonus if Nagano won the games. A consortium of Japanese businessmen promised $20 million for the construction of an Olympic museum in Lausanne if Nagano got the games. Nagano hosted the games. Salt Lake City lost out, but learned a lesson.

Joining the chorus, on January 22, 1999, John Coates, president of the Australian Olympic Committee and the point man in Sydney's bid to host the 2000 Summer Olympics, released various documents to the press. Among other things, these revealed that the day before Sydney's election, the Australian bid committee had offered $50,000 scholarships to the children of the Ugandan and Kenyan members of the IOC. Sydney won its selection by two votes.[45]

### Sharing the Spoils

As drama over payoffs was erupting between the IOC and the Olympic bid committees, a financial drama of a different sort was unfolding within the Olympic Movement. The rapidly growing television rights fees were not divided equally among the NOCs. Since broadcast rights in the United States went for much higher sums than those in other countries, the U.S. Olympic Committee (USOC) felt that it was entitled to a larger share of Olympic revenues than other NOCs. And for a while, the IOC seemed to agree.[46] During 1986–98, U.S. rights fees accounted for 83 percent of total Olympics television revenues. The U.S. share fell to 60 percent during 2001–04 and to 53 percent during 2005–08. Meanwhile, the United States received 12.75 percent of the IOC's total television distributions to the NOCs (and 20 percent of the IOC's sponsorship distributions) during 1985–2012.[47]

The NOCs felt this unequal distribution both violated the Olympic spirit and was inappropriate in light of the enormous resources available to support athletics in the United States. The NOCs also made an economic argument, to wit, much of the revenue earned by U.S.

sponsors and television advertisers, such as Coca-Cola, is generated outside the United States.

When the IOC voted in 2005 to drop baseball and softball as Olympic sports and to select London over New York City to host the 2012 Summer Games, many observers interpreted this decision as a reaction to the financially privileged position of the USOC in the Olympic Movement. The same was said when the IOC selected Rio de Janeiro over Chicago to host the 2016 Olympics. In 2012, the USOC and the IOC negotiated a new agreement whereby, beginning in 2020, the USOC share of revenues from television broadcasting rights would fall to 7 percent and its share of global sponsorship revenues would fall to 10 percent, with the USOC guaranteed a minimum of $410 million per quadrennium (adjusted for inflation).[48]

## Enter the BRICS

With the exceptions of Mexico City in 1968 and Moscow in 1980, the Winter and Summer Olympics were always held in Western Europe, North America, Japan, or South Korea until the Beijing games in 2008. "BRICS" is an acronym that refers to five large and erstwhile rapidly growing countries, Brazil, Russia, India, China, and South Africa. Since 2008, each of the BRICS countries has hosted either the Olympics or the World Cup or the Commonwealth Games. Each has made it clear that it perceives these mega-events as a sort of coming-out party signaling that it is now a modernized economy, ready to make its presence felt in world trade and politics.

One of the problems facing developing economies when they host mega-events is that their existing transportation, communications, lodging, entertainment, and sports infrastructure is lacking. Thus, the amount of investment necessary to properly host a mega-event is extraordinary. Beijing spent more than $40 billion in preparation for the 2008 Summer Games. Brazil reportedly spent between $15 billion and $20 billion to host the 2014 World Cup. Sochi spent more than $50 billion to host the 2014 Winter Games.[49] And Rio's cost to host

**TABLE 2-3. Decline in Number of Cities Bidding for Olympic Games**

| Bid year | Year of games | Host city | No. of applicant cities | No. of candidate cities |
|---|---|---|---|---|
| *Summer Games* | | | | |
| 1997 | 2004 | Athens | 12 | 5 |
| 2001 | 2008 | Beijing | 10 | 5 |
| 2005 | 2012 | London | 9 | 5 |
| 2009 | 2016 | Rio de Janeiro | 7 | 4 |
| 2013 | 2020 | Tokyo | 5 | 3 |
| *Winter Games* | | | | |
| 1995 | 2002 | Salt Lake City | 9 | 4 |
| 1999 | 2006 | Turin | 6 | 2 |
| 2003 | 2010 | Vancouver | 7 | 3 |
| 2007 | 2014 | Sochi | 7 | 3 |
| 2011 | 2018 | Pyeongchang | 3 | 3 |

Source: Arne Feddersen and Wolfgang Maennig, "Determinants of Successful Bidding for Mega Events: The Case of the Olympic Winter Games," in *International Handbook of the Economics of Mega Sporting Events,* ed. Wolfgang Maennig and Andrew S. Zimbalist (Cheltenham, U.K.: Edward Elgar, 2012), p. 72.

the 2016 Summer Olympics is expected to approach $20 billion.[50] Compounding these escalating infrastructure expenses, all hosts of mega-events face astronomical security costs, often rising to $1 billion or $2 billion.

At these investment levels, a positive economic return to hosting in the short run is improbable. Any justification for the investment would have to lie in a transformative long-run impact—or "legacy," in the PR vernacular of the IOC. The situation for the BRICS is, of course, only exacerbated where the planners do not have to be responsive to the populace, where the planning is incomplete or short-sighted, and where payoffs and corruption are rampant.

The massive costs of these recent events have given the IOC's new president, Thomas Bach, pause. Several applicants have announced that they are dropping out of the bidding for the 2022 Winter Games and the 2024 Summer Games. More generally, as shown in table 2-3, there has been a steady decline in the number of applicant and candidate cities over the last five bidding cycles.

Bach does not want the Olympics to price itself out of the hosting market and experience a return to the conditions of the early 1980s. Accordingly, Bach spent the first months of his tenure (which began on September 10, 2013) globetrotting to instigate more interest in bidding. At the IOC meeting prior to the Sochi games, Bach signaled his interest in reforming the bidding process. I discuss Bach's initial proposals, as well as some of my own, in the final chapter.

## Financing the Olympics

Table 2-4 shows the sources of revenue generated from the Winter and Summer Olympics during the last two quadrennia. Television revenue is the largest source, accounting for 47.8 percent of revenue during the Vancouver games and the London games. Of the $3.85 billion from television rights, 56 percent came from U.S. rights fees.

It is worth noting that the total revenue from both the Vancouver games and the London games was just over $8 billion. Of this, $5.2 billion came from London and $2.8 billion from Vancouver. The Beijing Summer Games generated approximately $3.6 billion. That one-time revenue of $3.6 billion is less than 10 percent of China's $40 billion-plus in investments and operating expenses. Making the contrast even more striking, the IOC does not share a large portion of the generated revenue with the OCOG. For instance, less than 50 percent of the TV revenue is shared with the OCOG.[51]

The details of the post-2010 television distribution schedule have not been made public. The new policy is to share a fixed amount, not a percentage, with the host city. As television rights have skyrocketed, the IOC has kept payments to the host basically flat. Today the host's share of the total revenue from the games is at its lowest level ever. IOC president Thomas Bach announced in July 2014 that the IOC "will contribute $1.5 billion to the [2016] games, which will leave a huge sporting, economic and social legacy."[52] Yet the 2016 Rio Games

**TABLE 2-4. Sources of Olympic Revenue**

| Source | 2005–08 (millions of current USD) | 2009–12 (millions of current USD) |
| --- | --- | --- |
| Television | 2,570 | 3,850 |
| International sponsorships | 866 | 950 |
| Domestic sponsorships | 1,555 | 1,838 |
| Ticket sales | 274 | 1,238 |
| Licensing | 185 | 170 |
| **Total** | **5,450** | **8,046** |

Source: IOC, *Olympic Marketing Fact File*, 2014, p. 6.

will generate well in excess of $5 billion in revenue. Bach has thus given a magnanimous spin to an increasingly parsimonious policy.

Of course, the local economy of the host city will also benefit from lodging and food expenditures by the visitors to the games, but the sum of money involved here is almost certainly less than $500 million; further, most or all of this money is not a net addition to the local economy because sports tourists replace regular tourists and a good portion of this spending leaks out of the local economy, a topic I take up in the next chapter.

## FIFA and the World Cup

FIFA—the Fédération Internationale de Football Association—was established in 1904, and the World Cup competition started in 1930. FIFA's mission has always been to promote soccer. Although FIFA's rhetoric has connected the growth of soccer worldwide to the promotion of a better world, it has never embraced political goals. The World Cup has not been a target of political movements and has never been boycotted by countries for political reasons.[53] Part of the explanation for the reduced political turmoil around the World Cup compared with the Olympics may lie in the fact that fewer countries participate (thirty-two today) than in the Olympics (204 in the Summer Games, eighty-eight in the Winter Games).

Nevertheless, by bringing countries together and having them confine their battles to the soccer pitch, the implicit promise is that tournaments like the World Cup can only lead to a more harmonious political environment. For those who had hoped that the World Cup would promote world peace, the events in Honduras and El Salvador in the summer of 1969 leading up to the finals in Mexico came as a bitter disappointment.

To set the context, El Salvador at the time had a population density eight times that of Honduras, and increasing numbers of emigrants from El Salvador were living in Honduras. The Honduran economy was struggling, and unemployment was high. Many Hondurans believed that the 300,000-odd Salvadoran immigrants were taking their jobs.

A three-game playoff between the two countries began in Tegucigalpa, Honduras, with the Honduran team prevailing 1-0 on a last-minute goal. The second game was played in San Salvador, El Salvador. The night before the game, the hotel where the Honduran team was staying was set on fire. The team was transferred to a new hotel, only to be greeted by all-night serenaders beneath their windows. It is little wonder that the Salvador team took the second game, but Hondurans took out their frustrations on some of the Salvadoran immigrants living in Tegucigalpa.

The rubber match was played in Mexico City. The Salvadoran team went ahead in the game's last moments to win. A violent riot ensued on the streets of Mexico City, and military skirmishes broke out on the El Salvador–Honduran border. Soon Salvadoran troops penetrated into Honduras, and four days of heavy fighting followed. The Organization of American States persuaded each side to sign a cease-fire agreement, but not before 2,000 to 3,000 people had been killed and more than twice as many wounded. Over 100,000 Salvadorans were expelled from Honduras, the border was shut, and

**TABLE 2-5. World Cup Attendance since 1930**

| Year | Host country | No. of teams | Total attendance | No. of matches | Average attendance |
|------|--------------|--------------|------------------|----------------|--------------------|
| 1930 | Uruguay | 13 | 590,549 | 18 | 32,808 |
| 1934 | Italy | 16 | 363,000 | 17 | 21,353 |
| 1938 | France | 16 | 375,700 | 18 | 20,872 |
| 1950 | Brazil | 16 | 1,045,246 | 22 | 47,511 |
| 1954 | Switzerland | 16 | 768,607 | 26 | 29,562 |
| 1958 | Sweden | 16 | 819,810 | 35 | 23,423 |
| 1962 | Chile | 16 | 893,172 | 32 | 27,912 |
| 1966 | England | 16 | 1,563,135 | 32 | 48,848 |
| 1970 | Mexico | 16 | 1,603,975 | 32 | 50,124 |
| 1974 | West Germany | 16 | 1,865,753 | 38 | 49,099 |
| 1978 | Argentina | 16 | 1,545,791 | 38 | 40,679 |
| 1982 | Spain | 24 | 2,109,723 | 52 | 40,572 |
| 1986 | Mexico | 24 | 2,394,031 | 52 | 46,039 |
| 1990 | Italy | 24 | 2,516,215 | 52 | 48,389 |
| 1994 | United States | 24 | 3,587,538 | 52 | 68,991 |
| 1998 | France | 32 | 2,785,100 | 64 | 43,517 |
| 2002 | South Korea/Japan | 32 | 2,705,197 | 64 | 42,269 |
| 2006 | Germany | 32 | 3,359,439 | 64 | 52,491 |
| 2010 | South Africa | 32 | 3,178,856 | 64 | 49,670 |

hostilities lingered on. Unfortunately, soccer contests spilling over into violence on the streets have not been a rare occurrence.[54]

As shown in table 2-5, participation in and the popularity of the World Cup have grown gradually over the years. Today, FIFA has a larger membership of nations than the IOC and considerably outdraws the Olympics in international television ratings.

## FIFA's Internal Struggles

While FIFA has not reflected the drama of world politics to the same degree as the Olympic Games have, the organization has been filled with internal leadership struggles and has seen more than its share of corruption scandals.[55] On multiple occasions there have been allegations of payoffs to individuals on the twenty-five-member Executive Committee prior to a hosting decision. Sometimes the charges have gone as high as the president or general secretary, and sometimes member nations have been sanctioned. Most of the allegations have not been proved, but circumstances suggest there is ample room for suspicion.

One internal struggle within FIFA has concerned equity among its six continental subdivisions with regard to hosting the quadrennial World Cup finals. The basic pattern had been to alternate host nations between Europe and the Americas. This pattern was broken in 2002 with the World Cup's first Asian finals, and again in May 2004, when the rights to host the 2010 finals went to the first African host. The new policy was to rotate the hosting rights among the six continents represented in FIFA. It was South America's turn to host the 2014 finals, but when the World Cup was awarded in October 2007, there was only one bidder from the continent, Brazil.

Without competition among potential hosts, FIFA would lose its leverage. So FIFA changed its policy of continental rotation. Henceforth the new policy held that countries that were members of the same continental confederation as either of the last two World Cup hosts would be ineligible. This way, rather than identifying a single continent that could bid to host the tournament, countries from four continental confederations would be eligible to bid.

The new policy seems to have engendered a desirable level of competition from FIFA's perspective. Eleven bids to host the 2018 finals were submitted to the FIFA Executive Committee in March 2009. After a couple of withdrawals and a deal that only European countries would compete for the 2018 tournament, the number of bidders was whittled down to four: Belgium–the Netherlands, Spain–Portugal, England, and Russia. Many considered England to be the favorite. As the tournament's birthplace, not having hosted the finals since 1966, boasting a superb infrastructure with modern stadiums, and the bid committee having spent more than $33 million in preparing and publicizing its plan, England seemed like the logical choice. Yet Vladimir Putin was able not only to push Russia's bid within his country, he was somehow able to successfully promote it with FIFA's Executive Committee.

On December 2, 2010, Sepp Blatter, FIFA's long-standing president, announced both that Russia would be the 2018 host and that Qatar would be the 2022 host. The latter selection also raised some eyebrows. Qatar was competing against Australia, Japan, South Korea, and the United States. Not only were the 1994 U.S. games the most heavily attended in World Cup history, the United States had the best infrastructure and was in the process of developing soccer as a leading professional sport. Further development of U.S. soccer would have been a great boost to the game internationally and to FIFA. Qatar, a nation the size of the Falkland Islands and lacking a football history or an enticing trajectory, and without the proper infrastructure or a suitable climate, was awarded the games. Worse still, analysts projected a high-level security concern in Qatar.

Some were left scratching their heads over the selection of Qatar; others were left cursing. According to a news report in London's *Sunday Times* in early June 2014, the Qatari vice president of FIFA, Mohamed bin Hammam, "used secret slush funds to make dozens of payments" totaling more than $5 million to senior officials "to create a groundswell of support for Qatar's plan to take world football by storm." The *Sunday Times* based its allegations on a cache of millions of e-mails and other documents. FIFA at first refused to comment. Then, following a subsequent report that a gambling syndicate had paid off field referees to fix games during the South African World Cup in 2010, FIFA president Sepp Blatter quixotically delivered "a tirade" in which he called the British newspaper racist.[56]

Meanwhile, politics within FIFA continue to fester, with the seventy-eight-year-old Blatter declaring his candidacy to remain for another term as president and Michel Platini, the president of the European Soccer Federation (UEFA), refusing to support him. In an attempt to round up votes for his candidacy, at the FIFA meeting in Brazil before the 2014 opening match Blatter opportunistically announced that he was tripling FIFA's annual distribution to its member countries' soccer federations. Subsequent to that came the decision to double the salaries of Executive Committee members.

## Financing the World Cup

FIFA has altered its approach to sharing revenue with the host country over the years. Until 2010, FIFA and the host country had split broadcast, sponsorship, licensing, and ticketing revenues according to varying formulas. In 2002, when there were two cohosts, Japan and South Korea, FIFA made an additional lump sum payment to each country to compensate them for the fact that each bore practically full administrative costs but received only half the revenue. In both South Africa (2010) and Brazil (2014), a new system was introduced. The host country now produces an operating budget, which is subject to FIFA's approval, and then FIFA covers virtually all of the operating expenses. FIFA also retains all of the revenue. The stated purpose of the new system is to ensure that the host country does not experience an operating deficit. FIFA also provided a legacy fund of $42 million to South Africa and intends to provide a similar amount to Brazil. The catch, of course, is that all infrastructure spending on transportation, communications, stadiums, and so forth is the responsibility of the host country. Such spending is several times greater than the operating costs of the games.

For the World Cup four-year cycle ending in 2010 with the South Africa tournament, FIFA took in $4.2 billion in revenue. FIFA's expenses over the same time period were $3.57 billion, leaving a surplus of $631 million. At the end of 2010, FIFA had an accumulated surplus of $1.3 billion.

In addition to appropriate infrastructure, tax preferences, and various hospitality services, FIFA requires the host country to have eight modern stadiums, each with a minimum capacity of 40,000, to include one stadium for the opening match with at least 60,000 seats and another for the finals of 80,000 capacity.[57] Without the proper stadium infrastructure, South Africa was obligated to build eight new or renovated stadiums, but ended up building ten and spending $5–$6 billion to host the World Cup finals. In 2002, South Korea reportedly spent $2.5 billion and Japan $5 billion. In contrast, with adequate facilities already in place, Germany (2006), the United States (1994), and France (1998) each spent under $1 billion.[58] As we shall see, the same countries that have to invest substantial sums in modern, new stadiums are also likely to be the ones that find little economically viable use for these facilities after the World Cup is over. In both the short and the long run, hosting a mega-sports event is likely to prove a present and future burden rather than a benefit to the host country's economy.

# 3 | The Short-Run Economic Impact

The claims are impressive. World Cup and Olympic Games organizers and their hired consultants would have us believe that hosting those events is one of the best tools of economic development since the steam engine. According to InterVISTAS Consulting, the 2010 Vancouver Games lifted output by $10.7 billion and created 244,000 jobs. The Dentsu Institute for Human Studies estimated that the part of the 2002 World Cup held in Japan raised that country's output by $24.8 billion. A 2010 study by the consultancy Grant Thornton projected that the World Cup that year in South Africa would attract 483,000 overseas visitors and generate $12 billion in output, and another Grant Thornton report estimated that the London Olympics in 2012 increased output by at least $17 billion and created 31,000 new jobs.

## Different Assumptions, Different Results

### Making Predictions—Ex Ante Studies

The studies cited above are promotional in nature and share a common method of estimating costs and outcomes.[1] Rather than looking at the economic results of the event and comparing them to preexisting trends, these studies made assumptions, or predictions, about the number of visitors and the amount of spending connected to the games—an approach known as the ex ante method—and then ran them through an input-output model of the country's economy.[2] (In other words, nothing specific to the event has yet happened that can be measured.) The input-output model describes the purported relationships among sectors of the economy in such a way that when one sector expands, it has a predetermined impact on a connected sector, which in turn has a predetermined impact on a third sector, and so on. For instance, let us say a tourist buys a $100 meal at a local restaurant. To produce that meal, the restaurant must buy some local vegetables, fish, and bread, as well as some tables, chairs, and plates, and so on. So the purchase of the meal helps not only the restaurant business but also businesses in other sectors of the economy. The owners and workers at these businesses earn additional income, a portion of which they spend on the services and products of still other businesses.

The purpose of the input-output model in these studies is to generate a multiplier. The multiplier is supposed to tell us when a visitor buys a $100 meal at a restaurant and, as the $100 works its way through the rest of the economy, how much new output has been created. Depending on the model, the multipliers employed in these promotional reports tend to be in the range of 1.7 to 3.5. Thus, $100 of spending to buy a meal would increase output by between $170 and $350.

There are lots of issues with this methodology. The first set of issues is that the input-output models generally are based on intersectoral relationships that evolve over a period of years, involve fixed coefficients, assume constant returns to scale, and are highly aggregated. For instance, the fact that restaurants need tables does not mean that if, during a mega-sporting event, a restaurant experiences a 10 percent increase in its sales revenue, it will buy 10 percent more tables. It could also mean that the restaurant makes fuller use of its existing capacity, or that it has the same number of customers but has raised its prices 10 percent. Further, if it raises its prices 10 percent, then the relationship (coefficient), measured in dollars (or the local currency), between sectors of the economy will change (decrease). So, because the input-output model (1) is based on longer-term patterns of trade and (2) assumes fixed coefficients, it will misrepresent what is happening in the local economy.

Another problem is that input-output models operate at highly aggregated levels, such as textiles, sports, and food, rather than at the level of individual products, such as blue denim jeans, tennis balls, or cheese enchiladas. A common model of the U.S. economy has only 144 branches, but there are tens of millions of products in the economy. This high level of aggregation renders the model less accurate in projecting the effect of an increased demand for a particular product.

An important aspect of how a multiplier functions is related to the fact that most economies depend significantly on trade. Thus, a restaurant in Vancouver may buy its potatoes from Idaho, its silverware from France, and its tables from Sweden. To the extent that Vancouver's restaurants or hotels buy their inputs from outside Vancouver or outside Canada, visitors' expenditures locally will have less impact on the Vancouver economy.[3]

Macroeconomic models of the entire U.S. economy have multipliers around 1.3. Since the U.S. economy is less open (depends less on trade) than most of the world's economies, the national multipliers in other economies are bound to be smaller. Further, when the economic impact of a mega-event on a single city is being considered, the multiplier must be still smaller, because cities must import (from outside the city) a much higher proportion of the materials and goods that they use. That is, such goods may be made in other areas of the same country as well as in other countries. Thus, the input-output models producing multipliers greater than 1.3 are simply not credible. City sports multipliers are more typically between 0.7 and 1.1.[4]

Still another problem is that when a foreign soccer fan spends $100 at a Brazilian restaurant during the World Cup competition, it might not be a net gain for the Brazilian economy. This is because between June 12 and July 13, 2014, there may have been tens or hundreds of thousands of people (tourists or businesspeople) who would otherwise have traveled to Brazil but instead chose to avoid the congestion, tight security, and high prices during the World Cup and either went else-where or stayed home. This plays out in real life: tourism in Beijing fell during the 2008 Summer Games, as it did in London during the 2012 Olympics. That is, even counting the athletes, the media, the adminis-trators, and the Olympic tourists, the total number of visitors to these cities fell during the month of the Olympic Games. Further, some local residents may have the same impulse that foreigners have: they believe their city or country will be excessively crowded and expensive during the mega-event and that the period of the competition would be a good time to take a vacation outside the country. The amount of outbound tourism from China grew by 12 percent in 2008, the year China hosted the Summer Olympics.[5]

Yet another issue is that profits earned by local businesses during the competition may not stay in the city or the country. If an interna-tional hotel chain owns a hotel in London and its typical price for a room for one night in late July is $400 but during the 2012 Olympics it is $800, then the hotel will reap an additional profit of $400 per room per night during the games (assuming the hotel has the same occupancy rate in both instances.) The hotel does not have to hire any additional desk clerks, chambermaids, or concierges during the games, so there is no gain to local employment or to employment income. Indeed, it is likely that the entire $400 extra profit will be repatriated back to the hotel's home office in another country. The standard pro-cedure for an ex ante, input-output study would be to take the $800 and multiply it by an inflated multiplier (1.7 to 3.5) and come up with an economic impact of $1,360 to $2,800 for the hotel spending alone from that one-night stay. The reality, in this hypothetical case, is that the impact would be zero if the Olympic fan were simply replacing a normal tourist, or it would be closer to $400 × (0.7 to 1.1) ($280 to $440) if the Olympic fan did not displace a normal tourist. In either case, the ex ante economic impact study produces a vastly inflated and unrealistic estimate.

Another major leakage from the local economy occurs when a local resident buys tickets to an Olympic or World Cup event. For instance, a good majority of the attendees at the 2014 World Cup were Brazilians. When Brazilians paid for tickets to the tournament, this money went to FIFA—it left the local economy. Total ticket sales for the 2014 World Cup competition were around $350 million, suggesting that over $200 million that would otherwise have contributed to domestic demand in Brazil did not do so.

There are still other reasons why the typical ex ante report might overstate any impact. Someone in the host city for a reason other than the competition (for example, normal tourism, visiting relatives, conducting business) may decide for an evening's entertainment to go to a competition rather than to the theater or a fine restaurant. No money is added to the local economy, but that individual will be classified as an Olympic tourist and deemed to be adding to the area's economy.

Yet another possibility is that an individual or family may have been planning a normal tourist visit to the host city for later in the year but instead moved up the vacation to take advantage of the games. Here too there is no added tourism, just a different timing of the tourist visits.

Finally, ex ante promotional studies leave out a vital economic element—how the games are paid for. If a government borrows $10 billion at 5 percent over a thirty-year period, then its yearly costs of financing that loan are $651 million for thirty years.[6] To pay for this debt service, the government must either raise taxes or reduce government services, either of which would introduce a drag on the local economy. This drag too must be seen as part of the cost of the games. (Of course, if politically palatable, the government could also choose to borrow more money to pay back the first debt, but this just pushes these costs further down the road.)

### Looking at Results—Ex Post Studies

In contrast to the ex ante studies, which have largely been performed by consulting firms hired by interested parties and have been marred by the use of an inappropriate methodology and unrealistic assumptions, a growing number of disinterested, scholarly studies have attempted to gauge the economic impact of hosting the

Olympics and World Cup. These studies use an ex post methodology: the authors wait until the tournament is over, then examine the actual economic data generated before, during, and after the event. The common approach is to use econometrics and to attempt to control for all the other relevant variables that could have affected output or employment over the period of the study. Generally, the month or year of the competition is treated as a binary (dummy) variable. Table 3-1 summarizes the findings of major studies on the economic impact of hosting the Olympics or World Cup.[7]

The results of these studies can be summarized as follows (some studies cover more than one mega-event): in sixteen cases, the games were found to have no statistically significant effect on employment or income, in seven cases a modest positive effect on income or short-run employment was found, and in three cases a negative effect on income was found.[8] Where there was a modest short-term positive employment effect, it was in each case a fraction of the officially projected effect and must be measured against the large public investment in all cases, except Los Angeles, where public funding was diminutive. Later I consider the conditions under which a positive effect might be created; here I attempt to explain the much more common outcome of no positive effect.

The first step is to grasp that, despite the enormous cultural penumbra of the World Cup and the Olympics, the events are really quite small quantitatively in relation to the economy of the host country. If one adds up all the sources of World Cup revenue in 2014 (from ticket sales, sponsorships, international television rights, and so forth), the sum is likely to approach $4.5 billion. FIFA does not share any of this revenue with Brazil, but it does pay for local operating expenses during the World Cup. Let's assume that these expenses come to $2 billion, and that all of that amount goes to buying goods and services only from Brazil. The GDP in Brazil is approximately $2.5 trillion, so the amount of World Cup money staying in the country, optimistically gauged, is about one-twelfth of 1 percent of Brazil's GDP in the year of the competition.

## TABLE 3-1. Studies on the Economic Impact of Hosting the Olympics and the World Cup

1.  Feddersen, Grötzinger, and Maennig (2009). FIFA World Cup 2006. The games had no significant impact on employment or income in urban areas where new stadium construction took place compared to other urban areas.

2.  Baade and Matheson (2004). FIFA World Cup 1994. Comparing income across the thirteen host cities, the authors found the average income was $712 million below trend, versus boosters' claims of $300 million gains.

3.  Du Plessis and Maennig (2011). FIFA World Cup 2011. International tourists numbered 40,000–90,000, versus ex ante forecasts of approximately 400,000.

4.  Hagn and Maennig (2008). FIFA World Cup 1974. The authors found no significant positive impact on long-run employment in the host cities through 1988.

5.  Hagn and Maennig (2009). FIFA World Cup 2006. The authors found no significant employment impact on the cities that hosted games compared to other German cities that did not host the games.

6.  Allmers and Maennig (2009). FIFA World Cup 1998, 2006, 2010. The authors found no significant impacts on hotel stays, income, or retail sales in France (1998). Significant positive impacts on hotel stays and income were found in Germany (2006).

7.  Szymanski (2002). World Cup, various. Hosts experienced slower growth during year of event, amounting to a loss of 2.4 percent of nominal GDP in the host country.

8.  Du Plessis and Venter (2010). FIFA World Cup 2010. The authors estimate that the World Cup lifted GDP by 0.1 percent in South Africa.

9.  Jasmand and Maennig (2008). Summer Olympic Games 1972. The authors found a significantly positive impact on income in some host regions but an insignificant impact on employment in host regions.

10. Porter and Fletcher (2008). Summer Olympic Games 1996, Winter Olympic Games 2002. The authors found no significant impacts on taxable sales, hotel occupancy, or airport usage.

11. Feddersen and Maennig (2013). Summer Olympic Games 1996. The authors were unable to reject the null hypothesis that the games provided no employment boost in the U.S. state of Georgia.

12. Feddersen and Maennig (2012). FIFA World Cup 2006. The authors found no statistically significant general economic impact but did identify a small, short-run impact on employment in the hospitality sector.

13. Giesecke and Madden (2011). Summer Olympic Games, 2000. The effect of Sydney hosting was to reduce Australian household consumption by $2.1 billion.

*(continued)*

**TABLE 3-1 (*continued*)**

---

14. Billings and Holladay (2012). Olympics, multiple years. The authors developed a difference-in-difference estimator for all Olympic host cities between 1950 and 2005 and found no long-term impact on real GDP or trade openness.

15. Von Rekowsky (2013). Olympics and World Cup, various years. Based on a study of Olympic and World Cup Games between 1990 and 2010, the author concludes these mega-events offered no meaningful lasting economic benefits.

16. Baumann and others (2012). Winter Olympics 2002. The authors found a short-term impact on the leisure industry amounting to an increase of between 4,000 and 7,000 jobs in Salt Lake City, but no effect on employment after twelve months.

17. Baumann and Engelhardt (2012). World Cup 1994. The authors found no statistically significant increase in employment in the nine cities that hosted this World Cup, no impact on the leisure and hospitality sectors, and a negative impact on the retail sector.

18. Baade and Matheson (2002). Summer Olympics 1984 and 1996. The authors found a modest short-run employment effect in Los Angeles amounting to an increase of 5,043 jobs and in Atlanta of between 4,500 and 42,500 jobs, but no long-run effect in Los Angeles.

19. Hotchkiss, Moore, and Zobay (2003). Summer Olympics 1996. Using difference-in-difference methodology, the authors found employment gains, but not wage gains, in counties hosting Olympic venues and counties nearby Olympic venues, when contrasting the economic performance of 1985–93 and 1994–2000.

---

Sources: See note 7 on p. 145.

It might be objected that the foregoing does not include the revenue generated through hotels, meals, local transport, and so on by visitors attending the games. Here it is important to recall the displacement and substitution effects considered earlier. It is quite possible that there will be no net increase in tourist spending during the competitions, and that if there is an increase, it is bound to be considerably smaller than that projected by the event organizers. For example, the organizers of the 2010 World Cup in South Africa initially projected 400,000 international tourists would come to the games; subsequent academic research found that the actual numbers were between 40,000 and 220,000.[9]

But let us be optimistic and assume that a country experiences a net increase of 300,000 international tourists, that each spends $300 a day (and all on goods and services produced in the host country, excluding event tickets), and that each spends five days in the country.[10] The sum total of expenditures in this circumstance would be $450 million. So, if this hopeful figure is added to the $2 billion of revenue staying in the country from the World Cup, the total would now be almost $2.5 billion.[11]

We can now compare the $2.5 billion with how much World Cup or Olympic budgets have been in recent years: for Athens in 2004, $16 billion; for London in 2012, $15–$20 billion; for Beijing in 2008, $40 billion; for Brazil in 2014, $15–$20 billion; for Sochi, $51–$70 billion, and so on. Two points need to be made. First, a good chunk of these costs relates to nonsports infrastructure (transportation, telecommunications, energy), and much of this investment may be beneficial to the country going forward. Hence, any fair appraisal of the economic impact of the games would have to include an assessment of how appropriate these investments were in relation to the city's or country's long-term development needs. Second, and complementing the first, since the short-run benefits are extremely unlikely to offset the costs, any economic justification for hosting the competition must be found in the long-run or legacy benefits. I consider legacy benefits in the next chapter. First we must take a closer look at the costs.

## Hosting Costs

### Bidding

The first cost, and one that applies not only to the city eventually selected as host but to all those cities that would be hosts, is the bidding expense. There are the upfront payments to the IOC or FIFA for being considered in the preliminary applicant stage and then again in the final candidate stage. For the IOC, these payments are $150,000 and $500,000, respectively. Well beyond these costs are those required to put together a plan, to hire consultants, to make fancy brochures and videos, to host IOC and FIFA executives, to travel to IOC and FIFA meetings, and so on. Chicago spent more than $100 million in its failed bid to host the 2016 Summer Olympics. Other cities and countries have reported similar sums, or more. Tokyo reportedly spent $150 million in its failed bid to host the 2016 Summer Games.

The Netherlands has been considering a bid to host the 2028 Summer Games. According to a study by RTLnews, the largest commercial broadcaster in the country, as of 2012 the Dutch had already spent $105 million in direct costs to study the feasibility of hosting, draw up preliminary plans, mobilize relevant parties, and organize events "to entice IOC members to vote for us."[12] As of late July 2014, the Netherlands had not made a decision on whether or not to bid for the 2028 games.

### Opening and Closing Ceremonies

Another, often underappreciated expense for Olympics hosts is producing the opening and closing ceremonies. Cities and countries frequently see these ceremonies as their big opportunity to promote local history, culture, and beauty—their main shot at creating an enticing image of their city or country and attracting worldwide tourism for years to come. Accordingly, they spend lavishly. China, for instance, reportedly spent $343 million (in 2014 prices) on its opening ceremony.[13]

### Sports Venues and Nonsport Infrastructure

The most obvious costs are those associated with building sports venues (which number more than thirty for the Summer Olympics) and nonsport infrastructure. Depending on the material conditions of the country (its level of economic and sport development), either a modest or a substantial investment will be required—these days running between roughly $5 billion and $50 billion (although the strange 2022 World Cup in Qatar may go well over $200 billion). And, of course, sometimes we don't know the true costs, because either (1) the host engages in dissimulation or cover-ups, or (2) the host committee has the financial records destroyed (as was the case with Nagano in 1998), or (3) there is disagreement about what infrastructure spending should be attributed to the sporting event and what should be considered to be independent of the event.

### Business Disruption

A related cost is that the intense period of construction for the games may disrupt local business. Retail businesses from London, Sochi, Athens, Capetown, and elsewhere tell of high expectations, investments to expand their operations, and then slumps in sales as surrounding streets are cordoned off to foot traffic or become too noisy to attract customers.

### Security

There are also increasing costs for security. Ever since the events of September 11, 2001, security expenses have escalated rapidly. Athens in 2004 was the first post-9/11 host of the Summer Games. Athens initially forecasted a security budget of $400 million. The European Tour Operators Association (ETOA) put Athens's final security cost at $1.5 billion.[14] More recent competition hosts have reported security costs in the $1 billion to $2 billion range.

### Cost Overruns

One of the more interesting and important dilemmas facing host cities and countries is the phenomenon of cost overruns. Overruns are ubiquitous, and most are massive, as reflected in table 3-2. What is notable about these numbers is that in each case, the overrun is not of a normal order of magnitude but instead is fourfold to tenfold (or more) than the initial estimate.

How can we explain the consistency and the degree of these cost overruns? First and foremost, a significant part of the story is deliberate deception. The main promoters of hosting are the economic interests that stand to gain the most, such as construction companies and their unions, insurance companies, real estate interests, architectural

**TABLE 3-2. Cost Overruns**

| Host city or country | Year of games | Initial bid (billions of USD) | Estimated final cost (billions of USD) |
|---|---|---|---|
| Athens | 2004 | 1.6 | 16 |
| South Africa | 2010 | 0.3 | 5–6 |
| London | 2012 | 4.0 | 15–20 |
| Sochi | 2014 | 12.0 | 51–70 |
| Brazil (stadiums only) | 2014 | 1.1 | 5 |

Sources: E. Cottle, ed., *South Africa's World Cup: A Legacy for Whom?* (University of KwaZulu-Natal Press, 2011), and P. Alegi and C. Bolsmann, eds., *Africa's World Cup* (University of Michigan Press, 2013). Interestingly, the Commonwealth Games in India in 2010 were initially budgeted at $250 million. *Business Today* magazine estimated the final cost at $9.2 billion. If these numbers are accurate, then the overrun was on the order of 36 times! See Nalin Mehta and Boria Majumdar, "For a Monsoon Wedding: Delhi and the Commonwealth Games," in *International Handbook on the Economics of Mega Sporting Events*, ed. Wolfgang Maennig and Andrew S. Zimbalist (Cheltenham, U.K.: Edward Elgar, 2012).

firms, the investment bankers who will float the loans and their lawyers, local media companies, and some hotels and restaurants. It is in their interest to convince the relevant government body or bodies to support the bid effort. If a realistic estimate of costs were provided, the probability of getting a political green light would diminish substantially. The clear strategy is to lowball the cost estimates with a bare-bones plan, and then, once it is approved, to add the bells and whistles.

Second, it is important to remember that prospective hosts are involved in an eleven-year (or longer) process, facing first domestic competitors and then international ones. Along the way there is constant and strong pressure to outdo other competititors' designs, extravagance, amenities, and security features. An eleven-year process of one-upmanship, along with meeting direct demands made by the IOC or FIFA, leads to ever more elaborate and expensive plans.

Third, the long lag time between the initial plan and the competition itself means there are many years of intervening inflation. Especially when a lot of production is concentrated in a few areas, the increasing demand for construction materials, engineers, and manual labor pushes up the prices of all the inputs.

Fourth, cities and countries invariably fall behind in their construction schedule—because of political encumbrances, or deficient planning or sloppy administration, or bad weather, or labor disputes. As hosts fall behind their timetable, construction must be rushed. This leads to relaxed bidding rules, which raises prices, and to premium prices demanded by construction companies for quick delivery (which often also leads to inferior workmanship and higher maintenance costs down the road).

Fifth, along with higher construction prices, it is common for real estate prices to rise in the run-up to the games, and, in anticipation of wealthy foreign tourists, prices tend to rise more rapidly throughout the local economy. The generalized price increases in turn feed protests coalescing around the games. The *Los Angeles Times* aptly described this dynamic in Rio de Janeiro prior to the 2014 World Cup competition:

Fed-up Rio residents have taken to social media to share photos of price tags, receipts and menu items so pricey, it almost seems they could only have been dreamed up by the Spanish surrealist artist.

There is a shrimp omelet, now famous, that costs $41 at a simple bar and beachside restaurant in the Copacabana neighborhood. At a nearby snack stand, a side of fries goes for $13. A fruit salad at another beach kiosk is $17, and one establishment charges passersby $1.75 to use the bathroom.

Normally laid-back *cariocas,* as Rio inhabitants are known, are getting steamed, said George Patino, a spokesman for the Technological Park of Rio who hosts a Facebook page dubbed Rio Surreal.

In that online forum, locals gripe daily about the prices of taxi rides, color copies, liquor, produce and more. Some have organized "cooler" parties outside popular bars, drinking their own beer on the streets rather than paying steep tabs inside.

"We've been seeing price increases in all sectors in Rio for a long time. But things have gotten worse, and people are now really upset," Patino said. "With the World Cup and other big events coming, it seems everyone has lost their sense of perspective. Everyone is trying to make money as if this was their last chance ever to do so."[15]

### Other Costs

Then there are the rest of the operating costs of the games: the PR and advertising campaign, the provision of sumptuous food and lodging for IOC and FIFA executives, the underwriting of at least a portion of the food and lodging for the athletes, the costs of maintaining the sports venues and practice fields, and covering the expenses of administration, sanitation, utilities, traffic control, ticket sales, forgone tax revenues, ushers, and so on.

Next, there is the cost of payoffs and corruption. Government officials in charge of doling out contracts tend to be large beneficiaries of considerations from construction companies. Stories of this behavior are legion and are sprinkled later into the text.

There is also the opportunity cost of the human capital invested by engineers, planners, and politicians in the preparation for and implementation of the games. Their skills and time could have been dedicated to other, perhaps more beneficial activities.

Finally, there are the human costs, which may appear in the form of heavily exploited migrant labor, human rights violations, construction-related deaths, environmental degradation, architectural anomalies, and eviction and community destruction.[16] Examples of these problems are discussed in chapters 5 and 6.

## Hosting Benefits

Several short-run benefits are commonly touted in connection with hosting the Olympics or the World Cup. An evaluation of the key benefits mentioned in this regard suggests that the vast majority do not play out in reality.

## Overcoming Political Gridlock

A common and often sensible claim made by mega-event boosters is that without the pressure that comes with being thrust onto the world stage, the local political system would be incapable of appropriating money for sorely needed infrastructure. For instance, in 2004, when New York City was bidding to host the 2012 Summer Olympics, it was frequently argued that a major benefit was that the Javits Convention Center on the west side would finally be expanded and modernized. Various funding proposals had been presented to the state legislature in Albany over the years, but the Republicans and Democrats could not agree. While there may be some validity to this reasoning, it might also be argued that the planned investment in the expansion of the Javits Center was ill conceived in the first place.

A similar argument was made for Brazil being the host of the World Cup: it would create enough urgency for infrastructure investment and pacifying the favelas that it would finally get done. The question here is whether the Brazilian political morass was actually overcome or whether the morass precluded the effective installation of needed infrastructure and constructive development.

## Higher Real Estate Prices

Higher land prices are often cited as a benefit of hosting mega-events. Land prices do tend to rise where infrastructure and facility construction is taking place. Such price increases undoubtedly benefit landowners, real estate agents, and speculators, but they are also likely to hurt lower-income families, who are evicted or unable to afford rising rents. These families are often obliged to relocate miles away, disrupting travel to work and to school for their children, as well as compelling a social and emotional adjustment to a new community.

## Feel-Good Effects

Being at the center of the world stage creates excitement, as does the buildup to the several weeks of fame and glory. Survey work in host cities confirms that, with some exceptions, the mood and spirit of the local population tend to be uplifted. (Brazil 2014 is arguably an exception to the rule.) Host committees organize thousands of local residents to do volunteer work for the games, and this engenders a greater sense of community and cooperation. To the extent that this effect takes hold, however, it tends to be ephemeral. When the planet's attention disappears, life and spirits return to normal.[17]

### Construction

Most promotional studies for mega-events include a section that estimates the employment and output gains from the period of construction leading up to the games. These studies generally do not take into account two crucial factors: the future effect of the debt incurred to finance the construction and the macroeconomic (and labor market) conditions during the construction phase.

Other than in Los Angeles (where public spending was minimal), there has been a significant financial contribution from the public sector. Such a contribution must be financed in one of three ways: (1) by cutting back on other public services, (2) by raising taxes, or (3) by government borrowing. The first two methods reduce income, output, and employment, tending to offset any gains from spending for games-related construction. The third method (assuming away the rational expectations and complete crowding-out positions) will have a positive short-run effect on output, but it will require debt service going forward, and this debt service (other things being equal) will entail either future reductions in public services or increases in taxes, or both.

If increases in public construction spending did not have to be funded eventually, maintaining full employment would be trivial. Each city could simply hire a thousand workers to dig a big hole every week, and then hire another thousand to fill it up. Too bad economics is not so simple. If the object being built has no or little value, then it is a bad investment for the city. A good investment would return enough value not only to retire the relevant debt service but also to cover the return on the next best available public investment at the time (the opportunity cost).

Another consideration is the state of the economy and the labor market at the time the investments for the games are made. If the economy is booming and labor markets are tight, then the most likely outcome will not be additional output but a reallocation of output toward the sports and nonsports facilities for the games and away from existing areas of investment. Moreover, since there will be excess demand on the scarce resources of building materials and construction labor, the prices of these inputs are bound to rise, creating inflationary pressure. This pressure in turn may lead to contractionary macropolicy and eventually to lower output.

Alternatively, if the economy is weak and the labor market slack, then the games-related investments may lower unemployment and lead to output growth. The question in this case is whether there are other investments that would have the same salutary short-run impact but would also be more likely to raise productivity in the longer run. Because public debt is being incurred, it is important to evaluate the long-run effect of public spending.

Beyond these considerations, it is necessary to keep in mind that the bidding process for the Olympics or the World Cup is not synchronized with a country's business cycle. When a city or country bids, it bids on the IOC's or FIFA's timetable. It would be a fool's errand to bid to host either the Olympics or the World Cup on the assumption that when the bulk of construction took place, the local labor markets would be slack.

Finally, the sheer volume of sport and infrastructure construction for a host of the games usually results in a shortage of construction labor. It becomes necessary to import migrant labor, either from other areas of the country or from other countries. Under these circumstances, migrant labor is generally mistreated and underpaid. For instance, early reports out of Qatar are horrifying: the Qataris have confirmed that during 2012 and 2013, nearly a thousand migrant laborers died as a result of the unsafe working conditions and dismal living conditions at construction sites for the 2022 World Cup. According to a report in London's *Guardian,* pay slips revealed that workers building the first stadium for the 2022 Cup were paid as little as $0.76 an hour.[18]

### Tourism

The evidence for a boost in tourism during the Olympics or the World Cup is uneven. The so-called Olympic and World Cup communities (the athletes, the coaches, the judges or referees, the media, the families, the sponsors and their guests, the administrators from FIFA or the IOC) are large and, depending on the event, run in the 10,000 to 25,000 range. These visitors alone would seem to guarantee additional tourist income for the host city or country during the games.

But it is not always so. Some hosts have experienced a modest increase in tourist revenue, while others have had a decrease or no appreciable change. For instance, an econometric study of the Atlanta Summer Olympics in 1996 that examined monthly data found that when other factors were controlled for, there was no statistically significant change in retail sales, hotel occupancy, and airport traffic during the Olympics. The only indicator that increased was hotel rates, and, not surprisingly, most of additional revenue from this source went to the headquarters of hotel chains in other cities.[19]

In another example, the number of foreign tourists visiting China in 2008 was 24.3 million, or 6.8 percent fewer than the 26.1 million who visited in 2007. Beijing received 30 percent fewer foreign arrivals in August 2008 than in August 2007, and the number of hotel bed nights in the city dropped 39 percent during the games compared to a year earlier. Beijing had anticipated 400,000 foreign visitors per night during the Olympics, but the actual number was 235,000.[20]

China is not the only host country to forecast the number of foreign tourists overly optimistically. Sydney anticipated 132,000 foreign visitors daily but received only 97,000. Athens expected 105,000 per night but received only 14,000.[21] According to the European Tour

Operators Association, the problem is universal: "No city has yet predicted with any accuracy the number of people who attend."[22]

For the London games, the U.K.'s Office for National Statistics reported that in July and August 2012, there was a net decrease in overseas visitors to the United Kingdom of 6.1 percent relative to the number in July and August 2011 (from 6.57 million visitors in 2011 to 6.17 million in 2012). In Salt Lake City, the number of visitor skier days in Utah during the Olympic year of 2001–02 was 2.98 million, 9.9 percent below the 3.28 million in 2000–01 (and 5.3 percent below the 3.14 million in 2002–03). Foreign tourism during the 2002 World Cup in South Korea equaled 403,406, which was 37 percent below the forecasted level and 12.4 percent below the number for the same month in 2001.[23]

In contrast, the number of foreign visitors to Sydney increased modestly, from 2.5 million in 1999 to 2.7 million in 2000, the year the city hosted the Summer Games. That was the good news for Sydney. The bad news was that the city anticipated 27 percent more visitors than it received, and the number of tourists fell steadily over the next three years, to 2.3 million in 2003, as neighboring New Zealand's numbers soared. Moreover, Sydney hoteliers imprudently expanded room capacity by 30 percent for the games, which led to a fall in the occupancy rate to a reported 57 percent during the Olympics.[24]

British Columbia also experienced a modest increase in tourism in 2010, the year that Vancouver hosted the Winter Olympics. The hotel occupancy rate rose from 58.8 percent in 2009 to 60.1 percent in 2010 and tourist entries increased from 5.61 million in 2009 to 6.19 million in 2010—still well below the annual average during 2005–07 of 6.88 million.[25] Employment in tourism-related industries (air transport, accommodations, food and beverage, arts and entertainment), however, after growing at 3.2 percent annually between 2005 and 2009, fell by 1.1 percent in 2010.[26] The drop in employment is all the more notable because the North American economy had begun to recover from the 2007–08 financial crisis.

Brazil's 2014 World Cup also appears to have increased foreign tourism. According to preliminary estimates, although the government projected that the Cup would bring 600,000 international tourists to Brazil, the Ministry of Tourism released a report in mid-July claiming 1 million foreign visitors between May 23 and July 13. (The first game of the Cup was on June 10.) This figure did not jibe with that issued by the Brazilian Airline Association, which projected in the middle of the competition that total air travel would fall between 11 and 15 percent during the Cup.[27]

The Brazilian Ministry of Tourism also increased its projected tourist revenue from the Cup from R$1 billion (Brazilian reales; the real was worth approximately 45 cents in July 2014) to R$4.4 billion. The revenue figures are based on survey work done by consulting groups.[28] The 67 percent increase in number of foreign tourists, according to the ministry's figures, in conjunction with the 4.4-fold increase in revenue from tourists' spending implies that the average spending per tourist was 2.65 times above what was originally projected. Something appears to be significantly off in these estimates. The disparity becomes more glaring when it is considered that most of the foreign tourists came from the neighboring countries of Argentina, Uruguay, Colombia, and Chile, all of which had teams in the final sixteen. In Rio, for instance, which enjoyed the largest influx of foreigners, Argentine tourists led the way, with 77,000, Chile was second, with 45,000, and Colombia was third, with 31,000. The United States had 24,000 visitors in Rio, while France had 16,000 and England and Germany each had 10,000. According to various anecdotal reports, the tourists from nearby South American countries in large numbers slept on the beach or in trailers and used public restrooms.[29] Their spending was minimal. Thus, the special geographic and competitive circumstances of the Brazilian games helped to raise the number of international visitors but probably did very little to raise foreign exchange earnings for the economy.

In any event, it is problematic to simply look at the change in number of tourists from one year to the next because so many other factors could be moving the needle. As an example, the background trajectory of tourist numbers could well mask a drop during the Olympic year. Most countries that host the Olympics are in a growth phase for their economy and for their tourism industry. If tourism numbers had been growing at 4 percent per year prior to a country's hosting the World Cup and then grew at 2 percent per year afterward, it would be difficult to make the case that hosting lifted tourism, even though the numbers grew on a year-over-year basis after the games.[30] Changes in the world economy or political factors also come into play. The point is simply that the notion that hosting the Olympics or the World Cup is an automatic plus for the tourism industry is misleading. The long-run changes in tourism, discussed in the next chapter, also do not bear out the rosy picture painted by the organizing bodies' PR efforts.

# 4 | The Long-Run Economic Impact

As the costs for hosting the Olympics and the World Cup have skyrocketed over the past thirty years, rising into the tens of billions of dollars, the potential short-run increase in economic activity of between $2 billion and $5 billion has paled in comparison. To justify the enormous expense of hosting the competitions, the IOC has introduced the term "legacy" to refer to the presumed long-run benefits. "Legacy" was introduced into IOC parlance after the 2000 Games in Sydney and has become a broad, encompassing concept, seemingly limited only by the imagination of the employees in the IOC's PR office in Lausanne.[1] FIFA has been happy to adopt the legacy argument.

Here is a noninclusive list of what the IOC has asserted are potential legacy benefits for the host city and country:[2]

—Construction of sports venues

—Construction of transportation, communications, and energy infrastructure

—Construction of accommodations

—Boost for tourism

—Increased trade and investment

—Improved management practices; better coordination among government agencies

—Improved national spirit and mood

—Educational benefits

—Public health benefits—more exercise and sports participation and better standards of cleanliness in restaurant food preparation

—Greater accessibility for handicapped persons

—Improved sustainability policies and standards

—More effective cultural preservation

—Lower crime rates

—Higher real estate prices

—Reduced racism

—Greater social inclusion[3]

Several observations can be made about this list. First, since the changes enumerated all represent putative long-run benefits, the host city or country potentially must wait years to decades before experiencing the full gains. Second, since many other variables intervene in the long run, it is more difficult to tie any changes to the impact of the games themselves. Third, many of the envisaged benefits are intangible and not quantifiable. Fourth, the calculus for political leaders or members of the organizing committee of the games shifts dramatically. Those who promised economic and other advantages from hosting become basically unaccountable. If there are no apparent gains, the politicians can always proclaim that the benefits are on their way. Thus, in the short run the games' boosters can appeal to the promise of long-run legacy benefits, while in the long run the boosters can appeal to the expectation of still longer-run benefits down the road. By this time the politicians who originally appropriated public funds to finance the games may be long gone.

Let us turn to consider the evidence from multiple studies on the alleged legacy benefits.

## Long-Term Benefits

### Tourism

In the last chapter we considered the effect of the games on tourism in the short run; namely, whether tourism grows in the run-up to and during the games themselves. Here we consider the possibility of a branding effect that might increase the number of tourists in the years following the games.

One of the most frequently heard and stridently claimed benefits is that hosting the games provides wonderful advertising value and a unique opportunity to develop the host country's brand. Both the World Cup and the Olympics are watched on television and the Internet by billions of people worldwide, and there is no better occasion to trumpet the touristic glories and appetizing business opportunities of your city or country, runs the PR.

Here is Jacques Rogge (IOC head from 2001 to 2013) extolling the television reach of the 2004 Athens Games: "The Athens Olympics broke global TV viewing records, with nearly 4 billion tuning in . . . beating the previous record of 3.6 billion viewers for the 2000 Sydney Olympics."[4] The European Tour Operators Association (ETOA) mounted a biting response to Rogge's claims: "There are roughly 6.5 billion people on the planet. Of these, 1.6 billion have no access to electricity. A further 300 million may have access to electricity, but are under five years old."[5] That leaves 4.6 billion people who could have watched the Athens Olympics. So, Rogge was claiming that 87 percent of those who could have watched the games actually watched them. What Rogge's numbers seem to represent in reality is the number of people who could have *potentially* watched the Olympics, rather than a reliable tally of those actually watching.

Even if the IOC and FIFA exaggerate the number of eyeballs watching their competitions, it is true that the worldwide audience is enormous. The larger issue is not whether there are half a billion or 4 billion viewers, it is whether the actual viewers and television cameras are focused on the tourist attractions of the hosting country or on the outcomes of the sporting competitions. To the extent that viewers who are in an economic position to travel to or invest in the host country focus on the qualities of the country, there is the question of whether the viewers' take-away is positive or negative. Did viewers have a better impression of Mexico after the 1968 Summer Games, which were preceded by the killing of more than 200 student demonstrators by the military, followed by the political protests of U.S. black athletes—and all of this occurring against the background of broadcasters' repeated assertions of terrible air pollution? Similar questions could be asked about Munich in 1972, Montreal in 1976, Moscow in 1980, Atlanta in 1996, Athens in 2004, Beijing in 2008, Sochi in 2014, or Brazil in 2014. A 1991 study by J. R. Brent Ritchie and Brian H. Smith on awareness of the 1988 Calgary Winter Games found that the most common characteristic identified with Calgary among U.S. and European viewers was the cold. Moreover, Ritchie and Smith found that while there was strong awareness of Calgary as the host in 1988, there was also a rapid drop-off in awareness by 1989, just one year later. The authors concluded that the hosting impact "on levels of top-of-mind awareness decreases measurably after a short period of time."[6]

No matter how inherently charming and appealing a city or country may be, then, it seems that hosting always involves uncertainties and risks: the weather may be bad, popular protests may arise, terrorism may surface, or traffic snarls may infuriate. For countries with widespread poverty, problematic pollution, variable weather, a repressive political apparatus, rampant corruption, or an underdeveloped infrastructure, the risks are magnified.

The ETOA has conducted several studies on the impact of the Olympics on tourism. In each case the conclusion was pessimistic. One of the more telling arguments made by the ETOA is that Olympic and World Cup fans visit the host country to watch the sporting competitions rather than to enjoy the country's lasting tourist attractions. When sports fans went to London in 2012, for instance, they didn't go to the theater, to concert venues, to the Tate Gallery, to the British Museum, to Buckingham Palace, or to Hyde Park. They went to East London for the competitions. When they returned home, they might have described the excitement of the games to their friends, relatives, and neighbors, but the games are ephemeral, and no future tourist will go to London in 2015 because there were exciting games in 2012. And while Olympic fans may have had little or nothing to say about the enduring virtues of visiting London, they likely did have something to say about high-priced hotels and restaurants and endless traffic jams.

The ETOA claims that the most effective way to advertise tourism is by word of mouth. With mega-event tourists, the value of word of mouth is largely lost, and indeed, to the extent that the mega-event tourist chases away the traditional tourist who touts the enduring attractions of a city, the impact of the games on future tourism may be negative. In its 2010 report, the ETOA put the matter this way:

> The post Olympic blight was common to all the cities that hosted the Games since Seoul. As was pointed out in 2006, every Olympics displaces tourists: Olympic visitors do not behave like normal guests. Their presence is determined by their interest in sport. They do not come to sightsee, attend the theatre or recreate themselves on a beach. They come to attend a sporting event.
>
> This removal of visitors has a detrimental effect on subsequent demand. The most important motivator for visitors is example and word of mouth: this sales mechanism loses momentum as visitors are deterred. Their very absence is a suppression of marketing. This failure far outweighs any gains derived from the television audience, an audience whose size and propensity to travel is exaggerated.[7]

The dichotomy between normal and sports tourists may be sharper for the Olympics than for the World Cup. The World Cup takes place over roughly twice as many days, leaving more time for the sports tourist to visit traditional tourist sites. Thus, Brazil's Ministry of Tourism reported healthy increases in the number of visitors to the Christ the Redeemer statue, as well as to Sugarloaf Mountain.

Assessing the long-run impact of the World Cup or Olympics on a country's tourism is not an easy matter. One must parse the preexisting trend in tourism, the growth of the regional and world economy, changing transportation and hotel prices, visa regulations and costs, other domestic investments in promoting tourism, and so on. In a few cases, such as Barcelona in 1992, it appears that the games did provide a fillip to the tourism industry—though many other factors were also at work in Barcelona contributing to this effect. In other cases it is difficult to identify any clear impact, and in yet other cases the effect appears to have been negative.

The impact of the 2000 Sydney Olympics on tourism offers a cautionary example. An Australian tourism industry report based on detailed survey evidence offered a plausible explanation for the crucial American market's reluctance to see Australia as a newly desirable destination for tourism and investment:

> Given that the Sydney Olympics were considered as global entertainment, U.S. media-coverage of the Games and Australia, for the most part, simply reinforces the already-held imagery of Australia as a far-away exotic location peopled by friendly folk who seemed almost American. Given that there was no Sydney 2000 media coverage that served to fundamentally challenge already-held images and attitudes, American perceptions, not surprisingly, remained largely constant before and after the Sydney Olympics.[8]

In another study, *The Sydney Olympics: Seven Years On*, James Giesecke and John Madden of Monash University's Centre of Policy Studies concluded, "In terms of purely measurable economic variables the Sydney Olympics had a negative effect on New South Wales and Australia as a whole."[9]

Sydney increased its stock of hotel rooms by 30 percent to accommodate expected Olympic travelers. By the end of 2004, ten of the city's major hotels had closed.[10] David Mazitelli of the Australian Tourism Export Council put the matter bluntly:

> The Sydney Olympics had few long term positive impacts beyond 2000 on the growth of Australian tourism. . . . The forecast of a strong impact for the four years following the Games did not eventuate. As soon as the Olympics finished, we started to see a fall away in inbound activity. Australia went into three years of negative growth (2001, 2002 and 2003).[11]

International arrivals in Sydney went from 2.7 million visitors in 2000 to 2.6 million in 2001, 2.4 million in 2002, and 2.3 million in 2003.[12] While some attributed the decline to changes in the international political and economic environment, it is notable that foreign arrivals to New Zealand grew each year, increasing by 17 percent between 2000 and 2003.[13]

Jon Teigland, in an October 1996 study on the 1994 Lillehammer Winter Olympic Games and the two prior Winter Olympic Games, in Calgary, Canada, in 1988 and in Albertville, France, in 1992, found that the long-term impact on tourism was between nonexistent and very modest after what appeared to be about a "three-year" novelty effect. The impact on tourism after the Winter Olympic Games in Innsbruck, Austria, in 1976 was similar.

There is little to indicate that, even in the best of cases, the Olympics or World Cup boosted tourism beyond a couple of years, if at all. On tourism growth following the games, Teigland opined with regard to Lillehammer's experience:

> The tourism developments so far in the Norwegian host town and region are in many ways lower than expected by both private investors and public authorities. One effect of the too high expectations is a clear overcapacity of commercial accommodation supply afterwards. Another effect is serious economical problems in the host town, which now has decided to reduce its public budget by 12–15% from 1997 on. The recent sale of the major facility for 1 (one) U.S. dollar to prevent bankruptcy reflects also that the realities have been different from local expectations (and forecast by more or less serious advisers).[14]

Athens 2004 presents a somewhat more positive and complicated story. First, Athens was prudent to be more cautious in expanding its hotel capacity for the seventeen-day event. Hotel capacity was expanded by only 8 percent, less than one-third of Sydney's expansion. Second, a significant part of Athens's Olympic budget went into modernizing its airport, roads, public transportation, and communications system. Although Athens's tourism fell by 6 percent in the Olympic year of 2004, the improved infrastructure, together with the city's strong tourist reputation prior to the games, seems to have contributed to a healthy growth in foreign arrivals in 2005 and 2006.[15] After 2006, tourism suffered, but the decline was likely the result of external and domestic economic weakness. It is also notable, however, that despite its post-Olympic growth during 2004–06, Greek tourism growth was outpaced in those years by tourism to both Turkey and Croatia.

It seems clear that the post-Olympic or post–World Cup tourist trajectory will vary by country, depending on characteristics of the country, its previous tourist experience, and economic conditions, among other things. There is little evidence, however, that the world media exposure from the games will by itself launch the city or country onto a higher growth path. Each prospective host would do well to ask the question, if we have $10 billion or $20 billion or more to spend on promoting tourism, what is the most effective use of those resources?

### Trade and Investment

If there is advertising value from hosting, then presumably it might appeal not only to potential tourists but also to people interested in doing business with the host city or country. It is not surprising, then, that event promoters frequently trumpet increases in international trade and investment as a potential benefit. Until a 2011 study by Andrew K. Rose and Mark M. Spiegel, however, there was no independent scholarly study that attested to such a positive effect.[16] Rose and Spiegel found that Olympic host countries experience substantial and lasting increases in their exports.[17] They attributed this effect not to the actual hosting of the games but to the bidding to host the games. That is, the positive effect they identified holds equally for countries that bid to host and are not selected by the IOC to host and for countries that bid and are selected to host. Rose and Spiegel suggest that the causal effect is through each country's signaling an openness to commerce, as well as an interest and competitiveness in trade, by bidding to host the games.

A subsequent study by Wolfgang Maennig and Felix Richter, however, effectively critiqued Rose and Spiegel on the grounds that their sample of countries was not representative:

We challenge the empirical findings of Rose and Spiegel because they compare Olympic nations such as the United States, Japan, Germany, Canada, Italy, Spain, and Australia, which have been among the leading export nations for centuries, to all other nations. Their comparison of structurally different, nonmatching groups might suffer from a selection bias.[18]

When Maennig and Richter corrected for this bias by using only structurally similar countries, they found that the positive trade-signaling effect completely disappeared. Thus, we are left without any empirical evidence to confirm the touted benefit.

### Qualitative and Other Benefits

The list of alleged qualitative benefits associated with hosting the Olympics is long and reaches in many directions: improved management practices and business culture, uplifted mood, reduced crime, higher real estate values, increased exercise and participation in sports, better sustainability practices, and improved values. Here, too, independent corroborative evidence is lacking. While there have doubtless been improvements in some of these areas for some hosts, such improvements would likely have occurred with or without hosting. Other so-called benefits, when they do occur, can be a mixed blessing. Higher real estate prices are good for current property owners in the affected areas, but they are not good for current tenants or people and businesses hoping to move into the area. Nor are they good for the people who were evicted.

Still other claimed benefits do not appear to be benefits at all. A 2012 study that estimated the impact of sporting events and professional sports teams on local crime rates found that while franchises do not have a statistically significant impact on crime rates, the Olympics are associated with a 10 percent *increase* in crime rates.[19]

Sustainability is another area in which results may be mixed to poor, despite the IOC's recent rhetorical focus on this issue. Following pushback after the ecological losses sustained during and after the Albertville, France, Winter Games in 1992, the IOC announced its "Agenda 21"—henceforth to promote sustainable games—at the Earth Summit in Rio. At the Olympic Congress in 1994, the IOC stressed that environmental preservation was "an essential component of Olympism," and in 1995 it inserted mention of the environment into Rule 2 of the Olympic Charter, requiring that the IOC see that "the Olympic Games are held in conditions which demonstrate a responsible concern for environmental issues."

The example of South Africa, which hosted the 2010 World Cup, suggests the difficulty of making a net improvement on this dimension. There were advances in wastewater treatment, and technological knowledge was gained regarding more efficient energy use. However, there was also increased pollution from construction materials, as well as a massive carbon footprint from international air travel to and from the competition (more than 80 percent of the 2010 Cup's carbon footprint came from jet travel). While jet travel to games anywhere will leave a significant carbon footprint, when the host country is located in the southern part of the Southern Hemisphere and isolated from population centers longitudinally, the footprint grows measurably.

In the case of Brazil in 2014, the government's PR boasted of the BRT transportation system that was created in several cities. This system consisted of special lanes for rapid transit buses. At best, BRT connected airports with World Cup (or future Olympic) venues, but it did little or nothing to ameliorate the woeful inadequacy of public transportation for the Brazilian people in Rio, São Paulo, and other cities.[20] The main BRT line in Rio runs 39 kilometers from the airport to the upscale residential suburb of Barra da Tijuca (where the main Olympic cluster for 2016 lies) and rips through a dozen lower-income neighborhoods. From the perspective of sustainability, Brazil is a country without passenger train service and in desperate need of an effective light rail system. The commitment of billions of dollars to infrastructure for the World Cup and Olympics was an opportunity to address the glaring deficiencies in public transportation; instead, there was investment in the BRT bus system and airport expansion promoting the use of fossil fuels.[21]

Equally troubling is Brazil's plan to build a golf course in a low-lying, environmentally fragile area of Barra da Tijuca. Golf is returning to the 2016 Olympics for the first time since 1900. In Brazil, golf is exclusively the domain of the wealthy. Of Rio's two golf courses, neither is open to the public. Rather than preserving the natural beauty of the coastal land, the Olympics will yield a legacy of a third golf course for the city's elite. Christopher Gaffney, a mega-event and urban planning expert at Rio's Federal Fluminense University, concludes: "One of the few remaining areas of environmental protection in the Barra da Tijuca region has been appropriated by the government, opened up for toxic land use patterns and handed over to a private development firm for recreational and real-estate purposes."[22] In September 2014 a court in Rio de Janeiro ordered the local organizing body to make changes in their plans for the golf course. Citing potential ecological damage, the judge called for the course to be moved away from the lagoon and to the north. If the relocation occurs, it will interfere with a planned high-end residential development.[23]

Interestingly, while the IOC mentions promoting sustainability as one of its main goals (although it provides no metric or standard against which to assess any progress), FIFA's position is more modest. FIFA's goal is "minimizing negative impacts," thereby acknowledging implicitly that there will be environmental damage from hosting a World Cup.[24]

Brazilian communications have improved modestly through the investment in coordinating emergency services across sectors of the government and through installations in and around stadiums (although most of the twelve World Cup venues did not have the promised functioning wireless systems). In contrast, there was no broad-based expansion of communications technology across the Brazilian economy.

Brazil also listed combating racial prejudice as one of the gains to be expected from hosting the World Cup. This claim was no doubt ironic to the people of the Aldeia Maracanã indigenous community, who were violently removed from their land next to the Maracanã Stadium in Rio by shock troops. The head of the state agency responsible for the Maracanã complex at the time of the eviction commented, "The place for Indians is in the forest; that's why we're preserving the Amazon."[25]

To the extent that hosting the Olympics or World Cup brought benefits in any of these areas, the benefits must be weighed against the costs of providing them, and the opportunities forgone to devote resources to other areas. It is inevitable that any hosting experience will leave a positive residue of at least a handful of constructive infrastructure investments. Mega-event boosters will always be able to point to these, and some will claim that they justify the hosting of the event. The question is not whether there is a trace element of pro-development activity. Rather, the questions are: why couldn't these positive investments have been made without hosting the games, and why was it necessary to spend tens of billions of dollars to host the event in order to get several hundred million dollars, or even a billion or more dollars, of worthwhile infrastructural investments?

## Long-Term Costs

When specialized facilities are built for an event that lasts seventeen to thirty-four days, it is perhaps unavoidable that some of these facilities will not be effectively used when the event is over. When they are not utilized or are underutilized, they will still cost money to maintain and operate. The long-term costs in these cases involve the operating and maintenance fees going forward, the debt service on the loans that were issued to finance the original construction, and the opportunity cost of the land on which the facility sits. Such under- or unutilized facilities are commonly referred to as white elephants.[26] They seem to pop up ubiquitously after sport mega-events.

### White Elephants

The Bird's Nest in Beijing, which served as the Olympic Stadium for the 2008 Games, cost a reported $460 million to build. It had a capacity of 90,000 for the Olympics, with 140 luxury suites. One plan was for the Beijing Guo'an soccer team to play in the stadium after the Olympics, but the team backed out, afraid of the embarrassment of drawing its standard 10,000 fans to a venue with eight or nine times that capacity. Today it costs some $10 million a year to maintain, hosts an occasional event, and serves as a tourist stop for visitors to Beijing. According to a *CBS News* report from February 2014, "Few tourists are willing to pay more than $8 to tour the facility as enthusiasm for the 2008 Games fades, and the venue has struggled to fill its space with events."[27] The CBS report goes on to note: "But other venues have withered in neglect. A rowing park in the city's suburbs that cost $55 million has fallen into disuse, and visitors to this paid facility are few and far between. The cycling race tracks in another outlying district are covered in weeds, and the sand volleyball courts have been largely closed off to the public."[28]

While the Bird's Nest may be the best known of the white elephants, the Athens games seem to have spawned the largest number of them. Writing in the Toronto *Globe and Mail* in May 2014, Doug Saunders shared his impressions of the aftermath of the 2004 Athens Olympics:

> If you spend some time wandering the fields and hillsides outside of Athens, as I've done, you will see rising from the scrub a very different sort of Greek ruin. There's a crumbling volleyball stadium with nomadic families living in its stands. There's a 20,000-seat softball park largely reclaimed by trees. A barren, grass-covered hillside resembling a huge abandoned amphitheater turns out to have been a kayaking venue. All were built for the 2004 Olympic Games.[29]

According to one researcher, "Twenty-one out of 22 of the stadiums, arenas, sports halls and swimming pools built for the games are either derelict, in a state of disrepair, boarded up or unable to find a buyer and underused. As the Beijing games opened four years later Athens faced a bill estimated at $784 million simply to maintain this ghost town of Olympian extravagance."[30] Half of the 2,300 apartments in Athens's Olympic Village were still unoccupied in 2011, and most of the commercial properties on the site had closed, while promised schools were never finished. A 2011 article in the *The Telegraph* of London related some aspects of the depressing story:

> Despite grand plans for an Olympic legacy, municipalities ran out of money and the political will to maintain them.
>
> "We had some very good plans, well-laid plans," said Athanasios Alevras, a socialist MP from the ruling PASOK party and former deputy minister of culture in the run-up to the Games. "The idea was to build sites that could be then converted to benefit the lives of Atheneans afterwards. The Olympic Village was a great plan to regenerate an area."
>
> But, he admits, it went wrong. "We promised infrastructure and facilities that then weren't delivered. The plans were not respected. Basically, it's a disaster."
>
> He blames a change in the government and a lack of vision. "It isn't just that we ran out of money but that the administrative system just wasn't prepared to do what was needed," said Mr Alevras.
>
> Many on the streets of Athens see state overspending on the Olympics as a major contributor to Greece's runaway financial problems. Sofia Sakorafa, an MP thrown out of George Papandreou's ruling PASOK party after voting against the bailout package a year ago, estimates the Games cost Greece €27bn, vastly over the given €5.5bn budget. She added that no official figure for the cost has ever been published.
>
> "It was a hugely wasted opportunity and one that sticks in the throat of many people. We are left with installations that are rotting away because we don't even have the money to maintain them. A lot of entrepreneurs and property developers got rich very quickly," said Ms. Sakorafa.

Other former hosts have also had a hard time finding long-term uses for Olympic venues. In Nagano, five large structures from the 1998 Winter Games remain, but many complain that they are too costly for a town of less than 400,000 to maintain. Nagano's Olympic Stadium was converted into a baseball stadium, but there are no teams in Nippon Professional Baseball that play in Nagano. Atlanta's Olympic Stadium was converted into the Atlanta Braves' home park in 1997, but in 2013 the Braves announced that they would move to a suburb north of the city. Barcelona's Olympic Stadium from 1992 still lacks a primary tenant.[31]

Of the twenty stadiums that were built or remodeled for the 2002 World Cup, held jointly in Japan and South Korea, a majority have fallen into disuse.[32] Vancouver's Olympic Village was taken over by the city because the developer defaulted on its loans. A large number of its units remained unsold in early 2014, and the city projected a loss of $300 million on the project.[33]

The South African Premier Soccer League averages only 7,500 fans per match. The Cape Town stadium for the 2010 World Cup was originally to be built in the working-class community of Athlone, with plans for extensive investment to modernize the area's infrastructure. At FIFA's insistence, the new stadium was moved to Green Point, a white, affluent community on the waterfront, at a huge cost. Juliet Macur described her 2013 visit to the Cape Town stadium in the *New York Times:*

> Last fall, I paid about $4 to tour Cape Town Stadium, which was built for the 2010 World Cup in South Africa but had turned into a cavernous ghost town. Maybe 100 people a week buy tickets to get a close look at the Cup-generated waste. The space can be rented for weddings or other events, like the small fashion show that I saw there.
>
> Suites that once held World Cup parties were dusty and silent. The state-of-the-art locker rooms, with tiny safes at each stall and rows of sinks to wash dirt off cleats, remained untouched. Thousands of tiny lights glistened from the ceiling of a V.I.P. entrance.[34]

Of the ten stadiums employed for the 2010 Cup, five were newly constructed, with renovations at the others. One of the new stadiums was built in Polokwane, South Africa, just east of the existing Pietersburg Stadium. The latter was originally going to be updated for the Cup, but FIFA was not satisfied, and the decision was made to build the Peter Mokaba Stadium. The Mokaba Stadium has a capacity of 41,733, but it is rarely used by either professional soccer or rugby teams. Another new facility in Nelspruit, South Africa, is the Mbombela Stadium, with 40,929 seats. There were five worker strikes during the construction. After the last strike, the workers were fired and the project was completed with subcontractors. Serious corruption charges were made, and at least three persons were murdered in connection with the allegations. Many more received death threats. Mbombela is also rarely used, and both Mokaba and Mbombela may have to be demolished to avoid the crippling operating and maintenance costs. Green Point Stadium in Cape Town has yearly maintenance costs of $6.2 million. The Nelson Mandela Bay Stadium is still looking for an anchor tenant and will cost an estimated $8.7 million a year to run.[35]

FIFA has a 420-page stadium manual that explains that a new stadium "provides many benefits for the local community" and enhances community pride. In too many cases, this is fanciful nonsense, but either the executives at FIFA are willfully ignorant or they just don't want any facts getting in the way of their PR machine. The manual doesn't contain a section that elaborates the long-term costs and how to avoid building white elephants.

If finding long-term tenants for soccer stadiums and residential units is difficult, then one can only imagine the challenge in finding uses for lesser-used and more obscure venues such as velodromes, whitewater canoe/kayak runs, beach volleyball stadiums, speedskating ovals, and bobsled tracks. The list of underutilized, vacant, and demolished facilities is long. Some of them are discussed in chapters 5 and 6, which look in detail at specific host cities' experiences with mega-events.

## Long-Term Debt and Opportunity Costs

Just as rollicking parties often leave heavy hangovers, Olympic and World Cup games leave massive debt. Governments borrow to finance their sports extravaganzas. The legacy is that the debt has to be paid back, usually over periods of ten, twenty, or thirty years.

The *New York Times* commented on the residue of heavy debt from the Vancouver Winter Olympics:

> The immediate legacy for this city of 580,000 is a nearly $1 billion debt from bailing out the Olympic Village development. Beyond that, people in Vancouver and British Columbia have already seen cuts in services like education, health care and arts financing from their provincial government.[36]

The Brazilian economy is in dire need of light rail, metros, intercity train transport, roads, bridges, ports, and airport improvements, yet it spends only 1.5 percent of its GDP on infrastructure, compared to the global average of 3.8 percent. Among other things, Brazil's deficient infrastructure puts its businesses at a competitive disadvantage internationally. For instance, a Brazilian soybean farmer in the state of Mato Grosso may spend 25 percent of the value of his product getting it to port, whereas a U.S. soybean farmer in Iowa spends 9 percent.

The money that services the billions of dollars of debt cannot be used for worthy infrastructure projects, for health care, for education, or for promoting sustainability. In fact, paying off the debt has to mean either cuts in public services or higher taxes. Such a financial legacy can be economically justified only if the original investments made with borrowed money have positive consequences for the city's or the country's long-term development. Parties are fun, but promoting jobs and economic development is a more complicated matter.

# 5 | Barcelona and Sochi

Barcelona and Sochi stand at opposite ends of the spectrum in realizing gains from hosting the Olympics. The advance planning, the sources of funding, and the inherent potential based on cultural endowment and location dramatically separate the two cities' experiences and provide an illustrative and cautionary tale for prospective mega-event hosts.

## Barcelona

Barcelona is the poster child of success for cities hosting the Olympic Games. Each new host city studies and seeks to emulate the experience of Barcelona in hosting the 1992 Summer Games. In many ways, the Barcelona case does indeed represent how to do it right, and there is good reason for other cities to try to learn from Barcelona. In other ways, however, the circumstances in Barcelona were unique, and will not be easy for other cities to duplicate.

Some historical background helps set the context for Barcelona's success. From 1939 until his death in 1975, Francisco Franco was the authoritarian ruler of Spain. The Catalonian region, where Barcelona is located, was relatively neglected during this period. Development in Barcelona was characterized by real estate speculation, inadequate investment in infrastructure, and little thought given to urban design. Despite Barcelona's desirable climate, location on the Mediterranean Sea, rich architectural heritage, and interesting culture, the city was well down the list of European tourist destinations and business centers.

With the end of Francoism, the city anxiously anticipated a new opportunity to reshape its development. A positive spirit of cooperation between capital and labor and among the municipal, regional, and national governments fostered a proactive approach. In 1976 the city produced the General Metropolitan Plan (PGM), which established a new spatial framework for the city. A significant part of this framework entailed opening the city to the sea. This involved relocating rail lines that separated the Pobleneu neighborhood from the beach and placing a roadway below-grade at the bottom of the famous street, Las Ramblas. It also meant that an area of mostly abandoned warehouses and factories in Pobleneu would be razed and become the eventual site of the Olympic Village, to be converted to residential housing after the games. Other parts of the plan related to improving the road network around the city, extending the metro system, redesigning the airport, renovating public spaces and museums, and modernizing the sewerage system.

Thus, an early plan for urban redevelopment was formulated by 1976 and then elaborated in the following years. It was not until 1986 that the IOC selected Barcelona to host the 1992 Games.

In 1983, city planners put out a preliminary report on the feasibility of hosting the Olympics and concluded that the refurbishment of the 1936 stadium in Montjuic (which became the Olympic Stadium) and the construction of the Sports Palace and Swimming facility would be undertaken whether or not the city was selected to host the games.[1] Of the thirty-seven sports facilities ultimately used during the 1992 Olympics, twenty-seven were already built and another five were under construction at the time Spain was selected to host the games in 1986.[2] Thus, a central feature of the Barcelona experience is that *the plan preceded the games,* and hence the games were put at the service of the preexisting plan, rather than the typical pattern of the city development plan being put at the service of the games.[3]

Several factors further contributed to the salutary role played by being host to the games. First, of the $11.5 billion total cost of the games (as measured in constant 2000 dollars), $6.9 billion (or 60 percent) came from private sources. Of the 40 percent that came from public sources, only $235 million (5 percent of all public funds) came from the Barcelona city budget.[4] Out of all the investments in urban improvements connected to the PGM and the games, 83 percent went into nonsports facilities.[5]

Second, the macroeconomic conditions in Spain were auspicious. After an annual average rate of GDP per capita growth of 6.1 percent during 1960–74, the next eleven years brought near stagnation, with annual per capita growth falling to 0.8 percent during 1974–85. The protracted period of slow growth meant that the large infrastructural and facility investments of the PGM would stimulate employment and output increases rather than provoke strong inflation. Stated differently, the Barcelona economy was ready to receive and benefit from stimulus spending.

Third, the favorable macroeconomic conditions were enhanced by Spain's entry into the European Economic Community (today known as the European Union) in 1986. Spain's membership facilitated finance, trade, and tourism.

Fourth, and quite important, Barcelona was a hidden jewel. Its location, climate, architecture, and history meant that the city had a tremendous potential for tourism and business that had been unexploited for decades. While many prospective host cities would like to believe that they can emulate Barcelona, few would be able to bring together the special features that characterized Barcelona in the 1980s.

Between November 1986 and July 1992, unemployment in Barcelona fell from 127,774 to 60,885, corresponding to a drop in the unemployment rate from 18.4 percent to 9.6 percent.[6] With a new airport terminal and forty new hotels in the city, the number of passengers at Barcelona's airport almost doubled, from 5.46 million in 1985 to 10.04 million in 1992. Barcelona's ranking as a tourist and business meeting destination among European cities improved from eleventh in 1990 to fourth in 2009.

Of course, although there is a temporal association, it is not necessarily the case that these gains can be attributed solely to hosting the Olympic Games. In fact, the ETOA did a study in which it questioned whether any significant improvement resulted from the 1992 Games. The following is an excerpt from that report:

> Hotel occupancy actually dropped from 70 percent in 1991 to 64 percent in 1992, the Olympic year. Fears of construction and overcrowding played a role in deterring visitors. Further decreases in hotel occupancy followed in the two years after the Olympics registering just 54%. It then took a further two years for Barcelona's occupancy rates to recover. Only in 1998 did they exceed the 80% mark.
>
> Whilst Barcelona has undoubtedly grown as a tourist destination, the extent to which this growth is due to the Olympic Games is by no means certain. If there is any benefit to tourism from hosting the Olympics, then the biggest benefit should be immediately afterwards. This, after all, is when the image of the city would be freshest in the minds of the audience.
>
> But if you plot Barcelona's tourism growth against that of Venice, Florence and Lisbon, its performance is below average.
>
> But Barcelona was, even before the Olympics, the byword for urban cool, feted by everyone from Freddy Mercury to Robert Hughes. The nearest match to a "Barcelona without the Olympics" would be Dublin and Prague, both medium sized national centres which blended hedonism with considerable cultural appeal. If you track Barcelona's visitor growth against these cities, then the "Olympic effect" disappears.[7]

Yet a closer look at Barcelona's tourism numbers suggests that the ETOA's critical analysis may have been overstated.

Table 5-1 shows the number of domestic and foreign tourist bed nights (the number of tourists multiplied by the average number of nights per tourist), which is a more complete measure of tourism's economic impact than simply the number of tourists. (Three of the columns provide ratios comparing bed nights between years to depict the growth over the period.) While the number of bed nights in Barcelona did decline in 1993, the year following the games, it grew handsomely thereafter. If we compare Barcelona's performance with that of Florence and Venice during the 1990/1991 through 1994 period, we find that Barcelona's tourism increased more than Florence's whether we use 1990 or 1991 as the base year, and increased more than Venice's when 1990 is used as the base year for comparison. Barcelona also outperformed the growth of all other major European cities during either time frame. More significant, since 1993 Barcelona's tourism growth has far outpaced that of all the other European cities in table 5-1. The city's tourism rise has been remarkable by any standards.

What accounted for Barcelona's take-off since 1993? A 2010 English study, seeking to garner lessons for the upcoming 2012 London Games, observed about the Barcelona games: "However, hotels that had an average annual occupancy of 80% before the Olympic Games, now found that they had less than 50% occupancy. This, in turn, caused prices to fall with the very real prospect that the city would fade back into obscurity."[8]

This interpretation is consistent with that of the ETOA: the games by themselves greatly expanded the supply of hotel rooms without automatically increasing the demand for hotel rooms commensurately. Hotel prices fell, the hospitality sector fretted, and the city took action.

In 1993, Barcelona established its Bureau of Tourism (Turisme de Barcelona), a combination of public and private interests. The bureau is presided over by the city's mayor, while its executive committee is headed by the president of the Chamber of Commerce. The bureau undertook extensive market research and launched an aggressive promotional campaign. As well, new port facilities were exploited to develop a cruise market; today those facilities can accommodate

**TABLE 5-1. European Tourism by City**

| City | | | | Millions of bed nights, by year | | | | | | |
| --- | --- | --- | --- | --- | --- | --- | --- | --- | --- | --- | --- |
| | 1990 | 1991 | 1992 | 1993 | 1994 | Ratio, 1994/1990 | Ratio, 1994/1991 | 1995 | 2000 | 2010 | Ratio, 2010/1991 |
| London | 91.300 | 84.400 | 84.100 | 85.782 | 92.100 | 1.01 | 1.09 | 103.300 | 124.440 | 114.636 | 1.36 |
| Paris | 31.166 | 28.269 | 30.976 | 26.453 | 26.984 | 0.87 | 0.95 | 24.813 | 33.547 | 35.790 | 1.27 |
| Berlin | 7.244 | 7.668 | 7.661 | 7.292 | 7.344 | 1.01 | 0.96 | 7.530 | 11.413 | 20.803 | 2.71 |
| Rome | 12.915 | 12.019 | 12.406 | 12.367 | 14.374 | 1.11 | 1.20 | 12.828 | 14.781 | 20.395 | 1.70 |
| **Barcelona** | **3.796** | **4.090** | **4.333** | **4.257** | **4.705** | **1.24** | **1.15** | **5.675** | **9.276** | **15.342** | **3.75** |
| Madrid | 9.482 | 8.728 | 7.717 | 7.186 | 8.056 | 0.85 | 0.92 | 8.372 | 12.655 | 15.193 | 1.74 |
| Prague | 4.524 | 4.700 | 4.363 | 3.515 | 4.556 | 1.01 | 0.97 | 5.104 | 8.155 | 12.090 | 2.57 |
| Vienna | 8.079 | 7.617 | 7.606 | 7.226 | 7.493 | 0.93 | 0.98 | 7.623 | 8.235 | 11.676 | 1.53 |
| Munich | 6.924 | 6.608 | 6.541 | 6.095 | 5.932 | 0.86 | 0.90 | 6.127 | 7.756 | 11.096 | 1.68 |
| Amsterdam | 5.721 | 5.364 | 5.850 | 5.414 | 5.912 | 1.03 | 1.10 | 6.214 | 7.766 | 9.725 | 1.81 |
| Hamburg | 3.962 | 4.072 | 4.044 | 3.960 | 4.115 | 1.04 | 1.01 | 4.165 | 4.845 | 8.877 | 2.18 |
| Milan | 5.791 | 5.574 | 5.590 | 5.352 | 5.764 | 1.00 | 1.03 | 6.005 | 5.035 | 8.420 | 1.51 |
| Florence | 5.671 | 5.468 | 5.756 | 5.647 | 6.202 | 1.09 | 1.13 | 6.455 | 6.874 | 6.008 | 1.10 |
| Budapest | 6.586 | 5.032 | 4.519 | 4.149 | 4.373 | 0.66 | 0.87 | 4.328 | 4.873 | 5.854 | 1.16 |
| Venice | 2.432 | 2.209 | 2.388 | 2.583 | 2.809 | 1.16 | 1.27 | 2.944 | 3.563 | 5.761 | 2.61 |

Source: Data compiled from TourismReview.com (www.tourism-review.com/bednight-figures-in-european-cities-reach-for-the-sky-in-the-european-cities-marketing-benchmarking-report-news2847), various years.

more than 26,000 passengers daily. Serendipitously, the deregulation of European airlines in 1997 led to the emergence of new, private companies offering heavily discounted air service within Europe. Together, these factors, along with Barcelona's inherent attractions, catapulted the city onto its gilded path to tourism glory.

Thus, although hosting the games was hardly the only factor behind Barcelona's success, it appears to have been a catalyzing influence. It is not without reason that Barcelona has become a poster child of Olympic good fortune.

But Barcelona's hosting experience had some less appealing aspects, too. The development plan included the removal of old industrial and residential areas. Barcelona's widely published and well-known architectural critic Josep Maria Montaner leveled the following criticism at the changes to the city's urban landscape:

> [There was a] mistreatment of heritage, especially the industrial heritage in Poblenou. To understand this, one must understand that the underlying characteristic of the Spanish tradition, from dictatorship to democracy, was one of forgetting—wiping out the past and ignoring the responsibility of Francoism. . . . This programmed amnesia was similarly applied to urbanism. . . . The aim being to erase the city's working class memory, by demolishing popular and cooperative centers, old social housing and factories . . . and the total absence of any sustainability objectives. . . . In no building project . . . were any ecological criteria or sustainability standards implemented.[9]

Barcelona's new urban zones were redeveloped with improved public services and, in some cases, direct access to the sea. These parts of the city became gentrified, and hand in hand with gentrification came higher prices. Higher prices meant that lower-income people had to relocate, and, more generally, plans for public housing were underfulfilled.[10] One study noted the following impacts:

—Strong increases in the prices of housing for rent and for sale (from 1986 to 1993 the cumulative increase was 139% for home sale prices and nearly 145% in home rentals)

—A drastic decrease in the availability of public housing (from 1986 to 1992 there was a cumulative decrease of 5.9%)

—A gradual decrease in the availability of private houses for rent (from 1981 to 1991 the cumulative decrease was 23.7%)[11]

Thus, like the experience with mega-events elsewhere, hosting the games in Barcelona was accompanied by a redistribution of living standards to the detriment of lower-income groups.[12]

Finally, it is noteworthy that Barcelona made a major investment to host the 2004 Universal Forum of Cultures. The planning for this 141-day international event did not benefit from either the political euphoria of the 1980s or the cooperation of different sectors of the Barcelonan community. Indeed, there was vocal opposition from several NGOs, which argued the planning was controlled by big-business interests in the city. The cost of hosting the Forum was $2.3 billion, and the extended event was expected to draw more than 5 million visitors. The official attendance figure was 3.5 million, but various independent estimates were significantly lower.[13] According to one study, the physical legacy of the 2004 Forum had little to commend it:

> The coastal area built up around the forum district offers few amenities to pedestrians. What was left after the 2004 events are sprawling empty spaces on a scale useless for much else than future large events. The result, unsurprisingly, is a wasteland of plazas. Worse yet, the unpopularity of these plazas spreads to the parks and beaches that flank them (to the point where one feels unsafe in them).[14]

Barcelona, then, found it difficult to emulate its own experience, which should sound a strong cautionary note to would-be hosts of future Olympic and World Cup competitions.

## Sochi, Russia

If Barcelona is the poster child for how to host the Olympics successfully, then Sochi is the poster child for how to do it unsuccessfully. Plans to develop Sochi into a winter resort had existed since late Soviet times, and the bid for the 2014 Games was the third such visiting of the idea. The two previous ones in the 1990s failed owing to a lack of funds and the collapse of the economy after the fall of the Soviet Union.[15] Because of the 2014 Olympics, Sochi's "refurbishment" became much grander than it would have been otherwise. The initial plan was to spend $12 billion. For Vladimir Putin, the Winter Games were intended to elevate Russia's status worldwide to that of a superpower.

Sochi is a city of 350,000 inhabitants on the Black Sea. It has a subtropical climate, with warm summers and mild winters, and has long served as a summer retreat for Russia's elite. In addition to hosting the 2014 Winter Games, it will be one of the host cities for the 2018 World Cup.

Although the PR spin from Putin was that Sochi would become a year-round, stylish European resort, the evidence seems to suggest that not only will that not occur but that Sochi's historical draw as a summer resort may have been damaged. The price tag for this grandiose foray certainly exceeded $50 billion and may have reached above $65 billion.

Of course, the real cost of the Sochi games is a closely guarded state secret, and we will probably never know. Igor Nikolaev, director of the Strategic Analysis Department at FBK, one of Russia's most respected financial and accounting consulting firms, estimated the total cost at $66.7 billion.[16] But let us be conservative for the moment and use the figure most often cited by Russian officials and the media, $51 billion—still some $10 billion more than the previously most expensive games, in Beijing in 2008, and also more costly than all previous Winter Olympics combined. Even at $51 billion it represents five times the initial Sochi bid documentation for total costs at $10.3 billion.[17]

How much money would have to be made from Sochi tourism to justify an investment of $51 billion? A $51 billion loan financed over thirty years at an 8.25 percent interest rate, the Russian Central Bank's interest rate in late 2013, would require $4.7 billion in profits from Sochi tourism *a year* to make the annual debt payment. To put that tidy sum in perspective, the *total* annual personal income generated in Pitkin County, Colorado, home of the famous ski resorts of Aspen and Snowmass, in 2010 was under $700 million.

Now let's consider what we know about the "plan" for the Sochi games and its record investment. The ultimate goal of Putin in seeking the games was revealed by Deputy Prime Minister Alexander Zhukov in July 2007, when Russia was selected to host the 2014 Olympics. Zhukov declared, "This is international recognition of the new Russia." Boris Gryzlov, the leading Duma member, added, "Russia is once again becoming a world leader."[18]

Putin's vanity games involved little planning for the future. They were about proving that Russia could pull off this mega-construction project, in some ways similar to Stalin's superindustrialization project during the first Soviet Five-Year Plan of 1928–32. If enough resources were lavished on Sochi and sufficient payoffs made, then it could and would be done—or almost done. A lot went wrong.

### The Oligarchs and Private Funding

Originally, the idea was to have the private sector cover about two-thirds of the construction costs, which were supposed to total $12 billion (the estimate was increased from the initial $10.3 billion bid presented to the IOC). Putin went to his oligarch friends, whom he had set up with sweetheart leases to Russia's mineral wealth, and called in his chips. The oligarchs, somewhat reluctantly, went along at first, expecting a controlled amount of funding and subsidies from the state. As the required investments grew, the hoped-for subsidies were not forthcoming and the necessary payoffs to get the work done ballooned.[19] The oligarchs grew weary. Two such oligarchs were Vladimir Potanin (nickel) and Oleg Deripaska (aluminum).

Putin had suggested that Potanin finance the building of one of four ski resorts, some thirty-eight miles from Sochi, while the two of them were on a ski vacation together. Deripaska, who borrowed $1 billion from the state bank VEB and later undertook projects on the port, roads, airport, and Olympic Village worth an estimated $2.4 billion, was told that it would be highly advisable for him to go along with projected Sochi investments if he wanted future Kremlin support for his business ventures.[20]

Both Potanin and Deripaska gave numerous interviews to express concern about their investments and to call for enhanced government subsidies, tax benefits, and low-interest credit. Potanin told Reuters in 2012 that he wanted to sell the hotels he was building before the games, but pressure from the Kremlin dissuaded him. A study by the Center for Security Analysis and Prevention in Prague similarly found that "the developers who build new hotel complexes [in Sochi] are losing interest in these projects." The report went on to state that "some of the private investors have realized the impossibility of achieving a return on realized buildings and they demand a percentage subsidy on loans from the state bank and want the state to buy a share in their companies."[21]

Mikhail Kasyanov, a former prime minister under Putin, suggested the private investments were coerced: "If you want to carry on doing business in Russia, here's the tax you need to pay—the kind of a tax that [Putin] wants you to pay." Nonetheless, as the magnitude of the Sochi expenses escalated, the share of the private financing, although huge to the individual investors, fell. By some estimates, although originally projected to cover roughly 67 percent of all costs, private funds probably accounted for less than 10 percent. Public monies and the Russian people covered the rest.

To be sure, what originally appeared as private funding may end up as public funding because some loans from the state bank won't be repaid and additional budgetary appropriations are slated to subsidize private losses on certain investments. A July 2014 article in *Around the Rings* reported the following:

Russia's development bank, the VEB, has asked for the federal government to cover losses related to Sochi Olympic construction—as much as $5 billion.

A report in the Kommersant says Prime Minster Dmitry Medvedev told the finance ministry to include the losses in its 2015 budget, which will fund the government in 2016 and 2017.

VEB chairman Vladimir Dmitriev said nine borrowers were at risk of missing payments on construction. Included in that group are developers behind the Rosa Khutor and Gorki venues, the Olympic Village, the Sochi 2014 headquarters, and a group of hotels built for the Games.[22]

### Civil Rights, Worker Exploitation, and Forced Relocations

Human Rights Watch published a study in February 2013 that found extensive violations of Russian labor law. Investigators interviewed dozens of migrant workers—about 16,000 of whom came from outside Russia—at the various Olympic venues and transportation construction sites and found that it was common for workers to work seven days a week, more than ten hours a day, and to receive no overtime pay. The nominal pay range varied between $1.80 and $2.60 an hour, although some workers did not receive any pay, or received delayed or partial payments. The migrant workers were put in excessively crowded living conditions with inadequate nutrition. The report notes that this treatment is in direct contravention of the Olympic Charter, which pledges to promote and uphold human dignity.[23]

The report also notes that, as is common to Olympic construction sites, the investigators observed many instances of forced evictions and relocations, with below-market compensation to the displaced residents. Tatiana Skiba's new hillside home was ruined when vast amounts of concrete and rubble were dumped from an Olympic construction site. Skiba stated that while she was initially excited about the Olympics coming to Sochi, "Now the Olympics is hell for me and for everyone who lives along this street. It is hell and we are very bitter toward the government."[24]

### Pollution

Environmentalists have argued that venue and infrastructure construction around Sochi has been damaging to the sensitive mountain landscape, has hurt biodiversity, and has dumped toxins into the Black Sea. Here is Jules Boykoff:

By 2010, both Greenpeace and the World Wildlife Fund had severed ties with Russia's state-owned construction firm Olympstroi, which the NGOs blamed for dumping heavy metals and industrial waste. In 2009 the Russia-based group Environmental Watch on North Caucasus lodged a complaint that the natural gas giant Gazprom was illegally crossing into the Caucasus Strict Nature Reserve in order to build a road connecting to the Olympic Ski Complex. . . . In February 2013, the group issued an open statement to the IOC asserting that deforestation and the release of toxic effluents had degraded the natural landscape in the Sochi region.[25]

Notwithstanding the IOC's rhetorical embrace of sustainability, Sochi construction has left a problematic environmental footprint. A Reuters reporter observed, "Locals in Sochi say that chemicals used in Olympic construction have polluted the water and damaged the prospect of the city turning into a major Russian tourist destination anytime soon." A tourist from Moscow told the reporter, "You don't want to swim in the water here. Even the locals have stopped swimming here." The Human Rights Watch report echoed these concerns, citing innumerable complaints from residents and suggesting that much of the construction work for the games was performed without following the environmental review procedures mandated in Russian law.

An article in the *Moscow Times* reported: "Prominent among the critics are ecologists, who say that the massive construction projects are destroying local wildlife. In 2010, the United Nations Environment Program said in a report that the government had ignored the cumulative effects of the various projects on the regional ecosystem."[26]

Steven Meyers, writing for the *New York Times Magazine*, commented on the "rapacious development under way in the region's protected parks, including a supposed research center above Sochi that is widely believed to be a personal mountain resort, replete with helipads and several Swiss-style chalets, for Putin."[27]

The locals and the environmentalists who protested these ecological transgressions were subject to scorn and repression. According to an Associated Press 2013 report, the protesters "have been detained, put on trial and even barred from going on the beach."[28]

There was perhaps an even larger environmental fallout from the Sochi games—the relaxation of legislation for environmental protection around the country. Martin Müller, professor of urban geography at the University of Zurich, observed: "It is even more cause for concern that some of this environmental damage was facilitated through the targeted relaxation of environmental jurisdiction. This applies to the law on protected areas, which was modified to allow for sports mega-events to be held there, and the forest code, which was modified to allow for the cutting of rare species of trees."[29]

### Terrorism

As became painfully apparent following the two bombings of the railway station in Volgograd in December 2013, killing thirty-four, and the shootout in Dagestan, which killed another seven, the Sochi area is politically unstable and dangerous. Terrorist groups seeking independence are very active in Dagestan, Chechnya, and Abkhazia, among other nearby regions. A Chechen terrorist leader threatened to disrupt the Winter Games. While the Sochi area may have been thought of as a peaceful, subtropical retreat on the Black Sea prior to its exposure to the world press around the 2014 Olympics, now there are few who regard the region as safe.

### Weather

As many had feared, the weather did not cooperate for the Winter Games. For nearly a week, thermometers broke 60 degrees Fahrenheit at the ski resort in the mountains outside Sochi. The organizing committee had to use the tons of artificial snow they had stored under thermal blankets to spread over the competition areas. Even then, events were delayed, and competitors complained copiously.

Subtropical Sochi has served for decades as a summer retreat, mostly for Russian politicians and, more recently, wealthy business leaders.[30] The expressed hope was to convert Sochi into a year-round resort. The warm weather during the Winter Games, broadcast to the world on television, the Internet, and social media, could not have promoted the image of Sochi as a winter resort very successfully.

## Hospitality

As has often been the case with mega-sporting events, the scale of construction was so grand that it was inevitable that certain projects were not completed on time. For the hotel construction projects in Sochi, this problem was experienced in spades. The media outlets were swarming with jokes about hotels that did not open for the games despite having booked tourists or athletes, hotel rooms without water or with water pooling on the bathroom floor, rooms without phones or television sets, bathrooms without toilets or ceilings, and so on. There were abundant complaints about the lack of evening entertainment, the paucity of restaurant choices, and the level of service.

Alexander Maklyarovsky, the head of the internal tourism department at the major Russian tour operator company KMP, commented, "The city has no experience with foreigners and locals struggle to communicate in English." Sochi's mayoral adviser, Olga Nedelko, added that "hospitality is also an issue . . . locals are used to seeing tourists as a nuisance."[31]

## Impact on Tourism

The 2013 official report of the Sochi organizing committee noted that tourism in the Sochi area declined in 2010 and 2011, sending it back down to its 2006 level. The report speculated that the decline may have been due to excessive construction work in the region. With all the negative publicity from the games, there was little optimism that tourism would pick up. The facts that Sochi is far away from most population centers in Russia and Europe, difficult to get to, and encumbered by Russian visa requirements did not augur well. There were widespread concerns that the overbuilding of hotel rooms for the games (22,000 new rooms) would lead to occupancy rates as low as 30 percent and put downward pressure on room prices, which in turn would lead to extensive bankruptcies.

A comprehensive study on the prospects for Sochi tourism by the Czech Center for Security Analysis and Prevention was not sanguine. The study concluded:

> The developers who build new hotel complexes are losing their interest in these projects in Sochi. . . . The returns . . . after the Olympic Games are over remain the main investment risk. The emergence of competitive tourism seems to be the biggest problem with the investment. . . . Instead of staying in Sochi for three days, the Russians prefer to fly to Egypt or Turkey for one week, all inclusive and with services at a higher level. Some of the private investors realized the impossibility of achieving a return on realized buildings and they demand a percentage subsidy on loans from the state bank and want the state to buy a share in their companies.[32]

In fact, the massive Olympic construction was just that: construction for the seventeen days of the Olympics. Although there were visions of a new international, year-round, luxury resort in Sochi, no careful feasibility studies were done and there was no serious planning. After the games were over, David Segal, writing in the *New York Times*, made the following observations:

> It also seems that few people in the upper echelons of the Russian government have given the future of Sochi much thought.
>
> "I don't think anyone is sure what to do with it," said Sufian Zhemukhov, co-author of a coming book on the Sochi Games. "I say that because President Putin and Prime Minister Medvedev have changed the concept many times. First, it was going to become a kind of capital of southern Russia. Then they talked

about dismantling the arenas and taking them north. A few months ago, Medvedev said they were going to open casinos there. Virtually everything about the Sochi Games has been improvised, it seems, and their aftermath will not be any different."[33]

Brian Gleeson, the general manager of the Radisson Blue Beach Resort and Spa in Sochi, is not sure where the additional tourists will come from. He has written off U.S. and European tourists, who have better options closer to home for which they need not put up with the expense and hassles of procuring a Russian visa.[34] The annexation of Crimea is making things even worse: the beaches in Crimea are the one immediate competitor for Sochi in summer tourism. Once the Russian government annexed Crimea, it began pouring money into subsidizing flights and getting the tourism industry up and running again to hasten the integration of Crimea into Russia.

Complicating any constructive legacy still further is that the combination of corruption and the myopic vision of the overall project led to most of the building being done on the cheap. Martin Müller, who has spent five years studying the area, commented that he spoke with engineers in charge of quality assurance on the various construction projects and was told, "There is no quality to assure. Quality wasn't an issue. It wasn't demanded by investors, and nobody asked for it. Builders would sometimes even try to bribe their way through the quality assessment phase."[35]

As of the time of writing, July 2014, the Olympic venues and hotels appeared to be in financial trouble. The Russian government issued a rule in May 2014 that exempted Olympic-related businesses from regional property taxes. This move would reportedly cost the regional government $114 million in tax revenue during 2014. One official commented that the businesses did not have the money to pay the tax, so there was really no choice.[36]

Meanwhile, hotel vacancy rates soared, and officials scrambled to develop plans to entice tourism. Several ideas were floated, including the creation of an extreme sports park and a Russian Disneyland, but as of

July 2014 nothing had been decided. Some previous plans were scrapped, such as the conversion of the Iceberg Skating Palace into a velodrome.

Ironically, in June 2014 the government announced that the Sochi games had produced a record Olympic surplus of $261 million.[37] This figure refers to the *operating* revenues and *operating* costs directly connected to the staging of the games and has little economic meaning. The central government could write the Sochi Olympic Organizing Committee a check to boost its revenues or to reduce its costs for any amount to generate such a surplus. And the designation of *operating* surplus means that all capital costs are excluded.

Thus, in the end, Putin had an inordinately expensive mess on his hands, with the potential for political pushback. Although not so proficient at planning economic development, Putin is masterful at political and military strategy. So, either by serendipity or by design, Putin was able to divert the eyes of the Russian people away from Sochi just days after the Winter Olympics ended and toward a much weightier nationalist matter—the annexation of Crimea to Russia.

Russia is currently committed to hosting yet another "most expensive ever event" with the World Cup in 2018. That extravaganza is estimated to cost a minimum of $21 billion already four years before the event (with further cost increases likely to occur down the line, as seems to be the rule).[38]

The contrast between Barcelona and Sochi couldn't be starker. For Barcelona, the Olympics were put at the service of the preexisting city plan; for Sochi, the city plan was put at the service of the Olympics. Barcelona had deep, unrealized potential as a tourist destination, whereas Sochi's potential arguably had already been approached. In Barcelona, the financing scheme took full advantage of existing infrastructure and maximized the use of outside funds; in Sochi, virtually everything was built from scratch, and financing was overwhelmingly public. For Barcelona, management was intelligent and efficient; for Sochi, management was often feckless and corrupt. The different economic outcomes of the 1992 and 2014 Olympic Games reflected these underlying realities.

# 6 | Rio-Brazil and London

Brazil and London represent the two most recent experiences with hosting the World Cup and the Summer Olympics, and Rio, of course, will become the newest host of the Summer Games in 2016. The contrasts between the Rio-Brazil and London experiences are manifested along several dimensions: degree of economic development, planning model and goals, administrative style and efficiency, and the extent of buy-in from the local population.

## Rio and Brazil

Two for one. Not a bad idea. Brazil hosted the 2014 World Cup and Rio de Janeiro will host the 2016 Summer Olympics. In theory, there should be some savings, or what economists call economies of scale, from such a double engagement.[1] The final match of the World Cup was played at the refurbished Maracanã Stadium in Rio, and the same venue is slated to serve as the Olympic Stadium in 2016.[2] The Brazilian Ministry of Sport is overseeing both events, and many of the same executives are supposed to be involved. If all goes according to plan, a pacification of the favelas, a more efficient political and administrative apparatus, and various infrastructural improvements will result from the doubleheader, helping to carry Brazil's fame and fortune forward in the coming decades.

When Rio was awarded the host status for the 2016 Games, it became the first city in South America slated to host the Olympics. Rio's Organizing Committee for the Olympic Games (OCOG) took some interesting initial steps. It hired several outside consulting firms (AECOM from Los Angeles, Wilkinson Eyre Architects from the United Kingdom, Pujol Barcelona Architects from Spain, and IMG and McKinsey from New York) to design an urban strategy and style for the games. The final master plan for the 2016 Games was meant to emulate that of the successful 1992 Games in Barcelona—four urban clusters rather than one focal area, with new transportation routes and technologies connecting them. Superficially, the plan resembled Barcelona's. In substance and outcome, however, the two plans had little in common.

### The 2014 World Cup

But first things first. Although the 2014 World Cup was pulled off with relatively minor hitches evident to the international television audience, on the streets of the host cities the situation was far from normal. A *New York Times* reporter described the scene in Rio on July 13, the day of the final match between Argentina and Germany, this way: "The authorities had assembled what ranked as one of the largest security operations ever in Brazil, with 25,000 soldiers and police officers giving Rio a martial feel throughout the day with sirens blaring and motorcades halting traffic."[3]

Also not visible to the international television audience was that preparations on the ground lagged woefully. The transportation infrastructure was far from completed. Buildings around the stadiums were left half-finished. The building that was supposed to serve as the media center in the southern city of Curitiba, the capital of Paraná, for example, was left as a "six-story metal skeleton jutting out from the World Cup soccer stadium."[4] Other projects abandoned in midstream included the monorail to São Paulo's domestic airport, a passenger terminal at the Fortaleza International Airport, and WiFi networks at six of the twelve stadiums, among many others. Some construction was so rushed that quality was uncertain, such as the overpass on the way to the stadium in Belo Horizonte, which collapsed on July 3, leaving at least two people dead and nineteen injured.[5]

According to a Reuters report, "In Salvador de Bahia, construction of a planned subway system was handed over to a private company halfway through, and work will not be completed until after the tournament is over. A new runway was proposed for the World Cup at Rio de Janeiro's Galeão International Airport, but now it is unclear if it will be finished even in time for the 2016 Games."[6] Five of the twelve host cities admitted that they didn't complete the promised transportation infrastructure (bus lanes, metro, or monorail) on time for the Cup. Sinaenco, a trade group of architects and engineers, stated that nationwide, "only 36 of 93 major projects are complete" in time for the World Cup.[7]

FIFA requires that each host country have eight modern stadiums of at least 40,000 capacity, one of which must have 60,000 seats, for the opening match, and another with 80,000 capacity, for the final contest. That threshold alone would have been difficult enough to meet, but Brazil decided to go one better. In the hopes of exposing twelve of its cities to the world and resolving some internal political squabbles, Brazil committed to having twelve venues, each with a minimum 40,000 capacity.[8] In 2009 the Brazilian Football Confederation initially estimated that refitting or building the twelve stadiums required for the World Cup would cost about $1.1 billion. The total stadium budget eventually rose to over $4.7 billion.[9] Nine of the stadiums were new, and of these, seven were built on the site of existing stadiums that were demolished.[10] With the exception of the new stadiums in Manaus and Cuiabá, all the facilities were publicly financed yet are now under private management. In these so-called public-private partnerships, the taxpayers fund the construction and the private sector gains the usufruct rights. Manaus and Cuiabá, whose new stadiums were also built with public funds, are actively looking for private companies to manage their stadiums, which have little prospect of profitable use.

Estimates for the total cost (including all infrastructure, security, and operations) of the World Cup for Brazil run from $15 billion to $20 billion. (Of course, these estimates, like others concerning the cost of hosting mega-events, are affected by what auxiliary, infrastructural investments are deemed to be directly related to the event. The more tangentially related investments are included, the higher the cost estimates go.)

White elephants seem inevitable. Four stadiums were built in cities with no football team in the first division of Brazil's soccer leagues. In Manaus, there is a second-division team that draws an average attendance of around 1,500. Manaus now has a new stadium with a capacity of 42,374, built at a cost of $325 million.[11] It was used for a grand total of four games during the World Cup. Meanwhile, a sewerage system and monorail that were part of the Manaus Cup plans were never built.

New stadiums were also built in Cuiabá, Brasília, and Natal, all with lower-division teams and low attendance. In Natal, another perfectly good playing field was bulldozed so that a new stadium could be erected that met FIFA standards. Dave Zirin quotes Jan-Marten Hoitsma, a project manager brought in to make sure that Natal's new facility was completed on time: "There are no big football teams here—the biggest team gets gates of around 5,000 and we're building a 42,000-seater World Cup stadium."[12]

The Natal stadium cost $450 million, not including the cost of the new highway that leads to it. That highway cost Maria Ivanilde Oliveira her livelihood. She used to sell ice to locals on their way to the beach. The locals no longer travel on her street. She can no longer afford electricity for her house.[13] Marília Sueli Ferreira works at a stationery store next to the new stadium in Natal. During the competition, she raised the question, "What are we going to use this stadium for after the World Cup? The World Cup is made for tourists, not for residents, and the tourists are going to disappear very soon."[14]

The Mané Garrincha Stadium in Brasília cost a reported $900 million to build and has a capacity of over 70,000.[15] The stadium was initially budgeted at $300 million. An official audit of the stadium completed in May 2014 found that the tripling of the costs owed in large measure to construction company payoffs and price gouging. For example, the 140-page auditor's report states that the transportation of prefabricated grandstands was supposed to cost just $14,700, but the construction company billed the government $1.5 million. The auditors found $2.3 million in overcharges for materials that were listed multiple times on invoices. All told, the report estimates that one-third of the $900 million cost was due to fraudulent billing.

Brasília's professional football team, Brasiliense, is in Brazil's fourth division. They have chosen not to play in the Mané Garrincha Stadium. The team's coach, Marcos Soares, explains why: "You have to pay [to rent the stadium], you have the employees, cleaning, security staff, the clubs have to pay for this. It's a gigantic stadium, for 70,000 people; Brasiliense will not fill a stadium like that. To make a profit, you need, I imagine, 25,000 people and you're not going to get that in a fourth division match in the Brazilian championship."[16]

In Fortaleza, Recife, and Salvador they do have football teams in the first division, but the teams average around 15,000 attendance per game, with an average ticket price of $10. Recife already had three large, multipurpose stadiums. The populations in these cities do not come close to having the purchasing power to pay ticket prices high enough to maintain those stadiums, let alone to service the construction debt. In Curitiba, in early October 2013, with construction 78 percent complete, the new stadium construction was suspended because of numerous safety violations and out of fear that the structure would collapse. It was eventually completed in time for the competition.

Meanwhile, an Associated Press report found "skyrocketing campaign contributions by the very companies involved in the most Cup projects." And Renato Rainha, an arbiter at Brasília's Audit Court, stated, "These donations are making corruption in this country even worse and making it increasingly difficult to fight. These politicians are working for those who financed campaigns."[17]

Rainha speaks with good authority. Two mega-construction companies, Andrade Gutierrez and the Odebrecht consortium (which includes IMX and the Los Angeles–based AEG), received the bulk of World Cup construction projects. Political contributions from Andrade Gutierrez jumped 500-fold, from $73,180 in 2008 to $37.1 million in 2012, and those from Odebrecht went from $90,909 in 2008 to $11.6 million in 2012.[18] Fully 40 percent of federal members of congress had criminal cases pending against them in the nation's highest court.[19]

In São Paulo, the venerable Morumbi Stadium was excluded from the World Cup by FIFA because it failed to meet technical requirements.[20] The local organizing committee for the World Cup decided to build a new stadium that would meet FIFA's requirements. After its overview visit to Brazil in May 2011, FIFA required enhancements to the new facility's design. The enhanced design carried an estimated price tag of $650 million, a 30 percent increase in the total cost. The construction was disrupted in early 2014 when a crane collapse destroyed a good section of the stadium and killed two workers; a work stoppage followed. The construction company in charge of the venue admitted on May 19, 2014, that the glass covers for the roof would not be installed in time for the World Cup, meaning that the fans who were supposed to be protected from the elements would not be.[21] The final cost of the facility was expected to exceed $650 million by a substantial margin. The renowned Brazilian journalist and television commentator Juca Kfouri mused, "A stadium is built in São Paulo, with public money, to deliver to a private club [the Corinthian football team], when São Paulo has a stadium that for more than 50 years has served world football . . . and could perfectly host an event that lasts one month and would host a maximum of six games."[22]

At the famous Maracanã Stadium in Rio, which was originally built for the 1950 World Cup, there was a $200 million renovation for the Pan American Games in 2007.[23] That renovation was not suitable, in FIFA's judgment, so after the Pan American Games, Maracanã

Stadium was partly demolished and then rebuilt for over $500 million. The initial plan for the rebuild included the demolition of the Indigenous Cultural Center (the first indigenous museum in Latin America), as well as of a school and a gymnasium, to make room for a parking garage.[24] Fierce local resistance and social movements, however, have preserved the venues for the time being.

There was also the leveling of a nearby favela (Favela de Metro) and the relocation of its residents. The journalist Dave Zirin described the scene at this former favela in mid-June 2014:

> Two middle-aged men, former residents of Favela de Metro, sat around a plastic table between the sidewalk and a demolished home. We asked them why the city would hastily evict this community only to leave wreckage behind: "They didn't give us a reason why we had to leave. They just came, pushed us out, and knocked the building down."[25]

The land was slated to become a parking lot, but, as the World Cup matches began on June 12, 2014, there was no lot there. Seven hundred families had been displaced. The first 100 were removed at gunpoint and resettled two hours away in a western suburb of Rio. The remaining families protested and sued, and eventually received better treatment.

The plan was to have Brazil's most popular soccer team, Flamengo, continue to play at Maracanã after the games. The proximate problem was that the Consórcio Maracanã, a group led by Brazil's largest construction company, with the now fallen Brazilian billionaire Eike Batista's company IMX and the U.S-based AEG, was awarded a thirty-five-year contract to manage the stadium.[26] The consortium initially proposed to Flamengo that it pay the team a fixed sum per game and that it keep all the revenue generated by signage, concessions, and luxury seating. Flamengo demurred, but a settlement was eventually reached.[27]

The white elephants not only cost hundreds of millions of dollars each to build, they cost millions of dollars annually to operate and maintain. Anyone who has ever owned a car or a house knows that such maintenance costs are not trivial. They also present an aesthetic issue, for they are ultramodern facilities surrounded by a sea of parking lots anomalously situated in open areas or in communities with older, more modest construction.

These massive sports facility and infrastructure expenditures are taking place against a backdrop of sharp income inequality, a relatively low level of economic development, poor social services, increasing prices, and rising expectations. At $11,300, Brazil's per capita income is approximately one-fifth that of the United States. Measured by the Gini coefficient, Brazil's income distribution is roughly 40 percent more unequal than in the United States.[28] Approximately 20 percent of Brazil's 200 million-plus people live in poverty. The Brazilian GDP, which grew at close to 6 percent per year during 2000–10, slowed to a 2 percent rate during 2011–13. Meanwhile, inflation accelerated from the 3–4 percent range during 2000–10 to around 6 percent during 2011–13, and as the World Cup approached in 2014, prices rose at a still faster clip.

Housing prices spiked even faster. While gentrification is appealing to some, it means unaffordable housing to others. It is a pattern familiar to mega-events, as land becomes scarcer and demand often rises. According to the Knight Frank Global House Price Index, the rate of increase in home prices in Brazil during 2012 was the third highest in the world. The rate of increase in Rio was even higher, jumping 58.3 percent (in real terms) between August 2010 and June 2013.[29]

Rio has a housing deficit estimated at 500,000 units. The shortage was aggravated by the widespread evictions of slum (favela) dwellers to improve the visual appearances for the World Cup and Olympics and to allow developers to benefit from the rising real estate value of propitiously situated favelas.[30]

The provision of health services, public transportation, and education for most Brazilians is woeful. So, in hindsight it was not surprising when the announcement of a 9 cent increase in bus and metro fares in the summer of 2013 pushed hundreds of thousands of Brazilians over the edge.

During FIFA's 2013 Confederations Cup warmup for the World Cup, over a million Brazilians spontaneously poured into the streets, carrying placards declaring "Death to the World Cup" and "We Want a FIFA Level Education System." (At the time, Brazil's entire national education budget was $37 billion.) Many of the 2013 protests turned violent. A CNN reporter interviewed a teacher taking part in a demonstration in Belo Horizonte, who asserted that the World Cup was lining the pockets of the rich and corrupt while the poor continued to suffer. The teacher added, "Tonight this is about all of Brazil, we are moving against corruption. We have been suffering too long. And this year we rise. We have woken up."[31]

The protests continued well after the Confederations Cup and into 2014. During the last week of February 2014, a demonstration in São Paulo of more than a thousand people protesting the "waste" of $15–$20 billion[32] on hosting the World Cup turned violent as the protesters "went on a rampage, smashing bank windows and setting up roadblocks with garbage set on fire." Military police put down the protest and arrested more than 230 people.[33]

Toward the end of March 2014, less than eighty days before the start of the World Cup, the head of Rio's police pacification (of the favelas) program was shot during a wave of violence directed against the police. The popular movement seemed to confirm FIFA secretary general Jerome Valcke's observation: "Less democracy is sometimes better for organizing a World Cup."[34]

In the final weeks before the opening match, worker strikes broke out across the country, affecting police, teachers, and transit workers in São Paulo. Political groups threatened disruptive demonstrations, and the government sat down to reach a compromise with all of these groups.[35] According to an article in the *New York Times*, in the six months leading up to the first match on June 12, 2014, in São Paulo ten banks were vandalized (the front glass was shattered) and two car dealerships were damaged. In the same period, 505 people were arrested in São Paulo and 89 were injured (according to GAPP, a group of first-aid volunteers).[36] A poll conducted by the Pew Research Center in June 2014 found that only 34 percent of Brazilians felt the World Cup would have a positive impact on the country, and 72 percent were dissatisfied with the nation's direction.[37]

After the Confederations Cup, it was increasingly clear that the Brazilian government needed to take drastic security measures. The government announced the formation of a 10,000-member federal-level shock security force in addition to the normal public and private security personnel, complete with surveillance drones, to deal with expected protests during the World Cup.[38] The final security bill for the World Cup surpassed $1 billion. (The original contract for London's security force in 2012 was 10,000 as well. In the end, the London games required more than 20,000 military and security personnel.)[39] Protests during the first several Cup matches were decisively squashed by security personnel using tear gas, clubs, and reportedly bullets. At a joint meeting between the Brazilian security chief and FIFA after one week of the competition, it was decided to further beef up security procedures and personnel around the stadiums.

Fueling the resistance movement were concerns regarding FIFA's demands for special tax treatment. Romário de Souza Faria, the former Brazilian soccer star turned politician, claimed that FIFA would make a profit of $1.8 billion from the 2014 World Cup, which would normally yield $450 million in tax revenues. While Romário's assertion may lack accuracy (Brazil's Internal Revenue Service estimated the loss at $248.7 million),[40] it was enough to elicit anger. (It is true that FIFA does generate surpluses from the World Cup cycle approaching a billion dollars. However, since FIFA is a nonprofit organization, whether these surpluses are taxed is a function of the peculiarities of the tax code in each host country. FIFA did qualify as a tax-exempt nonprofit organization during the 1994 World Cup in the United States. There are other, smaller exemptions that FIFA insists on, such as the importation of materials and television equipment and some sales taxes. FIFA's tax privileges are similar to those received by other sports mega-event sponsors and organizations.)

Nor has Brazil's international embarrassment—the ever-present uncompleted projects, the deaths of at least nine construction workers, the crane collapse at the stadium construction site in São Paulo, the decertification of Rio's drug laboratory by the World Anti-Doping Association (necessitating the shipment of samples to Lausanne, Switzerland), and FIFA executives' statements that the preparations in Brazil were the worst they had ever seen—helped dampen the people's protests. Meanwhile, activists in Cuiabá and Manaus were motivated by the fact that their new stadiums cost 50 percent more than their cities' educational budgets.[41]

Further exacerbating local tensions was the shabby treatment of migrant construction workers at World Cup sites. A 2013 report released by the Brazilian Labor Attorney General's office stated that 111 workers on the renovation of São Paulo's airport were living in poor conditions next to the building site. They were lured from the northeast sector of Brazil on promises of monthly wages of $625. Many were not employed and had to stay in one of eleven makeshift camps in "slave-like conditions" next to the airport. Some had to pay more than $220 to secure the job.[42]

Protest passions were also stoked by the forced relocation of entire favelas. Estimates are that 250,000 people living near construction sites were displaced.[43] According to Clean Games, a transparency organization created to monitor the World Cup and Olympics, no government body communicated with the displaced.[44] The razing of favelas is for many reminiscent of a policy of Brazil's military dictatorships in the 1960s and 1970s. Most of the recent evictions took place without consultation with the residents, many of whom had lived in their favela communities for decades and had worked and schooled their children there. If they could prove title to their homes, they received compensation ranging from $1,500 to $5,000.[45] Many were relocated 10 or more kilometers away. Christopher Gaffney, a professor at Rio's Fluminense Federal University, commented, "These events were supposed to celebrate Brazil's accomplishments, but the opposite is happening. We're seeing an insidious pattern of trampling on the rights of the poor and cost overruns that are a nightmare."[46]

Many favelas not slated for destruction instead experienced siege-like conditions. The *Financial Times* reported that several favelas "now resemble no-man's land as military police clutch assault rifles to their bullet-proofed chests" and quoted Carlos Melo, a leading Brazilian political scientist, as saying that the World Cup had put Brazil in the spotlight and was encouraging gangs and other favela residents "to exploit a moment of visibility and the vulnerability of the government."[47]

While there was little question that Brazil needed massive infra-structure investment,[48] the popular sentiment questioned whether the best interests of the country's development were really being served by spending some $5 billion on soccer stadiums, the specialized nature of much of the infrastructure spending, and the ubiquitous waste and corruption.

Part of Brazil's World Cup dilemma seemed to emanate from a peculiarity in FIFA politics. FIFA president Sepp Blatter had prom-ised that South Africa would get to host the World Cup. When South Africa narrowly lost out to host the 2006 World Cup, Blatter per-suaded FIFA to change its selection system by introducing a continen-tal rotation. The African continent would go first, in 2010, thereby assuring South Africa as the host. The 2014 Cup would return to its continent of origin, South America. When 2007 rolled around and it was time to pick the South American host for 2014, there was only one bidder, Brazil.

The existence of only one bidder set up an interesting dynamic. Without competition from other countries, Brazil was not compelled to get its organizational act together. So, for instance, Brazil's initial bid did not designate which cities in the country would host the matches. Nor did Brazil take advantage of the absence of competition to lowball its bid; rather, the goal was to impress the world with Brazil's level of development and readiness to become a major economic player in world trade and tourism. So Brazil boldly declared that it would build or refurbish not the requisite eight but twelve stadiums, along with undertaking a variety of very ambitious infrastructural projects.

Aggravating Brazil's problem of finding domestic political compromise in the selection of the twelve locations, the final determination was not made until 2009—two years after the designation of Brazil as the host of the 2014 Cup.[49] This delay increased the construction costs and left less money available for important transportation and energy projects. Based on its unsatisfactory experience in Brazil, FIFA ended its experiment with continental rotation.

A key part of the initial Brazilian World Cup plan was former Brazilian president Lula's promise that the stadiums would be financed with private funds. But with the state on the hook for delivering the games to FIFA and the IOC, there was no incentive for the private sector to commit financing. Nearly all the stadium financing was paid for with public funds—another sore point for Brazil's World Cup detractors.[50]

Romário denounced the preparations: "The stadiums are constantly late, the rise in costs is way over the top, and public money is being used to build them before they are handed over to private firms who reap the benefits." A 2014 poll in Curitiba found that 58 percent of respondents were against Brazil hosting the World Cup and 87 percent were against using public money to fund the completion of the new stadium (over 70 percent of the funding for which came from the public treasury).[51]

There was more than a little irony, then, when Brazilian sports minister Orlando Silva declared there would be another special legacy of the World Cup: "The World Cup will leave us among other things more attractive stadiums. Clubs will be able to demand higher ticket prices, and our football will be able to finance itself better."[52]

### 2016 Olympic Games

Even though the Olympic Games last only seventeen days, compared to to thirty-four days for the World Cup, the Olympic Games are immensely more complicated to pull off than the World Cup.

The World Cup involves 736 athletes; the Summer Olympics involve 10,500. The World Cup has one championship; the Olympics have dozens. Host-generated broadcasting for the World Cup amounts to a few hundred hours; the Olympics in Rio are expected to generate almost 5,000 hours. The crowds and the traffic are concentrated in one city for the Olympics, rather than being dispersed among twelve.

Whatever deficiencies cropped up in hosting the 2014 World Cup, they appear to be magnified severalfold for the 2016 Summer Games. At Olympic Park, 2,500 construction workers went on strike during April 2014 for several weeks, just as various IOC officials were visiting Rio and declaring that the city was the most behind schedule they had ever seen. The IOC took the extraordinary step of sending a supervisory team to set up shop in Brazil and oversee the progress on the various construction projects over the final two years of preparation. Among other problems, facing environmental challenges, the planned Olympic golf course in Barra da Tijuca still hadn't planted grass as of June 2014, and at least two years is needed for course preparation to be done properly.[53]

At Guanabara Bay, the prospective site for sailing and water sports, pollution levels remain far above even the lax Brazilian standards, and, according to Rio's state environment secretary, Carlos Francisco Portinho, there is no longer any possibility that Rio can meet the pollution reduction metrics promised to the IOC. According to a May 2014 letter that Portinho sent to Brazilian sports minister Aldo Rebelo, it will take at least another decade to significantly reduce pollution levels in the bay, even if the requested $70 million for abatement facilities were immediately allocated. Meanwhile, several Olympic sports federations expressed fears that Rio's polluted waters could prove harmful to athletes' health, potentially exposing them to fecal matter that can cause hepatitis A, cholera, and dysentery.[54] Frustrated by the slow progress being made on Rio's new basketball arena, the head of the International Basketball Federation began looking into the possibility of holding the hoops tournament at an arena in São Paulo, 275 miles away.

In an interview with Brazil's *Colectiva* magazine, leading Brazilian journalist, television personality, and soccer commentator Juca Kfouri opined:

> I think that [hosting the Olympic Games] does not make any sense for a country that does even have a sports policy, as it has been admitted by the Minister of Sports. It is putting the cart before the horse. Sport should be handled as a factor of public health, disease prevention, following the dictates of the World Health Organization, which reveals that every dollar that you invest in democratization and mass sport, you save three in public health. ... What worries me is that the Olympics are in the hands of those who committed the debacle that was the Pan American Games in Rio de Janeiro. I have no reason to believe it will be different. And we should remember that we spent almost 10 times more public money than it was anticipated. From 400 million to nearly 4 billion, while leaving strictly no legacy for the city of Rio de Janeiro. The Bay of Guanabara was not depolluted, as had been promised. The Rodrigo de Freitas lagoon was not depolluted. The metro linking the Pan American Village to the Galeao Airport was not built. ... The Maria Lenk Aquatic Park is not good. The Velodrome is not good. Engenhão, which in theory is the most modern stadium of Brazil, is not planned to be used in the World Cup. At Maracanã ... a stadium was imploded and another is being built instead. I fear the lack of transparency of our spending and by the legacy promised to the city of Rio de Janeiro. We're seeing the displacement of people from their homes against the law, the *manu militari,* to take them much further from [where] they reside, from their jobs, their children's schools and everything else.[55]

Similar to Brazil's experience with the World Cup, the implementation of Rio's grand plans is proceeding at a slow pace. The IOC has expressed its concern over and over. After a three-day site visit in March 2014, the IOC delegation was as diplomatic as it could be in its assessment: "The delivery timelines of some of the venues for test events and the games have faced delays, and now leave no margin for any further slippages." The next month, John Coates, IOC vice president, stated, "We've become very concerned, to be quite frank. They really are not ready in many, many ways."[56]

The plans include extensive construction in four separate clusters of Rio (following one defining feature of Barcelona's Olympic plan),[57] encompassing sports facilities, bus rapid transit (BRT) lanes, metro connections, cleaning up of the port, a new golf course, an Olympic Village in Barra da Tijuca, new sewer systems, new parks, airport upgrades, and a museum, among other things. The Olympic village is scheduled to include 3,600 apartments, and all are slated to become luxury housing. Much of the new transportation network is intended to connect the airport to the hotel districts, the hotel districts to the Olympic sites (such as the BRT from Ipanema Beach to Barra da Tijuca), or the Olympic sites to each other. They appear either tangential or irrelevant to public needs or the city's economic development.

Equally significant, the TransOlímpica freeway that is slated to connect the four Olympic clusters to each other poses both human and environmental challenges. The $634 million freeway is expected to be 23 kilometers long, and its construction will require the relocation of at least 875 families. It will also have a major ecological impact because it will destroy 200,000 square meters of Atlantic shrub, an endangered form of vegetation in one of the largest conservation areas and the biggest urban park in Brazil. The affected residents will be moved some 2 kilometers away, and many are complaining that their new apartments are far inferior to their current homes. One sixty-two-year-old woman told a Rio newspaper, "I have a house with three bedrooms, three baths, a kitchen, a living room and space for my business. The apartments they are offering are very small. . . . I respect that they want us to leave, but I do not want to."[58]

## Assessment

It is too early to do a statistical assessment of the economic impact of hosting the World Cup and the Olympics on Brazil and Rio. It is not too early, however, to consider some of the factors that make economic success seem improbable.

Initially, it was projected that Brazil would have 600,000 foreign visitors during the World Cup. The Brazilian government has claimed that the actual number was 1 million. The large number owes to the participation of teams from four neighboring South American countries plus Mexico in the final sixteen.[59] The largest groups of foreign tourists came from Argentina, Chile, and Colombia. According to anecdotal reports, they were not big spenders. Large numbers of them slept on the beach or in trailers and used public restrooms.

Meanwhile, President Dilma Rousseff declared that the national workday for public employees would end at 12:30 p.m. every day on which a World Cup match was played. This meant shorter work days, so that the Brazilian people would all have the opportunity to watch and enjoy the World Cup. Though this measure might have lowered the intensity of popular protest, it might also have reduced worker productivity directly through shorter work hours and, perhaps, indirectly through the effect of extra celebration. One study estimated a drop in productivity of 30 percent.[60]

Brazil's political system is nothing short of a labyrinth. Years of trying to undo the authoritarian style of the country's long-standing dictatorship has produced a complexly encumbered decisionmaking process. Even once spending projects are approved, moving the funds from the national treasury to the institution that is supposed to spend them requires multiple departments and people to sign off. Not only can these steps take months, but inevitably many individuals may require payoffs to expedite the process. Sometimes state agencies even hire private consulting firms to make it all happen. At other times parallel government bodies or temporary authorities with no accountability are created.

It is hard enough for a relatively well-functioning democracy to pull off the gargantuan commitments for a sport mega-event. For a crippled system, it is next to impossible. Long delays are unavoidable, which leads to higher costs, which lead to less urgent projects being postponed or canceled.

Of course, autocratic political systems do not get a pass on mega-event construction delays and incompletions. Putin proved that in spades in Sochi. The sheer magnitude of the financial and physical commitments needed to host either the World Cup or the Olympic Games should serve as a code red warning to all developing countries. Olympic PR spin to the contrary, legacies can be negative, especially when they entail billions of dollars of debt.

Writing for the Atlantic Council, where he is a nonresident senior Brazil fellow, Ricardo Sennes casts a critical but ultimately hopeful light on the impact of mega-events. On the one hand, Sennes states that the coming-out party vision has backfired: "The image of Brazil as a global leader has given way to the image of a country experiencing an active democratic debate about its future." On the other hand, Sennes sees a possible, though unintended, silver lining:

> Governments will have to address the new social demands on the quality of life, reflected in the quality of public services and a path of inclusion for the new middle class, not only as consumers, but as citizens as well. This new process implies important changes in Brazil's political democratic system considering its representative model, the pattern of public resource allocation, and social participation in public policy decision-making processes.
>
> Change may be slow, but change will come. If the World Cup has had some role in clarifying and synthesizing these desired changes, that shall be the best legacy to expect from the 2014 championship in Brazil.[61]

These are hopeful words, though perhaps unrealistic. The political dynamic could instead turn toward more repression. If Sennes is right, then it is a rather twisted path toward social inclusion and deepened democracy. Mega-events, in his view, succeed because they first create crisis, and out of the ashes arises a more responsive, egalitarian society.

A more pessimistic and critical view is articulated by Christopher Gaffney:

Since the announcement of the 2016 host city in October 2009, the Rio de Janeiro city government has pushed through a revised master plan that was adopted to include the multiple Olympic projects. . . . The improvised revision of the city's master plan has been accompanied by an extensive list of executive decrees that have "flexibilized" urban space in order for Olympic related projects to occur. These measures have undermined Rio's fledgling democratic institutions and reduced public participation in urban planning processes.[62]

More growth or less? More equity or less? More democracy or less? Time will tell.

## London

The 2012 London Olympic Games distinguished themselves in several ways. Most significant, the legacy planning was more detailed and more ambitious than in any previous Olympics. The central legacy goal was to rejuvenate five depressed boroughs in East London— Newham, Hackney, Tower Hamlets, Waltham Forest, and Greenwich. Although they each have their distinct traits, as a group they are characterized by rising population numbers, a relatively young and minority demographic, and comparatively high levels of social deprivation (measured by levels of employment, income, health, skills, education, housing, and crime, and certain attributes of the living environment).

In the nineteenth century and much of the twentieth, East London was a center for manufacturing and the city's docklands. Accordingly, it was a working-class neighborhood and poor relative to western districts in London. During the 1970s and 1980s, however, in the wake of labor troubles and technological change, the docks closed, and East London suffered extensive job loss in traditional manufacturing and processing industries. By the late 1980s a regeneration process had begun, first with the new docklands project, which was followed in 1990 by the launching of the more dispersed Thames Gateway scheme,[63] and then by a movement of cultural and artistic businesses as well as nonprofit organizations into the area, seeking lower rents and prices. Small pockets of relative affluence began to appear in an area that was still economically depressed and crime-ridden. One outstanding problem was the paucity of public transportation connecting East London to the city center.

A major focus of London's Olympic Plan was to redevelop these five boroughs. It is important to emphasize, however, that a regenerative dynamic in favor of East London development had already begun in the 1990s. The London Docklands Development Corporation was established in 1985. The original scheme was to develop 8.8 million square feet of offices, hotels, shops, and restaurants and 8,000 parking spaces. The docklands light railway was the only form of public transportation connecting part of the area to the central city.

By the late 1990s, Canary Wharf, part of the docklands project, had begun to attract financial firms, and subsequently expanded to include other businesses and upscale housing. One study on the docklands project commented that "criticism has focused upon the removal of local democratic controls and the replacement of the existing population by a new, more prosperous group of young professionals. . . . Tower Hamlets, the borough in which Canary Wharf is located, experienced a significant change in population. . . . In 1981 the authority had 85 percent council (public) housing and 15 percent private housing and by 2008 nearly 60 percent was private housing."[64]

The new Stratford rapid train station and nearby housing are part of a project of the London and Continental Railways that was initiated in 1997.[65] Hence, by 2003, when the government decided to pursue its Olympic bid, an extensive transportation plan and related development plan were already in place.

### Short-Run Effects

In May 2011, the London Organizing Committee for the Olympic Games (LOCOG) put out a request for proposals (RFP) seeking to identify a group to produce an economic impact study. The RFP stipulated that LOCOG was anticipating significant public pushback with respect to the games because of the massive allocation of tax-payer monies to finance the necessary infrastructure and operations and that the LOCOG was therefore seeking a study that would be sufficiently robust to silence the critics. In the end, the consulting firm Grant Thornton got the contract and obliged with a study (for which it was paid a reported $2 million) that estimated a substantial economic boost. Stefan Szymanski, one of the economists working on the study but who was not involved in the final write-up, expressed alarm to Ari Shapiro of National Public Radio, calling the study "a political document . . . tantamount to a whitewash," and went on to say, "I'm very uncomfortable about the triumphalist tone of this which does not reflect what the data is saying."[66]

Let's take a look at the available evidence. Anne Power, professor and head of the London School of Economics program on Housing and Communities, has studied the impact of the Olympic construction on East London. The borough of Newham was the actual site and main host of the games. Because of the paucity of skilled local labor, only a small minority of the thousands of construction jobs created in preparation for the games went to Newham residents. Together with a growing population, this meant that the unemployment rate in Newham increased 42 percent between 2005 and 2012. Crime in the borough was 50 percent above the London average. The supply of subsidized housing declined during 2005–12, as the Olympic regeneration scheme removed thousands of homes, and the 1,300 homes in the Olympic Village that were slated to be affordable were still well beyond the financial reach of most Newham households.[67]

Dan Brown and Stefan Szymanski studied employment change in the five host boroughs in the run-up to the games and compared them with changes in the rest of London. They found that changes were more positive where Olympic construction was either nonexistent or minor and concluded that "the direct employment effects of the Olympics are small."[68]

What about the direct financial effect of hosting? The bottom line was certainly not helped by the special treatment in the IOC demands for the "Olympic family." The IOC required that LOCOG set aside 250 miles of VIP lanes for exclusive use by members of the Olympic family, to secure nearly 2,000 rooms for IOC bigwigs and associates in the finest five-star hotels, and to control commercial space in support of Olympic sponsors. In particular, the IOC's *Technical Manual on Brand Protection* stipulates that "candidate cities are required to obtain control of all billboard advertising, city transport advertising, airport advertising, etc., for the duration of the games and the month preceding the games to support the marketing program."[69]

As is the case for other host cities since 2010, corporate partners and foreign nationals participating in the Olympics (including athletes, media workers, and referees) were exempt from earnings taxation in England during the games. Since the status of some nonprofit organizations, such as LOCOG and the IOC, is likely to be tax-exempt even without the special tax treatment required by the IOC, it is not a simple matter to estimate what the cost of these privileges is to the London and English treasuries. One study put the costs of the tax exemptions at more than $130 million.[70]

As we have seen, a principal claim for sports mega-events is that they boost tourism both during the games and in the long run. The evidence for London tourism during 2012 is not encouraging. The number of London tourists during August 2012 was 5 percent below the level in 2011. Thanks to higher hotel prices and the purchase of tickets to Olympic events, total tourist spending increased. However, much of the increase had to be shared with the IOC and with the home offices of the hotel chains, many of which were outside London. Businesses in central London, from taxis, to restaurants, to museums and theaters, reported a reduction in demand of 20 to 40 percent. Not only were traditional tourists scared away by Olympic congestion and higher prices but Londoners by the hundreds fled or avoided the city.[71]

Despite an initial security snafu, the staging of the games went well.[72] LOCOG *operating* costs totaled $4.1 billion (infrastructure and facility costs are not included in this number), including

$185 million to put on the opening and closing ceremonies.[73] LOCOG itself broke even, but only after a significant infusion of $1.67 billion in public funds.[74]

At least up through the games, it does not appear there was a net gain in revenue to the national treasury or the London economy. On the other side of the ledger, the costs were high. As with other mega-events, there is always a good deal of subjectivity about what investments should be included in the budget of the games. Some infrastructural investments are peripheral to the games, others would have been undertaken without the games, and so on.

This is what we do know. When London won the bid in 2005, the initial total cost estimate was $5 billion.[75] The National Audit Report asserted that total costs up through the end of the games were £9.3 billion, or roughly $15.7 billion. Some estimates go considerably higher, up to £24 billion (approximately $40 billion).[76] Indeed, the December 2012 report of the National Audit Office refers to "the lack of realism in the original estimates."[77] Even if one uses the lowest of the final cost figures, the cost overrun was at least three times the initial estimate.

Thus, as in practically all other cases, the London games cannot be justified as a sound economic investment in the short run. If the investment can be justified economically, it must be on the basis of any long-run or legacy effect.

### Legacy Effects

London's legacy plan was ambitious, but many question whether it was realistic. In 2005, Jack Straw, England's secretary of state, commented in Parliament on the IOC's selection of London to host the 2012 Games:

London's bid was built on a special Olympic vision. That vision of an Olympic Games that would not only be a celebration of sport but a force for regeneration. The Games will transform one of the poorest and most deprived areas of London. They will create thousands of jobs and homes. They will offer new opportunities for business in the immediate area and throughout London . . . it reaches out to young people in two important respects: it will encourage many more to get fit and to be involved in sport and, whatever their physical prowess, to offer their services as volunteers for the Olympic cause.[78]

The various legacy goals included:

—Making the UK a world-leading sporting nation

—Transforming the heart of East London

—Inspiring a new generation of young people to take part in volunteering and cultural and physical activity

—Making the Olympic Park a blueprint for sustainable living[79]

—Demonstrating that the UK is a creative, inclusive, and welcoming place to live, visit, and do business

The National Audit Report of December 2012 estimated that the costs of implementing the legacy programs would be approximately $1.4 billion.[80] The $1.4 billion would be on top of the $15.7 billion-plus that had already been spent through the end of the games.

One of the key legacy projects was the conversion of the Olympic Stadium into the home field for the West Ham United soccer team. The stadium renovation was more complicated and expensive than it might have been. One reason for this was that the design of the Olympic Stadium did not anticipate the conversion needs of a soccer team, namely, the need to remove the running track so that the pitch (field) could be close to the stands. Had this been anticipated, then the last row of seats would have been higher and field seating could have been added on top of the track. The second reason is that the Olympic Stadium was far too big for the West Ham soccer team. The upper deck, with its 55,000 seats, had to be removed. In the end, the renovation carried an initial projected cost of $323 million, to be paid by taxpayers.[81] In early September 2014, according to a report by Sky News, the projected renovation cost rose by another $25 million, with further increases possible.[82]

Hackney is one of the five boroughs in East London where the games took place. It lies just west of the Olympic Park and about five miles east of the city center. In February 2014, *Sports Illustrated* ran a feature story about a community center in Hackney Wick, which lies a couple of blocks from the $735 million Olympic Stadium.[83] The area used to be home to a peanut factory, which closed in the 1970s. Other manufacturing firms closed as well, leaving behind vacant industrial buildings. Over time, many of these were converted into lofts for artists and a new, still low-income, community of artists and artisans developed.

When the Olympic planners arrived in the neighborhood after 2005, they promised a strong economic rebound. The community center invested in opening a café to cater to the expected Olympic visitors and growing workforce. But apart from higher rents, as of February 2014, little had changed in the local economy. The main metro stop, Stratford, was on the east side of the park, in the borough of Newham. There was next to no additional foot traffic in Hackney. Moreover, many of the planned investments were never made because public money ran out and private money was uninterested.

Lance Forman, owner of the H. Forman & Son salmon-smoking plant, commented, "People were not allowed to look out and see what East London had to offer. The Olympic Park could frankly have been in a big bubble on the moon. It was an opportunity missed. They said it would create great business opportunities. My experience is they failed spectacularly."[84]

Part of the transformation of East London entailed a plan to build 12,000 new homes and create 10,000 jobs. [85] The new-homes plan was scaled back to 8,000 in mid-2013. In spring of 2014, the Olympic Village conversion into housing had not been completed.[86]

The Olympic Village was supposed to cost £1 billion (approximately $1.7 billion) and to be financed privately by the Australian developer Lend Lease. (The head of London's Olympic Delivery Authority had been the CEO of Lend Lease until February 2011.) When the 2008 financial crisis hit, Lend Lease dropped out, and the Olympic Village was paid for out of public funds. In August 2011 the Village was sold to the Qatari ruling family's real estate company for £275 million (approximately $460 million), for a taxpayer loss in excess of $1 billion.[87]

More generally, there has been a decreasing commitment to afford-able housing (which carries a 30 percent discount to market rents). It is worth quoting Gavin Poynter, economics professor at the University of East London and a student of the London games, at length on the process:

> As part of the Mayor of London's *First Steps* programme, for example, tenants in social housing in London boroughs could apply to move into the Olympic Village. Those seeking to rent could secure a discount of up to 30 percent on the market rent for their property though they had to be in employment and meet other criteria. . . . But, as the Park's conversion gathered pace, such aspirations were much diluted. The first major mixed community development, Chobham Manor, provided about 25 percent affordable housing, 10 percent [age points] below the widely published target, and subsequent developments, to be completed by the early 2020s, are unlikely to achieve even this level. As the social or public gain dimension of the Games' urban legacy has waned, so the commercial has flourished. [88]

The Olympic, now East, Village has become part of a high rise, high density and high price area of development around the transport hub that is Stratford. The vision for the creation of affordable housing has receded. As developers have privileged scheme viability, the proportion of the value captured for invest-ment in social housing and public spaces has diminished particu-larly on the south side of the former Olympic Park and within the developments on its borders. In the absence of significant levels of public investment post-2012 (far more than that ear-marked in the LDDC's business plan), the social transformation focused on the needs of the local community has amounted to a wish list. Its achievement was undermined by a combination of insufficient public resources to deliver an ambitious city building programme, the impact of government social policies that capped housing benefit support for the lower waged and unemployed—putting the purchase or rent of new housing units out of the reach of many local people—and the operations of a London property market in which the activities of international investors pushed up rent and property prices in iconic locations such as the Olympic Park and its borders.[89]

What about the other legacy goals?

One goal was to advance the greening of London. The reduction of the carbon footprint from the games' facilities beyond the regulatory standards was accomplished, but the set targets were not met. For instance, one pledge was to supply 20 percent of the power for Olympic Park from renewable energy sources; according to the *New York Times,* the actual amount during the games was closer to 9 percent.[90]

Another goal was to transform the United Kingdom into a leading sports state and to inspire its citizens to engage in more physical activity. Here the early evidence is not as positive. Sports participation figures published in June 2013 by Sport England showed that nearly a year on from the 2012 Games, twenty out of twenty-nine sports recorded a fall in the number of adults taking part between April 2012 and April 2013. Overall, the numbers of people exercising for thirty minutes once a week fell by 100,000 to 15.3 million over the same period, or by an even greater margin of 200,000 since October. The number of those exercising three times a week also fell.[91] In its June 2014 report, the nationwide participation numbers for April 2013 to April 2014 were up slightly, but they were down again for London, where, one presumes, any positive Olympic effect would be more visible.[92] It appears that London is not alone in not reaching this goal. According to a 2007 study performed for the Culture, Media and Sport Committee of the British Parliament's House of Commons, "No host country has yet been able to demonstrate a direct benefit from the Olympic Games in the form of a lasting increase in participation."[93]

The goal to regenerate development in East London, to create thousands of new jobs, and to reduce poverty also has encountered difficulties. It is always possible to change the character of some micro-neighborhoods by displacing lower-income with higher-income groups. Such gentrification has necessarily occurred to a degree with the billions of dollars of new investments in pockets of East London. Such a process, however, is simply relocating, rather than producing, wealth.

In assessing the changes brought to East London from the games, Gavin Poynter comments that East London got a stadium it didn't need, more four- and five-star hotels it didn't need, and additional high-rise, high-priced developments it didn't need. Poynter adds that there was not much in it for lower-income people.

It is undoubtedly too early to make any definitive judgments, but a couple of take-aways seem appropriate. First, London gave careful thought to the legacy of the 2012 Games and made a bold attempt to redevelop a low-income, socially underserved, crime-ridden area of the city. London planners also provided for administrative continuity to allow ongoing attention to the legacy process after the games ended. These are certainly commendable aspects of the London games. The problem, however, appears to reside in the weakness in the plan's conception and the inadequate financial commitment to carry forward the ideals set out.

Second, from the time a plan is made to bid for the games to the time of the games themselves, eleven or more years pass. When there is an expectation of enticing private money to help finance construction, it is important to anticipate that financial markets may hit snags along the way. It is also important to understand that the dynamics of urban development can shift over the course of the decade-plus of gestation. In the case of East London, the low rents and low prices, together with some earlier government initiatives, were already beginning to transform the socioeconomic environment of the area. A rational plan for development would have understood and incorporated these changes.

A plethora of issues notwithstanding, London 2012 did a marvelous job planning and implementing its public relations. Sebastian Coe and his collaborators have spoken eloquently and repeatedly about the purported success of the London games, and the media have largely portrayed the games in a positive light. Impact reports from Grant Thornton, no matter how compromised they are in fact, help to further promote the triumphalist tone. One can only hope that the low-income residents of East London will one day come to experience the gains that the official line trumpets.

# 7 | Bread or Circuses?

The perennial claims that hosting the Olympics or the World Cup is an engine of economic development find little corroboration in independent studies. In the short run, the increasingly massive costs of hosting cannot come close to being matched by the modest revenues that are brought in by the games. The payoff, if there is one, must be realized in the long run. But even the legacy return is at best dubious. Much of the alleged legacy comes in the form of qualitative gains, and the rest comes over very long periods of time, difficult to trace back to the several-week period of the games or the prior construction. But more often than not, the main legacy consists of white elephants that cost billions to build and millions annually to maintain, along with mountains of debt that must be paid back over ten to thirty years.

## The Difficult Calculus of Economic Gain

Even where specific areas of benefits can be identified, they must be evaluated against not only the size of the financial investment in hosting but also the opportunity costs of land used and of the human talent committed to planning and implementing the games. Cities must ask themselves what the best long-term use of scarce land and other resources is. Areas that today are blighted or underutilized may face bleak prospects for the coming years, but filling these areas with stadiums for the next three decades or more may preclude a more productive use that may not become apparent for another five or ten years.

One of the more important rebuttals to the calculus that shows more expense than revenue in hosting is that much of the expense is connected to infrastructure that will support the city's or country's long-term development needs. This certainly may be true in theory, and may even be so in practice, but it requires very careful and clever planning, which is more noticeable for its absence.

That careful planning was certainly present in Barcelona for the 1992 Summer Games. But in Barcelona the city planners had begun reconceptualizing their city soon after the Franco regime ended in 1975. The Catalan region had been largely neglected under Franco, and Barcelona itself had suffered under decades of unregulated industrial development. As a result, people in this seaport city were cut off from the Mediterranean by blocks of manufacturing, warehousing, and railways. Together with poor traffic circulation and underdeveloped infrastructure, this situation made a city that could be a shining jewel of tourism, with its magnificent architecture, cultural history, climate, and location, mostly a tourist afterthought.

The new government began to hatch a master plan for Barcelona to change the entire picture in the late 1970s and elaborated the plan in the early 1980s. The plan preexisted the thought of hosting the Olympics, but hosting was seen as a vehicle to put the plan into action. Barcelona used the Olympics; the Olympics didn't use Barcelona.

If other cities were able to emulate Barcelona—and many have tried but failed—then the problems that have been discussed in this book may be attenuated, or even in some cases avoided. The difficulty is that the conditions that contributed to Barcelona's success are not present elsewhere, and the political systems in other countries have shown themselves increasingly unwilling or unable to engage in effective long-term planning.

Los Angeles in 1984 is another case that lends some hope. But Los Angeles mostly worked for a different reason. Hosting the Olympic

Games produced more negative than positive imagery during the period from Mexico City in 1968 through Montreal in 1976. When it came time to select a host for the Summer Games in 1984, there were no suitors. The IOC had no leverage, and Los Angeles and Peter Ueberroth (the head of the local organizing committee) took full advantage. Los Angeles passed an ordinance stipulating that it would not spend public money on the games and got the IOC to guarantee the city against any operating losses. The IOC further agreed to a minimal construction budget for minor venues only, and Ueberroth arranged for corporate financing of these. Ueberroth also profitably redesigned Olympic sponsorships. The end result was a surplus of $215 million and a new, positive image for hosting the games.

Bidding to host the Olympics since 1984, until recently, has been more competitive. Costs have skyrocketed and planning has been incomplete. Because the direct fiscal and economic impact has been neutral or negative, it is important to consider the opportunity costs of hosting.

One of the most significant costs is land use. The modern Olympic Games are huge affairs. At the 1896 Games in Athens, there were 295 athletes, 43 medal events, and 7 venues; at the 1936 Games in Berlin, there were 3,963 athletes, 129 medal events, and 25 venues; at the Tokyo Games in 1964, there were 5,151 athletes, 172 medal events, and 33 venues; and, most recently, at the 2012 London Games, there were 10,500 athletes, 302 medal events, and 31 venues. The IOC's guidelines for the *minimum* surface area for the footprint of the venues alone is 1,660 acres. For a smaller city like Barcelona, this represents almost 7 percent of the city's surface area. When ceremonial green space, large-scale public space, parking, transportation, and communication facilities are included, the amount of needed acreage can quadruple. Beijing used an estimated 8,400 acres of real estate to stage the 2008 Games.[1] The magnitude of these numbers suggests a substantial opportunity cost (opportunities forgone for alternative uses) from hosting the Summer Olympic Games.

If instead of spending some $5 billion tearing down old stadiums, then building new ones or renovating existing facilities, Brazil had spent $5 billion on public transportation networks in its major cities or on an intercity train system, what might have been the impact on the Brazilian economy? If instead of building an Olympic park in East London, London had provided rental subsidies or tax credits to artisanal industry and retail businesses or additional funding for, say, technical education, what enduring effect on employment in the surrounding boroughs might that have wrought? The questions about trade-offs are practically endless.

It is frequently argued that it is not possible to secure funding for more effective development projects. Political gridlock and partisan politics stand in the way of such appropriations in democratic countries, but somehow hosting the Olympics or World Cup breaks political stalemate. The irony is that in countries where political decisionmaking is so encumbered, the same obstacles that prevent more productive development projects without hosting the Olympics or World Cup are likely to thwart efficient implementation of mega-event plans. In authoritarian countries, gridlock is unlikely to be an issue, but skewed decisionmaking is common nonetheless.

In either democratic or authoritarian countries, the tendency is for event planning to hew closely to the interests of the local business elite. Construction companies, their unions (if there are any), insurance companies, architectural firms, media companies, investment bankers (who float the bonds), lawyers, and perhaps some hotel or restaurant interests get behind the Olympic or World Cup project. All stand to gain handsomely from the massive public funding. Typically, these interests hijack the local organizing committee, hire an obliging consulting firm to conduct an ersatz economic impact study, understate the costs, overstate the revenues, and go on to procure political consent. According to one study, in the buildup to hosting the 2010 World Cup, the average profits of five big construction companies in South Africa rose from R158 million in 2004 to R1.67 billion in 2009—a 10.5-fold increase.[2]

Inevitably, there are some short-term employment gains from the extensive construction required for the Olympics or World Cup.

The problem is twofold: first, the government has to pay back the money it borrowed over the ensuing decades, which reduces funding for other government projects and reduces public employment; and second, the typical pattern has been to import thousands of workers from other areas, often from out of the country, and pay them a pauper's wage. Further, when used after the games, the stadiums, ski slopes, golf courses, and road networks are more likely to serve the consumption habits of upper-income groups. Hosting sports mega-events, then, tends to reinforce the existing power structure and patterns of inequality.

## The Bidding Process Erodes Possible Gains

The fact that the existing power structure imposes itself on the bidding process has another unfavorable implication. Consider the following stylized model of the bidding process. In each of the three cases, there is a monopoly seller of hosting rights (either FIFA or the IOC).

### Case One

—Perfect information and no principal-agent problem

—Outcome: Expected net gains are bid away

In this case, it is assumed that the IOC or FIFA each has complete information about the bidders and each of the bidders has complete information about its own bid and those of its competitors. It is further assumed that there is no principal-agent problem. This means that the body representing the city or country (the local organizing committee) fairly represents the interests of the entire resident population. The local organizing committee is the agent of the entire resident population (the principal). With the assumption of perfect information, each bidder will know what its potential gain from hosting is and will continue to bid until just before its gain is fully eroded. (In theory, if each bidder also knows the gains of other bidders, it will stop bidding at just above the gain to the second highest bidder, leaving a small potential gain.) Note that if the overall return to hosting approaches zero, and if there are feel-good benefits from hosting, this implies that there will be a negative financial result. That is, the host will have to pay to achieve the feel-good effects, bringing the overall net return to zero.[3] This case is the most favorable for the bidding cities or countries. It is also the least realistic of the three cases.

## Case Two

—Imperfect information and no principal-agent problem

—Outcome: winner's curse and net loss

The sole difference between this case and the prior one is that the assumption of perfect information is dropped, making case 2 a better approximation of reality. In this case, each bidder does not know what its potential benefits and costs might turn out to be when it participates in the bidding competition. The winning bid in such a case usually goes to the most exuberant bidder, who not only outbids all the other bidders but also generally bids higher than the possible gain, an outcome known in game theory as the winner's curse. The result is a net financial loss and a net overall loss, even though the organizing committee (agent) in this case is still assumed to fairly represent the interests of the local population (the principal).

## Case Three

—Imperfect information and a principal-agent problem

—Outcome: outlandish overbid

This case moves yet closer to reality by acknowledging a principal-agent problem. That is, the local organizing committee, the agent, is controlled by the private interests that stand to gain the most from hosting, and these interests are not coincident with those of the host country's or city's population (the principal). The condition of imperfect information again facilitates extravagant bids from each of the prospective hosts. The expected outcome is substantial financial and overall losses, which will only be exacerbated by cost overruns.

## Cycles of Leverage

The foregoing discussion makes an implicit assumption, namely, that the good being auctioned—the right to host the Olympics or World Cup—is highly desired. We have seen that this has not always been the case in the past, such as with the bidding for the 1984 Summer Games. Indeed, monopolists (single sellers of a good or service) can exploit their situation only when they produce a good in demand. If I open up a fast food chain that sells hamburgers made of rubber, even though I may be the only producer of rubber hamburgers, it is improbable in the extreme that I will have any market power or leverage.

Alternatively, if I make edible hamburgers from beef, and if Burger King, McDonald's, Wendy's, and their ilk all go out of business, I will be able to raise my prices, and my chain will become very profitable. I will not, however, be able to raise my prices as high as I might want. The price will still be constrained by demand, even though I have a monopoly. The reason is that at some high price (say, $7 a burger), my customers will decide to patronize other fast food options, such as Taco Bell, Kentucky Fried Chicken, or prewrapped sandwiches at a convenience store.

Similarly, the IOC and FIFA have a lot of market power or leverage that enables them, within bounds, to extract excessive bids from prospective hosts. Yet if either body overplays its hand and if consecutive hosts have bad experiences, then the demand for hosting diminishes and the IOC and FIFA lose leverage. In the extreme case, no prospective hosts bid, as in the case of the Los Angeles Games in 1984, when the IOC lost all leverage.

At least since Beijing in 2008, as the BRICS began to dominate World Cup and Olympic hosting, the youthful exuberance of the developing countries has led to outlandishly expensive games. What may have been more subtle miscalculations and losses in Atlanta, Sydney, Salt Lake City, and Athens became glaring missteps in the cases of Beijing, South Africa, Sochi, and Brazil.[4] The negative news from the recent Olympics and World Cups has meant that the demand for hosting has fallen. FIFA thickened the imbroglio with revelations of corruption in its selection of Qatar to host the 2022 World Cup and of syndicate-rigged match fixing in previous Cups.[5]

From their behavior, it seems that both the IOC and FIFA see the writing on the wall. Table 2-3 listed the evidence: a diminishing number of bidders for the Summer and Winter Olympics since 2001. Over the last five bidding cycles, the number of applicant cities for the Summer Games has declined steadily from twelve (for the 2004 Games) to ten to nine to seven to five (for the 2020 Games), while the number applying for the Winter Games has gone from nine (for the 2002 Games) to three (for the 2018 Games).

Bidding for the 2022 Winter Olympics has almost ground to a halt. Early bids from Krakow, Stockholm, Munich, Davos, and Lviv were withdrawn in 2013 and 2014, leaving only Oslo and two authoritarian countries, China and Kazakhstan, in the hunt. Notably, a report commissioned by the Dutch government in 2012 predicted that in the future, it was likely that only nondemocratic countries would host the Olympics because only they would "have the centralized power and money to organize them."[6]

The IOC's selection of Oslo as a candidate city is also noteworthy. One of the explicit selection criteria in the IOC's rule book is broad support from the local population. Norway and Oslo hardly meet this standard. In a March 2014 poll, 59.2 percent of Norwegians and 55.8 percent of Oslo residents opposed the bid. Further, the bid still needs a financial guarantee from the government, and a decision is expected to be made by the parliament in the autumn of 2014. In selecting Oslo as a finalist, then, the IOC is choosing a city that has not yet committed to being the host. The tables may be turning on the IOC.[7]

The IOC is well aware of this problem. In a June 2014 study prepared by the National Olympic Committees (NOCs) of Austria, Germany, Sweden, and Switzerland and titled "Olympic Agenda 2020: The Bid Experience," the internal report had this to say:

In Switzerland and Germany, citizens rejected potential bids in public referenda with 53%, in Sweden national politics decided not to support a bid and in Austria public opposition even received 72% in a referendum . . . in Krakow 70% opted against hosting the Games.

What is the problem of established European nations to bid for the Olympics? The grounds cited sound very similar in all four countries: public and politics seemingly fear the high costs of bidding for and hosting the Games, especially in the aftermath of the increase of costs that was witnessed in Sochi as well as concerns relating to human rights and sustainability.[8]

The mayor of Paris, Anne Hidalgo, reflected an increasingly common perspective when asked whether her city would bid for the 2024 Summer Games: "I love sports. I love competitions. I know what it can bring to a society and a city. . . . But today we are all under financial and budgetary restraints that do not make it possible for me to say that I support such a candidacy. Parisians expect me to provide housing, public services, justice, economic ease."[9]

As the worker strikes and popular protests in South Africa and Brazil have underscored, it is not just the Parisians who have this expectation. A new protest movement in Japan has emerged in 2014 in opposition to Tokyo's extravagant plans to host the 2020 Summer Games. Street demonstrations in Tokyo in July 2014 denounced the projected $1.5 billion Olympic Stadium (already reduced in scale by almost 50 percent from the original bid) as ecologically damaging and financially wasteful. The protesters called for the renovation of Tokyo's existing Olympic Stadium from the 1964 Games, rather than the construction of another facility. John Coates, IOC vice president, responded that further changes in the venue plan could occur only if the IOC approved.[10]

When Thomas Bach replaced Jacques Rogge as head of the IOC in September 2013, one of his first projects was to tour prospective host cities around the globe to drum up interest in bidding for future games. His message in each instance was similar: the IOC would look very favorably on a bid from your city. Subsequently, Bach has discussed other reforms to put the bidding process back on track from the IOC's perspective. I discuss these reforms later in the chapter, along with other proposals.

Sepp Blatter and FIFA have also been tinkering. FIFA's basic pattern had been to alternate host nations between Europe and the Americas. This pattern was disrupted in 2002 with the World Cup's first Asian finals and again in May 2004, when the rights to host the 2010 finals were awarded to South Africa. The new policy was to rotate the hosting rights among the six continents. It was South America's turn for 2014. But when the World Cup was awarded in October 2007, there was only one bidder from the continent, Brazil.

Without competition among potential hosts, FIFA lost its leverage, so FIFA aborted its policy of continental rotation. The new policy is that countries of the same continent as either of the last two World Cup hosts are ineligible. This way, rather than identifying a single continent that could bid to host the tournament, countries from four continental confederations would be eligible to bid for each World Cup.

## What Is to Be Done?

### Reform from Above

On June 10, 2014, the United States Olympic Committee (USOC) gathered for a quarterly meeting on the MIT campus in Cambridge, Massachusetts. The expectation was that the USOC would announce a handful of finalist cities it had chosen to bid to host the 2024 Summer Games. Back in February 2013, the USOC had sent out letters to fifty cities inviting them to apply to be the host. It is not uncommon for U.S. cities that compete to represent the United States in the worldwide hosting contest to spend up to $10 million on the domestic selection process.

But Larry Probst, the head of the USOC, made no announcement of finalists. Rather, reminding the press that the U.S. entries for the

2012 Summer Games (New York) and the 2016 Games (Chicago) had been rejected by the IOC, Probst said that he wanted to see how the IOC would reform its selection process before announcing a final U.S. entry. It sounded a bit like a threat: guarantee that the United States will win the games bid or we won't play.

The IOC should have a natural inclination to have a U.S. city host, which it hasn't had for the Summer Games since Atlanta in 1996, because the largest TV contract comes from the United States. The IOC currently has a contract with NBC for nearly $8 billion for U.S. broadcast rights through 2032. NBC will get higher ratings if the games are held in U.S. time zones and the domestic population can watch the competition live during prime time. Higher ratings will keep their NBC partner happy and lead to a higher rights fee next time around. Further, most leading U.S. cities have large, wealthy populations who can fill the Olympic venues, buying high-priced tickets and catering services, while U.S. companies purchase signage in the facility.

Probst and the USOC believe that if a U.S. city gets the right to host in 2024, it will mark the end of a twenty-eight-year hiatus, and that is longer than it should be. So Probst said that the USOC would not show its hand until the IOC Working Group on reforming the selection process, created by Thomas Bach in 2013, made its report in December 2014. Strangely, two weeks later Probst announced the four U.S. finalists—San Francisco, Los Angeles, Washington, D.C., and Boston—anyway.

When Bach entered office in September 2013, he immediately recognized that there was a declining number of bidding cities and that the situation was untenable. He told *Inside the Rings*, a newsletter that covers the business of the Olympics, that the IOC's bidding process was too onerous and that he wanted to make it simpler and more flexible:

We are asking too much too early. We approach potential candidate cities like you would in business with a tender for a franchise. We are putting out our conditions. "You have to do this, you have to do that, here are our conditions, here are the guarantees." This leads to a situation that all the bid books are written by the same people [consulting firms] around the world. You get the same answers in all the bids and when you have the Q&A in the Session or in the briefing I could give you the answers beforehand. I would like to change the mentality. . . . I want to invite potential candidates to study how the Olympic Games would fit into their long-term city and regional and country development.[11]

These are all reasonable thoughts, and Bach went on to set up his working group to study how the process could be reformed. The previous IOC head, Jacques Rogge, also called for a reformed, more supple process in the early 2000s. Nothing substantial came of it; in fact, the process only became more involved and more expensive.

Early indications from the working group were not encouraging about more substantial change. At the IOC meeting prior to the Sochi Olympics in February 2014, two reform ideas were discussed. The first was to allow countries as well as cities to bid to host. Such a change might lower the burden on the city but raise it on the country, and would entail higher transportation costs (and carbon footprint) and security spending. As a reform, it is hardly a game-changer. The second was to reinstate the pre–Salt Lake City policy of having IOC members visit the bidding cities.[12] The idea here is that firsthand visits provide more information than videos, so the plausibility of each city's plan could be better assessed. Perhaps, but such visits would raise costs and reopen avenues for payoffs and bribes, which of course is why they were scrapped in the first place.

Any fundamental change would have to affect the monopoly power that the IOC and FIFA wield. One way this could be accomplished, at least in theory, would be to introduce competition to the Olympics and the World Cup. This has been tried before, and failed. Witness the Goodwill Games, spawned by U.S. media mogul Ted Turner back in 1986 and shown on his own network. Turner lost $26 million on the Goodwill Games in that year and another $40 million in 1990, after which the games died a slow death, taking their last breath in Brisbane, Australia, in 2001.[13] If Turner with his media empire and deep pockets couldn't compete, it is not likely others could. The Olympics and the World Cup have deep branding and appear to be natural monopolies. Worldwide fans don't seem to want two Olympics or two World Cups.

Another way to reduce the leverage of the IOC and FIFA would be to control the number of bidders. A sensible way to do this would be to reintroduce the continental rotation system that FIFA briefly tried in the early 2000s but quickly abandoned when it saw its leverage decline. Yet such a system, which would involve the six continents, would not only delimit the geographic span of the competition in each cycle, it would also save the bidding cities from continents not in play the energy and expense of bidding—an expense that can rise to $100 million per city or more. (Tokyo reportedly spent $150 million on its failed bid to host the 2016 Summer Games.)[14] The question is not whether such a reform would be desirable, engendering at least incremental improvements, but whether Bach's working group or a parallel effort in FIFA would accept such a change.

Of course, it would also help if (1) FIFA and the IOC accepted the use of older, more modest stadiums, (2) they encouraged repeat hosting, and (3) they made a more serious and professional effort to identify which bids made the most sense for a city's development. While the IOC and FIFA give lip service to a concern over development, sustainability, and other desiderata, the IOC and FIFA voters are ill equipped to make judgments about a city's or country's development needs.[15]

The IOC's selection in September 2013 of Tokyo over Madrid (and Istanbul) to host the 2020 Summer Games raises questions about the constituency for real reform. Madrid's bid anticipated extensive use of existing sports facilities and only minor infrastructure work. Its total budget, shared by three levels of government over seven years, was only $1.9 billion, one of the lowest in modern Olympic history. Tokyo's bid budget was approximately $6 billion, including a very elaborate and lavish Olympic stadium and village (initially projected to cost $4 billion). If the IOC was interested in sending a message that it wanted to avoid fiscal excess and financial imprudence, it certainly did not manifest that desire in its selection of Tokyo.[16]

There are also calls for Athens to be designated the permanent home of the Summer Games. It's not an awful idea, but too many nations would object to not having the opportunity to host the games, and the internationalist image of the Olympics might suffer.

The World Cup has a simpler solution because there are so many countries around the globe with mature professional soccer leagues that have at last eight suitable stadiums. If FIFA moderated its demands for stadium capacity and luxury seating, the investment demands on the host country would be more modest and manageable.

Both FIFA and the IOC could also opt to share more of the generated revenue from the games with the host city or country. The Summer Games currently generate around $6 billion from television and media rights, ticket sales, corporate sponsorships, and memorabilia sales. The Winter Games earn between $3 and $4 billion, and the World Cup earns nearly $4.5 billion.

As of December 2013, FIFA had over $1.4 billion in its reserve investment portfolio. These reserves grew to well over $2 billion following the 2014 World Cup. Why can't some of those riches be shared with host countries, especially those less-developed countries with the largest infrastructure investment requirements? Such a policy would allow a more even distribution of hosting between the richer and poorer nations.

In short, there are a variety of options for FIFA and the IOC to lessen the burden on their hosts. It is questionable, however, whether as monopolies, with little competitive challenge in the mega-event marketplace, they will yield much of their market power. Of course, to the extent that cities and countries lose interest in bidding or corporate sponsors insist on improved public relations, FIFA and the IOC will find themselves obligated to introduce some reform. It is a good bet that the reform will be calibrated to be just enough to spark the necessary interest among prospective hosts and the necessary legitimacy in the eyes of the media and corporate sponsors.

The June 2014 report, mentioned above, by the NOCs of Austria, Germany, Sweden and Switzerland, "Olympic Agenda 2020," outlined some possible tinkering reforms. The report's authors studied the bid process for the 2010, 2014, and 2018 Winter Olympics and discovered that the cost of bidding alone had quadrupled over this period while the size of the bid book had doubled. The proposal is to simplify the bidding process. The report lamented the increasing public opposition to hosting and suggested stronger propaganda campaigns to convince the public of the value of hosting, and even that "the IOC might also think about financial support to co-fund communication campaigns in interested countries."[17] The authors hinted that it might be possible to lower IOC-mandated venue seating capacities and to modify other requirements so that host countries could more often use existing facilities rather than build new ones. They also suggested that it might be acceptable to reduce the size of the Olympic family (which now requires 42,000 rooms for the Summer Games) so that hosts do not have to overbuild hotel capacity. Finally, the report noted that for all the IOC's talk of promoting sustainability since the 1990s, the IOC has lacked specific environmental standards, any monitoring protocol, and any system of penalties. The report stated that it might be desirable to establish a sustainability monitoring body, and that to be effective, such a body would need enforcement powers. These thoughts, of course, were nothing more than suggestions for the IOC to deliberate and, presumably, decide on at its December 2014 meeting.

The 2014 bribery scandal surrounding the awarding of the 2022 World Cup to Qatar commends another type of reform from above—transparency. The voters who award the World Cup and Olympic hosting rights are protected by anonymity rules.[18] (Unfortunately, FIFA seems to be moving in the wrong direction, announcing in July 2014 that the report it commissioned on the possible corruption in the selection of Qatar will not be made public.)[19] If the choices of each voter were made public, then the process would be more accountable and less prone to corruption.

Following the bribery scandal connected to the awarding of the 2002 Winter Olympics to Salt Lake City, the IOC reduced the number of voters and ended the practice of having its voting members visit the candidate cities. The IOC procedures are still far from democratic and cry out for further reform.

The current process for selecting the candidate cities and then the winning city involves 115 people, called IOC members. These members include fifteen active athletes who are elected by their peers at the Olympic Games; fifteen individuals chosen from NOCs and fifteen from the International Federations; and seventy individual members, who are self-perpetuating. Thus, a solid majority (60.9 percent) of the IOC members belongs to a self-generating elite and is accountable to no one, other than to the Olympic Movement and the IOC president. Members on the selection committee serve terms of eight years and can be reelected indefinitely, with an age limit of seventy years (except for those members who joined the IOC before 2000, whose age limit is eighty). Why not have all the IOC members be elected by a constituent part of the Olympic Movement every four or eight years, with limits of two terms?

### Reform from Below

Absent substantial change emanating from the international monopolies, cities and countries will have to be smarter and more responsible. Gigantism needs to be eschewed. Bids need to be more cautious and to take greater advantage of already installed infrastructure. If their bids don't meet the standards of FIFA and the IOC, then cities and countries must be willing to stand their ground.[20]

Tokyo's governor Yoichi Masuzoe may have adumbrated a new, more entitled approach to hosting in late July 2014 when he informed the IOC that Tokyo was reconsidering its approved plan for the 2020 Olympics. The Tokyo Organizing Committee has been under popular pressure not to build a new Olympic stadium but rather to use the existing one built for the 1964 Games. The governor noted that Tokyo had promised a compact games geographically but that it was also necessary for the games to be compact financially. Accordingly, Tokyo is considering moving some of the events as far away as 60 miles to save on venue construction costs. As Masuzoe explained, "Expenses can be 30, 40, 50 times more than the original plan. How can I persuade the taxpayers to pay this kind of money?"[21]

Cities would also be well advised to follow the examples of Los Angeles and Barcelona. To do so would require that the contexts and preconditions for the success of those cities be fully understood. Rio's plan for the 2016 Olympics attempted to emulate Barcelona by designing four urban clusters of Olympic activity—a strategy in distinct contrast to the more common single central complex model followed by Atlanta in 1996, Sydney in 2000, Athens in 2004, Beijing in 2008, and London in 2012. Unfortunately, Rio followed Barcelona in form but not in substance. The two cities and their circumstances were entirely different.

The most important aspect of Barcelona's plan for other prospective hosts is not the four clusters but the fact that the urban redevelopment plan preceded any thought about hosting the Olympics. The Olympics were made to work for the plan. The plan was not created posthaste to work for the Olympics.

Many other factors worked in Barcelona's favor as well. Among them, 60 percent of the financing for the games came from the private sector, and of the 40 percent of financing that came from public money, only 5 percent came from the city of Barcelona. Of the thirty-seven venues used during the games, twenty-seven preexisted and five more were already under construction. Fully 83 percent of the total cost was connected to nonsports facilities. Barcelona's location, climate, architecture, and culture, as well as its entry into the European Common Market, regional airline deregulation, and intelligent marketing, were also key elements.

However, just as monopolists won't surrender power voluntarily and will be inclined toward minimalist, cosmetic reform, city and country politicians will be concerned with not alienating their donors and the most powerful elements in their constituencies. They will be inclined, absent political reform, to shill for the interests of the construction, insurance, finance, and hotel industries.

In most cases, the electorate has been willing to settle for circuses and the promise of bread. When the electorate demands bread itself, as it has in Brazil, then politicians will be forced to take notice.

# Notes

## Preface

1. See, for instance, Roger G. Noll and Andrew Zimbalist, eds., *Sports, Jobs and Taxes: The Economic Impact of Sports Teams and Stadiums* (Brookings Institution Press, 1997).

2. Stefan Szymanski and I follow the same practice in our book, *National Pastime: How Americans Play Baseball and the Rest of the World Plays Soccer* (Brookings Institution Press, 2006).

3. For a humorous discussion of this etymological issue, see Sarah Lydall, "Up in Arms over 'Soccer' vs. 'Football,'" *New York Times,* June 19, 2014.

## Chapter 1

1. Only Los Angeles and Moscow had bid to host the 1980 Summer Games. Los Angeles has bid to host the Olympics more than any other U.S. city.

2. See http://leastthing.blogspot.com/2013/06/further-thoughts-on-sepp-blatters-fifa.html.

3. According to Dominico Scala, a member of the three-man Compensation Sub-Committee, the pay levels chosen are meant to emulate the compensation paid to executives in similarly sized companies in the private sector. See www.fifa.com/aboutfifa/organisation/footballgovernance/news/newsid=2384045/index.html.

4. Jonathan Calvert and Heidi Blake, "Fifa's Chiefs Pocket Secret 100% Pay Rise," *Sunday Times,* June 22, 2014.

5. Jonathan Calvert and Heidi Blake, "Calling Time on Fifa's Watch Scandal," *Sunday Times* (London), September 14, 2014 (www.thesunday times.co.uk/sto/news/article1459174.ece).

6. "Fifa ExCo Members Ordered to Return Watches," *The Guardian,* September 18, 2014 (www.theguardian.com/football/2014/sep/18/ fifa-exco-return-watches-gift-brazil-world-cup).

7. Prince Nawaf Faisal Fahd Abdulaziz resigned from the IOC on July 11, 2014.

8. See www.businessinsider.com/finances-of-the-ioc-2012-8?op=1. There is also a potential upside to having such elite members on the committee. As Wolfgang Maennig pointed out to me, at least these persons cannot be corrupted.

9. It is common for bid committees to add a former Olympic athlete as a figurehead.

10. Rick Burton and Norm O'Reilly, "Bach's History a Signal That His Leadership Will Be Proactive," *Sports Business Journal,* February 10–16, 2014. Stockholm's potential bid had special significance because Stockholm would have become the first city to host both the Summer and the Winter Games. Munich's bid had Thomas Bach's interest because he hails from Wurzburg, just north of Munich.

## Chapter 2

1. Coubertin's commitment to a modern Olympics was inspired by his contact with the English physician William Penny Brookes. See Robert Barney, Stephen R. Wenn, and Scott G. Martyn, *Selling the Five Rings: The International Olympic Committee and the Rise of Olympic Commercialism* (University of Utah Press, 2004), chap. 1.

2. Coubertin changed his mind on the importance of amateurism over time. See *Olympism: Selected Writings of Pierre de Coubertin,* ed. Norbert Muller (Lausanne: IOC, 1970).

3. International Olympic Committee (IOC), "Olympic Charter" (Lausanne, 2013) (www.olympic.org/documents/olympic_charter_en.pdf).

4. Brundage finished sixth in the pentathlon and didn't finish in the decathlon. See, for example, Bruce Lowitt, "Thorpe Becomes 1st Olympic Star," *St. Petersburg Times,* October 31, 1999 (www.sptimes.com/ News/103199/news_pf/Sports/Thorpe_becomes_1st_Ol.shtml).

5. Allen Guttmann, *The Olympics: A History of the Modern Games* (University of Illinois Press, 2002), chap. 3.

6. Roland Renson and Marijke den Hollander, "Sport and Business in the City: The Antwerp Olympic Games of 1920 and the Urban Elite," *Olympika: The International Journal of Olympic Studies* 6 (1997): 73–84.

7. Guttmann, *The Olympics,* p. 44.

8. Five countries sought to host the first World Cup: Italy, Holland, Spain, Sweden, and Uruguay. In the competitive bidding spirit, Uruguay, a country of but 2 million and about to celebrate the centenary of its independence, offered to pay the full travel and lodging expenses of visiting teams and to build a new stadium. Yet two months before the 1930 competition was to begin, no European countries were willing to make the three-week boat trip to Uruguay. The Latin American soccer federations threatened to withdraw from FIFA, and political arm twisting began in Europe. In the end, France, Yugoslavia, Romania, and Belgium—hardly the powerhouses of European soccer at the time—agreed to participate. See Brian Glanville, *The Story of the World Cup* (London: Faber and Faber, 1993), chap. 1.

9. Tensions between FIFA and the IOC have asserted themselves on several occasions over the years. Notably, FIFA refused to accept the stadiums designated for soccer in Southern California matches by the Los Angeles Organizing Committee of the 1984 Games. As a consequence, the 1984 Olympic soccer competition was played at four sites: Harvard University, the U.S. Naval Academy in Maryland, Stanford University, and the Rose Bowl. See Peter Ueberroth, *Made in America* (New York: William Morrow and Co., 1985), p. 104.

10. See Guttmann, *The Olympics,* chap. 4, for a fuller discussion of this and other issues confronting the 1936 Games.

11. There were, however, two "alibi" Jews, Rudi Ball (ice hockey) and Helene Meyer (world-class fencer). They had Jewish fathers but non-Jewish mothers. By Jewish custom, only someone with a Jewish mother is considered Jewish. For a more detailed discussion, see Arnd Kruger, "Germany: The Propaganda Machine," in *The Nazi Olympics: Sport, Politics and Appeasement in the 1930s,* ed. A. Kruger and W. Murray (University of Illinois Press, 2003).

12. Marty Glickman and Sam Stoller were the two replaced athletes. See, for example, Donald Harrison, "Jewish Athlete Still Bitter about Ruined Shot at Gold Medal," *San Diego Jewish Press-Heritage,* July 2, 1999 (www.jewish sightseeing.com/germany/berlin/olympic_stadium/19990702-glickman.htm). See also Marty Glickman and Stan Isaacs, *The Fastest Kid on the Block: The Marty Glickman Story* (Syracuse University Press, 1999).

13. Germany did, however, take home the most gold medals from the 1936 Games, with the United States coming in second and Hungary third.

14. The Melbourne games were boycotted by Egypt, Iraq, and Lebanon to protest Israel's takeover of the Suez Canal in 1956. They were also the site of a vicious and bloody water polo contest between the Hungarian and the Soviet teams following the Soviet invasion of Hungary in that year.

15. IOC, *Olympic Marketing File,* 2014 (www.olympic.org/Documents/ IOC_Marketing/OLYMPIC_MARKETING_FACT_%20FILE_2014.pdf), p. 22.

16. Barney and others, *Selling the Five Rings,* chap. 4. Mexico City's games in 1968 were the first to be broadcast in color (ibid., p. 84).

17. See ibid., pp. 80–98, for an extended discussion of these tensions and their compromises.

18. Guttmann, *The Olympics,* p. 113. There is one International Federation for each sport.

19. In his memoir of the Los Angeles games, Peter Ueberroth, the president of the Local Organizing Committee, states that the IOC received one-third of the U.S. television rights fee of $225 million (*Made in America,* pp. 66–68). As pointed out in the text, this is inaccurate. The IOC received one-third of the cash payment of $100 million only.

20. The technical services deduction allowed to Calgary for the 1988 Winter Games was set at 20 percent of the gross value of the rights fee. Barney and others, *Selling the Five Rings,* p. 207.

21. Ibid., chap. 8.

22. The Partido Revolucionario Institucional has held power for more than seventy years since its founding in 1929.

23. The Mexico City games witnessed another first. Some of the athletes were paid by Adidas and Puma to wear their running shoes. Apparently, endorsements by Olympic athletes continued quietly for the next decade, and most in the IOC looked the other way.

24. Neither scaling the fence nor entering the balcony posed major physical challenges. The Israeli team had asked to be transferred to a more secure location at the beginning of the games, but its request was denied.

25. John Gold and Margaret Gold, "Olympic Cities: Regeneration, City Rebranding and Changing Urban Agendas," *Geography Compass* 2, no. 1 (2008): 305.

26. See Guttmann, *The Olympics,* pp. 143–44, for a discussion of the causes of the massive cost overrun in Montreal. See also Barney and others, *Selling the Five Rings,* pp. 123–25.

27. The first recorded use of performance-enhancing drugs in the Olympics was during the 1904 marathon when the winner, Thomas Hicks, was found to be using strychnine. The use of steroids, erythropoietin, and other substances has been widespread beyond the East Germans; such well-known figures as Marion Jones, Ben Johnson, and many others have admitted to drug use or have tested positive.

28. See Ueberroth, *Made in America,* p. 83.

29. Most commentaries in the West state that the true finances of the Moscow games are unknown, held as state secrets by Alexei Kosygin and Leonid Brezhnev. Ueberroth, however, suggests that the 1980 Games cost the USSR more than $5 billion (*Made in America,* p. 60). Barney and others (*Selling the Five Rings,* p. 148) report that Moscow's official figure put the cost at $1.3 billion, while other estimates rose as high as $9 billion.

30. Ueberroth adds that "donations [to finance the games] were out of the question. . . . It would have been insensitive and ill advised to compete against churches, synagogues, hospitals, YMCAs, Girl Scouts and all the other worthy organizations that rely on charity for their survival. Also, the USOC relies almost entirely on donations and we didn't want to compete for the same dollars" (*Made in America,* p. 60).

31. Ueberroth, *Made in America,* p. 121.

32. The extent to which it does one or the other depends on what economists call the price elasticity of demand. The more sensitive consumers are to price changes (the higher the elasticity), the more the tax on hotels or car rentals will lower demand for travel to the city.

33. An exclusive product category refers to a type of product, for example beer, and a single company being the only one allowed to advertise in that category during the competition or in association with the Olympics. The company would also be allowed to promote itself as an official sponsor of the Olympics. Ueberroth states in his book that the idea of fewer, larger, and exclusive sponsorship contracts came from his aide, Joel Rubenstein (*Made in America,* p. 61). The IOC adopted this strategy in its TOP program immediately after the L.A. games.

34. Although different surplus amounts have been cited in the literature, $215 million is the figure that Ueberroth cites several times in his book (for example, *Made in America,* p. 369.) Ueberroth states that the figure was revised upward from the September 1984 report of a $150 million surplus. The surplus was given 60 percent to the USOC and 40 percent to Southern California, in both cases to benefit the development of youth sports. The official IOC report on the Los Angeles games also states that the surplus was $215 million, although it notes the possibility that the figure could increase with some additional revenue trickling in by the time the LAOCOG dissolved. See http://library.la84.org/6oic/OfficialReports/1984/1984v1pt2.pdf, 11.01.10, p. 309.

35. IOC official report, ibid., p. 370. Ueberroth contrasts Los Angeles' good luck with what happened in Lake Placid, New York, where an expected operating surplus of $1 million turned into a $6 million operating deficit when the organizing committee had to throw money at a series of last-minute problems.

36. ABC paid the IOC $225 million for U.S. rights, and managed to turn a nifty profit of more than $400 million. The U.S. ratings soared, and ABC was able to charge $250,000 for a thirty-second advertising spot. Meanwhile, Peter Ueberroth thanked the thousands of volunteers and paid himself a modest bonus of $475,000.

37. There was actually a crack in the armor of amateurism under Lord Killanin. In 1978, Rule 26 of the Olympic Charter was modified so that athletes were allowed openly to earn money from endorsements if the money

went to their national sports federation or their country's Olympic Committee. The receiving organization was then permitted to pay the athlete's expenses in connection with the games, including "pocket money." "Broken-time" payments for time away from the athlete's regular job were also authorized if the athlete had a regular job. But the rule continued to declare that professional athletes were ineligible.

38. The IOC at the time consisted of 109 men and seven women. Members elected prior to 1966 had life membership, and those elected subsequently until the age of eighty. Today, the age limit for new members is seventy years.

39. Because of the growing size of both the Winter and the Summer Games, alternating the events also made administrative sense.

40. Elmer Sterken, "Economic Impact of Organizing Large Sporting Events," in *International Handbook on the Economics of Mega Sporting Events,* ed. Wolfgang Maennig and Andrew S. Zimbalist (Cheltenham, U.K.: Edward Elgar, 2012), p. 340.

41. See, for example, Stephen Wenn, Robert Barney, and Scott Martyn, *Tarnished Rings: The International Olympic Committee Bid Scandal* (Syracuse University Press, 2011), chap. 6, and A. Jennings and V. Simson, *The Lords of the Rings: Power, Money and Drugs in the Modern Olympics* (Transparency Books, 2012).

42. See, for example, the story provided by Ueberroth about payoffs to IOC members from South Korea in its successful pursuit of the 1988 Games (*Made in America*, p. 106).

43. See, for example, Helen Lenskyj, *Inside the Olympic Industry* (SUNY Press, 2000), chap. 1.

44. "Nagano Olympics Records Destroyed," CNNSI.com, January 15, 1999 (www.sportsillustrated.cnn.com/features/1999/year_in_review/flashbacks/olympics1/).

45. Michael Payne, *Olympic Turnaround* (London Business Press, 2005), p. 234.

46. A similar imbroglio unfurled earlier with regard to the split of corporate sponsorship revenues. After the IOC introduced its TOP program of exclusive sponsorships in 1985, the USOC argued that since most of the large sponsors were based in the United States (and, if they didn't sign with the IOC, they would do a national sponsorship deal), it was entitled to a disproportionate share of TOP revenues. The other NOCs, of course, strenuously disagreed. The IOC sponsorship negotiator was ISL, and ISL offered the USOC 20 percent of all TOP revenues. The USOC successfully held out for 30 percent, but not until after a significant amount of ill will had accumulated. See Barney and others, *Selling the Five Rings,* pp. 174–80.

47. This and other financial data on the Olympic Games are available in the *Olympic Marketing File* from various years and also the official IOC reports on each Olympics.

48. "IOC, USOC Finalize Revenue Deal," ESPN.com, May 24, 2012 (http://espn.go.com/olympics/story/_/id/7967000/ioc-usoc-resolve-differences-revenues). See also Barney and others, *Selling the Five Rings,* chap. 11.

49. Some estimates for Sochi expenditures go as high as $70 billion. Putin has not released a careful accounting of the investments, so even though the figure of $51 billion is frequently cited, there is no authoritative estimate. The matter is further complicated because the ruble-to-dollar exchange rate has fluctuated significantly during and subsequent to the games.

50. This estimate does not include an additional $600 million that Brazil is planning to spend on athlete training, with the goal of earning enough medals in 2016 to be in the top ten medal-winning countries at the Olympics. The country's announced goal is to win thirty medals, thirteen more than were won in 2012. Tariq Panja, "Brazil to Spend Record $600 Million to Boost Olympic Medal Hopes," Bloomberg.com, July 23, 2014 (http://brazil portal.wordpress.com/2014/07/24/brazil-to-spend-record-600-million-to-boost-olympic-medal-hopes/).

51. To be sure, the London Organizing Committee for the Olympic Games reported that it received only $700 million from the IOC, substantially less than the IOC numbers suggest. See, for example, "London Olympics 2012: Where Does the Money Come From—And Where's It Being Spent?," *The Guardian,* July 26, 2012 (www.theguardian.com/sport/datablog/2012/jul/26/london-2012-olympics-money).

52. Zjan Shirinian, "Rio 2016 'Top Priority' after World Cup, Pledges Brazilian President," *Inside the Games,* July 11, 2014 (www.insidethegames.biz/olympics/summer-olympics/2016/1021254-rio-2016-top-priority-after-world-cup-pledges-brazilian-president).

53. Argentina and Uruguay boycotted the 1938 World Cup in France because of an internal dispute over FIFA procedures. They each believed that FIFA's policy was to rotate the hosts between Europe and the Americas. Since the 1934 competition was held in Italy, the choice of France for 1938 violated the presumed policy. Between 1958 and 2010, FIFA scrupulously followed the continental rotation policy, as discussed later in the text. Although it was not a boycott of the World Cup finals, in 1974 the Soviet team refused to travel to Chile for an intercontinental playoff match in protest over Pinochet's overthrow of Allende and the new regime's brutality.

54. For further discussion of soccer and violence, see Stefan Szymanski and Andrew Zimbalist, *National Pastime: How Americans Play Baseball and the Rest of the World Plays Soccer* (Brookings Institution Press, 2006); Franklin Foer, *How Soccer Explains the World* (New York: Harper Perennial, 2010); and David Goldblatt, *The Ball Is Round: A Global History of Soccer* (New York: Riverhead Books, 2008).

55. See, for example, Paul Darby, "Africa, the FIFA Presidency, and the Governance of World Football: 1974, 1998 and 2002," *Africa Today,* 2003.

56. "Qatar's 2022 World Cup Bid Hit with Fresh Corruption Claims, FIFA Refuses to Comment," *Sports Business Daily Global,* June 2, 2014. For an earlier report, see Claire Newell, Holly Watt, Claire Duffin, and Ben Bryant, "Qatar World Cup 2022 Investigation: Former Fifa Vice-President Jack Warner and Family Paid Millions," *The Telegraph,* March 21, 2014. On the match-fixing scandal, see "FIFA Report on Match-Fixing Casts Shadow over This Month's World Cup in Brazil," *Sports Business Daily Global,* June 2, 2014.

57. Following substantial pushback over the twelve new or fully renovated stadiums in Brazil, FIFA chiefs seem to be getting religion. A few days after the 2014 World Cup competition ended, Sepp Blatter announced that FIFA may ask Russia to build only ten instead of twelve new stadiums for the 2018 competition.

58. Dennis Coates, "World Cup Economics: What Americans Need to Know about a US World Cup," University of Maryland Baltimore County, Department of Economics Working Paper 10-121, pp. 18–20. For the 1994 World Cup in the United States, the only appreciable facility investments were $2.5 million to replace the artificial turf at the Silverdome outside Detroit, Michigan, and $2.8 million to slightly widen the field at the Cotton Bowl in Dallas, Texas. While most studies report that Germany spent under $1 billion on facilities to host the 2006 Cup, one article cites a figure of $1.9 billion. See Victor Matheson, "Were the Billions the Brazilians Spent on World Cup Stadiums Worth It?," Five-Thirty-Eight.com, 2014 (http://fivethirtyeight.com/features/were-the-billions-brazil-spent-on-world-cup-stadiums-worth-it/). This article seems to be confounding original stadium construction costs and facility preparation expenses for the 2006 World Cup.

## Chapter 3

1. Ex ante methodology means that the estimated impact is forecast before the event takes place. To create such an estimate, one must make assumptions about the number of foreign visitors, number of days spent in the city or country, amount of spending per day, and so on. It is a simple matter to inflate the estimates by making unrealistic assumptions. As discussed in the text, there are numerous other issues with this methodology.

2. To be sure, there is also a literature of ex ante event analysis that looks at how financial markets respond to the announcement of a city being selected as a mega-event host. The findings in this literature are mixed. In both Beijing and Sydney, the national stock markets did not experience a lasting boost from the awarding of the games to their cities, although the share prices of

construction companies in New South Wales did rise. See, for example, R. Brooks and S. Davidson, "The Sydney Olympic Games Announcement and the Australian Stock Market Reaction," *Applied Economics Letters* 7, no. 12 (2000); M. Leeds, J. Mirikitani, and D. Tang, "Rational Exuberance? An Event Analysis of the 2008 Olympic Announcement," *International Journal of Sport Finance* 4, no. 1 (2009); and N. Veraros, E. Kasimati, and P. Dawson, "The 2004 Olympic Games Announcement and Its Effect on the Athens and Milan Stock Exchanges," *Applied Economics Letters* 11, no. 12 (2004).

3. Most input-output models contain highly aggregated data on imports and exports.

4. John J. Siegfried and Andrew Zimbalist, "The Economics of Sports Facilities and Their Communities," *Journal of Economic Perspectives* 14, no. 3 (2000): 95–114.

5. See www.travelingguide.com/tourism/2008statistics.

6. This computation is based on the standard finance formula, Payment = Principal $* [r(1 + r)^\wedge n/((1 + r)^\wedge n - 1)]$, wherein part of the principal, as well as the interest, is paid off each year, such that the payments are spread out equally over the thirty-year period of the loan. The interest rate is denoted by $r$ and the number of years by $n$.

7. Sources for table 3-1 follow: A. Feddersen, A. Grotzinger, and W. Maennig (2009), "Investment in Stadia and Regional Economic Development: Evidence from FIFA World Cup 2006 Stadia," *International Journal of Sport Finance* 4 (4), pp. 221–39; R. Baade and V. Matheson (2004), "The Quest for the Cup: Assessing the Economic Impact of the World Cup," *Regional Studies* 38, pp. 343–54; S. Du Plessis and W. Maennig (2011), "The 2010 World Cup High Frequency Data Economics: Effects on International Tourism and Awareness for South Africa," *Development Southern Africa* 28 (3), pp. 349–65; F. Hagn and W. Maennig (2008), "Employment Effects of the Football World Cup 1974 in Germany," *Labour Economics* 15 (5), pp. 1062–75; F. Hagn and W. Maennig (2009), "Large Sport Events and Unemployment: The Case of the 2006 Soccer World Cup in Germany," *Applied Economics* 41 (25), pp. 3295–302; S. Allmers and W. Maennig (2009), "Economic Impacts of the FIFA Soccer World Cups in France 1998, Germany 2006, and Outlook for South Africa 2010," *Eastern Economic Journal* 35 (4), pp. 500–19; S. Szymanski (2002), "The Economic Impact of the World Cup," *World Economics* 3 (1), pp. 169–77; S. du Plessis and C. Venter, "The Home Team Scores! A First Assessment of the Economic Impact of World Cup 2010," Stellenbosch Working Paper Series WP21/2010 (Stellenbosch University, Department of Economics); S. Jasmand and W. Maennig (2008), "Regional Income and Employment Effects of the 1972 Munich Summer Olympic Games," *Regional Studies* 42 (7), pp. 991–1002; P. K. Porter and D. Fletcher (2008), "The Economic Impact of the Olympic Games: Ex Ante

Predictions and Ex Post Reality," *Journal of Sport Management* 22 (4), pp. 470–86; A. Feddersen and W. Maennig (2013), "Employment Effects of the Olympic Games in Atlanta 1996 Reconsidered," *International Journal of Sport Finance* 8 (2), pp. 95–111; A. Feddersen and W. Maennig (2012), "Sectoral Labour Market Effects of the 2006 FIFA World Cup," *Labour Economics* 19(6), pp. 860–69; J. Giesecke and J. Madden (2011), "Modelling the Economic Impacts of the Sydney Olympics in Retrospect: Game Over for the Bonanza Story?," *Economic Papers* 30 (2), pp. 218–32; S. B. Billings and J. S. Holladay (2012), "Should Cities Go for the Gold? The Long-Term Impacts of Hosting the Olympics," *Economic Inquiry* 50 (3), pp. 642–47; R. von Rekowsky (2013), "Are the Olympics a Golden Opportunity for Investors?," *Leadership Series—Investment Insights* (Boston: Fidelity Investments, August); R. Baumann, Bryon Engelhardt, and Victor A. Matheson (2012), "Employment Effects of the 2002 Winter Olympics in Salt Lake City, Utah," *Journal of Economics and Statistics* 232 (3), pp. 308–17; Robert Baumann and Bryon Eldon Engelhardt (2012), "Labor Market Effects of the World Cup: A Sectoral Analysis," in *International Handbook on the Economics of Mega Sporting Events,* ed. Wolfgang Maennig and Andrew S. Zimbalist (Cheltenham, U.K.: Edward Elgar), pp. 385–400; R. A. Baade and V. Matheson (2002), "Bidding for the Olympics: Fool's Gold?," in *Transatlantic Sport,* ed. Carlos Pestana Barros, Muradali Ibrahímo, and Stefan Szymanski (London: Edward Elgar), pp. 127–51; J. L. Hotchkiss, R. E. Moore, and S. M. Zobay (2003), "Impact of the 1996 Summer Olympic Games on Employment and Wages in Georgia," *Southern Economic Journal* 69(3), pp. 691–704.

8. J. L. Hotchkiss and others, "Impact of the 1996 Summer Olympic Games on Employment and Wages in Georgia," *Southern Economic Journal* 69, no. 3 (2003): 691–704. The Hotchkiss and colleagues' study may be interpreted to be picking up medium-term employment gains, as it goes four years past the 1996 Games. The authors claim that the main employment effect of the games begins to occur two years before the games, so they compare performance between two periods, 1985–93 and 1994–2000. They arrived at this division by testing dummy variables for different period breakdowns beginning with 1990, the year the IOC awarded the games to Atlanta, and then picking the breakdown that best fit the data. This technique arguably involves data mining and is further questionable because a good deal of Olympic construction takes place more than two years in advance of the games. It is also noteworthy that they do not conduct separate tests for counties with venues and counties nearby counties with venues. Also, without explanation, in two cases the counties included are not contiguous with counties with venues. These are included without explanation. Further, there are problems with serial correlation in their regressions. See also Arne Feddersen

and Wolfgang Maennig, "Employment Effects of the Olympic Games in Atlanta 1996 Reconsidered," *International Journal of Sport Finance* 8, no. 2 (2013): 95–111.

9. Stan Du Plessis and Wolfgang Maennig, "The 2010 World Cup High-Frequency Data Economics: Effects on International Tourism and Awareness for South Africa," *Development Southern Africa* 28, no. 3 (2011): 349–65; Thomas Peeters, Victor Matheson, and Stefan Szymanski, "Tourism and the 2010 World Cup: Lessons for Developing Countries," *Journal of African Economies,* January 2014, pp. 1–31.

10. Estimates for the 2010 South African World Cup have the average foreign tourist spending a total of $1,650 in the country, while estimates for the German World Cup in 2006 put total spending per visitor at $1,286. Our estimate in the example is in the upper part of this range, at $1,500. See Peeters and others, "Tourism and the 2010 World Cup."

11. As discussed later in the text, Brazil reported that the number of visitors during the period of the 2014 World Cup, including a few weeks before the beginning of the matches, was 1 million, denoting a gain of around half a million above normal levels. The majority of these visitors came from neighboring South American countries with teams in the final sixteen. Anecdotal reports suggest that these visitors in large numbers stayed on the beaches and trailers, used public bathrooms, and spent little money.

12. Michel de Nooij, "Mega Sport Events: A Probabilistic Social Cost-Benefit Analysis of Bidding for the Games," *Journal of Sports Economics* 15, no. 4 (2014): 412. Indirect costs are estimated at an additional $142 million.

13. Michael Feblowitz, "The Legacy Games: Social and Economic Impacts for Olympic Cities," *Social Impact Research Experience Journal,* January 1, 2012, p. 20.

14. European Tour Operators Association (ETOA), "Olympic Hotel Demand," ETOA Report 2010 (www.etoa.org).

15. See www.latimes.com/business/la-fi-rio-high-prices-20140314,0,54 3820.story#axzz2w95MLCBY.

16. For more on the human costs of poor design associated with mega-events, see, for example, Christopher Gaffney's June 30, 2014, discussion of the lack of design integration of Brazil's World Cup stadiums, surrounded by parking lots, in their communities, at geostadia.com. An extensive treatment of the human costs associated with mega-events can be found in Dave Zirin, *Brazil's Dance with the Devil* (Chicago: Haymarket Books, 2014), chaps. 6 and 7.

17. Kavetsos and Szymanski, using survey evidence, considered three mega-events in Europe and found that there is a short-term increase in self-defined happiness in two of the three host countries, but that the effect is not lasting. They also found that having the home team win does not produce a

significant increase in self-defined happiness. Georgios Kavetsos and Stefan Szymanski, "National Well-Being and International Sports Events," *Journal of Economic Psychology* 31, no. 2 (April 2010): 158–71.

18. *Guardian* report cited in "Pay Slips Show Qatar World Cup Stadium Workers Earn as Little as $0.76 an Hour," *Sports Business Daily Global,* July 31, 2014.

19. Arrivals at the Atlanta International Airport did increase in the four years following 1996, but they increased at a slower rate than in the previous four years. The Atlanta airport is a Delta Airlines hub and serves as an entry point into the United States for fifty-one countries, so there are many factors that affect Atlanta's airport arrivals besides the Olympic Games. P. K. Porter and D. Fletcher (2008), "The Economic Impact of the Olympic Games: Ex Ante Predictions and Ex Post Reality," *Journal of Sport Management* 22, no. 4 (2008): 470–86.

20. ETOA, "Olympic Hotel Demand," ETOA Report 2010 (www.etoa.org).

21. In 1996 in Georgia, home state of the host city Atlanta, hotel occupancy rates fell from 73 percent in the previous year to 68 percent. Sydney in 2000 saw hotel occupancy rates fall steadily as the games approached, from 83 percent in March to 68 percent in July and August, before a modest recovery to 80 percent during the games themselves. Cited in Mark Perryman, "Do the Olympics Boost the Economy? Studies Show the Impact Is Likely Negative," *Daily Beast,* July 7, 2012 (www.thedailybeast.com/articles/2012/07/30/do-the-olympics-boost-the-economy-studies-show-the-impact-is-likely-negative.html), p. 7.

22. Ibid.

23. M. Saayman and R. Rossouw, "The Economic Value of the 2010 Soccer World Cup" (www.actacommercil.co.za/index.php/acta/article/viewfile/55/55).

24. ETOA, "Olympics and Tourism," ETOA Report 2006 (www.etoa.org).

25. Vancouver bed nights followed a similar pattern, reaching 8.415 million in 2010, below the 8.91 million level set in 2007.

26. *Statistics Canada,* various years (www.statcan.gc.ca/start-debut-eng.html).

27. Talia Marcopoto, "Brazil Claims 'Victory' in World Cup," CNN.com, July 16, 2014.

28. See, for example, Eduardo Campos, "Gasto de Turista Estrangeiro Pode Chegar a R$2,4 Bi," *De Brasilia,* July 16, 2014 (www.valor.com.br/financas/3616670/gasto-de-turista-estrangeiro-pode-chegar-r-24-bi#ixzz37jqFNkjL).

29. Author conversations with Luiz Martins de Melo, Christopher Gaffney, and various journalists covering the World Cup.

30. Foreign tourism in Brazil had been growing at 5.7 percent annually from 2009 through 2012.

## Chapter 4

1. Christopher Gaffney, "Between Discourse and Reality: The Un-Sustainability of Mega-Event Planning," *Sustainability* 5 (2013): 3926–40.

2. IOC publications enumerate the perceived legacy benefits after each Olympic Games. See, for instance, IOC, *Fact Sheet: Legacies of the Games.* Update December 2013. See also Grant Thornton, "Report 5: Post-Games Evaluation: Meta-Evaluation of the Impacts and Legacy of the London 2012 Olympic Games and Paralympic Games," July 2013.

3. Points 15 and 16 were added in a June 2014 public relations brochure titled "What You Need to Know about the 2014 FIFA World Cup Brazil," put out by the Secretariat for Social Communication, Presidency of the Federative Republic of Brazil. The brochure was prepared by a New York City public relations firm, Fleishman-Hillard.

4. European Tour Operators Association (ETOA), *Olympic Report,* ETOA Report 2006 (www.etoa.org), p. 6.

5. Ibid.

6. J. R. Brent Ritchie and Brian H. Smith, "The Impact of a Mega-Event on Host Region Awareness: A Longitudinal Study," *Journal of Travel Research* 30, no. 1 (1991): 3–10.

7. ETOA, "Olympics and Tourism," ETOA Report 2010 (www.etoa.org), p. 1. It is perhaps reasonable to question the objectivity of the ETOA. On the one hand, as a tourist trade association, one would suspect that the ETOA would be a proponent of any event that lifted tourism and hence would be inclined to be supportive of the Olympics if the games indeed lift tourism. On the other hand, since the Olympics tend to concentrate any effects within one city of one country, it may be that the majority of ETOA members oppose them. I am not in a position to evaluate the internal politics of the ETOA, and it seems reasonable, a priori, to assume that it is in the best interests of the ETOA to understand the true economic impact from hosting the games.

8. The report, *The Sydney Olympics and Foreign Attitudes to Australia,* was written by authors that included Nancy Rivenburgh, a former professor at Barcelona's Centre for Olympic Studies. It is cited by Perryman in "Do the Olympics Boost the Economy?," p. 7.

9. Cited by Perryman, ibid.

10. ETOA, "Olympics and Tourism," ETOA Report 2006 (www.etoa.org), p. 15.

11. Cited in ibid.

12. Tourism New South Wales, "Facts and Figures" (corporate.tourism.nsw.gov.au/Facts_And_Figures_p10.aspx).

13. ETOA, "Olympics and Tourism," ETOA Report 2010 (www.etoa.org), p. 3.

14. Jon Teigland, "Impacts on Tourism from Mega-Events: The Case of Winter Olympic Games," *Western Norway Research Institute,* October 1996, p. 45.

15. ETOA, "Olympics and Tourism," ETOA Report 2010 (www.etoa. org), p. 3.

16. A. Rose and M. Spiegel, "The Olympic Effect," *Economic Journal* 121 (2011): 652–77. Interestingly, another 2011 study by Billings and Holladay found that Olympic host cities between 1950 and 2005 did not experience any increase in trade openness (or real GDP) as a result of hosting. S. Billings and J. Holladay, "Should Cities Go for the Gold? The Long-Term Impacts of Hosting the Olympics," *Economic Inquiry* 50, no. 3 (2012): 754–72.

17. Wonho Song, using the Rose and Spiegel data set, found increases to exports and to tourism. However, these findings suffer from the same selection bias found in Rose and Spiegel. W. Song, "Impacts of Olympics on Exports and Tourism," *Journal of Economic Development* 35, no. 4 (2010).

18. W. Maennig and F. Richter, "Exports and Olympic Games: Is There a Signal Effect?," *Journal of Sports Economics* 13, no. 6 (2012): 636.

19. Robert Baumann, T. Ciavarra, and B. Engelhardt, "An Examination of Spectator Sports and Crime Rates," *Economics and Labour Relations Review* 23, no. 2 (2012): 83–97.

20. In São Paulo there was also a metro line built that goes out to the new stadium and adjacent real estate development.

21. Of the total spending on the World Cup in excess of $15 billion, approximately $4 billion was spent on road, bus, and rail transportation, $3.8 billion on airport upgrades, $315 million on port improvement and $180 million on telecommunications. Deputy Sport Minister Luis Fernandes emphasizes the importance of the investment to extend the nation's broadband network to Manaus for the Cup. This was a minor investment and certainly could and would have been undertaken without hosting the World Cup. "Seeking a Silver Lining," *Sports Pro,* July 2014, pp. 56–65.

22. Gaffney, "Between Discourse and Reality," p. 3933.

23. Associated Press, "Rio's Olympic Golf Course in Turmoil," September 4, 2014 (http://espn.go.com/espn/print?id=11463567&type=story).

24. Gaffney, "Between Discourse and Reality," 3928.

25. Christopher Gaffney, "Hunting White Elephants/Caçando Elefantes Brancos," blog entry, June 6, 2014 (www.geostadia.com/).

26. The idiom "white elephant" derives from an ancient tradition of Southeast Asian monarchies. White elephants were very rare and were regarded as sacred. If the king gave one as a gift, it was an honor. However, the gift was a terrible burden to the person who received it. He had to feed and care for that elephant throughout its long life.

27. *CBS News,* "Olympic Challenge: How Do Host Cities Fare after the Games?," February 24, 2014 (www.cbsnews.com/news/olympic-challenge-host-do-host-cities-fare-after-the-games).

28. Ibid.

29. Doug Saunders, "Is the World Cup a Giant Waste of Money?," *Globe and Mail,* May 31, 2014 (www.realclearworld.com/2014/06/12/brazil_needs_more_than_a_world_cup_win_159149.html).

30. Perryman, "Do the Olympics Boost the Economy?"

31. In 2014, however, Barcelona turned its Olympic Stadium at Montjuic into an upscale sports theme park.

32. Gaffney, "Between Discourse and Reality," p. 3929.

33. *CBS News,* "Olympic Challenge: How Do Host Cities Fare after the Games?"

34. Juliet Macur, "When Dazzle of Stadiums Gives Way to Desolation," *New York Times,* June 29, 2014.

35. E. Cottle, ed., *South Africa's World Cup: A Legacy for Whom?* (University of KwaZulu-Natal Press, 2011).

36. Ian Austen, "Vancouver Journal: A $1 Billion Hangover from an Olympic Party," *New York Times,* February 24, 2010 (www.nytimes.com/2010/02/25/sports/olympics/25vancouver.html?_r=0).

## Chapter 5

1. Anna Sanchez and others, "Barcelona 1992: International Events and Housing Rights: A Focus on the Olympic Games" (Geneva: Center on Housing Rights and Evictions [COHRE], 2007), p. 20. See also Nadia Fava, "Tourism and the City Image: The Barcelona Olympic Case" (Universitat de Girona, Spain, 2012); COBI, "Barcelona: Urban Transformation and '92 Olympic Games," 2005 (http://www.mt.usi.ch/barcelona-123372.pdf); and London East Research Institute, "A Lasting Legacy for London?" (London, May 2007).

2. Sanchez and others, "Barcelona 1992," p. 21.

3. Of course, once the Olympic project was undertaken, the PGM was modified. It is also worth noting that Barcelona had a tradition of using mega-events to help transform the city. The 1929 World Exposition in Barcelona led to the construction of Parc Montjuic, and the 1888 International Expo led to the creation of the city's central park, Parc de la Ciutadella.

4. Ferran Brunet, "The Economic Impact of the Barcelona Olympic Games, 1986–2004," in *Barcelona: L'herencia deis Jocs,* ed. Miguel de Moragas and Miguel Botella (Barcelona: Centre d'Estudis Olimpics, 2002), p. 14. The percentages of private and public spending differ according to the

source. The discrepancies are most likely a product of what investments are considered to be part of the Olympic effort. For example, Barcelona Holding Olímpic S.A. made the following expenditure calculations: 33.8 percent of total Olympic activities were financed by private sector investment and 66.2 percent of total Olympic activities were financed by public sector investment. See Barcelona Holding Olímpic S.A., "Los Juegos Olímpicos Como Generadores de Inversión (1986–1992)" (Barcelona, June 1992), p. 7. In any event, it is clear that the share of private funding was substantial.

5. John Gold and Margaret Gold, "Olympic Cities: Regeneration, City Rebranding and Changing Urban Agenda," *Geography Compass* 2, no. 1 (2008): 307.

6. Ferran Brunet, "An Economic Analysis of the Barcelona '92 Olympic Games" (Barcelona: Centre d'Estudis Olimpics, 1995).

7. European Tour Operators Association (ETOA), "Olympic Report," July 2005 (www.etoa.org), pp. 11–14.

8. Iris HIllier and Rafael Isun, "Barcelona: Before and after the '92 Olympic Games," February 2010 (www.insights.org.uk), p. 3.

9. Josep Maria Montaner, "The Barcelona Model Reviewed: Leading Up to the 1992 Olympic Games," lecture presented at the "Learning from Barcelona" conference, Birkbeck, Stratford, January 28, 2011, p. 5.

10. Unlike in other mega-events, however, there were no forced evictions in Barcelona, and those who did relocate were provided with other homes or housing subsidies. Unfortunately, many were relocated to distant areas, often compromising their employment situation. Sanchez and others, "Barcelona 1992," p. 29.

11. Ibid., p. 48.

12. Other criticisms of Barcelona's plan include the 40 kilometers of ring roads surrounding the city (which promoted personal car use at the expense of public transport and did little to alleviate inner-city traffic), the widespread use of migrant labor with long hours, and the high import component of building materials for the planned construction. See the LSE Study on Barcelona games, 2010; and Miguelez and Carrasquer, "The Repercussion of the Olympic Games on Labour" (Barcelona: Centre d'Estudis Olimpics, 1995).

13. See "2004 Universal Forum of Cultures" (en.wikipedia.org/wiki/2004_Universal_Forum_of_Cultures), p. 3.

14. Parks, Promenades & Planning: Brand Management with the 21st Century Urban Waterfront, "Barcelona: Event as Catalyst" (urbanwaterfront.blogspot.com), p. 6.

15. M. Müller, "State Dirigisme in Megaprojects: Governing the 2014 Winter Olympics in Sochi," *Environment and Planning A* 43, no. 9 (2011): 2091–108.

16. RT.com, February 4, 2013.

17. Jules Boykoff, "Celebration Capitalism and the Sochi 2014 Winter Olympics," *Olympika: The International Journal of Olympic Studies* 22 (2013): 54. A number of news reports put the price tag at $51 billion already in February 2013. For instance, see an Associated Press article of February 5, 2013, published in the *Washington Times* and elsewhere (www.washingtontimes.com/news/2013/feb/5/one-year-out-sochi-gearing-winter-olympics-spotlig/). These news reports appear to be based on the last official announcement in January 2013 of a price tag for the Sochi Olympics (at 1.526 trillion rubles—not including operational costs and security) by Sports Minister Vitaliy Mutko. No official figures have been made public since then. This lacuna also helps to explain speculations about a much higher price. See "Zatraty na podgotovku k Olimpijskim igram v Soči sostavjat 1,526 trln rublej," Gazeta.ru, January 2, 2013 (www.gazeta.ru/sport/2013/02/01/a_4949973.shtml).

18. Quoted in Boykoff, "Celebration Capitalism and the Sochi 2014 Winter Olympics," p. 39.

19. Boris Nemtsov, a former Russian deputy prime minister, alleged that between $25 billion and $30 billion of the $50 billion-plus cost of the Sochi games was due to manipulated contracts and venality to the benefit of "oligarchs and companies close to Mr. Putin." Nataliya Vasilyeva, "Russian Oligarchs Foot Most of 2014 Sochi Olympics," Associated Press, May 20, 2013. See also *BBC News,* May 30, 2013, and *HBO Real Sports,* November 19, 2013.

20. Stephanie Baker and Ilya Arkhipov,"Rich Russians Sparring with Putin over $48 Billion Olympics Bet," Bloomberg.com, November 26, 2013.

21. Thomas Grove, "Special Report: Russia's $50 Billion Olympic Gamble," Reuters, February 21, 2013.

22. Ed Hula III, "Investment Bank Asks for Bailout on Sochi Losses," *Around the Rings,* July 7, 2014.

23. Human Rights Watch, "Race to the Bottom: Exploitation of Migrant Workers ahead of Russia's 2014 Winter Olympic Games in Sochi" (February 6, 2013).

24. Daniel Sandford, "Putin's Olympic Steamroller in Sochi," *BBC News Europe,* February 6, 2013.

25. Boykoff, "Celebration Capitalism and the Sochi 2014 Winter Olympics," p. 56.

26. Nikolas von Twickel, "Sochi Is a Hard Nut to Crack for PR Gurus," *Moscow Times,* February 7, 2013.

27. Steven Myers, "Putin's Olympic Fever Dream," *New York Times Magazine,* January 22, 2014.

28. Nataliya Vasilyeva, "Sochi Critics Get Terrorist Treatment," Associated Press, December 18, 2013.

29. M. Müller, "(Im-)Mobile Policies: Why Sustainability Went Wrong in the 2014 Olympics in Sochi," *European Urban and Regional Studies* 22 (2015): 13.

30. In the Soviet era, many workers' unions also had retreats in Sochi. Today Sochi is viewed as the patriotic place to go, and the Russian elite feel almost obligated to spend some time there on vacation.

31. Both quotations from Alexey Eremenko, "Can Sochi Become a World Class Resort after Olympics?," *Russia & India Report,* December 20, 2013 (indus.in/economics/2013/12/20).

32. Center for Security Analysis and Prevention, "Evaluation of the Investment Risks in the Field of Tourism Construction Industry in Sochi" (www.cbap.cz/?p=1253&lang=en#more-1253).

33. David Segal, "Now What? A City Fears a Flameout," *New York Times,* February 23, 2014 (www.nytimes.com/2014/02/24/sports/olympics/sochi-olympics-construction-weighs-on-citys-future.html).

34. Ibid.

35. Ibid.

36. Nick Butler, "Tax Breaks Announced for All Sochi 2014 Buildings in Bid to Reduce Financial Burden," *Inside the Games,* May 13, 2014 (insidethegames.com).

37. David Owen, "Sochi Unveils $261 Million Profit," *Inside the Games,* June 19, 2014 (insidethegames.com).

38. M. Müller and S. D. Wolfe, "World Cup Russia 2018: Already the Most Expensive Ever?," *Russian Analytical Digest* 150 (2014): 2–6.

## Chapter 6

1. To be precise, economies of scale would apply to the double use of Maracanã Stadium or other facilities as well as to administrative savings where the work of preparing for the World Cup and for the Olympics is duplicative. Where the work for the two events is distinctive (they are considered separate products), then any administrative savings would be considered to be economies of scope.

2. Maracanã will be used for the opening and closing ceremonies, and for soccer matches, during the 2016 Olympics. The nearby João Havelange Stadium, which was built for the 2007 Pan American Games, after a very expensive renovation is scheduled to be used for track and field events in 2016.

3. Simon Romero, "Brazilians Go Back to Real Life," *New York Times,* July 13, 2014 (www.nytimes.com/2014/07/14/sports/worldcup/world-cup-2014-brazil-was-embarrassed-but-an-argentina-victory-would-have-been-intolerable.html).

4. Dom Phillips, "Brazilian Officials Are Giving Up on Some Unfinished World Cup Projects," *Washington Post,* May 7, 2014 (www.washington post.com/world/the_americas/brazilian-officials-are-giving-up-on-some-unfinished-world-cup-projects/2014/05/07/cde52c2c-d17e-11e3-937f-d3026234b51c_story.html).

5. Emily Godard, "At Least Two Dead as Overpass Collapses in Brazil World Cup City," *Inside the Games,* July 3, 2014 (insidethegames.com).

6. Patricia Ray Mallen, "Brazil Skirts Organizational Disaster with the Most Expensive World Cup Ever," *International Business Times,* April 11, 2014 (ibtimes.com).

7. Quoted in "Brazilian Left Wanting by Flawed FIFA World Cup Investment," Reuters, May 19, 2014.

8. According to Christopher Gaffney, the government was originally contemplating using seventeen different cities and stadiums for the World Cup. See Gaffney, "Between Discourse and Reality: The Un-Sustainability of Mega-Event Planning," *Sustainability 5* (2013): 3926–40.

9. M. Bastos and R. Mattos, "Esportes," *Folha de São Paulo,* São Paulo, May 19, 2011.

10. Ibid.

11. Dave Zirin, *Brazil's Dance with the Devil* (Chicago: Haymarket Books, 2014), p. 33.

12. Ibid., p. 17.

13. Of course, most policies are likely to create winners and losers. The key is to understand the net welfare effect on a community. The experience of Maria Oliveira is not offered as definitive evidence that it was bad policy to build the stadium; rather, it is offered as evidence that often there are overlooked costs.

14. Juliet Macur, "When Dazzle of Stadiums Gives Way to Desolation," *New York Times,* June 29, 2014.

15. Tariq Panja, "Brazil's Flamengo Won't Make 'Stupid' Deal to Return to Maracanã," Bloomberg (www.bloomberg.com), June 18, 2013.

16. Brian Homewood, "Not Much Football to Look Forward to in Brasília," Reuters, July 7, 2014.

17. Bradley Brooks, "High Cost, Corruption Claims Mar Brazil World Cup," Associated Press, May 12, 2014.

18. Ibid.

19. Ibid.

20. The capacity of Morumbi stadium is over 80,000 and is the home field of Brazil's first division team, São Paulo FC. The stadium was built in 1952.

21. Tales Azzoni, "Brazil Holds Final Stadium Tests for World Cup," Associated Press, May 19, 2014.

22. Interview with Kfouri by Tulio Velho Barreto, *Colectiva* (www.colec
tiva.org), April–June 2012.

23. Some estimates for the renovation at Maracanã Stadium for the Pan
American Games go above $200 million. According to Christopher Gaffney,
the Pan American Games went ten times over budget. C. Gaffney, "Mega-
Events and Socio-Spatial Dynamics in Rio de Janeiro, 1919–2016," *Journal
of Latin American Geography* 9, no. 1 (2010).

24. Thêmis Aragão and Wolfgang Maennig, "Mega Sporting Events, Real
Estate, and Urban Social Economics: The Case of Brazil, 2014/2016," Hamburg Contemporary Economic Discussions No. 47 (University of Hamburg,
2014). See also Zirin, *Brazil's Dance with the Devil*, chap. 1.

25. Dave Zirin, "Dispatches from Brazil's World Cup: 'No One Lives Here
Anymore,' *The Nation*, June 15, 2014 (www.thenation.com/blog/180239/
dispatches-brazils-world-cup-no-one-lives-here-anymore). For an interesting discussion of life in favelas, the threat of razing several of them for the
World Cup or Olympics, and local movements to save them, see Zirin, *Brazil's Dance with the Devil*, chap. 7. For historical background on the favelas
and the recent eviction process, see Theresa Williamson and Mauricio Hora,
"In the Name of the Future, Rio is Destroying Its Past," *New York Times*,
August 12, 2012.

26. Batista is under investigation by the federal police for alleged financial
wrongdoings. His $60 billion EBX empire, including interests in oil, mining,
and logistics, crumbled in 2013. See *SportsPro Magazine*, June 2014, p. 31.

27. Panja, "Brazil's Flamengo Won't Make 'Stupid' Deal."

28. The Gini coefficient measures actual inequality relative to perfect equality. It ranges from 0 to 1, with lower numbers representing more equality.

29. Aragão and Maennig, "Mega Sporting Events," p. 18.

30. More precisely, the housing deficit was calculated by the João Pinheiro
Foundation at 522,607 units in 2008. See Aragão and Maennig, "Mega Sporting Events," p. 12. On the callousness of the eviction process and its connection to private profit, see Williamson and Hora, "In the Name of the Future."

31. James Montague, "World Cup Only Benefits Outsiders, Say Brazil
Protesters," CNN.com, June 18, 2013.

32. As of June 2013, the projected costs on infrastructure and stadiums for
the 2014 World Cup were as follows: $5.8 billion for transportation, $2.9
billion for stadiums (likely to have ended up close to $5 billion), $2.8 billion
for ports and airports, $2.3 billion for security and health, $1.9 billion for
telecommunications and energy, and $900 million for new hotels in host cit-
ies. These items total to $16.6 billion and do not include future cost overruns
and operational expenses during the games. *Sports Business Journal*, June
17–23, 2013, p. 19.

33. Cited in *Sports Business Daily Global*, February 24, 2014.

34. Quoted in Marina Amaral and Natalia Viana, "Why Are Brazilians Protesting the World Cup?," *The Nation,* June 21, 2013.

35. Facing the threat of additional layoffs, the transit workers in São Paulo agreed not to continue their strike on June 11, but workers at Rio's municipal and international airports declared a twenty-four-hour strike for the opening day of the World Cup, June 12. A court order required the union to maintain 80 percent staffing at each airport or face a heavy fine. Meanwhile, the hackers' group Anonymous claimed it "attacked a large number of websites associated with the World Cup, including Bank of Brazil's and that of the country's military police." There were also violent clashes between protesters and police in front of São Paulo's World Cup stadium before the opening match. See www.espnfc.us/fifa-world-cup/story/1874614/rio-de-janeiro-airport-workers-go-on-strike.

36. Vanessa Barbara, "Brazil vs. Brazil," *New York Times,* June 26, 2014.

37. Ricardo Sennes, "Will Brazil Get What It Expects from the World Cup?," Atlantic Council Policy Brief (Washington, June 2014).

38. By another accounting, Brazil's security forces are considerably more extensive. A special report in the magazine *Sport Pro* in July 2014 (p. 65) had the following to say: "The heart of Brazil's World Cup security operation across all 12 cities is the National Integration Command and Control Centre (CICCN), located in the capital, Brasília. The giant control room there features 56 monitors connected up to key locations across the country. The CICCN is effectively a hub, gathering, processing and responding to information provided by 27 mobile command centres, 36 elevated observation links and 157,000 agents, including law enforcement officers and members of Brazil's armed forces. 57,000 members of the military . . . will be involved."

39. National Audit Office, "The London 2012 Olympic Games and Paralympic Games: Post-Games Review," Report by the Comptroller and Auditor General (London, December 5 , 2012), p. 6. Reportedly, the United States was still concerned and sent 500 FBI agents to London to safeguard security. Jules Boykoff, "What Is the Real Price of the London Olympics?," *The Guardian,* April 4, 2012. Dave Zirin cites much higher estimates of London's security forces: "Forty-eight thousand security forces. Thirteen thousand five hundred troops. Surface-to-air missiles stationed on top of residential apartment buildings. A sonic weapon that disperses crowds by creating 'head-splitting pain.' Unmanned drones peering down from the skies. A safe zone cordoned off by an eleven-mile electrified fence, ringed with trained agents and fifty-five teams of attack dogs" (*Brazil's Dance with the Devil,* p. 164).

40. Interestingly, although FIFA took out withholding taxes on behalf of South Africa from the hundreds of millions of dollars in prize money paid to the thirty-two finalist country teams in the 2010 World Cup, in Brazil FIFA did not take out withholding taxes for the $576 million in prize money doled

out in 2014. So, other than possible taxes on income earned by members of the Brazilian team, the Brazilian treasury did not earn tax revenue on the prize money generated during the 2014 World Cup. Personal communication with Sunil Gulati, FIFA Executive Committee member, July 21, 2014. See also Kelly Phillips Erb, "World Cup Mania: Figuring Out FIFA, Soccer & Tax," *Forbes*, June 16, 2014 (www.forbes.com/sites/kellyphillipserb/2014/06/16/world-cup-mania-figuring-out-fifa-soccer-tax/), and John Sinnott, "A Fair World Cup Deal for Brazil?," CNN.com, July 24, 2013 (http://edition.cnn.com/2013/06/24/sport/football/brazil-protests-fifa-tax/).

41. "Seeking a Silver Lining," *Pro Sports*, July 2014, p. 64.

42. "Brazil World Cup Workers Face Slave-Like Conditions," *BBC News*, October 10, 2013.

43. Some estimates have gone much higher. Dave Zirin cites an activist who claimed that 1.5 million families from favelas would be relocated by 2014. Zirin, *Brazil's Dance with the Devil*, p. 180.

44. Sennes, "Will Brazil Get What It Expects from the World Cup?"

45. Amaral and Viana, "Why Are Brazilians Protesting the World Cup?"

46. Simon Romero, "Slum Dwellers Are Defying Brazil's Grand Design for Olympics," *New York Times*, March 6, 2012.

47. Cited in *Sports Business Daily Global*, March 28, 2014.

48. See, for instance, the discussion in "Has Brazil Blown It?," *The Economist*, October 8, 2013.

49. According to an ESPN article, Brazil actually knew unofficially as early as back in March 2003 that it would be chosen as the 2014 host. Arguments within the Brazilian soccer federation and between the federation and local politicians thwarted the decisionmaking process. Making matters worse, the head of the federation and also of the local organizing committee for the World Cup, Ricardo Teixeira, was a compromised figure who, in March 2012, facing charges of ineptitude and corruption, was forced to resign his posts. See Tim Vickery, "Will Teixeira's Ouster Lead to Change?," ESPN.com, March 14, 2012. When the local organizing committee for the World Cup was formed with Teixeira at the helm, the committee consisted of his daughter, his lawyer, his press secretary, his personal secretary, a personal adviser, and an ex-president of the Bank of Brazil from the military era, but nobody from the government. Simon Kuper, "Game of Two Halves: The Ugly Side of Brazilian Football," *Financial Times*, May 9, 2014. According to Christopher Gaffney, "Between 2007 and 2009, the 2014 Organizing Committee conducted a competition among 18 cities, engendering a bidding war full of political intrigue in which host cities and states scrambled to outspend their competition on new stadiums, highways and airport terminals" ("Mega-Events and Socio-Spatial Dynamics in Rio de Janeiro, 1919–2016").

50. Tom Vickery, "Can Brazil Protests Be Traced Back to a 2003 FIFA Decision?," *BBC News,* June 24, 2013.

51. Ibid.

52. Gaffney, "Mega-Events and Socio-Spatial Dynamics in Rio de Janeiro, 1919–2016."

53. Nick Butler, "Construction Workers Vote to Continue Strikes in Yet Another Blow for Rio 2016," *Inside the Games,* April 15, 2004 (www. insidethegames.biz).

54. "Brazil Won't Meet Water Pollution Reduction Target before Olympics: Official," *Sports Business News,* May 18, 2014. Rio invited sailing teams to test the waters in Guanabara Bay in late July 2014. The results were not encouraging. An Austrian boat was damaged by garbage in the water and a member of the sailing team said that he saw a dead dog. Other sailors complained that the Bay "smells like a toilet because of raw sewage and trash that flow into [the Bay] on a daily basis." Tariq Panja, "Olympic Boast Damaged by Rio Bay Garbage as Sailors See Dead Dog," Bloomberg.com, July 29, 2014 (www.bloomberg.com/news/2014-07-29/olympic-sailors-boat-damaged-by-floating-garbage-in-rio-s-bay.html).

55. Interview with Kfouri by Barreto.

56. Mike Sheridan, "Racing to Get Ready: Rio 2016 Olympics," *Urbanland: The Magazine of the Urban Land Institute,* May 5, 2014.

57. The problem is that this was an emulation of form, but not content, of Barcelona's plan. More important, the political-economic context of the games in the two cities was entirely different.

58. "Construction of TransOlímpica Freeway for 2016 Rio Games to Displace 800 Families," *Sports Business Daily Global,* September 29, 2024.

59. It is also noteworthy that, in a country where more than half the people identify themselves as black or of mixed race, the great majority of attendees at the World Cup matches were white and from Brazil's upper class. A Datafolha Polling Group survey published in the *Folha de São Paulo* newspaper said that at the June 28 Brazil-Chile match, 67 percent of attendees were white and 90 percent came from Brazil's top economic classes. *Yahoo Sports,* June 30, 2014.

60. See the blog post of Christopher Gaffney, "Hunting White Elephants / Caçando Elefantes Brancos," June 6, 2014. The *Wall Street Journal* quoted Daniela Ordonez, an economist at the financial firm Euler Hermes: "All the activity in consumpion and tourism [from the World Cup] was more or less offset by reduced productivity in other areas like construction and transportation. From an economic point of view, maybe it was not worth it." Ordonez also projected that hosting would raise the country's inflation rate. Vipal Monga and Emily Chasan, "When in Doubt, Blame It on the World Cup," *Wall Street Journal,* July 30, 2014.

61. Sennes, "Will Brazil Get What It Expects from the World Cup?"

62. Gaffney, "Between Discourse and Reality," p. 3931.

63. For a discussion of the Thames Gateway project, see Gavin Poynter, "From Beijing to Bow Bells: Measuring the Olympic Effect," London East Research Institute, Working Papers in Urban Studies (London, March 2006).

64. Iain MacRury and Gavin Poynter, "London's Olympic Legacy: A Thinkpiece Report Prepared for the OECD and Department for Communications and Local Government" (University of East London, November 2009), p. 96.

65. Stratford Mall was also planned prior to the Games' planning. Nonetheless, its construction is often pointed to as a positive outcome of hosting the Olympics.

66. Ari Shapiro, "Did London Get an Economic Boost from the Olympics?," *All Things Considered,* National Public Radio, February 4, 2014.

67. Anne Power, "The Olympic Investment in East London Has Barely Scratched the Surface of the Area's Needs," blog post, August 15, 2012 (http://blogs.lse.ac.uk/politicsandpolicy/archives/2022); National Audit Office, "The London 2012 Olympic and Paralympic Games: Post-Games Review," Report by the Comptroller and Auditor General (London, December 5, 2012), p. 25.

68. Dan Brown and Stefan Szymanski, "The Employment Effects of London 2012," in *International Handbook on the Economics of Mega Sporting Events,* ed. Wolfgang Maennig and Andrew S. Zimbalist (Cheltenham, U.K.: Edward Elgar, 2012), pp. 546–70.

69. Cited in ibid.

70. Tim Hunt, "How Tax Avoidance Schemes Now Lie at the Heart of the Modern Olympic Games," *Ethical Consumer,* July 27, 2012 (www.ethical consumer.org).

71. Peter Woodman, "London Tourism Struggles during Olympics," *The Independent* (www.independent.co.uk/news/uk/home-news/london-tourism-struggles-during-olympics-7994159.html). See also "British Tourism Slumped during London Olympics," Associated Press, August 13, 2012.

72. The National Audit Report of December 5, 2012, stated, "The planning for venue security at the games did not go smoothly" (p. 6). The number of guards required was initially estimated at 10,000. The final number was over 20,000. One month before the games began, the company contracted to provide security informed LOCOG that it would not be able to provide the full number of guards in the contract. Ultimately the military was mobilized to do the job.

73. National Audit Office, "The London 2012 Olympic and Paralympic Games: Post-Games Review," p. 10.

74. Ibid., p. 24. This and other dollar cost figures are converted from British pounds at the rate of $1.69 to £1.

75. Tripp Mickle, "Panel at GE Event Addresses City Changes, Legacy of an Olympics," *Sports Business Daily,* July 31, 2012.

76. Jules Boykoff and Dave Zirin, "Protest Is Coming to the London Olympics," *The Nation,* May 21, 2012.

77. National Audit Office, "The London 2012 Olympic and Paralympic Games: Post-Games Review," p. 31.

78. Quoted in Poynter, "From Beijing to Bow Bells," p. 23.

79. Gavin Poynter, "Afterword: A Postcard from Rio," in *London: Was It Good for Us?,* ed. Mark Perryman (London: Lawrence and Wishart, 2012), p. 4.

80. National Audit Office, "The London 2012 Olympic and Paralympic Games: Post-Games Review," p. 18.

81. "Olympic Challenge: How Do Host Cities Fare after the Games?," *CBS News,* February 24, 2014 (www.cbsnews.com). Matthew Saltmarsh, "Will the Olympics Save East London?," *New York Times,* July 28, 2011.

82. The original stadium cost a reported $706 million to build (www.dailymail.co.uk/sport/football/article-2741150/Cost-converting-Olympic-Stadium-use-West-Ham-rise-15m.html).

83. Bill Carey, "Do Olympics Fulfill Economic Promises? A Look Back at London," *Sports Illustrated,* February 6, 2014.

84. Ibid.

85. Iain MacRury and Gavin Poynter, "London's Olympic Legacy: A Thinkpiece Report Prepared for the OCED and Department for Communications and Local Government" (University of East London, November 2009), p. 8. Oliver Wainwright, "London's Olympics Legacy Faces Early Disqualification," *The Guardian,* July 21, 2013.

86. "Other promises, like the Olympic Museum due to open this year, have simply been quietly dropped." Wainwright, "London's Olympics Legacy Faces Early Disqualification."

87. Boykoff, "What Is the Real Price of the London Olympics?"; National Audit Office, "The London 2012 Olympic Games and Paralympic Games," p. 25.

88. Poynter, "Afterword: A Postcard from Rio," p. 5.

89. Ibid., pp. 6–7.

90. Saltmarsh, "Will the Olympics Save East London?"

91. Robin Scott-Elliott, "Significantly Fewer People Now Playing Sport Regularly Than before Last Year's Olympic Games," *The Independent,* June 14, 2013.

92. See http://sportengland.org/research/who-plays-sport/.

93. Quoted in www.parliament.uk/business/publications/research/key-issues-for-the-new-parliament/social-reform/2012-olympics-and-sporting-legacy/. See also www.publications.parliament.uk/pa/cm200607/cmselect/cmcumeds/69/69i.pdf, p. 37.

## Chapter 7

1. Acreage estimates are from Judith Grant Long, "The Olympic Games and Urban Development Impacts," in P. Esteves and others, *BRICS e os Mega-eventos Esportivos* (Rio de Janeiro: BRICS Policy Institute, forthcoming).

2. E. Cottle, ed., *South Africa's World Cup: A Legacy for Whom?* (University of KwaZulu-Natal Press, 2011).

3. However, cities and countries do not bid with dollar figures. Rather, they bid with fancy facilities, appealing infrastructure, and amenities. Since these have a price, their bids can be translated into dollar figures.

4. And India, in the case of the 2010 Commonwealth Games. See, for instance, Nalin Mehta and Boria Majumdar, "For a Monsoon Wedding: Delhi and the Commonwealth Games," in *International Handbook on the Economics of Mega Sporting Events,* ed. Wolfgang Maennig and Andrew S. Zimbalist (Cheltenham, U.K.: Edward Elgar, 2012), pp. 504–26.

5. See, for example, Declan Hill and Jere Longman, "Fixed Soccer Matches Cast Shadow over World Cup," *New York Times,* May 31, 2014; Andrew Critchlow, "IoD Attacks Fifa in Wake of Qatar World Cup Scandal," *The Telegraph,* June 11, 2014; and Owen Gibson, "Qatar Hits Back at Allegations of Bribery over 2022 World Cup," *The Observer,* June 14, 2014.

6. See www.dezeen.com/2012/08/01/democracies-find-it-very-difficult-to-host-games-say-authors-of-olympic-cities-book/.

7. The *Washington Post*'s Catherine Rampell commented, "Norway's government looks likely to nix the bid later this year, since polls show only 36 percent of Norwegians are on board," *Washington Post,* July 11, 2014.

8. International Olympics Committee (IOC), "Olympic Agenda 2020: The Bid Experience" (Lausanne, June 2014), p. 4.

9. Duncan Mackay, "Paris Mayor Unenthusiastic about Bid for 2024 Olympics and Paralympics," *Inside the Games,* May 31, 2014 (www.insidethegames.biz/olympics). See also "Bill de Blasio Rules out NYC Bid," Associated Press, May 28, 2014.

10. Nick Butler, "Protests Held as Opposition Builds against New National Stadium in Tokyo," *Inside the Games,* July 5, 2014 (www.insidethegames.biz).

11. Duncan Mackay, "Exclusive: 'We Ask Too Much Too Early,'" *Inside the Games,* September 11, 2013 (www.insidethegames.biz).

12. See Duncan Mackay, "Changes to Olympic Bid Process on Way as IOC Members Debate Ideas," *Inside the Games,* February 5, 2014 (www.insidethegames.biz/olympics/1018223-changes-to-olympic-bid-process-on-way-as-ioc-members-debate-ideas).

13. Wolfgang Maennig and Andrew Zimbalist, "Future Challenges: Maximizing the Benefits and Minimizing the Costs," in Maennig and Zimbalist, *International Handbook on the Economics of Mega Sporting Events,* pp. 571–86.

14. "Tokyo to Reduce 2020 Olympic Bid Budget," GamesBids.com, December 2, 2011.

15. Jules Boykoff, professor of political science at Pacific University and prolific analyst of the Olympic Games, calls for the IOC to "create an independent body comprising respected sports economists, urban planners and political scholars who can objectively assess whether bids' construction plans fulfill long-view development strategies." Jules Boykoff, "A Bid for a Better Olympics," *New York Times,* August 13, 2014.

16. Reportedly, there were IOC concerns about the weakness of Spain's economy. The Spanish economy was devastated by the post-2007 financial crisis in Europe and the United States and was indeed weak in 2013 (unemployment rates were over 25 percent). The Spanish economy, however, was already beginning to recover at the time of Tokyo's selection in 2013, and there was little basis for the IOC to condemn it to a recession seven years hence.

17. IOC, "Olympic Agenda 2020: The Bid Experience," p. 6.

18. Until the summer of 2014, FIFA rules provided for only twenty-four individuals to vote on the selection of the World Cup host. Many believed that with so few people involved, bribery was simpler and cheaper. Accordingly, in the wake of the Qatar vote-buying scandal, FIFA altered its voting procedures to include the entire 209-nation membership. Further democratizing reform in the voting procedure is proposed by Duncan O'Leary, "Football's Great Reform Act" (http://quarterly.demos.co.uk/aticle/issue-3/footballs-great-reform-act/).

19. See, for example, "FIFA Confirms Michael Garcia's World Cup Ethics Report Won't Be Made Public," *The Guardian,* July 21, 2014. FIFA did finally release a summary of the investigatory report in November 2014, but Michael Garcia promptly issued a denunciation, stating that the summary contained "numerous materially incomplete and erroneous representations of the facts and conclusions detailed in the investigatory chamber's report."

20. German Olympics expert Wolfgang Maennig called for Hamburg and Berlin to apply to host the 2024 Summer Games, but to do so with a twist: there should be no new permanent building, planning should be more participatory, and more music and art should accompany the athletic competitions, inter alia. Wolfgang Maennig, "Deutschland ist dran," *Frankfurter Allgemeine,* August 14, 2014. In early September 2014, both Berlin and Hamburg announced their preliminary bid plans for the 2024 Games. In both cases the plans were rather modest and scaled back, emphasizing the use of existing facilities. See "Berlin, Hamburg Reveal Olympic Concepts for Potential 2024 Summer Games Bid," *Sports Business Daily Global,* September 2, 2014, p. 1.

21. Jim Armstrong, "Tokyo Governor Defends 2020 Olympics Venue Relocation Plans," July 1, 2014 (http://wintergames.ap.org/article/tokyo-governor-defends-venue-relocation-plans).

# Index